A DAPPER MURDER

KEITH FINNEY

VINCI
BOOKS

By Keith Finney

Rex and the Dowager

For Joan

Vinci Books

vinci-books.com

Published by Vinci Books Ltd in 2026

1

Copyright © Keith Finney 2025

The publisher and the author have made every effort to obtain permissions for any third party material used in this book and to comply with copyright law. Any queries in this respect should be brought to the attention of the publisher and any omissions will be corrected in future editions.

A CIP catalogue record for this book is available from the British Library.

Paperback ISBN: 9781036710385

The EU GPSR authorised representative is Logos Europe, 9 rue Nicolas Poussion, 17000 La Rochelle, France

contact@logoseurope.eu

Chapter One

NORTHWARDS TO NORWICH

I put on my leather driving gauntlets and slipped into the driver's seat of the Rolls Royce.

The Dowager Duchess of Drakeford (or HG as I may address Her Grace in private) and I bade farewell to the Home Counties. Our destination? The verdant landscape of Norfolk.

'I hope you've packed enough iced fancies and lemonade, Rex,' came a crisp voice from the rear seat.

A smile tugged at my lips. I assured HG I'd prepared well for our lengthy journey.

The conversation flowed with an ease between us, a testament to the time we'd spent together as she tutored me in the art and science of the amateur sleuth. HG had a remarkable talent for attracting trouble, or better yet, for trouble to seek her out.

I helped her investigate, and did other things too, while Detective Inspector Whipple made sure we followed protocol.

'It feels like only yesterday we were on our last adventure in Norfolk. Poor Mr Farrier, what a sad case that was.'

As I pondered the case, a rush of satisfaction flooded over me. Despite the misdirection and utter evil at play, HG, Whipple, and I brought the perpetrator to justice.

I nodded to show empathy for Farrier.

'Yes, dear Rex, sad indeed, and so many lives ruined.'

I navigated the Rolls through narrow lanes, past village greens where older children played cricket. The younger ones favoured tag and skipping, as their laughter carried on the light breeze. As the occasional motor car and horse-drawn cart passed by, the drivers tipped their caps in friendly greeting.

We soon found ourselves in the bustling market town of Bury St Edmunds. The streets brimmed with activity. Shopkeepers arranged their wares and townsfolk tested produce for freshness between finger and thumb. The smell of fresh bread wafted from a nearby bakery, mingling with the earthy scent of livestock from the market square.

HG tapped on the glass partition. 'Rex, do slow down a tad. I think we are about to pass by the Angel Hotel.'

I wondered why the building piqued HG's interest.

'Ah, now that's an interesting question,' she began. 'In 1861, one of our literary giants stayed at the hotel. You see, Charles Dickens read *the Pickwick Papers* and *A Personal History of David Copperfield* to a paying audience at the Athenaeum - Look yonder. There it stands. My parents took me to a performance, although, of course, I was quite young. To my inexperienced eyes, he was an old gentleman with unkempt hair, when in truth he'd have been but forty-nine years old and in his prime.'

A car hooter sounded from the vehicle behind for the second time as I listened to HG. I looked into the rearview mirror to see a fellow gesticulating for me to get a move on. Reluctantly, I engage first gear, rotated my outreached right arm, and pulled away from the kerb. The angry chap stalled his motor car, which I thought just deserts for his inconsiderate actions.

As we left Bury St Edmunds, the terrain opened before us. A patchwork of green fields and golden wheat hugged the gentle undulations of the Suffolk landscape. The occasional windmill stood sentinel on the horizon, its sails turning in the mid-morning sun.

Crossing into Norfolk, the terrain flattened and gave way to the vast expanse of the Fens. Field drainage ditches lined the narrow roads, their still waters reflecting the sky above. In the distance, I made out the silhouette of a wind pump, a reminder of the constant battle against the encroaching waters.

I nodded, feeling a sense of anticipation building within me. After several months of feverish investigation, I looked forward to a peaceful interlude. Also, the hope I might meet up with a certain lady mechanic I'd met during our previous visit to Norfolk.

As I brought the vehicle to a halt, I stole a glance at HG. She had her eyes fixed on Thorpe Manor; Pride, certainly – this was her Norfolk seat after all, but also something else. A hint of nostalgia, perhaps, or touch of melancholy.

I mentioned to HG that the Manor looked splendid.

She didn't respond at first, lost in her own thoughts. I took the moment to survey the grounds. The lawns were immaculate, stretching out in a sea of green towards the distant tree line. The rose beds near the house offered a riot of colour, the result of the head gardener's continuing meticulous care.

'Indeed, Rex,' said HG as she finally spoke, her voice soft. 'Thorpe Manor always knows how to put on a show,

I stepped out of the car, happy at the chance to stretch my legs after the long drive. The air felt crisp and clean, carrying the scent of cut grass and fragrant flowers.

HG's gaze lingered on the upper windows of the Manor; so much so that I enquired if all was well.

She emerged from the car with her usual grace, patting my arm as she did so. 'Just remembering, dear boy. This old house holds so many memories for me. The emotional connection I have with the place catches me out each time I visit.'

I understood her reflective mood. For all her strength and sharp wit, even HG wasn't immune to the occasional interlude of sentimentality. We stood for a moment as we took in the Manor's splendour.

As we climbed the wide stone steps to the front door, Graham, the butler, negated my need to clasp an ornate wrought-iron bell pull by opening both leaves of the sumptuously carved Jacobean doors.

'Your Grace,' he said in a respectful tone as he offered a bow from the neck. 'So nice to see you again. All is ready for you, and the cook has just taken a fresh batch of your favourite fruit scones from the range. Refreshments in the saloon, perhaps?'

HG thanked the butler for his foresight. 'You've outdone yourself once again, Graham. And do convey our gratitude to cook for those delightful scones. Nothing quite compares to her baking.'

Graham's chest swelled with pride at the compliment. 'Thank you, Your Grace. I shall pass on your kind words to Mrs Palmer.'

HG then inquired about the programme for the

upcoming fashion show in Norwich. Graham assured her he'd received the document and would bring it to the saloon with our refreshments.

HG removed her gloves and placed them on an ornate side table. Her fingers traced the intricate carving of Tudor roses that adorned its surface.

'The craftmanship never fails to take my breath away,' she murmured. 'Eight generations of my family have touched this very spot.'

My gaze followed hers to the gallery above, where gilt-framed portraits of her ancestors gazed down upon us. Their stern faces seemed to soften in the warm light that filled the space.

A grand staircase curved upward; its oak balustrade polished to a mirror finish by countless hands over the centuries. The wood gleamed like honey where the sun caught it.

The gentle tick of a long-case clock marked time in the corner, its brass face catching glints of the afternoon sun. Through leaded windows, glimpses of the rose garden beyond added splashes of colour to the mellow tones of ancient wood and stone.

HG gestured toward the saloon doors, her silver hair catching the light as she moved forward. 'Rex, dear boy, would you care to accompany me to the fashion show tomorrow?'

I hesitated, my mind racing to find a polite way to decline. The thought of spending hours observing the latest women's fashions held little appeal. I'd much rather delve into the Manor's archives to discover its rich history, which I found fascinating.

HG's eyes twinkled with mischief as she observed my reticence. 'I assume your reluctance has nothing to do with a certain lady mechanic you encountered during our last visit?'

I felt heat rising to my cheeks. Trust HG to catch me off guard. I didn't even know her name. However, her clever hands and forward ways, had indeed crossed my mind more than once since I discovered we were to return to Thorpe Manor.

My face flushed as I stammered out a denial. 'No, no, HG, it's not that at all. I simply thought I might use the time to delve into the Manor's archives. There's so much history here, and I—'

'Oh?' HG's eyebrow arched, her amusement clear. 'And this sudden passion for local history has nothing to do with avoiding my company on the morro?'

I protested, my words tumbling out faster than I could control them. 'I'm merely interested in the architectural evolution of Thorpe Manor. The Tudor foundations, the Jacobean additions—it's all quite fascinating, really.'

'There's time enough for that,' she said, waving away my feeble excuses. 'So, we've reached an agreement. You shall accompany me to Norwich, where I shall teach you all there is to know about haute couture.'

I resigned myself to the inevitable, mumbling under my breath about the cruelty of fate.

HG eyed me with a hint of a smile. 'Did you say something?'

The game was up. 'Not at all, HG. I was just thinking to myself how much I'm looking forward to our refreshments.'

'Yes, I thought that was it.' She gave me a motherly smile, seeing right through my poor attempt at deflection.

I returned a tortured smile of defeat as we reached the rich oak doors of the saloon. The scent of warm scones distracted me from thoughts of tomorrow's ordeal by catwalk. I marvelled at the seamless blend of Tudor and Jacobean styles. The room exuded an air of timeless elegance, a testament to the centuries of history that had unfolded within the walls.

The grand fireplace, with its high mantle shelf adorned with intricate carvings, caught my eye. Above it, the great coat of arms of Elizabeth I commanded attention, a reminder of the Manor's illustrious past.

In contrast to the Tudor and Jacobean elements, the furniture was Edwardian. Luxurious chairs and sofas, upholstered in rich fabrics that matched the heavy curtain swags, and invited one to sink into their plush embrace.

On a side table, our refreshments awaited. A silver teapot sat atop a methylated spirit burner, keeping the brew at the perfect temperature. The aroma of the scones mingled with the subtle scent of Earl Grey, making my mouth water.

HG and I helped ourselves to the spread, balancing delicate plates laden with scones, clotted cream, and strawberry preserves. We took our seats in the comfortable armchairs, the weight of the journey melting away as we sank into the cushions.

On a side table next to HG's chair, a programme for Saturday's fashion show rested. The sight of it brought a small sigh to my lips, a reminder of the ordeal that awaited me.

I savoured the rich, buttery taste of the scone, letting the flavour linger on my tongue. HG and I sat in companionable silence, the only sound, the rhythmic beat of a grandfather clock. It struck me how comfortable we'd become in each other's presence over the years. The silence between us was never awkward, but a shared moment of contentment.

HG placed her cup on the small table with a soft clink.

She picked up the programme for the fashion show, her eyes skimming over the pages. After a few moments, she set it back down and turned her gaze to me.

'Rex, what do you remember about the children's home where you stayed before you became my Ward?'

The question caught me off guard, stirring memories I hadn't revisited in quite some time. I paused, gathering my thoughts before responding.

The home had been a haven, a stark contrast to the uncertainty that had plagued my young life after father's sudden absence. The staff had been kind and attentive. I recalled Miss Thompson, the matron, with her stern demeanour that concealed a heart of gold. The other children, a disparate group, found solace in each other. I had much to be grateful to HG for in easing my past struggles.

I mourned father during those days, his absence an ache that never subsided. Yet, looking back, I recognised how fortunate I'd been. Things could have turned out much worse. The streets of London were unforgiving, especially to a young boy alone in the world. The home had provided not just shelter, but a chance at a future.

As I shared these recollections with HG, I noticed a softening in her eyes, a hint of something I couldn't quite name. Compassion, or perhaps pride in her role in reshaping my destiny, may have motivated her.

Changing the subject back to the charity event, I asked HG if she was expecting a good turnout for the show.

She raised an eyebrow, her lips curving into a knowing smile. 'The upper class never miss an opportunity to be seen by their peers in the latest fashions, dear Rex'

The fashion show wasn't just about clothes; rather, a social battleground.

HG continued, her voice taking on a sardonic tone.

'Above all, they'll fight like cats to get a seat in the front row. Heaven forbid they're not prominently displayed in the press photographs. And seated with the fashion designers too.'

I chuckled at the image of Norfolk's elite clawing their way to the front seats and commented that it sounded more like a spectator sport than a fashion show.'

'Oh, it is,' HG agreed, her eyes twinkling with amusement. Forget the clothes; the real entertainment is the social climbing and jockeying for position among the wealthy.

I shook my head, marvelling at the intricacies of high society. 'And here I thought it was just about admiring new frocks and suits.'

'That, Rex, is precisely why you need to accompany me,' HG said, patting my hand. 'There's so much more to these events than meets the eye. It's a masterclass in social dynamics, political manoeuvring, and the art of subtle one-upmanship.'

I couldn't argue with that logic. At least now I understood why HG was so insistent on my presence. The issue transcended mere fashion.

Just then, Graham, the butler, entered the saloon and approached HG. I couldn't hear what he said, but watched HG's expression change. The mirth from our earlier conversation vanished. Now a firm look ruled.

'Thank you, Graham,' HG said, her voice calm but laced with an undercurrent of irritation. 'Did Lord Wentworth provide any further details?'

Graham shook his head. 'I'm afraid not, Your Grace. He seemed quite flustered and said he'd explain more when he sees you tomorrow.'

HG dismissed Graham with a nod, then turned to me. 'Well, Rex, it seems arrangements for my little fashion show have taken an unexpected turn. It appears young Milly Davenport is up to her old tricks. This time she has her claws into the Fairbridge twins.

I sought clarification if she was the young lady who regularly appeared in *The Tatler* magazine.

'The very same,' HG confirmed, her lips pursing. 'A young lady with more influence than sense, I'm afraid. She's developed quite a talent for stirring up trouble, then making sure it makes the headlines.'

I felt a twinge of curiosity and asked what the Fairbridge twins might have done to upset the young lady.

HG's eyes narrowed. 'The answer to that will invariably be, nothing. However, that won't stop the minx if its sensational publicity she's after. The twins are lovely girls, kind-hearted souls and we must nip Miss Davenport's intended attack in the bud.'

My confused expression encouraged HG to elaborate.

'Perhaps it results from her father's lineage,' replied HG. 'He, too, could be cruel for no apparent reason. In the end, he suffered what he'd done unto others.'

I asked what HG meant.

'Croaked it on the toboggan run in St Moritz several winters ago. He'd heard a rumour that the track was about to be closed because of a sudden rise in the air temperature, so he thought he'd beat the odds with one last run. Turned out the rumour was false; he pushed too hard and ended up shooting over the ice wall of the track and losing his head… literally.'

I recoiled in shock.

'Of course, he wasn't the first member of his family to end up in a coffin a little on the short side. Two of his forbears ended up kneeling at the block on Tower Hill. It goes to show that you can't go around spreading malicious rumours and walk away unscathed—at least not in the Middle Ages, when it came to kings and queens you couldn't.'

HG observed my reaction, breaking out into a broad smile as I considered if she'd just told me a tall tale, or spoke the truth.

'I can see you don't believe me. However, I can assure you it to be true. Speaking of which, we can't dismiss Milly Davenport entirely. If she follows through on her threat, it could cast a pall over the entire event. And more importantly, it could harm the twins' reputation.'

I watched as HG rose from her chair, pacing the room with measured steps. Her mind processed the problem, considering angles and possibilities I could only guess at.

'We'll need to speak with the twins,' she said at last, turning back to me. 'And perhaps have a word with Miss Davenport as well. There's more to this than meets the eye, I'm certain of it.'

Chapter Two

SHOWTIME

As I expected, HG had a full day of activities planned before the fashion show began at 7.30 pm. Not even the prospect of Mrs Palmer's delicious full English breakfast tempted my mentor to delay our departure. Instead, we made do with hot toast, Fortnum's strawberry jam and English breakfast tea served in our respective rooms.

I wolfed down my breakfast, the rich strawberry jam a fleeting pleasure on my tongue as I rushed through my morning ablutions. The clock ticked, each second bringing me closer to the Dowager's appointed departure time. I fumbled with my tie, cursing under my breath as I struggled to achieve the perfect Windsor knot.

With not a moment to spare, I dashed down to the garage, my polished shoes clicking against the gravel drive. The Rolls Royce purred to life, its engine a reassuring rumble in the crisp early October air. I manoeuvred the magnificent vehicle around to the front entrance.

As I stepped out to open the rear passenger door, I

caught sight of my reflection in the gleaming paintwork. A quick adjustment of my cap, and I was ready.

The grand doors of Thorpe Manor swung open at nine o'clock on the dot. HG emerged, a vision of elegance in a tailored travelling suit, her hat adorned with a jaunty feather that danced in the breeze.

I stood to attention, hand on the open door. 'Good morning, HG.'

The Dowager descended the steps with a regal poise, her eyes twinkling with anticipation for the day ahead. As she reached the car, she met me with a warm smile.

'To work, dear Rex, to work,' she declared, settling into the plush leather seat.

I closed the door with a soft click. What adventures awaited I wondered.

We had just set off when HG opened the glass partition that separated us. 'We go first to Lord Wentworth to discover what else he might tell us about Milly Davenport's little game. Head for Aylsham, Rex, I shall give further instruction anon.'

I guided the Rolls Royce through the winding Norfolk lanes; the countryside unfurling before us like a living tapestry. The morning mist hung low over the landscape, a mysterious blanket that cloaked fields and hedgerows in ethereal white. As our journey continued, the strengthening sun worked its magic, burning away the fog and revealing the lush green world beneath.

The transformation was mesmerising. Wisps of mist rose from the earth, twisting and dissipating into nothingness as the sun's rays pierced through. As if the land was exhaling, breathing new life into the day.

Ancient parish churches dotted the landscape, their weathered stone spires reaching skyward. These buildings stood as silent witnesses to East Anglia's prosperous wool trade era. Each church seemed to anchor its village to history, a tangible link between past and present.

As we drove, I marvelled at the timeless beauty of Norfolk. The patchwork of fields bordered by centuries-old hedgerows, the occasional windmill silhouetted against the brightening sky - a scene that had changed little in hundreds of years.

The Dowager remained silent in the rear, no doubt lost in her own thoughts about the day ahead. I focused on the road, enjoying the peaceful drive and the gradual awakening of the surrounding countryside.

Before long, I caught sight of a signpost ahead. As we drew closer, I made out the words: 'Aylsham - 3 miles'. Our destination was near.

'Rex, keep a sharp eye out for a left turn,' HG's voice floated from the back seat. 'There should be a sign for Cockleford Manor.'

I nodded, tightening my grip on the steering wheel. 'Yes, HG. I'll—'

The words died in my throat as the very turn she'd mentioned materialised before us. I stomped on the brake; the tyres screeching in protest as I wrenched the wheel to the left. The Rolls lurched, and I winced at the thought of HG being jostled about in the back.

As we swung onto the narrow lane, I caught sight of a farm-hand in a horse-drawn wagon. The poor chap had been about to turn right and now found himself face to face with our imposing vehicle. His weather-beaten face twisted into a scowl, and I braced myself for a barrage of colourful language.

Guilt gnawed at me. I glanced in the rear-view mirror, expecting to see HG's disapproving frown. To my astonishment, she grinned, her gloved hand raised in a cheerful wave to the farmhand.

Curiosity piqued; I looked back at the wagon. The farm-hand's scowl had vanished, replaced by an expression of surprise. As I watched, he lifted his ragged cap from his head and gave a curt, respectful nod in our direction.

I blinked, stunned by this exchange. It seemed that even here, in the depths of rural Norfolk, HG's influence held sway.

'Do watch out for the roe deer,' HG intoned as we made progress down the narrow lane. 'They are frightfully common in these parts and jump out of the hedges without a care for what might hurt them.'

I admit to being more concerned about the damage the beasts might inflict on the Rolls. I chose not to express this view to my mentor, who held all wildlife dear to her ample heart.

As we rounded the last bend, Cockleford Manor came into view. I couldn't help but raise an eyebrow at the sight. After the grandeur of Thorpe Manor, this place seemed almost quaint in comparison. The timber-framed structure, while charming, was a far cry from the sprawling estate we'd left behind.

I voiced my surprise to HG, remarking on the modest size of Lord Wentworth's abode.

'Ah, Rex,' she replied, a hint of amusement in her voice. 'This is an early medieval timber-framed house, built for a Gentleman Farmer who likely owned no more than a couple of hundred acres. Lord Wentworth acquired the house and grounds in the 1890s, at the pinnacle of his distinguished naval career.'

I stopped the Rolls before the historic building, its age clear in the worn wood and glass.

Once alighted from the car, I made my way around to assist HG. As she emerged, her eyes swept over the Manor with keen interest, no doubt piecing together its history from the architectural details.

We approached the oak front door, and I noticed an ornate brass door knocker fashioned in the shape of a wolf's head. Its eyes seemed to follow me as I reached out and grasped the cool metal. The sound of the knock echoed through the house, announcing our arrival to Lord Wentworth.

I watched in surprise as the door swung open, revealing not a butler or maid, but Lord Wentworth himself. His jovial face beamed at us, eyes twinkling with warmth. I felt a pang of shame, realising I'd judged the man's worth based on who answered his door. How foolish of me! A person's character isn't determined by the number of staff they employ; I chided myself.

'HG, my dear!' Lord Wentworth exclaimed, his voice rich with genuine pleasure. He stepped forward, planting a respectful peck on the Dowager's cheek.

I blinked, taken aback by the casual use of my mentor's initials. That level of familiarity was unusual outside our immediate circle.

Lord Wentworth turned his attention to me, his grin widening. 'And you must be Rex!' he boomed, letting out a hearty belly laugh that seemed to shake the timbers of the house. 'HG tells me about you every time we meet, and often in her correspondence. I daresay I know you as well as she does!'

I felt my cheeks flush, both flattered and embarrassed by the notion that I featured so much in HG's conversations and letters. The stark reminder highlighted my limited knowledge of my mentor's life outside our investigations.

'It's a pleasure to meet you, Lord Wentworth,' I managed, offering a polite bow from the neck.

His lordship ushered us into his home with a sweeping gesture. 'Come in, come in! Let's not stand on ceremony.'

I followed HG and our host through a narrow hallway, its walls adorned with faded portraits and nautical memorabilia. The floorboards creaked beneath our feet, each step a whisper of the house's long history.

We entered what I presumed to be the morning room, a cosy space that seemed to embody the very essence of a bachelor's existence. Mismatched furniture, chosen for comfort rather than style, filled the room. A well-worn leather armchair stood sentinel by the fireplace, its arms bearing the scars of countless evenings spent in quiet contemplation.

Books and newspapers were strewn across every available surface, creating a sort of organised chaos that spoke of a mind constantly at work. A half-empty teacup teetered on a stack of leather-bound volumes, a ring of tannin staining the saucer beneath.

As I took in the scene, a peculiar scent tickled my nostrils. It was earthy and slightly musty, not unpleasant, but certainly noticeable. I couldn't quite place it until a giant form lumbered into the room.

An English Mastiff, its jowls drooping and glistening with saliva, padded across the worn carpet. The beast's presence filled the room, dwarfing the furniture around it. It paused by my side, regarding me with doleful eyes, before continuing its leisurely journey to the fireplace.

With a heavy sigh, the dog lowered itself onto the hearth rug, sprawling out before the crackling flames. Lord Wentworth chuckled at the sight.

'That's Henry,' he explained, gesturing towards the

canine behemoth. 'He's supposed to keep his master safe. As you can see, he much prefers his own company and a roaring fire. The ungrateful hound only ever pays attention to me when it's time for food.'

Henry cocked his head, giving his master a "So?" look." The dog's expression was so human-like, I had to stifle a laugh.

Lord Wentworth gestured towards a pair of armchairs and a worn leather settee. 'Please, make yourselves comfortable.'

Each piece of furniture served as an impromptu storage space. I lifted a stack of nautical charts from one armchair, while HG moved a collection of newspapers from the settee. Our host made space on the chair by moving some books and a part-built model ship.

'I don't stand on ceremony here, young fellow, so let's dispense with formal titles, eh? Just call me Alfred,' he said, settling into his newly cleared seat.

The invitation caught me off guard, though I maintained what I hoped was a neutral expression. Such informality from a peer of the realm was unprecedented in my experience.

'What am I thinking of? I forgot the tea,' Alfred announced, rising from his chair. 'Just a tick. I'll arrange that now.'

I expected him to leave the room, wondering if he had any household staff at all. Instead, he made his way to the fireplace, having to step over Henry, who remained sprawled across the hearthrug.

Confused, I watched Alfred remove a brass stopper from a wall-mounted trumpet instead of pressing a service button.

'Ahoy there,' he bellowed into the device. 'Tea for three in the library.'

I exchanged an amused glance with HG as Alfred cupped his right ear in the brass cone he'd just shouted down to hear the response.

'Well, that's that sorted out. Now, I presume you both want to hear what young Milly has been up to?'

'She is certainly proving to be a nuisance on what is already a very busy day, so let's have it. Why is she picking on the twins?'

Alfred settled back into his chair, scratching behind Henry's ears as the massive dog had somehow dragged himself closer without any of us noticing.

'I was at Sir Charles Mountford's place - the Lord Lieutenant, you know - just two evenings past. Small gathering, nothing too formal. That Davenport girl was there, commanding attention as she does. Quite the show she put on.'

HG's eyebrows lifted a fraction. 'Do go on.'

'Well, the interesting bit came later. I'd stepped out to use the facilities when I overhead two maids chattering in the hallway. Normally I wouldn't pay attention to such things, but something caught my ear. One of them mentioned overhearing Miss Davenport in quite a state.'

'What exactly did they say?' HG asked, leaning forward.

'The maid claimed she heard the girl ranting about not receiving an invitation to some event, saying she'd show up regardless and create a scene. Something about the Fairbridge twins spreading tales about her.'

HG's eyes narrowed. 'Most peculiar. I know for certain she received an invitation to the fashion show.'

'That's not all,' Alfred continued, pausing as a knock at the door announced tea. An elderly maid entered with a laden tray, setting it down without ceremony before departing just as swiftly.

'I had a word with Charles afterwards,' he resumed, pouring tea into mismatched cups. 'He seemed troubled by the entire business. Said it felt orchestrated somehow - as if she meant to cause a distraction for some other purpose entirely. Though he couldn't fathom what that might be.'

'Did the Lord Lieutenant elaborate further?' HG asked, accepting a cup with a tiny chip on the rim.

'No, that was all he'd say on the matter. Though he appeared rather concerned about things.'

A shrill ring pierced our conversation. An ancient telephone mounted on the wall behind Alfred's desk demanded attention with its insistent jangling.

Alfred heaved himself up from his chair, navigating around Henry, who had sprawled across even more of the floor space. 'Pardon me,' he said, reaching for the earpiece. 'Cockleford Manor, Wentworth speaking.'

His expression shifted. 'Ah yes, one moment.' He extended the earpiece towards HG. 'It's for you, my dear. Your man Graham.'

HG rose with her usual grace and took the receiver. 'Yes, Graham?'

I watched as she listened; her face betraying nothing beyond mild interest. 'I see... Of course... Yes, I understand... I see... Very well, Graham.'

She replaced the receiver with deliberate care. 'It appears I'm needed in Norwich. The venue manager for tonight's fashion show is rather distressed about some sort of disagreement that's brewing.'

'Trouble?' I asked, already expecting our imminent departure.

'The tone, though lacking specifics, suggested urgency.'

HG smoothed her skirts. 'Alfred, I do apologise, but we must cut our visit short.'

'Not at all, not at all.' Alfred waved away her apology. 'Duty calls, what? Though I must say, this business with young Miss Davenport becomes more intriguing by the minute.'

I helped HG gather her things while Henry watched us, showing no inclination to move despite our flurry of activity.

The Rolls-Royce purred along the country lanes as I pressed the accelerator. The Norfolk countryside sped by. In no time, we were in Norwich's medieval city centre.

The transition caught me off-guard - one moment in the open countryside, the next a warren of crooked streets barely wide enough for our motor. Ancient buildings leaned together, their upper floors seeming to whisper across the streets below.

I chuntered about the narrow, twisting medieval streets as I swerved to avoid a cart pulled by a disinterested nag.

We emerged into a wider space, and I caught sight of a street sign that made me pause.

'Tombland? A macabre name for what appears to be the heart of the city. Something to do with the cathedral, perhaps?'

HG's laugh held genuine amusement. 'Not at all, Rex. The name comes from the Old English for "open ground" or "open place". This was Norwich's market square in Anglo-Saxon times. That is until the Normans invaded and decided they needed the space for something grander.'

She gestured ahead through the windscreen. 'See, the castle still stands, though not in its original form.'

I followed her pointing finger to where the massive square keep dominated the skyline, its pale stone walls a testament to Norman might.

'They moved the market to build that?'

'Indeed. The Normans didn't ask permission when they wanted something. The market's current location was their choice - and 900 years later, it's still there.'

In under a minute, I drove the Rolls Royce to the Assembly Hall's old carriage turnaround. A magnificent Georgian building with three wings surrounding a gravel courtyard and central lawn. A single majestic oak rose from its centre, casting its shadow across all three wings of the splendid establishment.

I stepped out and circled the Rolls, noting a fellow with polished black shoes kicking up clouds of gravel dust as he sprinted towards us. His morning suit coat flapped behind him like a distressed bird's wings.

The poor fellow's face blazed red as a summer strawberry, and perspiration dampened the edges of his waxed moustache. His hands wrung together in a constant motion that spoke of acute anxiety.

HG extended her hand with practiced grace as she emerged from the car. The manager seized it as though grasping a lifeline, pumping it up and down with such vigour I feared he might wrench Her Grace's arm clean off.

'Your Grace, such an honour, such a pleasure.' He fumbled in his trouser pocket, producing a handkerchief that had seen better days, and mopped his gleaming forehead.

HG's voice carried that blend of authority and kindness

she reserved for those in obvious distress. 'Do compose yourself, Mr...?'

'Pendlebury, Your Grace. Edward Pendlebury.' More dabbing at his forehead. The handkerchief looked utterly defeated by now.

'Mr Pendlebury, there's no need for such agitation. I'm certain everything is proceeding exactly as planned.'

His eyes widened to saucers. 'This way, Your Grace. Please, this way.' The words tumbled out in a breathless rush before he spun on his heel and dashed towards the building's entrance.

HG shot me a raised eyebrow before setting off after him, her heels clicking against the gravel. I lengthened my stride to keep pace, wondering what could have reduced a grown man to such a state of nervous excitement.

I followed HG and the flustered Mr Pendlebury into the main hall, where chaos reigned. The beautiful Georgian room had become a place of conflict and competing egos.

Two lighting technicians, high on ladders, directed the lighting above the runway. One shouted, 'It goes there!' While the other responded, 'Not unless you want them girls looking like ghosts!'

In the corner, a cluster of young women in various states of dress dabbed at mascara-streaked faces with delicate handkerchiefs. The show director, a severe-looking woman in a charcoal suit, sat slumped at a small table, her face buried in her hands.

Near the entrance, two men - one in shirtsleeves, the other in a rumpled jacket - stood nose to nose, fists clenched. Their angry mutterings carried promises of imminent violence.

HG surveyed this scene of pandemonium, her spine straightening like a steel rod. With deliberate steps, she strode to the centre of the hall, her silver-tipped walking stick striking the polished oak floor three times. The sharp crack echoed through the space.

'Enough. Stop this nonsense at once, do you hear?'

The effect was immediate. Silence fell like a heavy curtain. The quarrelling men stepped apart. The sobbing models froze mid-sniffle. Even the lighting technicians ceased their bickering to stare down at her commanding presence.

'Who,' HG's voice cut through the newly minted quiet, 'is in charge of this catastrophe?'

For a long moment, no one moved. Then, from behind a black curtain that shrouded the runway's wooden scaffolding, a slight figure emerged. He wore horn-rimmed glasses and a suit that looked as if he'd slept in it. His thin shoulders hunched forward as if bearing an invisible weight.

HG's eyes narrowed as she peered at the diminutive man. 'What, prey, causes this childish behaviour?'

The small man tried to speak, but no words followed. In the end, he gave up trying and shrugged his shoulders.

'I see,' said HG in an irritated tone. Dismissing the man, who appeared keen to vanish back behind the curtain, my mentor once more survey the scene.

'The show begins in six hours and it will begin on time. Do you all hear me?'

No one dared answer back. Instead, heads bobbled up and down.

'Then to work everyone; Models, please retreat to your dressing stations. You two up there. I want those lights fixed in the next ten minutes. You two by the door. If you don't behave yourselves, I'll biff you both about the head and have no doubt about it-do you understand?'

The two men gave HG a look of disobedient school

boys about to be caned by the headmaster. Their submission was complete.

Finally, HG approached the woman, who still held her head in her hands.

'And what's to do here?' she whispered. 'Tell me how I may help?'

From the distraught woman's demeanour, it seemed HG's enquiry was the first kind word she'd received all day.

Eventually the woman, who, once she'd shown her face, emerged much younger than her office attire, had me believe. In fact, she wore a kind countenance that I knew from experience, HG would warm to.

The lady appeared recovered at the end of the low-toned exchange.

'That's better,' began HG. 'Now, take yourself off somewhere quiet and have a nice cup of tea. I'm sure the wonderful Mr Pendlebury will arrange things, isn't that so?'

Pendlebury puffed out his chest, now returned to rude health. 'Of course I shall, Your Grace. If you will, young lady, please follow me and I'll find us a place of refuge among all this…'

Pendlebury didn't finish his sentence. Instead, he seemed to give a slight shiver at proceedings, before leading the young woman out of the vast hall.

At 7.30 pm, the fashion show began as the lights dimmed, to be replaced by two spotlights illuminating the show runway. A large contingent of the "Norfolk Set" was in attendance. HG had been correct to say few high society would dare miss the gathering. Their fear of missing out on the latest gossip, or the opportunity to seek influence from those above them in the rankings, won out.

I could see that HG had her wits about her, keeping an eye out for Milly Davenport, or indeed anything else that might impact on her ability to raise funds for her charity.

'Do you see here, Rex? I do wish I'd had a chance to nab her before the show started to stop her nonsense once and for all. Alas, we shall now just have to see what occurs. With luck, she's decided to abandon her silliness.'

Before I could answer, music signalled the beginning of the show. Soon, a procession of models paraded up and down the narrow runway. The crowd applauded each new appearance, though I must admit that to me, the frocks all looked the same.

Then came a sound that confused all present. A loud, crisp, bang. The crowd looked around, as did HG and I, to see if a piece of scenery had fallen, or some other object had hit the wooden floor with force. There followed a momentary silence, broken by a blood-curdling scream from backstage.

A loud commotion filled the hall as people struggled to see what had happened.

HG acted without a second's hesitation. 'Follow me, Rex. I think we both recognise that sound.'

As the house lights brightened, I followed HG at pace as we made our way down the side of the enormous room to the stage steps. Moving deeper into the bowels of the inner workings of the stage area, we found the models changing and preparation area. Fifteen feet to the right, we progressed into a small room without windows or doors, other than the one we'd just entered through. There we found a small gaggle of young women stood over a prone body.

'Her name is…I mean, was, Lucy Daws, said a blond-haired model still crouching down, cradling the victim's head in her lap.

HG stood to one side, observing all before her. 'Did anyone see what happened?'

The crouching girl cried. 'I was just speaking to her in the dressing room. Then she left. I heard a bang and came out to see what was going on. I came in here, and…'

The girl couldn't finish the sentence. Instead, she buried her head against the dead girl's shoulder.

HG gestured for me to join her a few feet away from the commotion.

'Get Pendlebury to ring the police. Tell him to keep things quiet.'

As I made to make off, HG caught hold of my arm. 'Whoever did this is may still be on the premises. Look, there's no way out of this room apart from that one door. We must do nothing that may provoke the murderer to kill again.

Chapter Three

A SAD INTRODUCTION

HG strode from the small room, leaving me to keep the dreadful scene secure. The blonde model had composed herself somewhat, though her shoulders still shook with silent sobs. The other models formed a protective circle around their fallen friend.

HG's voice rang from the main hall through the open door. Her tone commanded attention, brooking no argument.

'Ladies and gentlemen,' she began, 'because of an unforeseen incident, the show will not continue this evening.'

A ripple of murmurs swept through the assembled crowd, but HG's next words cut through the noise.

'I must ask that none of you speak to members of the press about what has occurred here tonight. The police will shortly be in attendance, and officers will be stationed at each exit. If any of you noticed anything unusual or suspicious during the evening, please do speak with them before you depart.'

The authority in her voice defied debate. Even from my position backstage, I sensed the crowd's compliance. HG had always possessed that rare ability to command a room without raising her voice above a civilised level.

More footsteps approached the small room - Pendlebury appeared in the doorway, his nervous disposition on full display. He gave me a nod, showing the police had arrived.

From my position, I caught sight of HG's return with Lord Wentworth in tow. The pair paused outside the small room, their forms casting long shadows across the dimly lit corridor that led from the stage. Wentworth's aristocratic profile looked more severe than usual. His angular features tightened with concern.

His lordship leaned closer and whispered, 'Strange business. I spotted Miss Davenport practically fleeing the premises moments after that dreadful noise.'

HG's eyebrows lifted a fraction. 'Indeed?'

'Tried to catch up with her, but the girl moves like a gazelle when she wants to. Straight out through the side entrance and into a waiting motor car.'

'Did you notice the direction the vehicle took?'

'Afraid not.' He tugged at his silk cravat. 'But I must say, her behaviour struck me as rather odd. One doesn't simply abandon a charity event of this calibre without so much as a by-your-leave.'

'Unless one has pressing reasons to do so,' HG's voice held a tone I recognised - the one that meant pieces of a puzzle were falling into place behind those shrewd eyes.

'Precisely my thoughts.' Wentworth glanced towards the room where Lucy's body lay. 'The timing seems...significant.'

I shifted my weight, careful not to draw attention to myself while straining to catch every word. The conversa-

tion proved Miss Davenport planned to trouble the Fairbridge twins.

Then an unfamiliar figure emerged, cutting HG and his
lordship's conversation short. The detective's long coat
swept behind him as he strode past them without so much
as a nod of acknowledgement. His sharp features and
serious demeanour struck me - he could have been a
younger version of my old friend Whipple. These police
types all seemed to favour the same fashion choices. Well-
worn coats, practical boots that had seen better days, and
that ubiquitous moustache that appeared to be standard
issue.

The tall fellow came to an abrupt halt at the threshold
of the crime scene. His eyes swept across the small room,
taking in every detail with clinical precision. Unlike Whipple, this fellow stayed silent.

'Detective Sergeant O'Brien,' he announced to no one
in particular, his gaze fixed on Lucy's prone form.

I caught HG's subtle frown at being overlooked. She
wasn't accustomed to such treatment, not from public
servants. The detective's lack of social grace irked Lord
Wentworth even more. His aristocratic nostrils flared with
indignation.

O'Brien planted himself at the edge of the scene, hands
clasped behind his back, still maintaining that unnerving
silence. The blonde model's sniffles were the only sound that
broke the heavy quiet.

'I want this room cleared now.' The sergeant's gaze
continued to survey the scene without bothering to engage
with its occupants. 'Wait on the other side of the stage. One
of my officers will interview you and advise when you may
leave the premises.'

HG's first impressions of the officer, if her current

demeanour counted as evidence, continued its downward trajectory.

HG tapped the sergeant on the shoulder with a gloved finger, causing O'Brien to turn around. 'I am the Dowager Duchess of Drakeford. Perhaps we might dispense with the dramatics and focus on more pressing matters?'

O'Brien stiffened his tall frame. For a moment, he looked over his shoulder at me, making the connection. The name sparked recognition. 'Ah, the interfering aristocrat who meddles in police business.'

A lesser person might have bristled at his tone, but HG's composure remained unruffled. 'If you harbour concerns about my involvement, contact Scotland Yard. The commissioner himself will be happy to discuss my credentials.'

She took a measured step closer, bringing herself within whispering distance. From my position, I caught her words as she faced towards me.

'Shall we start again, Detective Sergeant, and get on with the investigation?'

O'Brien remained motionless, his expression unreadable. The seconds stretched like hours in the cramped doorway. Then, with deliberate slowness, he shifted to one side, permitting HG entry to the crime scene.

Lord Wentworth's face split into a wide grin at this minor victory. He maintained his position, savouring the detective's grudging capitulation to HG's authority.

O'Brien watched from the doorway as HG went to Lucy Daws, whose body was surrounded by models and held by a weeping woman.

HG stepped forward, her presence transforming the tense atmosphere. Her voice emerged soft as silk, gentle in a way I'd rarely witnessed.

'My dears, might we give Lucy a moment of peace?'

The models parted like a curtain drawn back, each receiving a look from HG that spoke volumes of understanding. The grace with which she handled their raw grief left me in awe.

Despite her years and the constraints of her evening dress, HG lowered herself to crouch beside the blonde girl who still cradled Lucy's head. The young woman's tears fell onto Lucy's peaceful face, creating trails that caught the light.

HG placed her gloved hand on the girl's trembling arm. The rocking motion ceased at her touch, as natural as a mother calming a distressed child.

'What's your name, my dear?'

The girl's voice emerged, a mere whisper. 'Clara. Clara Brightman.'

'Clara.' HG's tone carried such warmth that even O'Brien's rigid posture softened a fraction. 'You may call me Violet.'

My eyebrows lifted of their own accord. In all our years together, I'd never heard HG grant anyone permission to use her first name. Even I addressed her formally when in public, despite our close working relationship. The significance of this moment struck me - HG had recognised something in this girl that called for more than mere sympathy.

Clara's tear-stained face lifted, meeting HG's compassionate gaze. The connection between them formed instantly, transcending the usual barriers of class and circumstance that defined English society.

'Did you know Lucy well?' asked HG in a soft tone, her hand still resting gently on Clara.

'We were best friends,' responded the still tearful young

lady. 'The fashion industry can be unpleasant. We looked out for each other. We didn't keep secrets from one another.' Clara paused as remembering something.

'Is there something you want to tell me? You seemed to hesitate.' HG moved her hand to move a clump of hair that had fallen over Clara's face. Her forehead showed the deep furrows of a tortured soul. 'Tell me what you were about to say.'

Copying HG, Clara tidied Lucy's hair, revealing her eyes staring at the ceiling.

Clara's internal struggle played across her features. Her hands trembled as she smoothed Lucy's hair one last time.

'There is a...I mean, a man that, oh, I don't...never mind.' Clara's voice trailed off, her eyes darting towards Detective O'Brien, who'd edged closer to listen.

HG caught my eye. She'd file this fragment of information for later scrutiny. My mentor possessed an uncanny knack for knowing when to press for details and when to let matters rest. This moment, with Clara's raw grief still so fresh, called for the latter approach.

Instead of pursuing the cryptic reference to the unknown man, HG helped Clara to her feet. Simultaneously, she ensured that Lucy's head rested on the wooden floor. The young model's legs wobbled like a newborn foal's, but HG's steady hand at her elbow prevented any stumbling.

'Perhaps we might find you somewhere more comfortable to sit?' HG's voice remained soft, maternal. 'I believe there's a quiet room just down the corridor.'

Clara nodded, allowing herself to be led away from her friend's body. As they passed O'Brien, his expression appeared to express approval, though it vanished so fast that I couldn't be certain.

I noted how HG kept her arm linked through Clara's. Supporting her, while establishing a connection that would make future conversations easier. Her ability to forge trust during tragedy—a technique I'd seen her use before—was impressive. Whatever Clara knew about this mysterious man, HG would uncover it when the poor girl had regained her composure.

While HG remained absent with Clara, I followed Detective Sergeant O'Brien into the model's changing room. He looked back at me but made no objection to my doing so. Inside the room, half a dozen young women hung about in silence. One or two sat in front of their make-up station, staring blankly into their lit mirror. Two others half-perched on a large central table on which an array of dresses and accessories sat. The final two women paced up and down the room as if waiting for something—anything to happen.

I watched O'Brien's demeanour shift as he entered the dressing room. Gone was the brusque officer who'd confronted HG moments ago. Instead, his approach became measured - as if he'd absorbed the lesson in human connection HG had demonstrated.

He paused a few feet into the room, hands clasped behind his back. The models continued their restless movements until his quiet voice broke through their private thoughts.

'Ladies,' he spoke barely above a whisper, yet commanded their full attention. 'I understand this evening has been traumatic for you all. My only purpose here is to establish what happened and bring Lucy Daws's murderer to justice.'

The word "murderer" struck like a physical blow. The women exchanged rapid glances, fear flickering across their

faces. One girl perched on the table grabbed her neighbour's hand.

O'Brien noted their reaction, his tone softening further.
'You're safe now. I give you my word - nothing will happen
to any of you.' He took a step closer to the group. 'My officers secured all exits the moment we arrived. As I speak,
my team are searching every corner of this building for
anyone who might have hidden, waiting for everyone to
leave.'

The tension in the room eased at his words. His sensi-
tivity impressed even me. Perhaps O'Brien had more about
him than it first appeared - though I'd reserve final judgement until I saw more of his methods.

O'Brien drew a small notebook from his coat pocket.
'Did any of you notice anything unusual before the show
began? Or perhaps around the time you heard that loud
noise?'

The models exchanged glances, their silence heavy with
unspoken thoughts. Finally, a tall brunette with sharp
features stepped forward. Her evening gown rustled with
the movement.

'I'm Pippa Longsdale.' She wrapped her arms around
herself, shoulders hunched. 'Truth is, fashion shows are
always chaos. Everyone rowing about everything. Models
fighting over who gets the best pieces, who walks first, who
closes the show.'

She perched on the edge of her makeup table, her
reflection multiplied in the surrounding mirrors. 'Once the
show starts, it gets worse. Designers are upset when a model
doesn't showcase a dress well, walks incorrectly, misses their
cues, or delays the photo shoot process.

Pippa's nervous laugh held no humour. 'Half the time I
wonder why I stay in the industry. It's horrible. Some of

these people...' She shook her head, dark curls bouncing. 'Well, they're truly awful to work with.'

O'Brien's pencil moved across his notebook. 'Anyone in particular cause trouble tonight?'

'Tonight?' Pippa's gaze drifted to the door, beyond which Lucy's body lay. 'Nothing out of the ordinary. Just the usual drama.'

I noticed how she avoided meeting the detective's gaze as she spoke those last words. He caught it too - his pencil paused mid-stroke, head tilting as he studied her face.

O'Brien broke eye contact with Pippa and moved on to ask each model where they were and what they saw the instant the gunshot rang out.

Their responses came in fragments, punctuated by sniffles and trembling hands. Most couldn't recall details - trauma had already begun its work of blurring their memories.

'I think I was adjusting my hat...'

'Everything happened so fast...'

'The noise... I dropped my purse...'

The shock rendered their statements near useless, as each woman struggled to piece together the evening's events. O'Brien's patience surprised me - he nodded, jotting down their halting responses without pushing too hard.

Then a sharp voice cut through the muddle of hesitant testimonies.

'Oh, for heaven's sake.' A woman with a fashionable bob stepped forward, her rouge-painted lips twisted in disdain. 'I'm Amber Longstone, and I'll tell you something worth writing in that little book of yours.'

She planted herself in front of O'Brien, hands on her hips. 'I couldn't stand Lucy Daws, and I don't care who knows it. Little Miss Perfect with her sweet smile and butter-wouldn't-melt act.'

The other models fidgeted, but Amber pressed on, her voice dripping with venom.

'Everyone here treated her like some sort of saint. Well, I knew better. She wasn't half as innocent as she pretended to be. We all have secrets, don't we? I'm the one that's just being honest about things.'

I glanced around the room, noting how the other models avoided eye contact, their expressions sheepish. Some fidgeted with their clothes, others developed a fascination with their shoes. Their behaviour spoke volumes - more lurked beneath the surface of this fashion show than anyone was letting on.

O'Brien's pencil flew across his notebook, capturing every bitter word of Amber's outburst, as I wondered what HG might make of this development.

Several seconds elapsed before the detective lifted his eyes from the notebook and engaged the outspoken young woman.

His eyes narrowed at Amber's declaration. 'And what exactly did Miss Daws do to earn such enmity?'

'She was a manipulator.' Amber tossed her bobbed hair. 'Always playing the innocent while stepping over others to get ahead.'

'Could you be more specific?'

'Let's just say she knew how to work certain influential people to her advantage.' Amber's painted lips curved into a knowing smile. 'The right words here, a flutter of eyelashes there.'

O'Brien's pencil paused. 'Miss Longstone, you do realise that disparaging the deceased might cast suspicion in your direction?'

The shift in Amber's demeanour was subtle but unmistakable. Her shoulders relaxed, and her voice lost its sharp edge.

'Detective, I've told you the truth, that's all. When the gunshot went off, I was on the runway. Everyone saw me and there will be photographs to prove it. I speak as I find and don't care who hears it. In the coming days, you will discover just how rotten this industry is. My outspoken nature will be the least of your problems, I promise you.'

I stood there, astounded by Amber's brazen attitude. Working with HG, I saw many personalities, but Amber's honesty during the murder investigation was remarkable. Her insights about the fashion world's corruption suggested she knew more about Lucy's death than she'd let on.

Just then, a uniformed police officer entered the room and whispered something into O'Brien's ear. Whatever passed between them resulted in the detective's immediate departure. However, before leaving, he left one last set of instructions.

'I apologise for having to interrupt our little chat. While I'm gone, I ask that you remain here pending my return. My constable will ensure you have anything you need in the way of refreshments, except alcohol, of course. ' O'Brien turned to me. 'Of course, you may do as you please. All I ask is that you inform me of anything you hear or see relevant to the case. Do I have your assurance?'

I agreed to the detective's request, after which the fellow departed. This left a young constable to manage a group of shrewd models, whom, I suspected, might tease him rotten.

Finding the police officer's conversation amusing, I excused myself to tell HG what I'd learned and hear her news from Clara.

Unsure of which room HG had taken Clara, I trudged

up and down myriad corridors before meeting my mentor head on.

'Ah, there you are, dear boy. What have you been up to in my absence?'

I spent the next few minutes in deep conversation, relaying O'Brien's actions and the results of his inquiries. At last, I asked HG if her time with Clara Brightman had revealed anything.

'An excellent question, dear boy. Once I managed to calm Clara Brightman down a little, she began to talk. Not fluently, you understand, but cogent enough to make sense of what the poor girl meant.'

I urged my mentor to reveal all.

HG smiled that smile of hers before picking a speck of something off my jacket lapel.

'Lucy Daws murmured the words "Mason Drange" just before she died. I think, Rex, we have a major clue on our hands to unmask that girl's vicious killer.'

Chapter Four

A CHANGED PLAN

Saturday's tragedy weighed heavily as we left for Norwich Cathedral for Sunday worship.

HG had also arranged, and paid for, the fashion models to remain in the city, so that they might recover. And to be available to communicate any further information about Lucy Daws they might recall.

'Rex, do hurry.' HG tapped her silver-topped cane against the parquet flooring of the Royal Hotel's foyer. 'We've precisely ten minutes to make the service.'

Before I could muster a response, she swept through the revolving door and onto the pavement outside. The click of her heels echoed off the stone buildings that lined the empty streets. Not a soul stirred on this bitter Sunday morning, save for a lone newspaper boy who huddled in a doorway, his stack of papers untouched.

These streets had witnessed centuries pass; their medieval timber frames and Georgian facades standing sentinel through plague, war, and peace. An east wind whipped around my collar. Strange to think the North Sea lay just twenty miles to the east. Its waters nipped away the Norfolk coast as they had done since before the Normans raised Norwich's magnificent castle.

'Really, Rex, one foot in front of the other.' HG's voice carried back to me as we turned onto Queen Street.

'Nearly there.' HG paused at the entrance to cathedral close, her breath forming clouds in the chill air. 'Though I dare say we'll be lucky to find a decent seat now.'

We need not have worried. So vast was the nave that plenty of seats remained.

As we settled into a central pew, I looked up at the remarkable soaring roof above us. The nave's high, wooden ceiling, with its intricate design, shimmered in the light from the stained-glass windows.

'Look there.' HG pointed with her cane toward a patch of wall where fragments of medieval painted figures still clung. 'Henry VIII's reformers missed a bit.'

Indeed, they had. Among the white-washed walls, splashes of vermillion and azure remained. These were the remnants of saints and biblical scenes that had once adorned every surface. A particular fragment showed what might have been Mary Magdalene's robe, its rich blue pigment defying the centuries of neglect.

I ran my hand along the cold stone of the nearest column, feeling the rough texture beneath my fingers. Generations of people carved countless marks, dates, and initials into its surface.

'Rather fascinating graffiti, wouldn't you say?' I whispered to HG.

'Indeed. Though I'm more intrigued by these.' She gestured to several crude pentangles etched into the stone. 'Our ancestors' attempts to ward off evil spirits. One wonders if they worked.'

The organ played, its deep notes reverberating through the vast space, drawing my attention back to the present. Yet my mind lingered on those mysterious symbols and the countless hands that had left their mark in this sacred place.

For the next forty-five minutes, we enjoyed a form of service that hadn't changed since the early sixteenth-century, yet that wasn't the entire story as far as this sacred space was concerned. For 500 years before Henry had his way, the cathedral, like every other place of worship in England, had owed its loyalty to the Pope. How things change, I reminded myself.

As the Dean gave a final blessing to the congregation, the organ soared into life with an uplifting Voluntary by Bach as the pews emptied in orderly fashion.

As we emerged from the cathedral's west door, HG grasped my elbow. 'No time to dawdle, Rex. Detective Sergeant O'Brien expects us at half-past eleven. We head for the Tin Hut.'

I glanced at my pocket watch. Twenty minutes remained before our appointment. But what on earth did HG mean by "The Tin Hut"?

'You shall see, dear Rex. The walk should take us no more than ten minutes.' HG's cane clicked against the flagstones as we crossed the cathedral close. This city's police station has, to put it mildly, an eccentric design.

We passed through the cathedral gates and into the medieval heart of Norwich. The streets twisted and turned, following paths laid down centuries before motor cars existed.

We rounded a corner onto Gentleman's Walk and into the market square. On our left stood the imposing white building of Lloyds Bank, while to our right stood…well, a large tin hut. What was such an odd construction doing in the heart of what was once the second city of England after London?

I immediately understood the building's nickname: its corrugated metal made it resemble a dilapidated cricket pavilion. Several notice boards covered the bottom half of the building's frontage, as if advertising the latest release at a picture-house.

To the left front-side, a single door offered a less than an inviting method of accessing its strange interior.

We exchanged bemused looks as HG pointed her cane at the black-painted door. 'Onwards, dear boy. Let us see what delights await.'

A sharp push on the heavy door saw us enter a dismal foyer dominated by the high counter of the desk-sergeant's position. A single window frame comprising several small glass panes threw a dull, yellowish glimmer of light into the threatening space.

To say the interior of the old building presented a forlorn setting is to do an injustice to the word. We appeared to have entered a different world, where the freedoms available to all citizens in other circumstances, did not apply in this place.

A tall, broad-shouldered police officer aged around fifty-years gazed down upon us. The man's countenance bore witness to a working life spent dealing with argumentative drunkards, and other volatile reprobates.

He paid no regard to HG, as if receiving a Dowager Duchess was an everyday occurrence.

'We are here at the request of Detective Sergeant O'Brien,' began HG. 'Will you please alert your colleague to our arrival?'

It took the fellow several seconds to answer the question.

In the interim, he looked from one to the other of us without remark.

'That will not be possible, madam,' the sergeant finally replied in a gruff, low voice.

'Your Grace will suffice,' HG said, declaring her expectations.

The sergeant raised an eyebrow, before partaking in an exaggerated sniff of the surrounding air. If my nostrils were to be relied upon, it did nothing other than fill the fellow's lungs with a musty odour.

'Your Grace, is it?' the man ventured. 'Well, Duchess or not, Sergeant O'Brien is incapacitated at the moment, and likely to remain that way for some days. It's the shingles, you see.'

I had heard of such an ailment and sympathised with O'Brien.

HG gripped the silver terminal of her cane with a ferociousness I should not wish to have experienced about my person. However, as far as the sergeant was concerned, she showed a calm and measured presence.

'Then may we see his superior?' asked HG.

'Superior?' responded the sergeant with a puzzled expression. 'There isn't one.'

I observed HG making herculean efforts to remain calm, although the tapping of her cane on the stone floor showed this to be a battle she might well lose.

'Are you telling me that a Detective Sergeant is the most senior officer at this establishment?'

'Afraid so mada—I mean, Your Grace. We're short staffed, you see. If O'Brien isn't back within a day or two, I'll have to arrange for a stand-in if I can borrow one. If not, it'll be up to London to sort it out.'

HG shook her head, causing her hat to wobble in

sympathy. 'And where is the commissioner? You do know a murder took place in this city last evening, and that your colleague is in charge of the investigation?'

The desk sergeant fiddled with the chain of his police whistle as if wishing HG's question away.

'And there's the rub. I'm aware of which you speak. Until other arrangements are in place, I shall pick up the reins,' responded the less than convinced police officer. 'As for the commissioner. He's based not fifty yards yonder at the old Guild Hall. Trouble is, he's away, too. '

Ignoring news of the Commissioner's movements, HG instead focused on the death of Lucy Daws.

'Have you headed an investigation like this in the past?' HG asked, half-knowing the answer from the fellow's peculiar interest in a fountain pen, the top of which he continuously unscrewed, then tightened again.

'Er...not exactly. You see, it's not something we experience often. I suppose that's a good thing, isn't it?'

I noted HG's eyes narrow.

'Very well,' she announced in a clear, strong, voice. I shall make the necessary arrangements. This is no time to delay matters. Please relate my best wishes to Detective Sergeant O'Brien and tell him I shall pray for his rapid return to rude health. In the meantime, I shall make certain enquiries of the Police commissioner of the Metropolitan Police in London.'

With that, HG turned on her heels and made for the heavy entrance door. Before leaving, she turned to speak to the desk sergeant one last time.

'Please ensure that O'Brien's notebook is available at your counter for collection by mid-day on Monday; Tomorrow.'

With that, HG breezed through the open doorway,

stopped to adjust her hat and rested for a moment as she gazed at the magnificent St. Peter Mancroft church. She had the bit between her teeth and all I could do was to hang on to her metaphorical coat tails.

———

Back at the Royal Hotel, we partook in a delicious Sunday Roast, which did wonders for HG's mood. After all, who could resist a steaming plate of roast potatoes, Yorkshire pudding, beef, and all the trimmings?

HG arranged her dessert spoon while collecting her thoughts. The dining room at the Royal buzzed with diners, the hubbub providing perfect cover for our discussion.

'Now Rex, let's establish what we know.' She dabbed her lips with her napkin. 'First, we have poor Lucy Daws' last words to Clara Brightman.'

I posited that "Mason" was a common name and would, therefore, prove difficult to link to any one individual.

'Yes, that does complicate matters a little,' HG began. 'And then there's young Miss Davenport rushed departure by car, the number plate of which Lord Wentworth failed to catch.'

I recalled Wentworth retelling of his desperate sprint "Like a man possessed," as he put it, which, for a gentleman of his age, might have led to disaster.

HG nodded as she selected a crisp roast potato.

I reminded HG she'd acknowledged having some prior knowledge of Miss Davenport's background.'

'Oh yes.' HG's fork paused midway to her mouth. 'The Davenports put on quite the show of respectability, but her father's gambling debts nearly ruined them last season.

Only a timely marriage proposal to her elder sister saved their reputation.'

'And how does this connect to Lucy Daws' murder?' I asked.

'That, dear Rex, is what we need to determine.' She carefully cut into her Yorkshire pudding. 'Miss Davenport's plan to ruin the fashion show is key to the case, but murder is excessive, even for her.'

I thought about Lucy's name clue, Wentworth chasing Milly, and Amber's hatred of the victim.

'There's something else bothering me,' HG continued. 'Clara is distraught about Lucy's death, yet she's holding something back. I think our next move is to have another chat with her. But that can wait until after our apple pie and custard.

After lunch, HG and I walked to the Station Hotel, where my mentor had booked rooms for the models. The late afternoon sun cast long shadows across the cobblestones, and a gentle breeze carried the scent of fresh-cut grass from the nearby gardens.

HG suggested the hotel's location near the shops and train station was perfect for young women needing a distraction.

Approaching the building, we noticed Clara sitting outside alone. Her blonde hair glinted in the sunlight as she lifted a coffee cup to her lips. Upon noticing us, she offered a demure smile, though her eyes betrayed her exhaustion.

'Mind if we join you?' HG's tone held its usual warmth.

Clara gestured to the empty chairs. 'Please do.'

We settled ourselves around the small round table, the

metal chairs scraping against the flagstones. HG leaned forward, her expression gentle. 'How are you feeling, my dear?'

Clara's hands trembled as she set down her cup. 'I keep seeing her there, on the floor. Every time I close my eyes, Lucy's just...lying there.' Her voice cracked.

HG reached across and placed a comforting hand on Clara's arm. The three of us sat in silence, broken only by the distant whistle of a train and the rustle of leaves overhead.

'Clara.' HG's voice was soft, but firm. 'Rex and I need to ask you a few more questions. I hope you understand.'

Clara returned her coffee cup to its saucer. She straightened her back, folded her hands in her lap, and met HG's gaze with newfound composure.

HG steered the conversation towards Lucy's past, her manner both gentle and purposeful. Clara's posture shifted, her shoulders dropping as she settled into her chair.

'Tell me about Lucy's background, dear. Where did she grow up?'

'In Norwich, actually. Her father owned a small printing press near the cathedral. She lived above the shop with her parents until last year when she moved to London.'

HG nodded. 'And her circle of friends?'

'We met at her first show in London. She kept to herself mostly but was kind to everyone.' Clara paused, twisting a silver bracelet around her wrist. 'Though lately, she'd become more...private.'

I asked what Clara meant by the comment.

'She'd disappear after shows, make excuses to skip our usual suppers. When I asked, she'd just smile and say she was meeting someone special.'

'A gentleman friend?' HG's eyebrow arched.

'She never gave me a name. Just said he was different from the usual sort who hang around models.'

HG looked thoughtful. 'Clara, there are only two explanations for what happened to Lucy. Either someone mistook her for another model, or...' She paused, her voice dropping. 'Someone harboured enough hatred to commit murder.'

Clara's face blanched. The coffee cup rattled against its saucer as her hand jerked. For a moment, she looked as though she might faint, but then colour returned to her cheeks, and she straightened her posture.

'Hatred?' Her voice barely rose above a whisper. 'But who would...' She stopped, pressing her lips together.

HG paused proceeding as she noticed a waiter passing by. 'My dear fellow, would you be so good as to bring three coffees, and perhaps some iced fancies if you have them?

The middle-aged gentleman, dressed in an immaculate white shirt and bowtie, black trousers, and matching shoes, smiled and nodded. 'At once, Madam.'

After he left the scene, HG continued. 'I know it's a dreadful thing to contemplate, but there we have it. Is there anything—anything at all you remember that stands out about Lucy's life as you knew it? Even minor details could help bring your friend's killer to justice.

I watched Clara's face as she wrestled with her thoughts. Her fingers traced the rim of her empty coffee cup, round, and round in an endless circle. HG caught my eye, and I noticed the subtle lift of her eyebrow. We both recognised that familiar look - the expression of someone on the cusp of sharing vital information. The waiter appeared with our fresh coffees and a plate of delicate iced fancies. Clara failed to acknowledge his presence.

The silence stretched, broken only by the distant sound

of a whistle that marked the departure of another train. Clara's gaze moved to HG to show she'd reached a decision.

'She did tell me that her father strongly objected to her seeing her gentleman friend. I can't believe he would do anything, but Lucy did say he had a ferocious temper since her mother died. She said he wanted to know her every move. That's why Lucy moved to London. To get away. That's what she told me, anyway.'

The tension lessened as our formal discussion eased into a light conversation. This I took as HG's decision to end the interrogation for the time being.

As HG shifted direction, her manner became more casual in tone.

'Tell me about your experiences in fashion, Clara. What aspects bring you the most joy?'

Clara's demeanour brightened. 'The travel, without question. Paris, Milan, even New York last autumn. Each city offers new possibilities, fresh connections.'

'Connections?' HG selected a second iced fancy from the plate. 'One must always look ahead in this industry. Today's model could be tomorrow's designer or fashion house director. Speaking of designers, which houses capture your imagination?'

'Poiret's designs are revolutionary.' Clara's eyes lit up. 'And Vionnet - her cut-on-the-bias technique is pure genius. Though personally, I favour Lucile's more romantic aesthetic.'

'Ah, Lucile—or Lady Duff-Gordon to use her formal title. Do you know she survived the Titanic disaster? Then, just three years later in 1915, narrowly avoided the Lusitania tragedy because she cancelled her ticket at the last minute.' HG dabbed her lips with a napkin. 'Anyway, I digress. Have you considered your own path? Where do you see yourself in five years?'

'I've been saving, actually.' Clara's voice grew stronger, more assured. 'My dream is to open my own boutique. Not in London - the rents are astronomical. But perhaps here in Norwich. Or back home in Bristol. Somewhere I could build a loyal clientele without bankrupting myself in short order.'

'A sound business strategy,' HG nodded approvingly.

After chatting with Clara for twenty more minutes, we returned to the hotel, whereupon HG said to make a call and asked me to wait in the conservatory.

A little over ten minutes later, HG appeared at my table and made an announcement.

'Tomorrow morning at 10.32 am we shall be standing on platform one of Norwich railway station. Detective Inspector Whipple will alight said train and take over the investigation into the murder of Lucy Daws.'

Chapter Five

A DETECTIVE ARRIVES

Monday morning dawned with a heavy sky and the sort of drizzle that soaked into every pore of one's skin. The only saving grace was that getting to Norwich Thorpe station in time to collect Whipple, still gave us time for a hearty breakfast, which HG and I took full advantage of.

Now, as I pulled the Rolls into a parking spot next to the entrance of the Victorian edifice, the clouds darkened. Perhaps a portent of things to come?

'Do come along, Rex. We must not keep Arthur waiting. You know that he is not an aficionado of rail travel and he will, I'm sure, be all of a doo-dah when he arrives.'

Whipple had an aversion to anything that moved quicker than a horse. HG recalled Queen Victoria's similar dislike of rail travel. She recalled that the old Queen had a connection from her carriage directly to the train driver. If the train went too fast, she pulled a lever to ring a bell, commanding the driver to slow the train.

'Ah, there he is,' remarked my joyful mentor. 'Look at his little face. He is in need of his friend.'

One might think it odd that a Duchess of the Realm used such terminology, in particular when the object of her affection was a police officer. Then again, HG and Whipple shared a rare friendship. She told me once that they met many years ago. Whipple was a newly promoted Detective Sergeant in serious trouble through no fault of his own. HG came to the rescue, and thus sprung an indomitable friendship based on absolute trust and mutual admiration.

'What ails you, Rex? Do come along.'

My mentor's urgent call called me back from my mental meanderings, to catch up with HG in haste.

There before us stood Detective Inspector Arthur Whipple of Scotland Yard. This was a man whose reputation as the finest detective brain England offered, went before him. Whipple's secret, although not one he cultivated, was to appear somewhat disorganised in his appearance. His ill-fitting clothes and habit of sucking "Everton" mints at the most inappropriate of times.

'I hate those things,' mumbled Whipple as he glanced back at the stationary train as if it were the devil incarnate.

The detective pulled his coat tighter around his shoulders and cast another dark look at the steam engine. 'Ghastly contraptions. The sulphur from that smoke gets into your lungs. I shall taste it for days.'

I watched him pat down his pockets, no doubt searching for one of his beloved Everton mints.

'And the food.' He shuddered. 'If you can call it that. Stale sandwiches wrapped in greasy paper. Tea that tastes of dishwater.'

'Come now, Arthur,' HG chided. 'Surely it wasn't all that dire?'

'And then there's the speed; fast enough to draw the

breath from me lungs, it was. It's not natural, I tell you. Not natural at all,' exclaimed the twitching detective.

HG reached for his hand, her gloved fingers wrapping around his. She gave it a gentle squeeze. 'Well, you're here now, so all will be well.'

Whipple's eyebrows shot up towards his hairline. 'What, with a killer on the loose?'

HG scoffed at Whipple's remark. 'Dear Arthur, you thrive on such challenges. Now, what do you wish to do first?'

'Make quick work of a plate of bangers, bacon, and beans,' came the instant response.

HG looked up at the large circular station clock as we made our way to the exit. 'It's only 10.45 am. Did you not have breakfast?'

I noted Whipple chose restraint over honesty. 'Let's just say my sister is not a morning person, so expecting her to light the range at such an early hour wasn't going to happen.'

'You should be thankful your sibling took you in all those years ago. What state you might be in now if responsible for your own home comforts, I do not know.'

Whipple chose not to answer. The fellow knew when to surrender. Instead, he pulled up his collar against the continuing drizzle as we made our way back to the Rolls.

I navigated the Rolls through Norwich's damp streets while HG and Whipple discussed the case. The detective twisted in his seat, speaking through the open glass partition to HG in the back.

'Tell me about this Clara Brightman,' Whipple pulled out his notebook. 'Your telegram mentioned she was the last to speak with Lucy.'

'Indeed. Clara spoke of Lucy's secret gentleman friend,

though she claimed not to know his identity.' HG adjusted her hat pin. 'More concerning was her revelation about Lucy's father - a controlling brute.'

'Controlling enough to murder his own daughter?' Whipple's pencil scratched across the page.

'The thought had crossed my mind. Lucy fled to London to escape his influence, you see. Perhaps he learned of the fashion show.'

'And this mysterious gentleman?'

'Clara seemed genuinely ignorant of his identity. Though Lucy confided in her about most things.'

I took the corner onto Prince of Wales Road with care, mindful of the slick cobblestones.

'What of the Davenport girl?' Whipple asked. 'Your message mentioned their hasty departure.'

'Milly Davenport left the show moments after the murder. Her family's finances are in dire straits - gambling debts primarily.'

'Could Lucy have known something about their situation?'

'It's possible. Models hear much gossip backstage.' HG tapped her chin thoughtfully. 'Though why kill her in such a public setting-and anyway, her public pronouncement was against the Fairbridge twins?'

'Sometimes killers make mistakes under pressure,' Whipple mused. 'Or perhaps that was precisely the point - to send a message. As for the twins- a red herring on her part, perhaps?'

'Lucy's last words were "Mason...Drange", or perhaps, "Mason range",' HG added. 'Clara seemed particularly affected when I mentioned it.'

'We'll need to look into that. Could be significant.' Whipple flipped his notebook closed. 'I'd like to speak with

Clara myself, get a feel for what she might be holding back. But first the crime scene beckons.'

I guided the Rolls to a halt outside the Assembly Hall. The grand Georgian building loomed before us, its Portland stone facade darkened by the morning's persistent drizzle. Gone was the sparkle and glamour of Saturday evening - now the building wore its grief like a widow's veil. Water streaked down the ionic columns, while puddles gathered in the worn steps leading to the entrance.

Whipple stepped out first, grimacing as raindrops pelted his already rumpled coat. HG followed with considerably more grace, her black umbrella unfurling into a protective dome. I brought up the rear, noting how the building's windows seemed to weep in the grey morning light.

Inside, our footsteps echoed through the empty foyer. The gilt-framed mirrors that had reflected society's finest now only captured our solemn expressions. Pendlebury materialised from a side door, his usually pristine uniform showing signs of a sleepless night.

He nodded respectfully. 'Your Grace. Everything remains untouched, as requested.'

'Most excellent, Pendlebury,' HG replied. 'The inspector will need to see the scene precisely as it was.'

Pendlebury led us through the building's maze of corridors. The smell of face powder and perfume still lingered in the air, mixing with the metallic tang that only death leaves behind. The main hall felt like a theatre frozen in time. Chairs remained scattered where panicked guests had abandoned them. The catwalk stood empty, while discarded programmes littered the floor like fallen leaves.

'The dressing room is through here, Inspector.' Pendlebury gestured to a door at the far end of the hall. 'We've kept it locked since...' His voice trailed off, unable to finish the sentence.

The small space where Lucy Daws met her end waited beyond that door, still holding its terrible secret. I watched as Whipple squared his shoulders, preparing to face what lay within.

He extracted a handkerchief from his trouser pocket and used it to guard his skin, coming into contact with the brass doorknob. 'I know the local police have dusted for fingerprints,' he began. 'Still, better safe than sorry.

The dismal space revealed itself as Whipple pushed the creaking door open to its full extent, then flicked the light switch. A sickly orange glow provided scant light, like a cheap tallow candle.

I hung back near the doorway as HG recounted the scene, we'd discovered that fateful evening. The small, empty room felt even more oppressive now, its windowless walls closing in around us.

'Lucy lay there, Arthur.' HG pointed to the spot where the young model had fallen. 'Face-upwards, one arm outstretched towards the door. Her evening gown - a beautiful creation in midnight blue silk - spread like a dark pool.'

Whipple crouched down, examining the floor. His ill-fitting jacket bunched up around his shoulders as he moved.

'The shot came from outside,' HG continued. 'Entry wound to the heart. Death would have been near-instantaneous, thank heavens for small mercies.'

'And your first thoughts when you arrived?' Whipple looked up from his examination.

'That the killer must still have been present. With no windows and only one door, they couldn't have left without being seen. The corridors were full of people responding to the shot.'

'Yet no one saw anyone suspicious leaving, other than your friend, Lord Wentworth, who saw the Davenport girl and raced after her?'

'That is correct.' HG's voice carried a note of frustration. 'Which suggests either the girl is our murderer, or remarkable timing by persons unknown...'

'Blended in with the crowd, eh? Whipple finished. 'Someone who belonged here. Someone who could walk away without drawing attention to themselves.'

HG paced the small space, her heels clicking against the pine floor. 'My other immediate thought was that this was no random act. It was all too deliberate: the location, the timing. Lucy's death was supposed to happen here, Arthur. In the middle of her moment of triumph.'

Whipple nodded, jotting notes in his ever-present notebook. 'Revenge. Or a message, perhaps?'

'That's what we must determine.' HG paused. 'Though I can't shake the feeling that Lucy's ultimate words hold the key to everything.'

I dropped Whipple off at the Station Hotel, since he suggested to HG that he interview Clara and the other girls on his own. He reasoned that a new, albeit official, face might elicit new information. It also occurred to me that the inspector might avail himself of a hot meal to make up for his absent breakfast without the scrutiny of his eating habits by HG.

Having accomplished my task, the Norwich Public Record Office loomed before me, its classical columns reaching skyward. Through heavy oak doors, the scent of old paper and furniture polish filled my nostrils. A brass desk bell gleamed on the reception counter, where a grey-haired woman peered at me through wire-rimmed spectacles.

'Good morning, sir. How might I assist?'

Her crisp accent marked her as one of the middling sort, though her manner suggested aspirations above her station. The clicking of her heels echoed across the marble floor as she guided me past rows of researchers bent over leather-bound volumes.

Oak cabinets stretched from floor to ceiling, their brass handles polished to a shine. Each drawer bore alphabetical labels in perfect copperplate script. The categorisation seemed endless - births, deaths, marriages, property deeds, business licences, court records.

'Looking for anything specific?' The woman's keys jangled as she unlocked a cabinet.

My task felt impossible. Mason Drange could appear in any of these thousands of records - if that was even his real name. Lucy Daws's last word had led us here, but without more context, searching the archives was like hunting for a needle in a haystack.

Two elderly gentlemen in tweed jackets huddled over a tome at a nearby table, whispering about parish boundaries. A young woman in a navy dress made rapid notes while consulting multiple volumes spread before her.

The reception lady pulled out a drawer. 'Shall we start with the basic indices?'

My heart sank at the sight of hundreds of alphabetised cards. This could take days, perhaps weeks, and we had no guarantee Mason Drange's name would yield anything of value to our investigation.

'Why don't you interrogate the latest census?' said the receptionist, which I thought an excellent idea.

Thirty fruitless minutes later, I hadn't found a single entry that matched the supposed name, or any derivative thereof. For all I knew, the fellow might not be local. I'd had enough.

And so I said my goodbyes, braved the heavy drizzle, and bolted for the Rolls.

As I pulled up outside the Royal Hotel, the drizzle had turned into a proper downpour. The weather matched my mood after my failed mission at the records office.

HG stood in the reception; arms folded across her chest. 'And where exactly have you been?'

My mouth went dry. I muttered something about taking in the sights of Norwich - the Castle, Elm Hill. The words tumbled out in an unconvincing jumble.

'Really?' HG's eyebrow arched. 'Talking about sights, I have a very damp detective drying himself off after waiting for you to pick him up.'

My heart sank. In my quest at the records office, I'd forgotten about collecting Whipple. The intensity of HG's disapproving stare became too much.

'I went to the records office,' I confessed, heat rising in my cheeks. 'To look up the latest census for any mention of...but...'

'Well, well. I commend you for your enthusiasm, Rex. Though perhaps next time you'll remember were you should be, rather than following flights of fancy.'

I nodded sheepishly, grateful that HG found humour in my misadventure rather than further cause for reproach.

We had just settled into a pair of the hotel's plush armchairs with a fresh pot of Darjeeling when Whipple appeared in the doorway, looking like a half-drowned cat. Water dripped from his coat onto the polished floor as he fixed me with a glare that could have curdled milk.

With theatrical flair, he pulled out his handkerchief and wrung it out, each twist sending droplets spattering across the carpet. The other hotel guests cast sideways glances at the spectacle.

HG's eyes sparkled with barely contained mirth. 'Oh, do stop being so dramatic, Arthur. Come and sit down - I've ordered you a hot chocolate.'

Whipple's expression remained thunderous as he squelched his way to our table.

'And,' HG added with a hint of mischief, 'I took the liberty of requesting one of those chocolate eclairs you're so fond of.'

My stomach growled at the mention of the hotel's famous pastries. I'd been eyeing them in the display case earlier, but HG had steered me away.

As if reading my thoughts, she turned to me. 'I'm afraid you'll have to do without, Rex. Consider it penance for abandoning poor Arthur to the elements.'

Whipple took off his overcoat and settled into his chair. I caught the subtle quirk of satisfaction at the corner of his mouth as he smoothed his damp moustache.

As tempers cooled and our beverages took effect, HG asked Whipple what he'd learned, apart from the rain being wet. I must confess to wishing HG had let the matter drop with my pastry penance. Instead she gave me a polite smile, daring me to respond. This I thought better of. HG presented far too formidable a foe. In any event, I hoped for a pastry before the afternoon was out.

I settled back in my chair, watching HG and Whipple trade observations. The rain drummed against the hotel windows, creating an oddly soothing backdrop to their discussion.

'Clara's quite broken up about it all,' Whipple said, dabbing at his moustache with a napkin. 'Poor girl could barely string two sentences together without dissolving into tears.'

'She repeated much of what she told us yesterday,' HG asked. 'About Lucy's secret gentleman friend and her father?'

'Word for word.' Whipple paused to sip his hot chocolate. 'Though she did let something slip that might be of interest. Apparently, Lucy had caught the eye of an American agent. Not just any small-time operator either - one of the big New York agencies.'

'Really?' HG leaned forward. 'Further cause for jealousy, then?'

'Indeed. It was common knowledge that Lucy was headed for bigger and better things. Clara seemed quite proud of that fact,' Whipple replied.

'And what of our friend, Amber Longsdale?'

Whipple's expression soured. 'Now there's a piece of work. Spent half an hour telling me what a two-faced snake Clara was. How she's always plotted and schemed. Went on and on about it.'

'A touch too emphatic, perhaps?' HG's eyes narrowed.

'My thoughts exactly. The fashion world,' Whipple shook his head, 'it's a viper's nest. Half of them seem to despise each other, the remainder are just playing at it because that's what's expected. Makes it dashed difficult to separate the wheat from the chaff.'

'Or, to paraphrase, the murderer from the merely malicious,' HG added.

Chapter Six

A FATHER'S LOVE?

In keeping with Whipple's professional outlook on life, my morning lapse soon faded, and I found myself back in the detective's good books again. I'm pleased to say that HG also let the matter drop, and so we enjoyed a hearty lunch in the Royal Hotel restaurant before a busy afternoon of interviews and checking of alibies.

The establishment lounge offered a welcome respite from the morning's drama. Whipple sank into one of the plush armchairs while HG perched elegantly on the edge of her seat, both nursing steaming cups of coffee.

'Two matters require our immediate attention,' HG began. 'Lucy Daws's father and that troublesome Miss Davenport.'

Whipple's sharp features hardened. 'The father concerns me most. A controlling parent with a violent temper - that's quite the combination.'

'Indeed.' said HG. 'Clara mentioned he opposed Lucy's modelling career rather forcefully. 'Do we have an address for him?'

'Not yet, but I'll ring Clara Brightman - I forgot to ask for his address when we spoke earlier.'

I watched as Whipple jotted notes in his leather-bound notebook, his pencil scratching against the paper.

'And Miss Davenport?' He glanced up. 'The one who threatened to cause a scene before the show?'

HG's lips curved into a knowing smile. 'She's somewhat of a social butterfly. Milly flits between country houses like a bee between flowers. Finding her current location might prove challenging.'

'But you have ideas?'

I will contact Lady Thorpe, the Knowls-Brabhams, and Lord Wentworth to see if they have any information. Someone must know where she's landed.' HG sipped her coffee. 'Though I suspect she hasn't strayed far from Norwich. Milly does so love to be where the drama unfolds.'

'And there's been plenty of that,' Whipple remarked.

I reminded my colleagues that we had yet to recover Detective Sergeant O'Brien's notebook from the Tin Hut, a description that baffled Whipple.

'Fear not, Arthur,' remarked HG. 'Rex eludes to the operational headquarters of your fellow officers. All shall make sense when you clap eyes on the…er…eccentric construction.'

Whipple flipped through his notebook one last time before closing it with a snap. His brow furrowed as he considered something, then turned to HG.

'About the models and staff - how long have you arranged for them to stay at the Railway Hotel? I've already told them to remain local for the next few days.'

HG set down her coffee cup with a delicate clink. 'I've arranged an open booking with the hotel management.

They understand the situation and will accommodate our witnesses for as long as necessary.'

'Most generous.' Whipple's usually stern expression softened. 'That will make investigating this matter considerably easier. No rushing interviews or hunting down scattered witnesses across the county, except for Milly Davenport.'

'My thoughts exactly,' said HG. 'The last thing we need is key witnesses disappearing before we've had a chance to question them.'

Whipple nodded his appreciation, clearly impressed by HG's foresight in handling the practical aspects of the investigation.

'Of course,' began Whipple, 'assuming our killer lies not among the young ladies, they'll have wasted no time in scarpering - and for now, that includes Miss Davenport.'

HG and I waited in the Rolls to the rear of the Tin Hut while Whipple navigated his way around to the front. We both giggled as the fellow looked the remarkable building up and down. So engrossed was he in taking in the strange sight that he almost bumped into a chap coming in the opposite direction. A nod and cap-lift settled things, and the detective went inside the corrugated building without further incident.

HG and I exchanged knowing glances as Whipple stormed back to the Rolls, his face a picture of indignation. He yanked open the passenger door and dropped onto the leather seat with a huff.

'The absolute cheek of it. That desk sergeant had the gall to ask if I was selling insurance. Insurance! Can you believe it?' Whipple's moustache twitched with irritation.

'Asked me if I had any inexpensive policies for the constabulary.'

I caught HG's subtle smile in the rear-view mirror.

'Soon put him straight,' Whipple continued, waving O'Brien's notebook. I identified myself as a Met Police officer and explained I might have to report on the station's performance.

He smoothed his rain-dampened suit. 'You should have seen how quickly his attitude changed. Nearly fell off his chair, apologising. Though I can hardly blame him entirely. What self-respecting police station operates out of a tin shack? It's barely fit for storing garden tools.'

'They all used to be crammed into the Guild Hall not fifty-yards away, but as the force grew in number, they needed temporary accommodation. Except it turned out to be not so temporary,' HG responded.

'Ridiculous. How anyone's expected to conduct serious police work in that oversized biscuit tin is beyond me.' Whipple flipped through O'Brien's notebook with disdain. 'At least the sergeant managed to locate this without too much fuss once he knew who I was. Though I did make it clear, I might pop back to ensure things are running ship-shape in his superior's absence.'

By the time we reached the home of Lucy Daws' father, Whipple had calmed a little, though his moustache continued to twitch from time to time.

'Here we are,' announced HG. '52a Grapes Hill.'

The brick-built dwelling rested in the middle of a row of terraced houses as they traced their way up a steep incline. Every three or four houses saw a step in the roofline to consider the changing elevation.

The street bustled with activity as we pulled up to the kerb. A coal wagon clattered past, its heavy-hooved horses straining as they made their ascent up the steep hill. Behind them, a Morris Commercial lorry inched forward, the driver drumming his fingers impatiently on the steering wheel. Several private motorcars were parked along the street, their polished bonnets gleaming despite the overcast day.

Through gaps between the buildings, I caught glimpses of the new Catholic cathedral reaching skyward at the summit of Grapes Hill. Its clean stone facade standing in stark contrast to the red brick terraces that lined our approach.

Number 52a sat midway up the incline, identical to its neighbours, with its modest front garden barely large enough for a dustbin. A low brick wall, weathered and spotted with moss and dirtied by decades of winter smog, separated the property from the busy pavement. The wooden gate, its green paint peeling at the edges, creaked as Whipple pushed it open to access the front path.

Smoke curled from the chimney pots, caught by the breeze and stretched at an angle before dissipating into the grey Norwich sky. The same scene repeated all along the terrace - dozens of plumes being tugged sideways, creating a rhythmic pattern above the roofline. The scent of coal smoke hung heavy in the air, mingling with the exhaust fumes from passing vehicles.

A horse-drawn milk float clattered down the uneven road, its bottles tinkling. Its driver called out a cheerful greeting to a group of children playing hopscotch on the pavement opposite. They paused their game to wave back before returning to their chalk-drawn squares.

We huddled in line before the front door of No. 52a, with just enough room for me to close the low gate behind us. HG rapped on the panelled door with the silver tip of her walking stick. After what seemed like an eternity, the door opened to reveal a gruff-looking fellow in need of a good shave and haircut. He wore a dark pair of worn trousers held up with braces that rested askew on his chest owing to more than one button being missing from said trousers. To complete his apparel, the gentleman wore a collarless shirt, made decent by an off-white scarf around his neck.

'Well?' was the extent of the chap's welcome, his gruff voice offering only menace.

'Am I speaking to Mr Daws, father of Lucy Daws?'

The man gave HG a piercing stare, before turning his attention to Whipple and I. Behind me I heard a man's voice acknowledge Mr Daws. He did not reply.

Daws then turned to HG and wiped his nose on an upturned shirt sleeve. 'Well?'

'You are speaking to the Dowager Duchess of Drakeford, and it is news of your daughter that I and my associates come with. Now, do we stand here on the street like beggars, or will you grant entrance to us?'

Mr Daws' eyes narrowed at HG's commanding tone. His shoulders hunched forward, and he planted his feet wider apart in the doorway like a guard dog marking its territory. A vein pulsed at his temple as he scratched at three days' worth of stubble.

'How do you know my Lucy?' His voice carried the rough edge of someone who'd spent too many years shouting over machinery.

HG lifted her chin. 'That's not of import for now, Mr Daws. What matters is that we have information concerning your daughter that you need to hear.'

A low rumble emanated from deep in Daws' chest - the sort of sound a bear might make before deciding whether to charge or retreat. His bloodshot eyes darted between the three of us, lingering longest on Whipple's police-issue note-book clutched in his hand.

The silence stretched thin as a wire. Behind us, the children's game of hopscotch had gone quiet. Even they seemed to sense the tension radiating from number 52a's doorstep.

At last, Daws shifted his considerable bulk to one side. He didn't speak, just jerked his head toward the narrow vestibule behind him. The gesture wasn't exactly welcom-ing, but it was clear enough - we could enter.

The movement caused one side of his loose braces to slip further down his shoulder. He yanked them back up with a rough hand as HG stepped past him into the gloom beyond the doorway. Whipple followed, and I brought up the rear, catching a whiff of stale tobacco.

HG made to open the nearest door, which led to the small parlour.

'Not in there,' Daws growled. That's for best. He pushed past us, making no allowance for HG's impeccable wardrobe, and led us into the tiniest living space I'd come across.

The contents of the room comprised a moth-eaten armchair pulled close to an open hearth, two wooden chairs, and a sideboard that had seen much better days. Above the mantle hung a mirror with its rusted chain looped over a nail. An open door only four paces from our position allowed sight of an even smaller room with a Belfast sink and a single tap. To the open doorway's left, a window punctured the wall, previewing a narrow backyard and outside toilet.

Daws sat in the armchair without offering the remaining chairs to his guests. The fellow leaned forward and took his filled pipe from the fire hearth, pulled a wood taper from a sort of stoneware tube and lit its end in the fire. Next, he held the flame to his pipe bowl while sucking. Satisfied with his lit pipe, he gestured without looking for HG and one other to take the remaining chairs.

I remained standing while HG and Whipple took the seating. The floorboards creaked beneath my feet as I shifted my weight, seeking a comfortable position. Coal dust motes danced in the weak sunlight that filtered through the grimy windowpane.

Daws settled deeper into his armchair, its ancient springs protesting. His gaze fixed on the small window opposite, taking in the view of his neglected yard. A tin bath hung on one wall, its surface dulled by exposure to the elements. Across from it, a dolly tub slouched against the brickwork, cobwebs stretching between its handles. Neither looked as though they'd seen soap and water in months, perhaps years.

Pipe smoke curled around Daws' head, adding to the yellowed stains on the ceiling. The clock on the mantle ticked away precious minutes while we sat in uncomfortable silence. A cart rattled past outside, the horse's hooves striking, pounding the cobblestones.

HG cleared her throat. 'Mr Daws, do you not wish to hear what we've come to tell you about Lucy?'

The pipe stem clicked against his teeth as he clenched it tighter. His eyes never left the window, as though the crumbling yard held secrets, only he could see. Another long moment passed, marked by the steady drip of a tap from the kitchen.

'Don't have a daughter,' he growled, the words emerging in a cloud of blue-grey smoke. His gaze remained

70

fixed on the window; his profile was hard as granite in the dim light.

HG turned her gaze to Whipple and me. A sadness fell over her features, heralding the dreadful news to come.

'Mr Daws. I know a little of why you say such a thing. However, we are here to tell you a sad truth.'

HG leaned forward in her chair, her voice taking on that gentle tone she reserved for delivering tough news.

'Mr Daws, I regret to inform you that Lucy died on Saturday last at the Assembly Hall.'

The pipe smoke continued its lazy dance toward the ceiling. Not a muscle twitched in Daws' weathered face as he stared through the grimy window opposite. Only the quickening rhythm of his draws on the pipe betrayed any reaction to the news of his daughter's death.

The clock on the mantle marked each heavy second. A dog barked somewhere down the street. The coal in the grate shifted with a soft hiss.

'Mr Daws?' HG's voice carried a note of concern. 'I should explain that Detective Sergeant O'Brien, who initially led the investigation, fell ill before he could notify you. That's why you're only learning about this now.'

Still, Daws said nothing. His gaze remained fixed on the yard outside, as though the crumbling brick walls and rusted tin bath held more interest than news of his daughter's murder. The pipe stem clicked against his teeth again as he drew harder, more frequently now. Blue-grey smoke wreathed his head like a storm cloud.

'Mr Daws, did you hear what I said about Lucy?'

The question hung in the air, unanswered. Through the window, a sparrow landed on the dolly tub, pecked at something invisible, then fluttered away. Daws tracked its flight with the same detached interest he'd shown to everything else.

Through the thick pipe smoke, Daws finally spoke without turning his head. 'I told you, I don't have a daughter. Are you deaf, woman?'

His words carried enough venom to make me wince, but HG remained composed. I'd seen her deal with far ruder characters than this grief-stricken father. And grief it must be, I thought, even if he refused to show it. He came from a tough background, where showing emotion showed weakness.

HG smoothed her skirts, unruffled by his coarse manner. 'Mr Daws, there is much about Lucy's death that remains unknown to the police. Perhaps you might have information that could help us understand why it happened? Even the smallest detail could prove valuable.'

The pipe smoke continued its lazy spiral toward the ceiling as Daws shifted in his chair. The ancient springs creaked beneath him, a counterpoint to the steady tick of the mantle clock.

'Information?' He spat the word like it tasted bitter. 'Told you already - no daughter means no information.' His fingers tightened on the pipe stem until his knuckles showed white through his weathered skin.

HG's voice became firm. 'The police are particularly interested in understanding more about Lucy's life before she moved to London. Any insight you could provide about that time would be most helpful.'

I watched as something inside Daws snapped. He lurched forward in his chair, pipe clattering to the hearth, spilling hot tobacco across the cracked tile hearth.

'You want to know about before? Do you? We were happy - the three of us. A proper family. My Ethel kept this place spotless, not a speck of dust anywhere. Lucy'd help her with the cleaning every Saturday morning while I was at the foundry doing overtime. Sunday dinners round that very table.' He jabbed a finger toward the rickety construction. 'Church in the morning, walk in the afternoon, rain, or shine. That's what families do, isn't it?'

His voice hardened. 'Then the flu came. Spanish flu, they called it. Took my Ethel in less than a week. Barely time to say goodbye, she was gone so quick. And what does the girl do? Before her mother's even cold in the ground, she announces she's off to London. Says she can't stay here anymore; wants to better herself.'

The bitterness in his voice could have curdled milk. 'I told her straight - you walk out that door, you're no daughter of mine. But she went anyway. Chose London over her own flesh and blood. So that's it. What happened after is no concern of mine, nor my fault.'

HG's voice cut through the heavy silence that followed, quiet but sharp as a razor. 'Who said anything about it being your fault?'

Silence fell across the tiny room like a heavy blanket, broken only by the occasional snap and crackle of coal settling in the grate. Daws' anger vanished, replaced by deep sadness. Tears tracked down his cheeks, cutting paths through the foundry ash that seemed embedded in his skin.

He made not a sound as he continued to stare through the window, as though transfixed by something in that neglected yard. I followed his eyeline, wondering what held him so captive. At first, I saw nothing but the rusted tin bath, the dolly tub, and the crumbling brick walls.

Then I spotted it. There, perched in one corner of the narrow windowsill, sat a small picture frame I hadn't noticed before. The image inside had faded to sepia tones, but I could still make out two figures - a petite woman in a full-length dark skirt, holding a tiny child. Her smile beamed across the decades, radiating joy despite the photograph's age. Behind her hung the same tin bath that still adorned the yard wall, though in the picture it gleamed with care and polish.

Now I understood why Daws couldn't tear his gaze from the window. Every time he looked out there, he saw not the current decay, but that moment frozen in time - his wife and daughter, when they were still his entire world.

The tears continued to flow down his face, yet still he made no sound. I swallowed hard against the lump forming in my throat. Though our circumstances differed, I too knew the hollow ache of abandonment all too well.

Chapter Seven

CUCKOO IN THE NEST

We stood in silence on the pavement outside Mr. Daws' house, still in shock after witnessing the sombre scene inside No. 52a. The breeze had vanished, made real by a thousand domestic chimneys spewing sulphurous smoke vertically. A smog had formed while we three had been talking to Daws, which hung heavy in the air; its acrid content sticking in the throat like sandpaper.

I ventured that Lucy's father gave the appearance of a man destroyed by grief at the loss of a daughter he'd tried to forget.

Whipple offered a different interpretation.

'I'm not so sure,' he said, pulling at his damp collar. 'Of course, all may be innocent. Then again, was it guilt we observed in there? Not at disowning his daughter, but for ending her life, and so making real his deranged view of past events?'

A coal cart clattered past, the driver touching his cap to us as his horse's hooves struck sparks from the cobbles. HG watched it pass before turning back to our little group.

75

'You have a point, Arthur. We must guard against being swept up in the emotions of the moment.' HG's fingers tapped against the silver handle of that ever-present cane. 'It wouldn't be the first time a person with an absolute love for another turns apparent rejection into a fury so intense that it destroys the very thing they love.'

The smog thickened around us, turning the neighbouring houses into grey shadows. A clock struck somewhere in the murk, its notes muffled and distant.

'We must dig into Daws' movements over recent days,' HG said. 'To prove his innocence or uncover opportunity on top of the motive and means he may have had.'

We each took a final look at Daws' dwelling without conscious coordination, as if hoping the damp bricks and tearful windows might speak the truth to us.

In the end, we drifted back to the Rolls and HG entered as I held the rear door open for her. Whipple did not try to alight. Instead, he pointed toward the city centre.

'I shall hang around for a little. The occupants of the Tin Hut may yet provide me with valuable information about what went on at the Assembly Hall.'

HG nodded, then sat back into her sumptuous leather seat. 'Very well, Arthur. I'm pleased to say that my ring around earlier this morning revealed Milly Davenport's current location, and it's not too far from here. We shall see what the troublesome "Bright Young Thing has to say for herself.'

Whipple's form faded into the thickening smog, his silhouette dissolving like a spectre from The Hound of the Baskervilles. The grey tendrils curled around him until there was nothing left but the echo of his footsteps on the wet pavement stones. A haunting sight that would stay with me.

Settling behind the wheel of the Rolls, I adjusted my

cap and checked the mirrors - more from habit than necessity.

'To Frettenham, Rex,' HG's voice drifted from the back seat. 'Sir Walter Simms-Watts' residence. Our Miss Davenport has taken up temporary residence there, uninvited but impossible to turn away.'

The Rolls purred to life, and I guided her through Norwich's narrow streets. As we left the city, HG filled me in on the situation.

'My ring around earlier paid off. It seems Milly appeared on their doorstep claiming friendship with their daughter Jenny. The Simms-Watts is far too well-bred to turn her away, despite their misgivings.'

A twenty-minute journey saw us pull up to Frettenham Hall's impressive entrance. A footman appeared to escort us inside, where Lady Tilly was crossing the entrance hall. She drew HG aside, speaking in hushed tones.

'We simply don't know what to do,' Lady Tilly wrung her hands. 'She's taken over the Blue Room, rearranged the daily routine to suit herself, and my daughter — you remember Jenny, well, she's quite overwhelmed; you know what a strong character Milly is. Walter is beside himself but won't say anything - you know how he hates confrontation. The girl simply invited herself, and we...'

'Found yourselves unable to refuse,' HG finished gently. 'The Davenports have always had that effect on people. But perhaps we can help resolve this situation.'

Lady Tilly escorted us to Milly Davenport's temporary lair and pointed at the leaf-inspired brass door handle.

'I'd rather not come in. You do understand?'

HG smiled, 'Of course, my dear. You just leave this to me. I have a plan that will relieve you of your interloper!'

This came as a surprise to me, although why I did not

know, since I'd been around HG long enough now to know how frequently she pulled rabbits out of hats.

In the few seconds it took me to depress the heavy door handle and step aside to allow HG entry, Lady Tilly had vanished as if by a magical trick worthy of my dear father.

I followed HG into the Blue Room, where Miss Davenport reclined in a French bergere chair; a leather-bound volume balanced on her knee. Her fingers held an exquisite teacup, its surface alive with delicate Chinese brushwork depicting cranes in flight. At our entrance, her head turned, those famous calculating eyes widening a fraction.

HG swept forward, her smile radiant and disarming. 'Milly, my dear, what a surprise. I've called on Jenny to give my best wishes for her upcoming birthday, and here you are. What a thoughtful young woman you are.'

Miss Davenport's eyebrows drew together in momentary confusion. The teacup wavered, threatening to spill its contents onto the Turkish carpet below. I shared her bewilderment.

Then I realised. The casual mention of Jenny, the implied friendship. HG revised the story, implying Miss Davenport was a thoughtful guest. She'd trapped Miss Davenport, preventing a graceful denial without admitting her own mistake.

Miss Davenport's lips parted, but no words emerged. For perhaps the first time in her glittering social career, the queen of cutting remarks found herself without a ready response.

'I...er, well yes, of course. It's the least I can do,' Milly said as she closed the book on her lap and stood to greet her unexpected guests.

I observed Miss Davenport perform a perfect curtsy - the kind drilled into young ladies at those expensive Swiss

finishing schools. Her graceful movements, honed by countless hours of practice, conveyed both respect and a touch of
petulance.

HG accepted the proffered seat with her usual dignified
air, settling into the blue damask chair. As Miss Davenport's
gaze flickered in my direction, I caught the slight narrowing
of HG's eyes - nothing eluded her attention.

'Allow me to introduce my Ward, Rex,' HG said, her
tone carrying that familiar blend of warmth and authority.

Miss Davenport looked confused, but then she recovered
her composure. The transformation was remarkable - like
watching a theatre curtain drop and rise again to reveal a
different scene.

Taking my cue, I moved to position myself in the chair
to Miss Davenport's right. I positioned myself so HG could
see me, but our hostess couldn't. This was a tactic HG had
taught me.

'Can I offer you some tea?' Miss Davenport's voice
carried that tone of practiced hospitality that marked her
class.

The sheer audacity of it made me smile. Here she sat,
an uninvited guest in someone else's home, playing hostess
as if she owned the place. It encapsulated everything about
Milly Davenport. The entitlement, the arrogance, the absolute certainty that the world must bend to accommodate her
wishes.

HG accepted the offered tea with grace, though we both
knew she had no intention of drinking it. She chatted
politely, leaving the beverage untouched. My mentor had
perfected this technique over decades - the art of putting
someone at ease before delivering the unexpected thrust.

The late autumn sun struggled to penetrate the bleak-
ness, although at least the city smog failed to reach the Hall.

HG chatted about friends and London happenings, encouraging Miss Davenport to relax with each passing minute, her shoulders dropping from their defensive posture as she warmed to familiar social territory.

'Tell me, my dear, how long have you known the family?' HG's question floated across the space between them, gentle as thistledown.

Miss Davenport's face brightened. 'Oh, Jenny and I practically grew up together. We were inseparable during our childhood years.'

The trap had been laid and sprung. HG's smile remained warm, but her eyes sparkled with that familiar gleam that always preceded a devastating observation.

'How fascinating. Though I could have sworn there was quite an age difference between you both - seven years, if memory serves?'

The colour drained from Miss Davenport's face faster than flour through a sieve. Her fingers tightened around the teacup's handle.

'Well, yes,' she recovered swiftly, though her voice had lost its earlier confidence. 'But you see, my family spent summers here when I was quite young. Jenny was like an older sister to me, really. Terribly kind to the little girl always trailing after her.'

The explanation sounded plausible enough, but the damage had been done. Miss Davenport's composure had cracked, revealing the careful fabrication beneath. HG merely nodded, allowing the subject to drift away like a feather on the wind. She had achieved her purpose - demonstrating to Miss Davenport that her carefully constructed narrative wasn't as watertight as she believed.

Miss Davenport rose from her seat with the fluid grace of a dancer and drifted towards the window. The late autumn sun caught her blonde hair, creating a momentary halo effect that seemed at odds with her character. Through the glass panes, the lake stretched out like polished steel, its surface occasionally disturbed by falling leaves. A weathered rowing boat bobbed gently against a small boathouse; its paint peeling in long strips.

'Spring feels an age away,' she sighed dramatically, one perfectly manicured hand pressed against the windowpane. 'Everything looks so dreary.'

I caught the obvious deflection - a classic socialite's trick to redirect uncomfortable conversations. My gaze met HG's, and the slight curve of her lips told me she'd noted the same transparent manoeuvre.

HG allowed the silence to stretch for a moment before speaking. 'Your thoughts on the events at the Assembly Hall would interest me greatly, Miss Davenport.'

The young woman's shoulders stiffened. She remained facing the window, though her reflection showed a brief flash of something - fear, perhaps?

'Such a tragedy,' she murmured after a pause that lasted a fraction too long. 'That poor model. Dreadful.'

'Murder usually is, my dear,' HG's voice carried an extra edge. 'Though I wonder why you felt the need to flee the premises so hastily? Lord Wentworth mentioned catching sight of you running away.' The police do not yet know this fact. However, you must see how it looks?'

Miss Davenport snatched her hand from the window as if it were suddenly on fire. She turned to face her inquisitor; her eyes fixed on the carpet.

'Flee, Your Grace?' Dreadful though events were, my exit was purely coincidental. You must see that?'

I observed HG lean back in her chair. Her expression remained neutral, but I recognised the slight tilt of her head

- the same movement a cat makes before pouncing on an unwary mouse.

'Of course, my dear,' HG's voice dripped honey. 'These unfortunate events can cause all manner of misunderstandings. We're all prone to acting peculiarly when shocked.'

Miss Davenport's shoulders relaxed a fraction. She drifted back towards her chair, settling into it with practiced elegance.

'Then again,' HG continued, 'You must provide an explanation concerning why you left the proceedings. And account for your movements thereafter, you open yourself to being regarded as a suspect. We don't want that, do we and I'm sure there is an innocent explanation, should you care to share it with Rex and I?'

The colour drained from Miss Davenport's face. Her fingers found the delicate chain at her throat, twisting it back and forth in a nervous gesture that betrayed her carefully maintained composure. The silence in the room grew thick as treacle, broken only by the distant chime of a grandfather clock in the hall outside.

Miss Davenport's fingers released the chain at her throat, and her composure snapped back into place like an elastic band.

'The truth is quite simple,' she declared, smoothing her skirts. 'My dear friend Becky Wilbert became terribly distraught when the gun went off. She needed someone to escort her home immediately. Being a close friend, naturally I volunteered.'

The lie flowed from her lips as smoothly as honey from a spoon. My gaze flickered to HG, noting the slight arch of her eyebrow - the only visible reaction to this blatant fabrication. We both knew Lord Wentworth had witnessed Miss Davenport climbing into a sleek black motorcar alone. To cap it all, it had then roared away from the Assembly Hall before anyone could stop it.

'Such a thoughtful gesture,' HG murmured. 'And how did you convey this "friend," home?'

Miss Davenport's perfect mask slipped for just a fraction of a second. Her fingers found the chain again, twisting it so tightly her knuckles went white.

'Fortunately, a taxicab drove past, which I hailed.'

HG leaned forward and touched Milly's arm as if to offer comfort. 'There. That wasn't too hard, was it? Once the police check your alibi with the taxi company, it will be all over. No more questions and you will be able to get on with the rest of your busy social life.'

The grandfather clock in the hall struck three, its deep resonance filling the awkward silence that followed. Through the window, clouds gathered over the lake, turning its surface from steel to slate.

What was HG up to? She knew as well as I what Lord Wentworth had said. Why had my mentor not challenged Miss Davenport with the facts? As I continued to mull over this strange development, HG rose and repositioned herself on one arm of Miss Davenport's chair.

'And talking of busy lives, Milly. Your hosts are busy people and far too polite to raise the subject of your proposed leaving date from the house with you. I wonder if you might do me an immense favour?'

Miss Davenport cranked her neck to look up at HG from her much lower position in the chair.

'Oh…er, yes. Of course. I had intended to—'

'Yes, I thought as much, Milly. I tell you what. Why don't I give you a lift back to Norwich, or perhaps Lord Wentworth's abode? I know how fond you are of him, and it's only a few miles from here. I'm sure he'd be delighted to see you again. What do you say?'

My mind raced as I attempted to fathom HG's true intentions. What was going on?

'Well, if you think he'll have me for a few days, that would be splendid.'

'Then that settles matters. We shall head over there now. Rex, might you ready the Rolls while Miss Davenport collects her belongings, and we give our farewells to Sir Walter and Lady Simms-Watts?'

Miss Davenport and I shared bemused looks, although I suspected for very different reasons. What would his lordship have to say when we arrived unannounced?

The Rolls-Royce purred along the narrow Norfolk lanes, its gleaming bonnet parting the thick hedgerows like a ship's prow through yielding waves. Dark clouds had swallowed the afternoon sun, casting a stern pallor over the landscape. The fields beyond stretched out in various shades of brown and ochre, dotted with the occasional farmhouse or windmill.

My eyes darted between the road ahead and the hedgerows, watching for any wildlife that might dart across our path. A pheasant burst from the undergrowth, its copper feathers flashing as it took flight. The Rolls didn't falter.

In the rear-view mirror, Miss Davenport sat rigid as a poker, her hands folded neatly in her lap. She hadn't spoken a word since we'd left Frettenham Hall, though her eyes kept sliding towards HG as if expecting some revelation. The silence in the car grew heavier with each passing mile.

What game was HG playing? She'd orchestrated Miss Davenport's removal from the Simms-Watts household with surgical precision, but to what end? Lord Wentworth hadn't struck me as the type to welcome unexpected guests, particularly ones connected to a murder investigation.

A rabbit bounded across the lane, forcing me to tap the brakes. The action seemed to startle Miss Davenport. She shifted in her seat, adjusting her hat with trembling fingers.

The familiar gates of Cockleford Manor appeared around the next bend. Henry, Lord Wentworth's massive mastiff, would no doubt be sprawled somewhere in the entrance hall, drooling on the lush carpets. The thought of Miss Davenport's reaction to such an ungainly welcome brought a smile to my lips.

The gravel drive crunched beneath our wheels as we approached the Manor. Whatever HG had planned for our reluctant passenger, I suspected the next few days would prove rather interesting.

The tyres crunched to a halt on the gravel drive beside Cockleford Manor's weather-beaten entrance doors. Through gaps in the ancient stonework, moss peeked out like green whiskers on an old man's chin. The familiar sight of Sir Alfred rounding the corner caught my attention - his plus-fours and tweed ensemble matching perfectly with his flat cap. A fishing rod dangled from one hand, while the other clutched a folded canvas chair. The distinct lack of fish suggested his afternoon had been less than productive.

Stepping out to open HG's door, my boots settled into the loose gravel. She emerged with her usual fluid grace, her heels finding perfect purchase on the uneven surface.

'HG, what a splendid surprise!' Sir Alfred's voice boomed. His weathered face broke into a broad smile as he propped his fishing rod against a nearby large decorative urn.

Moving to stand a few feet from the Rolls, HG positioned herself with her back to the vehicle where Miss Davenport remained seated. The gentle breeze carried their conversation with just enough force that I could overhear their conversation.

'I've brought you a little bird, albeit a cuckoo,' HG said.

Sir Alfred's jovial expression melted into bewilderment, his bushy eyebrows drawing together.

'I need you to keep Miss Davenport occupied for a few days while Inspector Whipple digs deeper into the investigation of poor Lucy's murder.'

A deep frown creased Sir Alfred's forehead. 'Of course, if you need me to. Luckily, I've got some people coming to stay for a few days, so they will keep the young lady busy, but why?'

'Because, Alfred, I have good reason to believe Milly Davenport is our killer.'

Chapter Eight

GOING UNDERGROUND

Although HG was not one to flee from a difficult encounter, nor decline a challenge. There could be no doubt that our departure from Cockleford Manor might have appeared somewhat rushed to Lord Wentworth. I remain unsure whether HG's request that he host the young lady, or her assertion Milly might well be our killer, surprised him the most. In any event, the fellow took it all in his stride as he waved HG and me off.

The autumn sun pierced through dissolving clouds, casting long shadows across the Norfolk fields. My hands gripped the steering wheel of the Rolls Royce as we meandered along country lanes bordered by oak and ash trees, their leaves ablaze with amber and crimson.

The landscape stretched before us; a patchwork of harvested fields lay ready for ploughing. A fox darted across our path, disappearing into the hedgerow, where late-season blackberries still clung to thorny branches.

Norwich Cathedral's spire rose above the medieval rooftops as we entered the city. The streets bustled with motorcars and horse-drawn carts, while shoppers darted between them like startled pigeons. Market traders called their wares from wooden stalls, their voices carrying over the clip-clop of hooves on cobblestones.

'Gentleman's Walk, if you please, Rex,' HG shifted in her seat, folding away her tiny notebook. 'Coleman's Mustard Shop awaits.'

I asked why we stopped for mustard when the hotel had plenty.

'You misunderstand, dear boy. Besides selling their excellent mustards, which, I'll have you know, are manufactured not more than one mile from our current location, they offer refreshment facilities to those of a certain sort. Why, their scones alone have caused more than one society lady to break her diet vows. The pastries, well, they're spoken of in hushed, reverent tones from here to London.'

Threading our way through the narrow lanes, the Rolls Royce's gleaming bonnet reflected the golden afternoon light. Timber-framed houses leaned together on Gentleman's Walk, like gossiping neighbours.

After parking and alighting from the Rolls, we progressed into the Royal Arcade and soon arrived at our venue. As I pushed open the heavy oak door, a delightful scent greeted us—rich and tangy, with a hint of the warmth of freshly baked goods. The small cafe area nestled at the back was modest but charming, adorned with floral tablecloths and bright painted mustard pots that lined the shelves. A smiling woman in a crisp apron stood behind the counter, ready to take our order.

"Rex, what better place to review our work than among the town's culinary delights?" HG exclaimed.'

We approached the counter, where the woman greeted

us with a polite nod. 'Good afternoon. What might you like today?'

'We will have two cups of your finest tea, scones with clotted cream, and a selection of sandwiches, please,' HG replied with her characteristic authority.

As I looked out of the window, who should pass, but Whipple? I waved frantically, which drew the attention of several people strolling through the arcade; one or two waved back, perhaps thinking they knew me. Several others avoided eye contact and scurried on. Fortunately, Whipple, although bemused, acknowledged me and joined us.

'Ah, Arthur. What a timely rendezvous!' HG said as she twisted back to the lady behind the counter. 'Can you add a further serving in honour of our dear friend?'

The lady smiled, then vanished through a swing door into the kitchen.

As we settled into a table by the window, I observed the passers-by outside, each face a story to tell.

'Do you know,' began Whipple. 'I've been in that tin hut of a police station since you dropped me off. The place is a shambles and falling to bits. It's alright for the commissioner. His predecessors stayed at the Guildhall when everyone else relocated to that corrugated metal monstrosity.'

Whipple pointed to a building we couldn't see from our position, although I knew the building of which he spoke; an ornate brick structure of great antiquity and beauty.

'And do you know,' Whipple continued in an agitated tone, That—'

'Arthur…do take a breath. I see all too clearly that the day so far has not met your expectation. However, please do the other patrons, and your blood pressure, the honour of calming yourself. See, our refreshments are about to arrive.

I urge you to think of nothing other than a warm scone and limit your energies to deciding whether to put the jam, or clotted creme on your scone first.'

HG's urging did the trick, at least outwardly as Whipple took a deep breath, unbuttoned his suit jacket and positioned a crisp linen napkin across his lap.

'There, now isn't that better, dear Arthur?'

Whipple offered HG a diminutive smile, before watching which topping his friend applied to her scone first. With the relevant guidance delivered, Whipple copied her actions.

The electric lights from the arcade filtered through Coleman's windows, casting a warm glow over our table. Norwich's medieval streets stretched beyond, their ancient stones holding centuries of stories. Watching the people pass by, my thoughts drifted to the countless generations who had walked these same paths, from merchants to monarchs.

'The cathedral's quite spectacular in this light,' Whipple remarked between bites of his perfectly prepared scone. 'Though nothing beats the view from Mousehold Heath at sunset.'

HG nodded, dabbing her lips with a napkin. 'Indeed. Also, the Norman keep of the castle still stands proud after all these years. Such history in every stone and timber.'

'Now that we're all assembled,' HG set down her teacup, 'perhaps we should share our latest findings. Arthur, you first…any developments from your point of view?'

Whipple straightened in his chair. 'As a matter of fact, yes. One of our constables, young Roberts, was stationed at the Assembly Rooms' front entrance during the fashion show. He observed a young woman running from the premises shortly after the shot was heard. She jumped into a waiting motorcar.'

'But we already know that dear Arthur?'

'Indeed,' Whipple smiled. 'However, Roberts, being the thorough chap he is, noted down the vehicle's registration number.'

HG's eyes sparkled. 'Excellent news! Now, I should mention that we've just left Milly Davenport in the capable hands of his lordship at Cockleford Manor. The young lady seemed rather eager to avoid our questions about her hasty departure from the fashion show.'

'Did she now?' Whipple raised an eyebrow, reaching for his notebook.

'She did indeed, however I'm confident that Rex and I caught her out and, shall we say, persuaded to spend a few days at Cockleford Manor was just the ticket. Of course, we didn't confront or contradict her frankly laughable alibi of hailing a taxi, and she doesn't know Lord Wentworth was hot on her tail. Not to put too fine a point on matters, I'm convinced Milly Davenport is closely involved in the murder, if not the dastardly assailant herself.'

Although generous of HG to accredit me with a hand in the interrogation of Miss Davenport, I felt it necessary to correct the record. However, my mentor would hear nothing of it, and insisted we take shared credit.

Setting down her teacup, HG pulled out her notebook. 'Let us review our suspects while we enjoy these excellent refreshments.'

Watching her arrange her papers brought a sense of order to the chaotic events of recent days.

'First, we have Clara Brightman, Lucy's closest friend. Though she claims to know about a mysterious gentleman friend, her story remains vague. Her behaviour suggests she knows more than she's telling.'

Whipple nodded, dabbing cream from his moustache.

'The relationship between Clara and Lucy warrants deeper investigation.'

'Then there's Amber Longstone,' HG continued. 'Her hatred for Lucy was palpable during questioning. Professional rivalry can be a powerful motive.'

'And Mr Daws,' Whipple added. 'Lucy's father denied having a daughter at first. That estrangement after his wife's death from Spanish flu - quite odd.'

My thoughts drifted to our visit to the Daws residence, recalling the man's barely contained anger when discussing Lucy's departure to London.

'Which brings us to Miss Milly Davenport,' HG's eyes sparkled. 'Currently enjoying Lord Wentworth's hospitality at Cockleford Manor. Her hasty departure from the fashion show places her firmly in our sights.'

'Not to mention,' Whipple interjected, 'the registration number of her getaway vehicle, courtesy of Constable Roberts.'

'Indeed.' HG tapped her pencil against the notebook. 'We mustn't forget Lucy's last word: "Mason Drange." Whatever secret that holds could be crucial to solving this case.'

The afternoon light cast long shadows through Coleman's windows as we pondered these connections. Each suspect had motive, means, and opportunity - yet something still eluded us.

HG's teacup clinked against its saucer as she set it down with sudden purpose, her eyes lighting up with that familiar gleam that always preceded one of her revelations.

'Of course!' She pressed her palms flat against the tablecloth. 'We've been approaching this all wrong. Looking at suspects individually when we should be examining the collective.'

Whipple paused mid-bite of his second scone. 'The collective. Are you suggesting a fifth column of communists is at work?'

HG gave Whipple a sympathetic glance as she raised her eyebrows. Whipple shrugged his shoulders and took another bite of his scone, unconcerned that clotted cream dribbled from its interior onto his napkin.

'These girls, Arthur. Models operate as a tight-knit group. They share secrets, fears, dreams - but only amongst themselves. Notice how they clam up the moment anyone official appears?'

My hands wrapped around the warmth of my teacup as HG continued, her voice dropping to hardly above a whisper.

'What we need is someone on the inside. Someone who blends in naturally, become part of their world without raising suspicions. The girls will open up to such a person far more readily than to any of us.'

'But surely they'd spot an impostor straight away?' Whipple dabbed at his moustache with his napkin.

'Not if we choose the right person.' HG's fingers traced a pattern on the tablecloth. 'Someone who already has connections to their world, someone they might accept as belonging there. The key is to avoid any hint of investigation or authority. The moment they sense that, we'll lose any chance of learning their secrets.'

'And you have someone in mind?' Whipple leaned forward; his scone forgotten.

HG's smile dimmed. If we had time, but as of now, no.'

As Whipple frowned in confusion, I sensed HG's gaze beginning to fall on me.

'But we do…well, I say "we". Rex, here, knows someone who I think might fit the bill perfectly.'

Now I had two sets of eyes burning into me. I protested I knew no such person.

'Ah, but you do,' HG countered. 'You spoke so much about a young mechanic you came across when we were last in Norfolk. You remember, the Cumming's case?'

I joined Whipple in a mutual frown. Again, I protested and pointed out that I didn't even know the person's name, and that, anyway, she was a mechanic, not a fashion model.

'She's a young woman, and that's all that counts, 'HG asserted. 'Anyway, nipping over there in the Rolls will serve as a perfect opportunity to reacquaint yourselves with each other. If memory serves, you didn't stop talking about the girl for days after you first me her...including how, now, how did you put it? Oh, yes. How "forward" she was.'

By now I knew I was on a losing wicket. Thoroughly beaten, I finished the rest of my refreshments and departed for North Norfolk, leaving HG and Whipple to walk back to the Royal Hotel at their leisure.

Rolls Royce motor cars are famed for their quiet running. Indeed, it's said that the only thing one hears inside the cab is the ticking of the dashboard clock. As I neared the garage which my quarry owned, a thumping heart rate gave the clock a run for its money.

As I pulled the Rolls off the narrow lane and into the concrete surface of the garage yard, I spied a shock of blond hair behind the dusty glass of a ramshackle office. Its owner had their head tilted downwards, which I assumed meant the young woman was completing paperwork or some other administrative task.

So muted was the car's approach that my arrival had

gone unnoticed by the proprietor. It was only when I purposely slammed the driver's door shut (which I'd have frowned had any of my passengers done so in normal circumstances) that the mop of hair parted to reveal facial flesh.

For a moment we looked at one another, neither making a move. I concluded this was not the time to be bashful, and so began closing the short distance between car and office.

'Well, well,' began the young lady as she now stood at the open door to her office. 'You never did come back for that pint and game of darts, did you?'

Although still ten feet from her, I know she noticed my reddening cheeks.

'Since I guess this isn't a social call, I assume you're up to your Sherlock Holmes act again?'

I confess to being disappointed she'd seen through me so easily, I mumbled an answer 'Funny you should say that.'

The young lady opened the door wide, placed a hand on each hip, and stood back, allowing me to enter the eccentric construction. Inside looked no better than the building's exterior. Bits of thin sheet metal held planks of wood together; thick string looped around strategically placed nails held the roof onto the sides of the shack.

'Well,' she said. 'Don't stand there like an oily spark plug. Sit down and I'll make a cuppa.'

Looking around the small space, I couldn't for the life of me see one, never-mind two chairs.

'There…the oil drum. You're alright, it's empty,' she said. So that was it. I moved a pile of papers to reveal said oil drum, took the precaution of laying an old towel across its top, and sat.

One matter stood out above all: the need to find out

each other's names. And so, summoning up enough courage, I asked.

'That took you long enough,' she said as two steaming mugs of tea found themselves plonked on a small, untidy desk…or to be more accurate, a piece of plywood spanning two timber trestles. 'It's Poppy. And yours?'

'Rex,' I blurted out.

'Have you a dog?' Poppy enquired.

'Er…no?'

'Good job, I suppose. Folk wouldn't be sure who they were talking to.'

She sensed my confusion.

'Rex. Well, it's a popular dog's name, isn't it? Anyway, we had a dog when I was young, and we called him Rex. A bit smaller than you, with more hair.'

Still unsure how to react, I mumbled, 'Er, oh, I see,' then felt stupid and picked up my mug of tea, hoping to distract Poppy.

Instead, she giggled until I thought she'd burst. 'For heaven's sake. Lighten up, will you? I'm taking the rise out of you.'

Now I felt even more embarrassed.

She eventually gained control and pulled a mysterious item from the trouser pocket of her cotton boilersuit.

'Here, have some Fry's Chocolate Cream.'

How did she know that was my favourite? I thought, before eagerly accepting the two pieces, she'd broken off the bar for me.

As we drank and nibbled our chocolate in silence, Poppy's perpetual smile did its work in calming my nerves. I knew I'd eventually have to tell my host why I'd turned up, and why I hadn't taken her up on the offer she made the last time, we'd met.

While accepting my excuse for the beer and darts, Poppy had more to say about my proposition.

'Let me get this straight. A fashion model died last Saturday. You think you have the killer hold up with some Lord or other, but you've several other people who might also have killed that poor Lucy girl…including her father? And you want me to pretend to be a fashion model and see what information I can get out of all these other girls?

Poppy's summary made me realise what a crazy idea HG had proposed. After all, why should a woman I'd only met once before, and who had never met Whipple, or my mentor, get herself involved in such a hare-brained, not to say, dangerous, endeavour?

'A good job I did a bit of part-time modelling then, isn't it? Sounds fun to me. When do I start?'

Chapter Nine

NEW FRIENDS

As I waited for Poppy to arrive at Thorpe Manor for a late supper, and to meet HG and Whipple for the first time, I attempted to hide the mixture of excitement and nervousness that coursed through my body.

'It is no use,' my mentor began. 'You fizz with intoxicated fervour. The young lady we await has certainly captured your…imagination, I shall put it no stronger than that for the moment.'

She glanced at the inspector, who stood by the fire overmantle inspecting a teardrop shaped burn mark on the wall; a talisman to ward off evil spirits.

HG's eyes sparkled with mischief as she settled into her favourite wingback chair. The leather creaked beneath her, a sound that usually meant trouble for me.

'One assumes our young mechanic will need careful guidance in the art of feminine refinement, Inspector. Though perhaps Mr Watson here might require some instruction himself in maintaining professional distance while offering such guidance.'

Whipple's moustache twitched. 'Rather like teaching a grease monkey to waltz, what?'

'Not at all,' HG countered. 'Miss Poppy possesses natural grace from what Rex tells me. Though he did seem rather focused on her ready smile and quick wit during his rather lengthy report.'

My cheeks burned as I straightened the already pristine silver service laid out for supper.

'Come now,' Whipple chortled. 'Surely better a mechanically minded miss than that amorous librarian who sent our man fleeing into the street.'

'Indeed.' HG lifted her sherry glass. 'Though we must ensure Mr Watson remembers this is an investigation, not a courtship. Perhaps you might supervise his supervision, Inspector?'

'Capital idea. Can't have young Watson getting oil on his collar while showing the lady the finer points of society comportment.' his face its usual mask of dignified servitude.

'The young lady has arrived.'

The butler's announcement came as a huge relief, since Poppy's arrival caused the verbal exchange at my expense to cease. Although good humoured, its cessation lifted my embarrassment.

A few seconds later, Graham reappeared, looking rather discombobulated. Behind him stood a small figure

The butler's measured footsteps in the hall saved me from further torment. Graham appeared in the doorway, swathed in an ankle-length leather riding coat. In her right hand, a leather skull cap and goggles hung lazily; swinging gently in the warm air of the saloon.

'Miss Poppy,' Graham announced with as much decorum as the man could muster.

My heart skipped as Poppy shrugged off her leather

coat, revealing a smart woollen jumper and dark slacks beneath. Graham accepted the coat, helmet, and goggles with a bow from the neck, though his eyebrows lifted a fraction at her attire.

HG rose from her chair with the fluid grace that marked her every movement. 'My dear Miss Poppy, what an absolute pleasure to meet you at last.' She extended both hands in welcome. 'Rex has told me so much about you, truly, you feel like family already.'

Both women turned to look at me, Poppy's eyes dancing with amusement as colour flooded my face. Whipple remained by the fireplace; his expression carefully neutral as he observed the scene.

'Ah, you came by motorcycle.' HG's voice held warmth and approval. 'Those wonderful machines - such freedom they offer. What make is yours, my dear?'

Poppy's face lit up. 'The new BSA 500cc model. Father gave it to me when he handed over the garage a few months ago.'

'What a generous father you have.'

A touch of pink coloured Poppy's cheeks. 'Yes, he's always supported me, even when others thought a girl shouldn't be working with engines.'

'And quite right, too. There is nothing at all that us ladies cannot do. If ever there was any doubt, the Great War put an end to that nonsense.'

A short silence fell over the room. Any mention of that dreadful event still held raw emotions for all of us. Nevertheless, the moment soon passed as if a dark shadow had passed and allowed the warm sun to once more fill our hearts.

HG guided Poppy towards the fireplace where Whipple stood, examining his shoes with peculiar intensity.

'Allow me to present Detective Inspector Arthur Whipple.' HG's voice held a note of pride. 'Scotland Yard's most famous taker of thieves and other assorted villains.'

Whipple's left eye twitched at the introduction, his moustache following suit with a nervous quiver. His right hand strayed to his collar, tugging at it as though the starched fabric had suddenly grown too tight.

'How do you do?' Poppy extended her hand with natural grace.

The inspector's fingers tapped against his thigh before he managed a slight bow. Rather than shake her offered hand, he plunged his right hand into his jacket pocket and extracted a single black and white boiled sweet.

'Everton Mint?' His voice cracked slightly on the second word.

'Not now, dear Arthur,' HG said with a raised eyebrow.

A weak smile flickered across Whipple's face as he returned the sweet to his pocket. His shoulders hunched forward slightly, making him appear more like a schoolboy caught passing notes than London's finest detective.

Poppy's eyes met mine across the room, sparkling with barely suppressed mirth at the inspector's discomfort. The corner of her mouth twitched upward in that familiar teasing smile that never failed to quicken my pulse.

'And I suppose no introduction is necessary when it comes to that young man.' HG jokingly pointed in my direction as Poppy's eyes met mine.

'Oh, I don't know. He's a bit of a dark horse, that one.'

Both women smiled as Poppy closed the distance between us.

'And that's enough of the formality,' HG replied. 'In private, it is, "HG," as it is for these two reprobates.'

Without waiting for Poppy to respond, HG moved

effortlessly over to the drinks tray. 'Now, before we get down to business, anyone for drinkies?'

Whipple's eyes lit up as he coveted a lead-glass decanter two-thirds full of Scotch Whisky. He pointed, which prompted HG to smile and pour the man a generous measure into a gleaming glass that caught the light like a handful of cut diamonds.

'You two will have to make do with mineral water; Poppy, because you're driving a motorcycle, and Rex, because that's the polite thing to do when your guest declined to imbibe.

Poppy and I exchanged a playful glance, although why I felt so elated, I do not know.

Once seated, HG reminded us of the purpose for coming together.

HG settled into her chair, swirling the amber liquid in her glass. 'Now then, Miss Poppy - or rather, Poppy - how much has our young man told you about last Saturday's unfortunate events?'

My stomach tightened. In my eagerness to secure Poppy's help, perhaps too much had been shared over tea and chocolate biscuits at her garage.

Poppy sat forward, her natural confidence evident even under HG's penetrating gaze. 'Rex explained about the fashion show at the Assembly Hall and the murder of Lucy Daws. He mentioned she was shot in a small room with no windows, and that her last word was "Mason Drange, or range." Also, something about a woman called Milly Davenport acting suspiciously and fleeing the scene.'

'Anything else?' HG's eyebrow arched in my direction.

'Only that you need someone to mix with the models, try to learn what they know.' Poppy's hands clasped together in her lap. 'And that you think there might be a connection to an American modelling agency.'

Relief flooded through me. Despite our lengthy conversation at the garage, Poppy had maintained professional discretion about the case details.

'Very good.' HG nodded approvingly. 'Rex showed admirable restraint in sharing only the essential information. Though perhaps he was distracted by other matters during your discussion.'

Whipple nearly choked on his whisky while Poppy's eyes danced with barely contained amusement at my expense.

Setting her glass aside, her expression grew serious. The firelight cast dancing shadows across her face as she began outlining our suspects.

'First, we have Clara Brightman, Lucy's closest friend. Although not a suspect, Clara is key to understanding the tragic event as it unfolded.'

Poppy nodded, absorbing each detail with keen interest.

'Then there's Amber Longstone, who openly expressed hatred for Lucy during questioning. Professional jealousy can be a powerful motive for actions normally out of character for the individual,'

Whipple extracted his notebook, flipping through the pages. 'She claimed Lucy stole several of her modelling contracts.'

'Next, Lucy's father.' HG's voice hardened. 'A controlling man with a violent temper who became estranged from his daughter after she moved to London. His denial of her existence speaks volumes about their relationship.'

The flames crackled in the grate as HG continued.

'Milly Davenport remains our most intriguing suspect. Her hasty departure from the Assembly Hall, combined with her family's financial troubles and her pattern of destructive behaviour, places her firmly in our sights. She currently resides at Cockleford Manor under Lord Wentworth's supervision.'

'And finally,' HG picked up her glass again, 'we must consider Lucy's mystery gentleman friend. Known only to Clara, who guards his identity like a precious jewel. His connection to Lucy's final words may prove crucial.'

Whipple cleared his throat. 'There's also the American modelling agency angle to consider. Their representative was due to attend the show but never appeared according to two of the models.'

'Indeed.' HG's eyes narrowed. 'An absence that bears investigation, particularly given Lucy's recent correspondence with them.'

Poppy took a sip of her mineral water, before placing the tall, plain glass, back onto a side table. 'And where are the girls? Are they still local, of have they returned to their normal routine?'

Whipple stirred himself from his libation. 'Thanks to the generosity of HG, we've managed to keep them altogether at a local hotel in Norwich.'

'And how do they feel about that? If I were them, I'd want to get out of Norwich as fast as I could. Innocent or guilty, the city would hold nothing for me but danger or dreadful memories.'

I caught HG studying Poppy with rare intensity, and detected a look of satisfaction at Poppy's quick grasp of the facts, and insightful response.

Whipple took a chiselled stopper from the whisky decanter and offered HG a top up. Her acceptance gave him permission to refill his own glass, which may have been his ambition all along.

'You are correct, my dear,' HG began. 'I, too, should

wish to vacate the city if I were in their situation. However, I'd wager each one of those girls has weighed up the risks of running for it, whether for wholly innocent reasons, or the killer lurks among them and knows a wrong move might bring the police down upon them. Either way, I doubt any of them wish to stick their heads above the parapet, so to speak. Each will be harbouring secrets and ambitions they do not wish exposed.'

Poppy played with her glass of mineral water, deep in thought - perhaps considering how difficult the task we had in mind for her might prove.

'You said earlier that Milly Davenport had shaped up to be your prime suspect. Yet you encourage the fashion models to remain in Norwich. Have you doubt as to Miss Davenport's guilt?'

'An excellent observation, my dear,' HG responded, mirroring Poppy's actions in gently tumbling the golden liquid in her whisky glass. 'We do not have the slightest physical evidence to arrest Milly. It is only my station in life that obliges the girl to do as I bade her. Where she to vanish, there is little we might presently do to prevent such an action. Yet I doubt Milly will undertake such an action, for she knows the rules. A troublemaker she may be, but the risk of being cast out by society is too great a fall for one such as that lady. Without a powerful protector, she is, for the time being, in my thrall.'

Poppy locked eyes with HG. I sensed two women who understood how to use personal power and influence. In HG, I observed such traits in action often. Poppy was another thing entirely. For one, her age gave no indication of having the experience necessary to hold such attributes, and it only added to my sense of awe for the mechanic. What was it that gave her such a presence?

'Then what is our plan?' Poppy asked HG, making no secret of her desire to press on with her task.

Whipple dragged himself away from the warming fireside to sit in an armchair opposite Poppy. Rather than provide an answer to her query, he looked to HG as she finished off the last of her whisky.

'I've been formulating a plan since the idea of asking you to help arose. It seems to me that although our investigations remain at an early stage, our thoughts must turn to honouring Lucy Daws' life. My plan is to run a second fashion show, dedicated to Lucy in the same venue. Now, to some, this may sound macabre. However, I think it is fitting. When the show will happen I do not know, but let us assume our talented Inspector here will have the matter rapped up in a matter of days rather than weeks. So, I shall introduce you to the girls tomorrow and inform them of my plan. That will explain your presence. I shall say you are a distant relative of Miss Daws and have a little experience in the fashion world. My hope is that the models will have sympathy for your loss and accept you.'

The room fell silent as we took in HG's clever plan. With so many variables to consider, the silence continued for what seemed an age. At last, HG brought each of us back to the present.

'Now, I suggest we get an early night. There is a lot to consider and tomorrow will be a busy day. Poppy, I should be honoured if you'd stay the night. Not least it will save you driving home in the dark, and I'm sure I heard a clap of thunder earlier on?'

Poppy looked over to the large bay window. Outside, all was dark; the rose stems flexed in a strengthening breeze.

'Thank you for your kind offer,' Poppy began, 'but I've

quite a lot to sort out if I'm to be away from the garage for a few days. I hope you don't mind?'

HG smiled at her guest. 'Of course not, my dear. Just be careful out there. I share your love of motorcycles. However, I'm also all too aware that they bite back at the slightest provocation.'

Poppy smiled back as HG moved to the fireside and pressed a button on the wall. In seconds, Graham appeared.

'Miss Poppy is leaving now. Perhaps you might show her out?'

The butler gave his usual nod and stood aside to allow Poppy to pass through the wide doorway.

After a minute or so, I heard the distinctive engine noise of the BSA and wandered over to the vast window. The distinctive "clunk' of the motorbike slipping into gear floated across the heavy air as raindrops began to spatter the window glass. A single red light gave witness to Poppy beginning her journey across the gavel driveway in front of the Manor. She looked back and waved at me. I pondered how she knew I'd be watching?

Mr Pendlebury looked his usual flustered self as he welcomed our party back to the Assembly Rooms. HG returned his outstretched hand with a smile and thanked him for arranging matters at such short notice.

Whipple exited the Rolls, and surveyed his surroundings, then patted his jacket pocket to confirm he hadn't forgotten his Everton mints. 'At least it's stopped raining.'

I admit to being taken aback that the creme de la creme of Scotland Yard commented on the climatic conditions, instead of alluding to the lamentable incident from the weekend prior. Then again, for Whipple, I imagined murder and other villainy to be an everyday job of work.

'Do come along, you two, we have much to do,' scolded HG as she first pointed her silver-handled cane in our vicinity, before waving the implement in a broad arc to indicate the main doorway.

Trailing behind HG and Pendlebury as they crossed the Assembly Rooms' majestic threshold, my heels reverberated against the polished stone beneath, matching Whipple's steady stride. The vestibule still exuded its former splendour - elaborate mouldings adorned the overhead perimeter, while copper light fittings shimmered in the Dawn's rays that streamed through the lofty panes.

Pendlebury wrung his hands as he scurried ahead. 'Everything remains exactly as it was, just as you requested, Your Grace.'

'Very good of you, Mr Pendlebury,' HG's cane tapped a steady rhythm against the hard floor.

The main hall doors swung open to reveal the cavernous space where, mere days ago, Norfolk's finest had gathered for what should have been a celebratory evening. Now the room held a different atmosphere - heavy with memories of panic and tragedy. Several chairs lay scattered across the polished oak flooring, their positions marking where patrons had fled at the sound of gunfire.

The runway still dominated the centre, its surface now dulled by dust. Stage lights hung dormant above, their previous sparkle replaced by morning shadows. My gaze drifted to the wings where Lucy had died.

Whipple pulled out his notebook, already scribbling observations.

The morning sun caught the gilt frames of portraits lining the walls - generations of Norwich nobility watching our investigation with painted eyes. Below them, programmes from the ill-fated show still littered the floor, their glossy pages reflecting fragments of light.

HG led our small party across the hall, leaving Pendlebury hovering near the entrance. His anxious form grew smaller as we approached the backstage area, though his wringing hands remained visible until we rounded the corner.

The narrow corridor stretched before us, its wooden floorboards creaking beneath our feet. Paint flaked from the walls where countless shoulders had brushed against them over the years. A musty smell permeated the air - a mixture of greasepaint, perfume, and something else I couldn't quite place.

My footsteps slowed as we passed the doorway on our right. HG's cane paused mid-tap, and Whipple's steady stride faltered. None of us spoke, but our heads turned in unison toward the small room where Lucy Daws had died.

The door stood ajar, revealing a slice of the cramped space beyond.

Whipple cleared his throat and quickened his pace, the sound of his polished shoes echoing off the walls. HG's cane resumed its rhythmic tapping against the floorboards, leading us toward the models' dressing room.

The space felt different in daylight - less mysterious, perhaps, but somehow just as oppressive. Each step brought back memories of that night: the gunshot, the screams, the chaos that followed.

I pushed open the aged wooden door, expecting to find a half-dozen worried and jaded young women staring back at me anxiously. Instead, the scene before us was quite the opposite. The fashion models had gathered in a tight huddle, their faces alight with enthusiasm as they chatted and smiled at one another. And at the centre of this lively group was none other than Poppy.

I paused, taking in the unexpected sight. Poppy, who I had first thought was simply a skilled mechanic, now effortlessly captivated the attention of the glamorous models. Her confident, outgoing nature drew them in.

When we had first met, she had done the same to me, her ready smile and teasing manner putting me at ease. Now, as I watched her interact with the models, I realised Poppy possessed a formidable set of social skills.

Before clearing my throat, I checked to see where HG and Whipple were since neither had spoken since pausing at the murder scene. They had vanished, leaving me somewhat perplexed.

I stepped forward. Poppy glanced up, her eyes sparkling with amusement as she caught sight of me. "Rex," she greeted, her tone warm and familiar. 'Come and join us. We were discussing the merits of different types of thread for haute couture gowns.'

I felt a sudden pang of self-consciousness, realising that I had much to learn when it came to the world of fashion. Nonetheless, I steeled my nerves and approached the group, determined to support Poppy in her undercover investigation.

Poppy's grin broadened, and I sensed she'd picked up on my self-consciousness. Yet instead of mocking me, she launched into an account of diverse fabric qualities, speaking with an assured poise that belied her covert mission's challenges.

After several minutes of a baffling array of technical discussion among the women, I bade my leave, confident in Poppy's skills to insert herself successfully into the close-knit group. My task now was to track down my two colleagues.

As I stepped into the hallway, veering leftwards, I found myself staring directly at the cramped chamber where disaster had unfolded just a few days before. At that moment, a barely audible whisper of "Rex...Rex" reached me from behind, and despite its softness, I recognised Whipple's distinctive deep voice.

As I turned, HG and Whipple came into view. The detective appeared to wave his handkerchief at me, which I thought odd. Yet as I approached, quietly closing the door to the changing room as I passed it, Whipple, was, in fact, cradling a small object between finger and thumb, protected by his kerchief. This meant only one thing: evidence.

HG's excited demeanour left no doubt. They had come upon something of the utmost importance for our investigation.

As I neared, I recognised the small, misshapen object. A Bullet!

'We had another look at the murder scene as you were getting on so famously with all those young ladies,' Whipple teased. 'I thought it odd that I couldn't find signs of the bullet in the room. I assumed at the time that the evil object must still be in the victim's body. Yet something told me that was unlikely to be the case because I spotted gunpowder residue on both Lucy Daws' hands, and—'

'Why am I only hearing about this now, Arthur?'

HG's tone sounded unusually harsh, and I pondered how Whipple might now handle the situation. Instead of taking a submissive stance, Whipple stood his ground. I saw before me a professional senior policeman, and not one of HG's close associates.

'I kept it to myself at first because I didn't want to panic people. The situation was fraught enough as it was, and that room was, and remains, filthy. The substance I noticed could just as easily have been the detritus she picked up from being on the floor.

'And what has caused you to reveal this vital information now?' HG said, her tone still harsh.

'Because I had assumed Lucy was already in the room when her assassin struck. However, as you and I stood in that small space just now, it hit me like a steam train. What if it was the murderer who was already in the room when Lucy arrived? That means she'd of had her back to the door…and if it remained open when she took the bullet, its trajectory would have been stopped by this wall. That's why I suggested we look.'

HG toyed with the handle of her cane and alternated her gaze between the object in Whipple's fingers, and a small hole in the black-painted brick wall behind her.

Whipple carefully wrapped the bullet in his handkerchief and placed it into the inside pocket of his jacket.

'Now all we have to do,' he began, 'is find the gun.'

Chapter Ten

A SECRET SIGN

Standing in that pallid corridor, my mind raced with possibilities about the gun's whereabouts. HG tapped her cane against the floorboards, lost in thought, while Whipple scratched notes in his little book.

'It might be anywhere by now,' Whipple muttered, closing his notebook with a snap.

'Or still in this building,' HG countered. 'We must consider every—'

The click of a door handle interrupted her train of thought. Poppy emerged from the dressing room, her face brightening at the sight of us huddled in conference.

'You look as though you've found a penny and lost sixpence,' she said, smoothing down her borrowed dress.

HG beckoned her closer, lowering her voice to a whisper. 'We've recovered a bullet from the wall. Detective Inspector Whipple found something on Lucy's hand that he first thought was dust from the floor, but now believes it was gunpowder. The evidence suggests she walked in on her killer and shot at close range. Mind you, it looks as though the brave girl put up a valiant fight for her life.'

The playful spark in Poppy's eyes dimmed. 'This is getting real for me now.' She glanced back at the dressing room door. 'Look, I need to get a move on. Only came out to powder my nose. Don't want my newfound friends getting suspicious and coming to look for me.'

'Of course, my dear,' HG said. 'You're doing splendidly. Let's meet up at the Royal Hotel at 3.00 pm for afternoon tea and share what we've learned.'

Poppy nodded; her usual confident demeanour some-what subdued as she headed towards the powder room. The gravity of the situation had hit home - she wasn't playing at being a fashion model anymore but helping to catch a killer who could be among the women she was busy befriending.

The stark overhead lighting cast harsh shadows across the corridor as HG turned to Whipple. Her eyes held that familiar gleam - the one that meant she'd spotted something others had missed.

'May I see the bullet again?'

Whipple reached into his jacket pocket and produced his handkerchief with meticulous care. He unwrapped the twisted piece of lead, holding it flat in his palm.

'I thought as much,' HG said. 'See the scalloped edge? Can that tell us anything of use?'

My stomach churned as Whipple inspected the gnarled lump of lead. 'I don't want to put you off your lunch, but that was likely caused when the bullet grazed one of Lucy's ribs. Unfortunately, that will have sent the projectile spinning, which means the exit wound will be none too pretty. Of course, we won't know until I get the autopsy report. If I'm correct, it also explains why the bullet ended up askew when it hit the wall. See the crushed edge?'

He pointed to the damage without touching the grisly object. The metal gave off a dull glint under the electric lights, its misshapen form a stark reminder of the violence that had ended Lucy's life.

It was then I notice Mr Pendlebury watching events from a doorway that rested between the changing room and the small space in which Lucy met her end. He appeared to flinch and move out of view when he realised I'd seen him, then thought better of his plan, and re-emerged into the dank corridor.

The sight of Pendlebury lurking in doorways sparked an odd feeling in my gut. His hovering, nervous hand gestures, and darting eyes made him seem like a worried venue manager dealing with a disaster. But something nagged at me.

Whipple had barely glanced at that side room when we'd first arrived, declaring it nothing more than storage space. Yet Pendlebury had found a use for it.

His high-pitched voice carried down the corridor as he approached our group. 'Is there anything else you need? More lighting, perhaps? I could fetch some chairs?'

HG waved away his offers with her usual grace, but I noticed how Pendlebury's gaze fixed on the bullet still on view in Whipple's palm. His moustache twitched, hands clasping and unclasping in that familiar nervous dance.

The man certainly played the part of the helpful, anxious manager well - perhaps too well. My time working with HG had taught me that the most obvious explanation wasn't always the correct one. People wore masks, played roles, presented what they thought others expected to see.

Pendlebury hovered nearby as we discussed the bullet's trajectory, offering unnecessary comments about the building's history and suggesting various ways he could assist. His eagerness to insert himself into our investigation struck me as peculiar. Most venue managers would keep their distance from a murder inquiry, not seek ways to remain involved. A stance Pendlebury had upheld…until now.

That storage room beckoned like an itch that needed scratching. What drew Pendlebury there? Why did he feel the need to monitor our movements now? Perhaps it was time to take a closer look at both the room and the man who suddenly seemed so invested in our investigation.

Through the conservatory's soaring glass panels, shafts of autumn sunlight caught the crystal glasses and silver service, casting prismatic reflections across the Royal Hotel's finest linen tablecloths. The murmured conversations created a soothing backdrop as Norfolk's elite took their afternoon refreshment.

Whipple consulted his pocket watch for the third time in as many minutes, sighing on each occasion. The afternoon crowd ebbed and flowed around us, and HG held court with the passing gentry.

The waiters moved with practiced grace between the tables, their black waistcoats pristine and shoes gleaming like mirrors. They balanced silver trays laden with delicate pastries and steaming pots of tea, weaving through the maze of chairs and guests in an elegant dance that spoke of years of training. Not a drop spilled, not a step misplaced as they executed their carefully choreographed service.

A particularly deft young waiter pirouetted around a lady's outstretched arm, his tray of petit fours remaining perfectly level as he delivered them to an adjacent table.

Another glided past with fresh scones, the warm aroma of butter and currants trailing in his wake.

My gaze drifted to the entrance every few moments, watching for Poppy's arrival. The conservatory had filled considerably since we'd taken our seats, forcing newcomers to wait in the reception area. A party of ladies in the latest London fashions occupied the table nearest the door, their conversation punctuated by delicate laughter and the occasional gasp of society gossip.

The head waiter, resplendent in his tailcoat, directed his staff with subtle gestures and quiet words, maintaining the seamless flow of service like a conductor leading an orchestra. Fresh tea appeared just as cups emptied, used plates vanished without fanfare, and every request was anticipated before it could be voiced.

At last Poppy entered as if she didn't have a care in the world, her shoulder-length honey blond hair danced from side-to-side as she joined the staff in dodging an array of wide-brimmed hats and flailing arms to reach our table.

'Ah, there you are, darling Poppy,' exalted HG as she pointed to an empty chair. 'And now for afternoon tea. It remains to be seen if the arrival of scones and clotted cream do anything for Arthur's mood. However, that is a matter for him since I make it a point never to eat when irritated. It causes dyspepsia and is most unladylike.' Did you know that?'

Poppy flashed a brilliant smile at HG. 'My father's always telling me off for gulping down my food. Says I eat like a farm hand rather than a lady.'

'My dear, the young have the benefit of a sturdy constitution.' HG dabbed her lips with a napkin. 'Though do be careful - a bout of hiccups might displace your temporary immunity from indigestion.'

Poppy nodded with exaggerated solemnity, then turned her head to throw me a saucy wink that sent my pulse racing. The playful gesture caught me off guard, and my teacup rattled against its saucer.

Across the table, Whipple's scowl deepened. He'd barely touched his tea, and his mood had grown darker with each passing minute. The contrast between his brooding presence and the elegant surroundings couldn't have been starker.

HG set down her cup with a decisive clink. 'Out with it, Arthur, what causes your foul mood?'

Whipple's silver fob watch snapped shut once more, the sharp click drawing stares from nearby tables. The sound had become as regular as a metronome over the past hour, marking time with mechanical precision. My fingers tightened around my teacup, resisting the urge to snatch the timepiece from his hands.

'I spoke about the autopsy report a little earlier. Well, the laboratory at the Norfolk and Norwich Hospital promised me faithfully they would deliver it to me this afternoon. It's only around the corner on Ipswich Road, so hardly a hardship to send a lad on a bicycle to bring it to me.'

The detective's words came out in a frustrated rush, his London accent more pronounced than usual.

HG's expression softened as she regarded him across the table. 'Dear Arthur, you really must calm yourself. The general populace of this place knows who you are and might think your dour manner is a harbinger of some great misfortune about to descend on us all.'

Now my mentor's eyes lit up as she spotted the approaching waiters. 'Ah, here comes our sustenance.

Arthur, do remember what I said about dyspepsia. A calm mind aids digestion.'

The senior waiter, grey-haired and ramrod straight, guided his young apprentice with subtle gestures as they reached our table. Their synchronised movements spoke of hours of practice, the younger man mirroring his mentor's precise steps. Between them, they carried silver trays laden with an afternoon feast.

His apprentice's hands trembled as he placed delicate finger sandwiches before us - cucumber, smoked salmon, and egg mayonnaise arranged in perfect rows. His mentor deposited a three-tiered stand bearing fresh scones, still warm from the oven, alongside dainty cakes topped with glossy icing and fruit.

Fresh cups and saucers appeared before us, followed by steaming silver teapots wrapped in crisp white cloths. The young waiter's movements grew more confident under his mentor's watchful eye as he arranged everything just so.

'Such wonderful service,' HG beamed at them both. 'You've made this afternoon quite special.'

The apprentice's face broke into a broad smile at her words, his chest puffing with pride. His mentor acknowledged the praise with the barest inclination of his head, maintaining his professional composure as he steered his charge away from our table with a gentle touch to the elbow.

HG selected a cucumber sandwich with surgical precision. Poppy's eyes widened at the array of treats, her hand hovering between the cucumber and egg mayonnaise before choosing both. Her enthusiasm brought a smile to my face as she arranged them on her plate with far less ceremony than our hostess.

Whipple's mood visibly lifted at the sight of the fresh

salmon sandwiches. His shoulders relaxed as he helped himself to three, stacking them neatly beside a plain scone. The man even managed a small nod of appreciation as HG watched him like a hawk.

The teapot made its way around our table, filling each cup in turn with fragrant amber liquid. Steam curled upward in delicate spirals, carrying the bergamot scent that seemed to chase away the last of Whipple's earlier frustration.

My own plate soon held an assortment of sandwiches and a fruit scone that promised to be still warm from the oven. The clotted cream sat in a silver dish between Poppy and me, thick enough that the spoon stood upright.

'Now then, my dear,' HG said, turning to Poppy after taking a delicate sip of tea. 'Do tell us how you found your first encounter with our fashion friends. Tell me, did they swallow your cover story?'

Poppy dabbed her lips with a napkin, having just taken an enthusiastic bite of a sandwich. 'Yes; after gently probing my background, and especially how close I was to Lucy, which I stressed was limited to our childhood and early teens, they seemed fine. I have to say, they're quite the dramatic bunch, aren't they? Clara took me under her wing straight away - seems she's appointed herself as everyone's mother hen since...' She paused, glancing around before lowering her voice. 'Since Lucy.'

'And the others?' HG prompted, breaking a scone in half with practiced ease.

'Amber Longstone keeps to herself, mostly. Sits in the corner filing her nails and making catty remarks about everyone's outfits. The Cunliffs are friendly enough, though they speak so quickly to each other it's hard to follow their conversations.'

HG's eyes sparkled with satisfaction as she listened to Poppy's report. Her teacup paused halfway to her lips, steam curling around her face like a delicate veil. Our mechanic had proved herself more observant than any of us might have expected.

'Excellent work, my dear. Most illuminating.' HG set her cup down with a gentle clink. 'Now, did any material facts about that dreadful evening come to light during your conversations?'

Poppy leaned forward, her voice dropping to match HG's conspiratorial tone. 'There was quite a bit of peculiar chatter. The girls kept asking each other where they'd been when the shot rang out - all wrapped up in giggles and jokes, mind you.'

She paused to add a dollop of cream to her scone. 'Though as my Aunt Peggy is always saying, "Many a true word is said in jest".'

'Do elaborate,' HG prompted, her attention wholly focused on our newest recruit.

'Well, Clara asked Amber if she'd been powdering her nose at the crucial moment. Amber shot back, wondering if Pippa had been writing another letter to her mysterious friend. The Cunliffs kept needling each other about who'd borrowed whose lipstick and when.' Poppy's finger traced the pattern on the tablecloth. 'Seems to me there are several comments worth following up on.'

She reached for her teacup, pausing mid-motion. 'Yet they were definitely on their best behaviour - Almost like they were performing for my benefit.'

Despite what I considered important information arising from Poppy's feedback, Whipple remained distracted. The result? We lacked the detective's keen insight into what impact the revelations might have on our investigations. I resolved to fix the situation by asking for Whipple's view.

My question hung in the air as Whipple stared into the middle distance, lost in his own thoughts.

The pause stretched uncomfortably long. HG raised an eyebrow, while Poppy glanced between us with barely concealed amusement. Three pairs of eyes fixed on the detective until he finally registered our collective attention.

Whipple feigned a light cough and reached for his teacup, stirring the cooling Earl Grey with studied concentration.

'The models' behaviour suggests they're all hiding something,' he said at last, setting the spoon down with precision. 'Each seems to have been somewhere else when the shot was fired, yet they discuss it almost playfully. That strikes me as odd.'

He paused to take a sip of tea, grimacing at its temperature. 'Miss Longstone's isolation particularly interests me. In my experience, those who distance themselves often know more than they're willing to share. And these mysterious letters Miss Pippa writes - we'll need to look into those.'

His professional demeanour returned as he warmed to the topic. 'The way they're testing each other's alibis through casual conversation shows they're nervous. They may not be directly involved in the murder, but they likely know something important.'

'Most telling is how they modified their behaviour in front of Poppy here.' Whipple nodded toward her. 'That performance, as you called it, suggests they're very aware of being watched. People with nothing to hide don't usually feel the need to act differently around strangers.'

Watching HG's expression change from thoughtful to determined told me she had reached her own conclusions.

She dabbed her lips delicately with the napkin before responding to Whipple's assessment.

'Your analysis has merit, Arthur, but perhaps we should consider a different angle. These young ladies aren't necessarily hiding secrets about the murder - they're protecting their own small indiscretions. The fashion industry breeds competition, jealousy, and petty rivalries. Each model likely has something to conceal, but it may be as innocent as borrowing another's cosmetics without permission or meeting a gentleman caller between costume changes.'

She turned to Poppy with a gentle smile. 'Their performance, as you noted my dear, suggests they view you, quite naturally, as an outsider - but not necessarily because they fear detection. Models are a close-knit group, like a theatrical troupe. They present a united front to newcomers until they decide whether to accept them into their circle.'

Her fingers traced the rim of her teacup. 'The way they discussed their whereabouts through playful banter rather than direct questioning tells me they're more concerned with maintaining their social dynamics than covering up a murder. If they were truly involved, they would avoid the topic entirely or stick to carefully rehearsed stories.'

'However, what interests me more is Miss Longstone's isolation. Not because she's hiding something, Arthur, but because she's been excluded. The others mock her openly about her whereabouts - suggesting they don't view her as part of their inner circle. That makes her both vulnerable and potentially more willing to share what she knows, provided we approach her correctly.'

The logic of HG's assessment struck me as characteristically astute. Where Whipple saw conspiracy, she recognised the complex social dynamics of young women in a competitive environment. Her understanding of human nature often revealed insights that pure detective work might miss.

Before we could discuss the matter further, the Maitre D approached Whipple with a large, sealed envelope in his gloved hand. The detective's eyes lit up.

Whipple's demeanour transformed at the sight of the envelope. 'Ah, at last,' he breathed, snatching it from the Maitre D's white-gloved hands. The short man stood perfectly still, his pristine uniform a testament to decades of service, while Whipple tore into the envelope with uncharacteristic eagerness.

'Thank you so much,' HG called after the retreating figure, compensating for Whipple's oversight with an extra measure of warmth.

The detective spread the papers across the table, pushing aside his half-eaten scone without a second thought. His sharp features tensed as he absorbed each detail, eyes darting back and forth across the pages. The rest of us sat in uncomfortable silence, watching his face for any hint of revelation.

Poppy fidgeted with her napkin while HG maintained her usual composure, though her teacup remained suspended halfway to her lips. My own breath seemed too loud in the hushed atmosphere.

After what felt like an eternity, Whipple looked up from the report. 'Lucy Daws was shot at close range, which we'd already deduced. However, the pathologist noted a small tattoo on Lucy's left shoulder blade showing three interlocking circles.'

'Heavens, I know what that symbol means,' HG cut in, her teacup clattering against its saucer.

Chapter Eleven

BROADWAY BECKONS

HG's face had gone pale, her usual composure momentarily shaken. The revelation about the tattoo seemed to affect her deeply.

'That symbol,' she said, her voice dropping to barely above a whisper, 'represents membership in a particularly unpleasant organisation. The Three Circles society.'

Whipple leaned forward, his scone forgotten. 'Never heard of them.'

'Few have, Arthur. That's rather the point. They're a secretive group of influential people - aristocrats, politicians, industrialists - who use their combined power to protect their interests at any cost.'

Poppy shifted uncomfortably in her chair. 'At any cost?'

'Murder, blackmail, corruption - nothing is beneath them.' HG's lips pressed into a thin line. 'What puzzles me is Lucy's involvement. The society is incredibly selective about membership. They typically only admit those born into privilege or who've accumulated significant wealth and influence.'

'Lucy was just starting her career,' Whipple mused.

'Precisely.' HG nodded. 'A young model from Norwich hardly fits their usual profile. She must have had a connection to someone of extraordinary influence to receive that mark. Either that...' She paused, studying her reflection in the silver teapot. 'Or there are aspects of Lucy Daws's life we've yet to uncover.'

HG pulled out her leather-bound notebook. My eyes followed her elegant handwriting as she began listing what we knew about Lucy.

'Let's review the facts,' HG said, her fountain pen hovering above the page. 'Lucy Daws, aged twenty-one, murdered at close range in a small, windowless room. Gunpowder residue suggests she faced away from her killer.'

Whipple nodded, dabbing his mouth with a napkin. 'And that peculiar name spoken to Clara Brightman by Lucy.'

'Which led nowhere,' HG continued. 'The record office showed no connection, yet the word must hold significance.'

Poppy sat forward in her chair, her blue dress standing out against the conservatory's refined decor. Her eyes darted between HG and Whipple as they spoke, absorbing every detail.

'Then there's her father,' Whipple added. 'Claims estrangement after she left for London, but something feels off about his story.'

HG's pen scratched across the paper. 'The American modelling agency connection remains unexplored. And what of Milly Davenport's hasty departure?'

'Currently under Lord Wentworth's watchful eye,' Whipple reminded us.

'The bullet's distinctive markings trouble me,' HG said. 'Custom ammunition, suggesting our killer has means and connections. Add to that Mr Pendlebury's peculiar behaviour near that storage room...'

'And now this Three Circles tattoo,' Whipple finished.

Poppy's face showed the same fascination mine had worn when first working with HG - that mixture of awe and determination to keep pace with her lightning-quick mind.

HG closed her notebook with a snap. 'We have multiple threads, but no clear pattern. Lucy's secret gentleman friend, mentioned by Clara. Her controlling father. The society membership. These pieces should fit together, yet they refuse to align.'

Watching HG's expression change, I knew another revelation was coming. Her fingers tapped the leather notebook as realisation dawned across her features.

'Good heavens,' she muttered, shaking her head. 'How could I have been so careless?'

Whipple raised an eyebrow. 'Something else?'

'Two something's, Arthur? Rather, two "someones" we've completely overlooked.' HG straightened in her chair. 'Emily Brown, the show director. Remember her state when we arrived? Nearly hysterical over the preparations. And that peculiar fellow who scuttled out from beneath the runway - neither has been questioned about the events leading up to Lucy's death.'

My mind flashed back to that chaotic scene - Miss Brown's tear-stained face, the odd little man emerging like a theatre ghost from beneath the black curtilage.

'A serious oversight on my part.' HG's mouth tightened with displeasure. 'Both were present during those crucial hours before the show. Miss Brown would have known everyone's movements, schedules, preparations. And the mysterious little man- what exactly was he doing under that runway?'

'We can rectify it now,' Whipple offered. 'Better late than never.'

'Indeed, we must, Arthur.' HG rose from her chair. 'Would you accompany me to track down Miss Brown? She may be more forthcoming with a female presence.'

Poppy cleared her throat. 'Should I return to the models? Keep up appearances?'

'Yes, excellent thinking.' HG nodded approvingly. 'Rex can drive you back to the Assembly Hall. Arthur and I will make our way to Miss Brown's lodgings, the address of which she gave me when I offered her a friendly shoulder to lie against.'

The evening air cut sharp and clean across my face as we strolled through Eaton Park. Gas lamps cast pools of yellow light across the gravel paths, their glow catching the moisture-tipped grass beyond. Behind us, a colonnaded pavilion stood sentinel against the darkening sky, its white pillars gleaming.

HG pulled her coat collar tight against the chill. 'Miss Brown proved rather illuminating, wouldn't you say, Arthur?'

'Most peculiar woman.' Whipple's boots crunched on the path. 'Kept wringing her hands raw while we spoke.'

'She claimed no knowledge of Lucy's personal affairs,' HG continued, 'yet her eyes darted about like a trapped sparrow whenever we mentioned the victim's possible society connections.'

Our footsteps echoed off the pavilion walls as we rounded the formal gardens. The scent of Hellebores hanging in the air.

Whipple paused beside a marble statue and asked, 'Did you notice how she reacted when you mentioned the backstage preparations, HG? You know, stammering about costume changes, lighting cues and the like.'

'Indeed.' HG narrowed her grey eyes, almost as if she feared saying too much. 'What strikes me as odd is her reputation in fashion circles. Twenty years directing shows across Europe, yet she nearly collapsed from nerves over basic preparations.'

Whipple mused, 'Something spooked her that day.'

HG faced us both and said, 'Or someone.' 'Rex, you were there when we first arrived. Did Miss Brown's behaviour seem genuine to you?'

That chaotic scene returned to my mind, and I believed the director's tear-stained face and trembling hands were genuine. Now the question arose as to why she took on so?

The park's trees rustled in a breeze, showering discarded leaves across our path. The sight of them dancing in the lamplight reminded me of the chaos we'd witnessed at the Assembly Hall.

HG's voice cut through my reverie. 'Miss Brown seemed particularly agitated when discussing that peculiar little man who emerged from beneath the runway.'

'Angus Stirling?' Whipple pulled out his notebook. 'The name's written here.'

'Precisely.' HG traced her finger along the iron railing beside us. Miss Brown stated that he maintained the show's timing sequence. Rather vital in fashion presentations, yet she'd never collaborated with him before.'

Whipple scratched his pencil against the paper and said, 'It sounds like she won't ever again.

HG paused beside a marble fountain and said, 'No, indeed. She was quite emphatic about that. Called him an absolute disaster - the source of much of that afternoon's bedlam we witnessed.'

The memory flooded back of models rushing about, technicians shouting, and that diminutive fellow appearing, then vanishing like a Will-o'-the-wisp.

'Most telling perhaps,' HG continued, 'is that he failed to appear for the evening performance. Left poor Miss Brown managing the timing sequences along with her other duties.'

Whipple looked up from his notes. 'Rather convenient disappearance, wouldn't you say?'

'Most convenient.' HG's eyes glinted in the gaslight. 'And most peculiar that no one seems to know where he went.'

We continued our slow progress through the park in silence, and pondered how this new information might impact our investigation. One thing became clear: the more we dug, the more complicated matters became.

With an unexpected suggestion, HG interrupted our contemplative silence. 'Perhaps, let's set aside our investigative toil for one evening. The Theatre Royal has quite a production running.'

Whipple's eyebrows rose, sensing bad news.

'The Head Porter at the Royal Hotel spoke most highly of "Broadway Jones".' HG's face brightened. 'Apparently, it's a most delightful farcical comedy show - and has toured many locations, including London and Australia, no less.'

Whipple's reaction was entertaining to watch. He began to twitch his right eye, followed by a rapid succession of blinks that made him look rather like an owl caught in unexpected sunlight.

His voice cracked on the first syllable as he said, 'A…

'Oh yes,' HG continued, either missing or choosing to

ignore Whipple's distress. 'They say it's much better than the silent picture version, which I saw at a private viewing at Sandringham House not two years ago.'

My own feelings about spending an evening watching a theatre show about a theatre show, no matter how comedically matched Whipple's, although I thought discretion served the better form of valour. Turning away from HG's line of sight, I allowed the gathering darkness to hide my expression.

'The porter mentioned several excellent scenes.' HG's enthusiasm showed no signs of waning. 'I do so love a good giggle, and we are so fortunate to have as the lead character, Mr Harry Piddock. He does so enjoy playing with the audience.'

Whipple's blinking reached a most concerning velocity.

'But HG,' the inspector began, 'I have so much work to catch up on, I really do—'

'Thank me for ensuring you take a break from our investigations? Think nothing of it, Arthur. It's my treat.'

Whipple gave up; the fight unequal.

'Now that's settled, let us perambulate over to our august venue. With luck, we should just be in time for the 8.40 pm show. Come along, you two. No time to dawdle.'

Through the darkened streets of Norwich we walked, HG setting a brisk pace while Whipple dragged his feet several yards behind. The detective's shoulders slumped forward like a schoolboy facing detention, his normally precise stride reduced to an awkward shuffle.

'Do keep up, Arthur.' HG's voice carried back through the evening air. 'We don't want to miss the opening scene.'

A grunt emerged from behind us, followed by the sound of deliberately slow footsteps.

The golden glow of Theatre Street's lamps revealed the

Theatre Royal in all its Georgian splendour. The magnificent facade rose before us, its Portland stone gleaming pale against the night sky. Tri-columned porticos flanked the central entrance, their Corinthian capitals catching the lamplight. The building's perfect symmetry spoke of an era when architecture aimed for classical grace rather than mere function.

'Rather magnificent, wouldn't you say?' HG paused to admire the view.

Behind us, Whipple's footsteps grew even slower, each one seemingly more reluctant than the last.

'The renovations of 1913 did wonders for the old place,' HG continued, gesturing toward the freshly painted woodwork around the entrance. 'Though they kept the original 1826 design intact, thank heavens.'

The theatre's windows blazed with warmth, and well-dressed patrons climbed the steps between those stately columns. Their excitement for the evening's entertainment stood in stark contrast to Whipple's evident dismay.

'Arthur?' HG called back again. 'We really must hurry if we're to secure decent seats.'

The detective's response came as a barely audible mumble, something about case notes needing urgent attention.

HG's declaration about seats drew my attention to a poster advertising the evening's entertainment; the bottom of which displayed the price of various seating positions. These were as follows:

Boxes: 15/6

Orchestra Stalls: 2/4

Dress Circle: 2/-

Pit Stalls: 1/3

Upper circle: 1/-

Gallery: 5d

As I waited for Whipple to catch up, I observed HG securing a box for us three. A treat indeed.

Following HG's lead, we climbed the carpeted stairs to our box. Red velvet drapes framed the entrance, their gold tassels swaying as we passed through. The box offered an intimate view of the stage, nestled just above the left orchestra pit, where musicians tuned their instruments with quiet precision.

Gilt-edged mirrors lined the curved walls behind our seats, reflecting the warm glow of crystal chandeliers that hung like frozen raindrops from the ceiling. The theatre's dome stretched above, its elaborate plasterwork depicting classical scenes in cream and gold. Cherubs and garlands intertwined around the central rose, from which the grandest chandelier descended.

The auditorium buzzed with anticipation. Ladies in evening dress sparkled under the lights, their jewels catching and throwing back tiny points of brilliance. Gentlemen in dinner jackets filled the stalls below, while up in the gallery, dozens of faces peered down at the red velvet curtain.

Our box's position revealed details others might miss - the ornate ironwork of the balcony rails, painted in cream and picked out with gold leaf, curved in elegant arabesques. The proscenium arch framed the stage like a window into another world, its decorated borders matching the ceiling's classical theme.

Whipple sank into his plush seat with the air of a man facing execution, while HG leaned forward in eager antici- pation. The smell of beeswax polish mingled with perfume and tobacco, creating that heady theatre atmosphere that spoke of countless performances past.

Behind the safety curtain, known in theatrical circles as

the 'iron', stagehands sounded in a hurry, making final adjustments to the set. The orchestra struck up the overture, strings soaring toward the decorated ceiling, brass instruments gleaming under the dimming lights.

And so, into the limelight strode the lead characters... followed by a round of applause as the famous thespians set about their glorious illusion.

Up in the gallery, where working folk paid their five-pence for standing room only, raucous laughter accompanied the farcical interludes on stage, while good-natured heckling met the romantic moments. Their enthusiasm infected the whole theatre, breaking through the more reserved response of the dress circle below.

A flash of movement caught my attention - in the adjacent box, a lady in emerald silk kept glancing our way. Her attention focused on HG, who remained absorbed in the performance. The lady's jewels sparkled as she shifted position, trying to catch HG's eye without appearing obvious about it. Her companion, an elderly gentleman who had dozed off during the quieter scenes, seemed oblivious to her efforts.

The lady's attempts grew more determined as the play progressed. She dropped her programme twice, each time retrieving it with a flourish designed to attract notice. When that failed, she began fanning herself rather vigorously with it, causing her ostrich feather hat to bob in time with each movement.

HG remained focused on the stage, either unaware of or choosing to ignore the lady's increasingly desperate attempts at attention. Whipple, however, had noticed - his right eyebrow twitching higher with each new theatrical gesture from our neighbour.

From my position beside HG, the lady's increasingly

dramatic gestures became impossible to ignore. Her fan now moved with such vigour it threatened to launch her ostrich feathers into orbit. The emerald silk of her gown rustled with each exaggerated movement, drawing disapproving glances from other theatre-goers among her class.

Leaning closer to HG, my whispered words barely carried over the orchestra's crescendo. 'The lady in the next box seems rather desperate for your attention.'

'I am only too aware of Lady Leggit's uncouth behaviour. I shall have nothing to do with that person.' HG's eyes never left the stage. 'Do you know she and her husband once ran away when confronted by a frightened horse bearing down on several children in Hyde Park. Disaster was only averted when a brave shoe-shine grabbed the poor beast's reins and calmed the anxious steed. Ever since then, they've been known by society as "Leggit by name; Leg-it by nature."'

The corners of her mouth twitched ever so slightly as she delivered this assessment, though her gaze remained fixed on the performance before us. In the soft glow of the theatre lights, that subtle expression spoke volumes about her opinion of both Lord and Lady Leggit.

The final scene before intermission ended with a humorous flourish, prompting thunderous applause from every level of the theatre. My hands joined the enthusiastic response while observing the distinct reactions across the social strata. The gallery erupted in high-pitched whistles and loud roars, their unbridled appreciation echoing down to the stalls below.

As the red velvet curtain descended, the audience began their practiced exodus. The working folk from the gallery rushed down the back stairs; their footsteps creating a drumroll effect as they headed straight for the nearby

Theatre Royal Tavern. Their voices carried back through the open doors, filled with animated discussions about the first act's comedic moments.

The gentry rose with measured grace, ladies adjusting their evening gloves while gentlemen offered their arms. They drifted toward the theatre's own refreshment room, where champagne and delicate pastries awaited. The middling-sort followed in their wake, though their path led to the less expensive tea room where coffee and biscuits provided more modest refreshment.

HG turned to face us both, her eyes bright with enjoyment. Whipple, meanwhile, had perfected the art of appearing simultaneously awake and asleep - a talent no doubt honed through years of tedious police interviews.

The contrast between the various social groups grew more pronounced as they separated into their designated spaces. Through the theatre's open doors, bursts of raucous laughter drifted up from the tavern, while the gentle tinkling of champagne glasses echoed from the refreshment room.

Lady Leggit made one final attempt to catch HG's attention before sweeping out of her box, her emerald silks rustling with determination. Her elderly companion jerked awake at her departure, blinking in confusion at finding himself suddenly alone.

The refreshment room offered a stark contrast to the bustling corridors outside. Crystal glasses clinked with delicate precision while hushed conversations floated across tables draped in pristine white linen. Watching the assembled gentry sip their champagne reminded me of a carefully choreographed dance - each movement measured, each word weighed.

My peaceful observations shattered as Lady Leggit's emerald form bore down upon our table like a ship under full sail. HG could no longer pretend ignorance of the woman's existence.

'Your Grace!' Lady Leggit's voice carried just enough to draw attention without appearing vulgar. 'What an absolute delight!'

'Lady Leggit.' HG's eyebrows rose. 'What a surprise to see you here. I hadn't noticed you at all.'

The exchange of pleasantries threatened to overcome my composure. Desperate to maintain decorum, my attention shifted to Whipple.

'Would you mind passing the sugar-tongues, Inspector?'

Whipple's forehead creased. 'But I gave them to you not sixty seconds ago.'

By the time he looked back toward HG, she stood in a distant corner with her pursuer. The woman leaned so close that her ostrich feathers seemed to tickle HG's ear. Their conversation looked intense, the woman's gestures becoming increasingly animated, while HG remained perfectly still.

When HG returned to our table, pink spots coloured her usually pale cheeks. She sat with unusual stiffness, her fingers drumming a rapid pattern on the tablecloth.

'Are you quite all right?' Whipple's concern showed in his furrowed brow.

HG's grey eyes fixed on him. Her voice dropped to barely above a whisper. 'I've been warned off.'

Chapter Twelve

NIGHT SKY

Through the remainder of the performance, Lady Leggit's box remained conspicuously empty. Both she and her elderly companion had vanished, leaving behind only the faintest trace of expensive French perfume. The vacancy appeared to unsettle HG more than she cared to admit - her shoulders tensed each time her gaze drifted toward those velvet-draped seats.

We departed before the final curtain, slipping out during a particularly rousing musical number. The Royal Hotel's cocktail bar provided a welcome sanctuary from the evening's peculiarities. Art Deco style and plush cream leather chairs created an atmosphere of subtle luxury, while soft lighting cast gentle shadows on our worried faces.

'Your usual, madam?' The waiter materialised at our table with practiced efficiency.

'Yes, thank you, Charles.' HG's voice carried a hint of strain beneath its usual composure.

Charles returned moments later bearing our drinks on a silver tray - a Gin Fizz for HG, my Tom Collins, and a pint of Guinness for Whipple. The stout's creamy head formed perfect layers as it settled in the glass.

HG lifted her drink and took an uncharacteristically large swallow. Her eyes closed briefly, head shaking ever so slightly as she processed whatever warning Leggit had delivered. The ice clinked against her glass as she set it down with precise control.

Whipple's fingers caressed his glass while we waited for HG to share the detail of the woman's message. The normally vibrant cocktail bar was eerily silent, the other patrons seemingly sensing the seriousness of our situation and speaking quietly.

HG sat motionless, staring into her Gin Fizz as though the floating lemon twist might reveal answers. The ice cubes began to melt, creating delicate swirls in the cocktail that matched the troubled expression on her face. HG's normally precise posture had softened, shoulders dropping ever so slightly.

The bar's soft lighting caught the cut crystal of her glass, casting prism patterns across the polished wood table. My Tom Collins remained untouched, beads of condensation rolling down its sides.

At last, she broke the silence.

'Do you know, the Leggit woman smirked as she delivered her master's message. Oh, she observed the protocol of my rank, of course, yet the obsequious wretch nevertheless enjoyed her bit part in current proceedings.'

Whipple leaned forward, his Guinness forgotten. 'You know who this master is?'

HG lifted her glass, took another mighty swig, and replaced it on the low oblong table. 'That's the irritating part. If she knows, she's not saying. However, given her rocky status in society, my feeling is she will do the bidding of any person of superior standing to get in their good books.'

From my position near the window, the waiter's attention to HG's empty glass caught my eye. His practiced movements spoke of years serving the upper classes, each gesture a carefully choreographed dance of deference and timing. The crystal tumbler had barely touched the table before he materialised at her elbow.

'Another?' The waiter bent forward to recover the item, his white-gloved hands hovering with practiced grace.

'A splendid idea,' HG gestured to include Whipple and me in the offering. My head shook in gentle decline - someone needed to keep their wits sharp tonight.

'I'll have a half, if you'll be so kind,' Whipple said.

The waiter nodded and retreated to the bar to deliver his order, his polished shoes clicking softly against the parquet flooring.

HG reached for her silver chain clutch bag. The delicate clasp made a satisfying click as it opened. Her fingers dipped inside, emerging with the familiar leather-bound notebook she always carried.

The pages rustled as she thumbed through them, her expression growing more focused with each turn. The delicate lamplight caught the gold embossing on the cover - a gift from her late husband, if memory served correctly. Several loose papers threatened to escape, but she tucked them back with practiced ease.

After scanning several pages filled with her copperplate handwriting, she placed the notebook face down on the polished table surface.

'Gentlemen,' HG's voice cut through the ambient murmur of the cocktail bar, 'this investigation has become rather more complicated than initially anticipated. Perhaps we should review our list of potential suspects and their motives.'

Her fingers traced around the notebook's edges. 'We must consider not only the immediate players but also the implications of Lady Leggit's warning.'

Whipple leaned forward in his chair, his half-finished Guinness forgotten. The bar's soft lighting cast shadows across his weathered face as he nodded.

'The timing of that warning,' HG continued, 'suggests our investigation may have stirred up matters we have yet to unravel, or, perhaps, even recognise. An individual, or group clearly wishes us to abandon our inquiries. Before we go much further, we must ask ourselves why?'

Just then the waiter returned and deposited HG's cocktail and Whipple's Guinness, before departing into thin air.

HG's notebook looked comfortable in her hands, its well-worn leather bore the patina of constant use, and edges softened by countless openings and closings. HG fingers found the slim pencil tucked into the spine - a clever device my mentor always found amusing.

The cocktail bar's hushed atmosphere wrapped around us like a blanket. She positioned the notebook between her fresh Gin Fizz and the table's edge. A blank page presented itself, ready to receive our collective thoughts.

'Arthur, shall we begin?' HG adjusted her position, pencil poised above the cream paper. 'We must endeavour not to go into too much detail. Let us instead list the individuals, and our concise concerns about them.'

Whipple set down his half-pint and leaned back into the soft leather folds of his chair.

Whipple's methodical mind clicked into gear as he settled deeper into his chair.

'First, we have Clara Brightman,' he began, watching

HG's pencil move across the page. 'Best friend, confidante, yet clearly withholding information about Lucy's mystery man. Could be protecting someone dangerous.'

HG nodded, her neat handwriting capturing each word.

'Then there's Amber Longstone.' Whipple took a measured sip of his Guinness. 'Professional rivalry, openly hostile towards Lucy, and conveniently positioned near the room in which Lucy died.'

The pencil scratched steadily across the paper.

'Mr Daws, the father.' Whipple's voice hardened. 'Estranged relationship, violent temper, and peculiar behaviour when questioned about his daughter's death.'

Listening to Whipple, I knew now why he had gained such a reputation at Scotland Yard. His instant recollection, logical thought process and ability to use the fewest words to capture the essence of the case truly inspired me as he continued his exposition.

'Milly Davenport - fled the scene suspiciously fast, has financial troubles, and demonstrated a pattern of deception.'

HG's pencil paused momentarily, before continuing. Almost as if she required time to take it all in.

'Mr Pendlebury,' Whipple's eyes narrowed. 'His behaviour around that storage room warrants scrutiny, plus he had access to the entire building and holds the passkey for all locks.'

The list grew longer as HG's precise handwriting filled the page.

'Emily Brown and the missing stagehand, Angus Stirling.' Whipple's tone became thoughtful. 'Both unaccounted for during crucial moments, both disappeared rather conveniently.'

A waiter passed nearby, his shoes clicking against the parquet flooring, as Whipple leaned forward.

'And now, perhaps most intriguingly, we must consider the Three Circles Society connection. Lucy's tattoo suggests involvement with powerful people who might have wanted her silenced.'

'Could they be behind the warning I received this evening?' said HG.

'It has to be a distinct possibility,' replied Whipple, before sinking the last of his Guinness.

I ventured with eight possible suspects that we'd already identified. Aside from the unknown hands behind HG's warning and the mysterious Three Circles, perhaps we needed to concentrate on reducing the number to make our investigation more manageable.

My suggestion about narrowing down suspects caused HG to turn towards me, her expression brightening despite the late hour and gravity of our discussion.

'Rex, that's rather astute. We risk becoming tangled in too many threads at once.' Her pencil tapped thoughtfully against the notebook. 'What do you think, Arthur? Should we focus our attention on our most likely suspects?'

Whipple shifted in his chair, the leather creaking softly beneath him. 'The danger is, HG, eliminating suspects prematurely could prove disastrous. The killer might slip through our fingers simply because we deemed them less likely to kill than others.'

The cocktail bar's soft lighting caught the worry lines etched across his face as he continued.

'Take the Whitechapel case of '19. Three promising suspects dismissed early on because they seemed peripheral to the investigation. Turned out one was our man - we spent months chasing shadows while he was free to continue his spree.'

HG's pencil stilled against the paper.

'Mind you,' Whipple lifted his empty glass, studying it thoughtfully, 'I understand the temptation to streamline our inquiry. Nobody wants to waste time chasing red herrings when a killer walks free. But there's no substitute for proper police work - following where the evidence leads, regardless of how unlikely it might seem.'

'Even if that evidence points in eight or more different directions?' HG intoned.

'Especially then,' Whipple replied. 'Because somewhere within the confusion lies the truth about who killed Lucy Daws.'

A refined gentleman wearing a smart suite and carnation buttonhole began to loiter about our table. At length, he gave a stilted cough, placing his gloved hand over his mouth.

'Might there be anything else?'

HG took the hint after glancing around the empty cocktail bar and glimpsing an onyx mounted clock on the far wall.

'Ah, I see we have overstayed our welcome. Come, gentlemen, we shall retire to my room for a nightcap.'

The startled fellow looked concerned as he took each of us in, in turn.

'Er…shall I have drinks delivered, Your Grace?'

HG looked at the chap with kindness. 'No need, my suite is perfectly stocked with all we require.'

And so we relocated to the Nelson Suite, situated on the top floor of the establishment, and which afforded an excellent view of Norwich city. Decorated and furnished in the traditional English style, HG's suite proved the perfect location in which to continue our discussions.

'A whisky, Arthur,' asked HG as she hovered over the amply stocked drinks trolly. 'And for you, Rex; a G&T perhaps?'

Whipple wrapped his fingers around the crystal glass as if the delicate hue of his whisky might be the elixir of life. For my part, I'd learned to treat gin with the utmost respect after an unfortunate incident when, having drunk too large a measure at a dinner party, I'd lay on my bed by way of a brief respite, only to arise the following morning still dressed in my dinner suit with little recollection of how I'd got there.

I took particular note that on this occasion, HG dispensed a small measure of "Mothers Ruin", topped up with a copious amount of tonic. Her glance left little doubt as to her intention...to eliminate any repeat of my previous eccentric behaviour.

From my position near the window, the city's lights twinkled below like fallen stars. The whisky in Whipple's glass caught the opaque glow of the table lamp as HG settled into her favourite armchair.

'Gentlemen, before we retire for the evening, there's one matter we must address.' HG's fingers traced the rim of her glass. 'The "Three Circles". We need to determine if that subversive band plays any role in our investigation, or if Lucy's tattoo is merely an interesting distraction.'

Whipple's eyes narrowed, his weathered face showing keen interest. 'You know more about this organisation than either of us, HG. What's your assessment of their potential involvement?'

'The Three Circles began as a philosophical society at Oxford in 1851,' HG's voice took on a scholarly tone.

'Their original mandate was to promote progressive thinking among the elite. However, in the lead up to the Great War, they evolved into something far more sinister.'

The ice in her glass clinked as she took a measured sip.

'They now operate as a shadow network of influential figures - politicians, industrialists, even members of the aristocracy. Their symbol, the three interlocking circles, represents their core beliefs: power, secrecy, and influence. They're known to eliminate threats to their interests.'

Whipple's expression darkened. 'And you think Lucy somehow crossed paths with them?'

'Consider this - a young model from modest beginnings suddenly bears their mark. Either she was recruited for some purpose, or she discovered something that granted her entry, yet made her dangerous to them. The question is: which scenario led to her death, if indeed, they are involved at all?'

The weight of HG's words hung in the air as we contemplated the implications. My G&T remained untouched as I processed this new dimension to our investigation.

Whipple's brow furrowed at HG's mention of the Great War. He placed his whisky on the side table, the crystal making a soft clink against the polished wood.

'What exactly did you mean about the war, HG? Your tone suggests something rather unsavoury.'

HG's eyes focused on some distant point beyond the room's confines. The lamplight cast shadows across her face, deepening the gravity of her expression.

'Let us just say that certain persons saw the conflict as an opportunity to benefit their own interests.'

The statement hung in the air like gun smoke. Whipple's weathered face tightened, his police instincts clearly sensing the weight behind her carefully chosen words. My own memories of that conflict stirred uncomfortable recollections of those who were, and remain, affected by the tumult.

HG lifted the glass but didn't drink, instead studying the liquid as though it might reveal secrets best left buried in the mud of Flanders.

Whipple reached for his whisky again, his hand slightly less steady than before. The distant chime of Norwich Cathedral's bells marked the late hour, yet none of us moved to check the time. The implications of HG's words commanded our full attention.

'What if Lucy stumbled onto something?' Whipple's voice dropped lower. 'Something about one of these war profiteers you mentioned. Perhaps she discovered evidence of their activities during her modelling work - overheard conversations at social events, or documents...remember her last words?'

HG's expression remained neutral, but her fingers tightened almost imperceptibly around her glass.

'Rather than silence her immediately, they could have attempted to control the situation by drawing her into Three Circles membership. Perhaps this flattered Lucy, you know, her "importance."'

'An interesting theory, Arthur,' HG murmured.

'Once they gained her trust through flattery and false inclusion, she likely revealed what she knew,' Whipple's weathered hands gestured as he spoke. 'After that, she became a liability. The very act of sharing her knowledge sealed her fate. They couldn't risk her eventually realising the truth about their war activities and speaking out.

'The shooting wasn't just about silencing her,' Whipple continued. 'It was a message to others who Lucy might have shared her secrets. I venture that the Three Circles tattoo was put there to warn anyone who attempted to contact them understood the price they would pay.'

I ventured that if Whipple's hypothesis held up, then Clara Brightman might be at particular risk as Lucy's best friend. Neither HG nor Whipple replied. Their drawn features said enough.

A subdued silence fell over the room. We had come so far over recent days, yet when measured against the cold truth of a life lost too early, all we had achieved was to identify a melee of suspects. The risk of being busy fools felt too real for comfort.

As I wandered over to the large picture window, the cloudless sky drew my attention. Pegasus shone brightly, its shape resembling a winged horse. If only our investigation showed the same clarity. Instead, it felt more accurate to compare our effort to Andromeda, which I could just make out in the far night sky as a faint smudge; shapeless and out of reach.

As the constellations above Norwich twinkled with cold indifference to our earthly troubles, HG's quiet words floated across the elegant room.

'What occupies your thoughts, Rex?'

I turned from the window to face her, noting how the lamplight caught the silver threads in her hair. The weight of our discussion about the Three Circles and Lucy's murder pressed heavily on my mind, but before I could form a response, Whipple's gravelly voice cut through the silence.

'Like us, he's pondering which tendril of the great octopus we are grappling with to pull at first. Is that not so, young Rex?'

I offered a half-smile, appreciating his apt metaphor, and moved away from the window to re-join my colleagues.

'It seems to me,' began HG, 'that we must talk to Clara again, if only to warn her that she may be in grave danger, and to press the young lady on the subject of the Three Circles and any information Lucy may have shared.'

The shrill ring of the telephone interrupted our conversation. The bedside table's brass and oak creation demanded attention with its insistent chorus. HG rose from her chair with fluid grace, crossing to answer it.

Whipple caught my eye, his raised eyebrow matching my own curiosity at such a late caller. The cathedral bells had only recently struck an hour when most respectable folk were tucked safely in their beds.

We watched as HG lifted the receiver, her responses coming in measured tones. 'Oh,' she said, followed by a thoughtful pause. 'I see.' Another few seconds of silence. 'Is that so?'

The exchange appeared entirely one-sided, with HG offering nothing more than these brief acknowledgements. Her face remained impossible to read, though I noticed her free hand toying with the telephone cord - a rare display of restlessness from someone usually so composed.

When the call ended, HG replaced the handset with deliberate slowness, as if each fraction of movement required careful consideration. She stood there, one hand still resting on the telephone, gathering her thoughts before turning to us.

'That was Lord Wentworth,' she announced, her voice carrying a hint of frustration. 'He wanted to let me know that Milly Davenport has "Bally well jumped ship," as he put it. Now, I ask myself why she would do that?'

Chapter Thirteen

A PAST PHANTOM

Following our heated debate the night before, we made up our minds over the breakfast to divide our forces.

Whipple was assigned to investigate the histories of our persons of interest. However, Milly Davenport and Lady Leggit were still being handled by HG. I was also under HG's purview.

The gravel crunched beneath the Rolls' tyres as we pulled up to Cockleford Manor. His lordship stood at the open door; his usual confident bearing replaced by a stoop that spoke of defeat. His attire appeared more rumpled than usual, as if he'd slept in it.

'My deepest apologies.' He wrung his hands. 'That minx played us for fools. Young Freddie Montague - one of my house party guests, drove her to the station late last night. She spun him some tale about her mother being desperately ill.'

HG patted his arm. 'My dear Alfred, no young blade could resist Miss Davenport's particular charms. Might I have a word with this Freddie?'

'Of course, of course,' Wentworth gestured us inside. 'The whole sorry lot are in the morning room, nursing their headaches with coffee.'

We followed him down the oak-panelled hallway to a spacious room overlooking the rose garden. Three figures occupied the space - two men sprawled in leather armchairs and a woman perched on the window seat. Each wore tweeds and boots; dressed for a day's exploration of the estate.

The moment HG crossed the threshold, they leapt to their feet. The taller man almost upset his coffee cup in his haste to stand. Their faces showed a mix of awe and trepidation at HG's presence.

'Your Grace,' the woman breathed, executing a small curtsy. 'So wonderful to see you again.'

'Lady Langly, my pleasure entirely. And the pigs?'

I must confess to some confusion at HG's strange greeting until the lady explained all.

'Ah, the pigs. Yes, indeed. Under the constant supervision of my dear husband, they thrive. Which is more than I can say for the Hall. If only Peregrine would pay as much attention to the roof as he does to the pig styes, all should be well.'

There followed a brief silence as the others offered a sympathetic sigh.

'No matter,' continued Lady Langly. 'I suspect you are here to speak with young Monty, and not about my husband's Wessex Saddlebacks.

HG offered her a warm, friendly smile that lit up her entire face. The kind of smile that made everyone feel at ease, even in the most awkward of situations.

'Indeed, it is. Perhaps we might take a turn around the knot garden, Mr Montague? The morning air is quite mild for the time of year, and perhaps the earthy fragrance of the Chrysanthemums might stimulate our cerebral cores. What do you say?'

The tall, thin young man practically bounced on his heels. His eagerness to escape the Drawing Room matched only by the pink tinge creeping up his neck. No doubt the poor chap wished to spare himself further embarrassment over being so thoroughly duped by Miss Davenport.

'Rather! Splendid idea.' Monty strode towards the French doors. 'I do so love knot gardens.'

My companions and I made our farewells to Lord Wentworth and in an instant, we stepped out into the mild October morning. The grass path made for easy progress as we headed towards the renowned Cockleford knot garden.

Glancing back at the Hall, the gaggle of house guests pressed their noses against the French doors like children at a sweetshop window. Their attempts at subtlety failed miserably as they jostled for position, each trying to catch snippets of conversation. My stern look sent them scattering like startled pigeons, though Lady Langly maintained enough dignity to retreat at a stately pace.

The corners of my mouth twitched. Whether in grand Manor houses or village shops, human nature remained remarkably consistent - everyone loved a bit of gossip. The urge to eavesdrop knew no class boundaries.

Keeping a discreet distance behind HG and our young quarry, my boots sank into a soft cushion of grass. Close enough to hear, far enough to give them privacy.

'Might I call you Monty?' HG's voice carried clearly in the morning air.

'Oh yes, rather! All my friends do.' The young man's enthusiasm bubbled over.

'And how should I address you?'

'Your Grace will suffice.'

The words dropped like pebbles into a still pond. Without breaking stride or changing tone, HG had masterfully reminded young Montague of the social gulf between them. My shoulders shook with suppressed mirth - HG employed the tactic when necessary to dominate any exchange-and in this case, it meant Monty feeling obliged to tell HG the truth.

Poor Monty stumbled slightly, then executed an awkward half-turn toward a scraggly patch of heather.

'I say, what magnificent... er... specimens.' He gestured vaguely at the plants, his face flushed pink to the tips of his ears. 'Most... um... vigorous growth for the time of year.'

HG allowed a companionable silence to settle over us as we strolled past a weathered sundial. The morning dew still clung to the precisely trimmed box hedges, their geometric patterns a testament to the gardener's skill. Young Montague's shoulders gradually relaxed, his earlier embarrassment fading like morning mist.

'What remarkable knowledge you possess of herbaceous borders, Monty.' HG's voice carried the perfect blend of warmth and authority. 'So rare to find someone of your generation with such appreciation for the finer points of horticulture.'

The transformation in Monty was immediate. His spine straightened, chin lifted, and a genuine smile replaced his nervous fidgeting. 'Really? I mean to say, one does try to keep up with the latest developments in garden design. Been following old Gertrude Jekyll's writings rather closely.'

My lips curved into a knowing smile as HG worked her particular brand of magic. The pattern never varied - first the gentle reminder of her status to establish control, then the carefully measured praise to restore confidence. Like a master angler playing a fish, HG knew precisely when to apply pressure and when to give line.

'Indeed?' HG's interest appeared genuine, though my service had taught me to recognise the subtle signs of her technique. 'Do tell me more about your thoughts on Jekyll's approach to colour harmonies.'

Monty launched into an enthusiastic discourse on garden design, completely at ease now and utterly devoted to pleasing his distinguished listener. The transformation from nervous youth to eager confidant was complete. Once again, HG had masterfully engineered the perfect conditions for gathering information.

From my position a few paces behind, the scene unfolded like a well-rehearsed play. Every moment since we entered the garden had built towards this - HG's careful cultivation of trust, the measured praise, the shared interest in horticulture. Now, as naturally as leaves falling in autumn, HG took Monty's arm and asked, 'Now, Monty, what happened last night-you know, between you and that young minx?'

The question hung in the crisp morning air. HG taught me to recognise these pivotal moments. The gentle pressure on his arm, the conspiratorial tone - HG knew the young man would crack like a fresh egg. And crack he did.

'Well, you see,' Monty's words tumbled out, 'Miss Davenport - Milly - she's absolutely topping. Never met anyone quite like her. The way she listened, hanging on every word about my thoughts on modern garden design. Even asked about my plans for improving father's rose garden back at our estate.'

He paused to catch his breath; the colour rising in his cheeks. 'We'd been alone in the Drawing Room - I know it's not the done thing, you know, no chaperone, but it is 1922 after all, isn't it? Anyway. we were having the most fascinating discussion about herbaceous borders. When she returned after stepping out briefly, everything changed. Tears in her eyes, absolutely distraught about her mother being terribly ill in London. Begged me to help her catch the late train. What else could a chap do? Couldn't leave a lady in distress, could I?'

HG's expression softened at Monty's obvious distress. My heart went out to the young chap - clearly another victim of Miss Davenport's particular brand of manipulation.

'My dear boy, you acted precisely as any gentleman would.' HG patted his arm. 'While Miss Davenport's performance may have been genuine - one never knows with absolute certainty - my previous experience suggests otherwise. But you have nothing whatsoever to reproach yourself for.'

The relief on Monty's face was palpable. His shoulders relaxed, and the colour began to fade from his cheeks. The morning sun caught the brass buttons of his tweed jacket as he straightened his spine.

'Tell me, Monty,' HG's voice took on that gentle, probing tone that never failed to draw out information, 'did Miss Davenport say anything else during her stay? Either to you directly or perhaps something you overheard? The smallest detail might be significant - anything that made your ears prick up?'

Monty's brow furrowed in concentration as we passed a fine example of topiary. The sculpted peacock seemed to watch us with its leafy eye as Monty pondered the question. His hand stroked the crisp morning dew from a box hedge.

'Well, there was one thing.'

The air sizzled with expectation as HG and I waited to hear what young Monty might reveal. For the first time since we'd entered the garden, he turned to face HG directly, his lanky frame casting a shadow across the grass path.

At dinner, I overheard Milly talking to Lady Langly about a gentleman. I was shocked. The two women giggled at whatever Milly shared, which I thought uncouth in polite society.'

HG's eyes widened just a fraction - enough that my years of service allowed me to catch the subtle change.

'A name, perhaps?' HG's voice remained steady, though her fingers tightened ever so slightly on her silver-tipped walking stick.

Monty's face scrunched up in concentration, like a schoolboy trying to recall a particularly troublesome Latin conjugation. 'That's the strange thing. It wasn't a fellow's name, rather some sort of nick-name. For all the world, it sounded like "Pinstripe." All rather odd if you ask me.'

The colour drained from HG's face so rapidly that my hand instinctively moved toward her elbow, ready to offer support if needed. We both knew what that name implied. The reclusive "Pinstripe" had surfaced again. The question arose...what was he up to this time?

HG remained subdued as we made our way to the home of Lady Leggit. Although I knew a little of the distaste HG held for the nameless gentleman, I had not appreciated until now, that an element of fear might also be at play.

The grey clouds hung low over North Norfolk as we drove towards the Leggit residence. My curiosity about HG's evident unease finally got the better of me.

'May I ask about the individual who seems to cause you such concern?'

HG's fingers drummed against the leather armrest. 'That person first crossed my path when my eldest son went up to Oxford University. They were born in the same year; both joined the rowing club. My son told me the fellow dabbled in politics and was a firebrand on the merits of dictatorship. Fortunately, my son steered clear of the fellow. This proved fortuitous, given what the ubiquitous "Pinstripe" as he became known, got up to a few years later, and of which I do not wish to speak at this juncture.'

The vehemence in HG's tone made me grip the steering wheel tighter. Something in those words suggested wounds yet to heal.

'Twenty years is a long time to maintain such antagonism.' My voice remained neutral, probing gently.

'Some actions cannot be forgiven, Rex. Some betrayals cut too deep.' HG turned to watch the rain streak across the window. 'However, there is a positive in all this. We may not know where Milly Davenport has gone, other than checking with her mother's residence, but I know how to lure Pinstripe from the shadows, so let us focus on the Leggits' for now. The suited one can wait a few hours.'

The remainder of the journey to King's Lynn slid back into an uncomfortable silence, and I thought it better not to push my luck with my unsettled mentor.

Our reception at the substantial home of our quarry proved less hospitable than one might have expected on the arrival of a duchess. However, HG took in her stride the cool reception the Leggit woman offered us as the butler showed us into the spacious Morning Room of Fairview House.

Before our unwilling host could muster her evident displeasure at our arrival, HG swept forward with the grace of a duchess and the timing of a master swordsman delivering a Touché.

I wanted to express my gratitude for your wisdom at the Theatre Royal, my dear.

The woman's mouth hung open for a fraction before she collected herself. Her fingers fluttered at her throat, touching a string of pearls that spoke more of aspiration than achievement.

'How... kind of you to say so.' The words emerged stilted, uncertain.

'Might we impose upon you for tea?' HG's smile could have melted granite.

Lady Leggit had no choice but to ring for refreshments. She gestured towards two comfortable armchairs - not the antique pieces that graced most of HG contemporaries, but serviceable, nonetheless.

The transformation in our hostess proved remarkable to witness. Where moments ago, she had bristled with barely concealed hostility. Now she perched on the edge of her seat like a sparrow attempting to beguile an eagle. HG's masterful opening gambit had completely wrong-footed the woman, leaving her defensive posture in tatters.

Watching HG settle into the armchair with perfect poise, a familiar warmth of admiration spread through my chest. Once again, my mentor had demonstrated the art of social warfare with devastating effectiveness. Now she would, to utilise a fishing term, reel the lady in.

The butler delivered tea with a studied precision. Our host's hands shook as she poured.

HG leaned forward, those piercing eyes fixed on our hostess. 'Now, my dear, let us talk more about the danger you have saved me from. One cannot be too careful these days, especially with organisations like the Three Circles becoming so...influential.'

Lady Leggit's cup froze halfway to her lips. A splash of tea escaped onto the saucer.

'Three Circles?' Her voice emerged as barely more than a whisper. 'I... I don't know what you mean.'

'Come now, surely the person who sent you must have mentioned their association. After all, they wouldn't trust just anyone with such a delicate message.'

The woman's complexion paled further. 'I simply passed along what I was asked to convey. Nothing more.'

'By someone who clearly moves in the highest circles. Someone who understands the importance of... discretion.' HG's tone carried a hint of conspiracy. 'Someone whose good opinion might prove valuable to those seeking to restore their social standing.'

That last comment struck home. He ladyship set down her cup with trembling fingers.

'Lord Carstairs,' she blurted, then immediately pressed her fingers to her lips. 'Oh dear, I shouldn't have...'

'Lord Carstairs?' HG's eyebrows rose fractionally. 'How fascinating. And did he mention anyone else when giving you these instructions?'

'Only that he was acting on behalf of... of...' She twisted her hands in her lap. 'A gentleman who prefers to remain unnamed. Someone quite important in government circles.'

My eyes met HGs for the briefest moment. The pieces

were beginning to align. Andromeda had emerged from its haze.

'I must admit that it took all my finishing school training not to show my amusement when the woman froze like a startled rabbit,' HG began as she relayed our afternoon adventure in King's Lynn to Inspector Whipple. 'And do you know, that trick you taught me about getting suspects to say more that they meant to? Well, it worked a treat.'

And so, for the next fifteen minutes, HG and I related our busy day to Whipple and Poppy as we dined on Dover Sole with Pineapple Upside-Down cake to follow in the Maid's Hotel, one of Norwich's finest establishments.

Whipple dabbed at his mouth with the crisp linen napkin. 'Most impressive work with Lady Leggit, HG. The way you drew her out shows your talent for investigation hasn't dimmed.'

HG smiled at the compliment, but her eyes remained sharp. 'And your own enquiries, Arthur?'

'Productive, though that Tin Hut grows more depressing by the day.' Whipple shook his head. 'Muddleford's office festers more than O'Brien's shingles, if such a thing were possible. Still, I've made headway with our suspects.'

The waiter topped up our wine glasses as Whipple pulled out his notebook.

'Clara Brightman checks out - her story aligns perfectly with witness accounts. The Cunliffs were indeed in the powder room when the shot rang out, confirmed by three separate sources. Emily Brown's theatrical outburst masks a simple case of stage fright rather than murderous intent.'

'That narrows the field considerably,' HG remarked.

'Indeed. I've moved most to my unlikely list, save for three: Amber Longstone - her hatred for Lucy runs deeper than mere professional rivalry. Pendlebury - his behaviour around that storage room grows more suspicious by the day. And Mr Daws - a father's rage can drive men to terrible acts.'

'The others?' HG leaned forward.

'Under review, naturally. Fresh evidence could shift perspectives.' Whipple tucked his notebook away. 'But for now, these three warrant our closest attention.'

I turned to Poppy, who had remained silent, and enquired if she agreed with the inspector's assessment.

Poppy set down her fork and straightened in her chair. Her eyes sparkled with that characteristic gleam that meant she had something important to share.

'Your assessment makes perfect sense, Inspector, except for one glaring omission.' She glanced around the table. 'Remember the peculiar fellow who spends hours hiding beneath the fashion runway? The girls say his name is Phillious Cowpepper, although they've nicknamed him as "the phantom".'

The name caused Whipple to pause mid-bite.

'Strange little man,' Poppy continued. 'Balding, nervous sort who's always fiddling with his tie. The girls think he's creepy. Won't look anyone in the eye and scuttles away like a frightened crab whenever anyone approaches.'

My gaze shifted to HG, who had gone very still. She placed her dessert spoon beside her half-finished pudding with deliberate care.

'Arthur, we've been remiss,' she said. 'Here we sit, discussing suspects without consulting our most valuable source of information.' She turned to Poppy with genuine warmth. 'My dear, you've been privy to conversations and observations we could never access. Tell us more about this, Mr Cowpepper.'

Whipple pulled out his notebook again, this time with renewed interest. The waiter approached to clear our plates, but HG waved him away with a subtle gesture. All attention focused on Poppy, who clearly had more to share about our mysterious phantom.

Chapter Fourteen

OLD ENEMIES

After coffee, HG rose from the table with that determined look she wore when pieces of a puzzle started falling into place. 'Time to make a rather delicate telephone call from my room at the Royal. The Old Enemy won't be pleased to hear from me, but needs must.'

Whipple followed suit moments later. 'I'll put my team at the Yard to work calling in a few favours.'

Their departures left an oddly charged atmosphere at our corner table. Poppy sat across from me, absently tracing patterns on the tablecloth with her finger. The last time we'd been alone together was at her garage, sharing tea and chocolate biscuits while discussing her undercover role. Now, my collar felt uncomfortably tight.

Poppy glanced up, catching me staring. A smile played at the corners of her mouth. 'Penny for your thoughts, Mr Watson?'

I reached for my water glass, not knowing what to say. My mouth felt dry.

'Anyone there, Rex?' she asked with a teasing lilt. 'Or should I say Reginald?'

The way she said my full name sent an unexpected shiver down my spine. Perhaps sensing my discomfort, she leaned back in her chair, that familiar sparkle of mischief in her eyes. Even in her day dress, she carried herself with the same confidence she showed in her mechanic's overalls.

The waiter appeared at my elbow, breaking the moment. 'Will sir and madam be requiring anything else this evening?'

Never had an interruption felt more welcome - or more frustrating.

'Would you care for a drink?' The words tumbled out before my nerve could desert me.

Poppy giggled, her eyes dancing with delight. 'Let's be wicked, shall we? I'll have a Clover Club. What about you? And don't you dare say you're driving because you can leave the Rolls here overnight. The Royal is only around the corner.'

Whipple followed suit moments later. 'I'll put my team at the Yard to work calling in a few favours.'

Their departures left an oddly charged atmosphere at our corner table. Poppy sat across from me, absently tracing patterns on the tablecloth with her finger. The last time we'd been alone together was at her garage, sharing tea and chocolate biscuits while discussing her undercover role. Now, my collar felt uncomfortably tight.

Poppy glanced up, catching me staring. A smile played at the corners of her mouth. 'Penny for your thoughts, Mr Watson?'

My hand trembled slightly as I reached for my water glass. The evening light streaming through the hotel's windows caught her blonde hair, creating a golden halo effect that made my mouth go dry.

'Rex,' she corrected herself with a teasing lilt. 'Or should I say Reginald?'

The way she said my full name sent an unexpected shiver down my spine. Perhaps sensing my discomfort, she leaned back in her chair, that familiar sparkle of mischief in her eyes. Even in her day dress, she carried herself with the same confidence she showed in her mechanic's overalls.

The waiter appeared at my elbow, breaking the moment. 'Will sir and madam be requiring anything else this evening?'

Never had an interruption felt more welcome - or more frustrating.

'Would you care for a drink?' The words tumbled out before my nerve could desert me.

Poppy giggled, her eyes dancing with delight. 'Let's be wicked, shall we? I'll have a Clover Club. What about you? And don't you dare say you're driving because you can leave the Rolls here overnight. The Royal is only around the corner.'

My favourite excuse crumbled before I even spoke. She'd seen right through me. 'A Bee's Knees, then.'

The waiter nodded and disappeared, leaving us in nervous silence, at least on my part. My gaze drifted to the window again, where the bright moonlight caught the bronze memorial standing proudly in the middle of Tombland.

'That's a memorial to Edith Cavell, you know. Such a brave woman.'

The playfulness vanished from Poppy's expression. She rose from her chair and came to stand beside me, her hand settling on my shoulder. The warmth of her touch paralysed me, my muscles tensing beneath her fingers.

'Isn't it amazing what some people are capable of in extreme circumstances?' she said softly. 'We all owe a great deal to that lady, and others like her. Such an inspiration.'

Poppy's hand lingered on my shoulder a moment longer before she returned to her chair, moving with the natural grace she possessed, whether in oiled-stained work-ware or a dress. My gaze followed her.

This time, when our eyes met, something shifted inside me. The usual impulse to look away dissolved. Her warm brown eyes held mine, gentle yet unwavering, offering a silent encouragement that made my chest tighten. The nervousness that had plagued me all evening began to melt away beneath that steady gaze.

The bustling dining room faded into the background. The clink of glasses, the murmur of conversations - all became distant, unimportant details. My world narrowed to those sparkling eyes across the table, filled with warmth and understanding.

A shadow fell across our table. The waiter appeared with our cocktails balanced on his silver tray - my Bee's Knees glowing amber in its glass, her Clover Club a delicate shade of pink. For the first time in my life, the arrival of drinks felt like an unwelcome interruption. My hands clenched beneath the table, frustrated at having our moment broken.

The waiter placed our drinks with practiced efficiency, but my attention remained fixed on Poppy. Her eyes hadn't left mine, and in them danced a light that made my heart skip several beats.

The spell between us shattered as two large hands

descended onto Poppy's shoulders. My stomach clenched at the unwelcome intrusion.

'I thought it was you, Popps. Didn't recognise you in a dress.'

The fellow loomed over her, swaying ever so slightly. His evening suit bore the rumpled look of someone who'd spent too long at the bar, his bow tie hanging loose around his neck.

My fingers gripped the edge of the table, ready to spring up, but Poppy's subtle head shake stopped me cold. Her raised eyebrows carried a clear message - stay put.

'Hello, Timothy.' Her voice held none of the warmth it had moments ago. 'Enjoying yourself this evening?'

Timothy's hands remained on her shoulders, his thumbs making small circles that set my teeth on edge. The possessive gesture spoke of familiarity - too much familiarity. Heat crept up my neck as questions crowded my mind. Who was this fellow? What right did he have to touch her so casually?

'Not as much as you seem to be.' His words carried an edge that made my jaw clench. 'Never thought I'd see you dolled up like this. Remember when you used to help me tinker with father's motor?'

The mention of motors explained something - but not enough. My chest felt tight as Timothy's hands slid down to rest on her upper arms. The urge to stand grew stronger with each passing second, despite Poppy's silent warning.

'That was ages ago, Timothy.' Poppy's tone remained steady, but her fingers tightened around her cocktail glass. 'And if you'll excuse us, we were in the middle of something.'

Confusion loomed within me with an unfamiliar surge of jealousy as I watched and listened to their exchanges. The easy way he touched her, the shared history in their words - it spoke of a connection I didn't understand and wasn't sure I wanted to.

In one fluid motion, Poppy shrugged off Timothy's hands and stood. Her head caught him square under the chin with a satisfying thud. The impact sent him reeling backwards, arms windmilling.

My muscles relaxed as a hovering waiter - whose approach hadn't escaped my notice during Timothy's increasingly loud declarations - stepped forward to catch the stumbling fellow. The waiter's timing seemed choreographed, though his expression remained professionally blank as he steadied Timothy.

'Oh dear, how clumsy of me.' Poppy's voice dripped with mock concern. 'Are you quite alright, Timothy?'

Timothy rubbed his chin, his face flushed with equal parts embarrassment and alcohol. The waiter maintained a steadying grip on his elbow while managing to look both attentive and disapproving.

Across the table, Poppy caught my eye and gave me a saucy wink. Her lips curved into that teasing smile that made my heart race. The penny dropped - she'd calculated that move perfectly. The realisation only increased my admiration for her quick thinking and precise timing.

Timothy mumbled something unintelligible as the waiter guided him away from our table with gentle but firm efficiency. The other diners had already returned to their conversations, the brief drama forgotten in the gentle murmur of evening chatter.

The waiter's footsteps faded, along with Timothy's muttered protests. My mouth opened, the question burning on my lips, but Poppy held up her hand.

'Don't ask.' Her eyes sparkled with mischief as she

settled back into her chair, smoothing her dress with a swish of her hands.

The silence stretched between us, filled with unspoken questions. She took a delicate sip of her Clover Club, leaving a faint pink stain on the rim of the glass. My own drink sat untouched, forgotten in the drama of the moment.

'If you must know, he's always had an itch for me. A couple of years ago, he thought his father's wealth would get him anything he wanted. He found out the hard way that wasn't so...' She paused, then brightened. 'Anyway, how's your cocktail?'

The abrupt change of subject caught me off guard. My fingers found the stem of my glass, but my mind still lingered on the scene that had just played out. The calculated precision of her movement, the perfect timing of her 'accident', and her ability to brush the incident off - it revealed yet another fascinating layer to this remarkable woman.

The cocktails worked their magic, melting away the lingering tension from Timothy's interruption. Poppy regaled me with tales of her father's garage, of learning to fix engines before she's mastered copper-plate writing, and the satisfaction of proving wrong every man who doubted her abilities. Her animated gestures and bright laughter drew envious glances from nearby diners.

My own reserve crumbled as she coaxed stories from me - adventures with HG, memorable cases, close calls that seemed funnier in retrospect. The ice in our glasses clinked, marking time's passage until the dining room had nearly emptied.

'Shall we call it a night?' Poppy stretched, cat-like, then glanced at the clock. 'Though it seems a shame to end such a lovely evening.'

My heart leapt. 'May I walk you back to your hotel?'

'Such a gentleman.' That teasing smile again. 'How could I refuse?'

The night air hit us with a brisk slap as we stepped outside, stars twinkling above Tombland's varied skyline. Medieval houses thrust their thatched peaks skyward, jostling against the broader frontages of coaching inns. Above it all, Norwich Cathedral's spire pierced the night sky like a stone arrow.

Warmth flooded through me as Poppy's hand slipped into mine, her fingers intertwining with my own. The contact sent electricity racing up my arm. My breath caught in my throat as we strolled along Tombland.

Something profound had shifted tonight. The usual walls guarding my emotions lay in ruins, replaced by an unfamiliar lightness. Each step beside Poppy felt right in a way nothing else ever had. For the first time in my life, walking too quickly felt like a crime - each moment too precious to rush.

Whipple's fork clinked against his plate as he shovelled another piece of sausage into his mouth. His obvious enjoyment of the Royal Hotel's full English breakfast seemed at odds with the drumming rain outside. Steam rose from his baked beans as he mixed them with chunks of bacon, humming between mouthfuls.

My own appetite had disappeared, replaced by memories of Poppy's hand in mine, her perfume lingering in the night air. The walk through Tombland kept replaying in my mind, each remembered moment bringing fresh warmth despite the gloomy morning.

Across the table, HG stirred her porridge without eating, her spoon making endless circles in the bowl. Her usual sharp gaze had turned inward, focused on something none of us could see. The morning paper lay unopened beside her tea cup.

Whipple paused mid-bite, his fork hovering. His eyes darted to me, then to HG, his brow furrowing. He tilted his head slightly in HG's direction, raising his eyebrows in silent question.

My shoulders lifted in a small shrug. The cheerful inspector's concern was plain as he watched HG push her breakfast around. Whatever thoughts occupied her mind had stolen her usual appetite and morning vigour.

Thunder crashed outside, rattling the windows. The rain's intensity matched the heavy silence that had settled over our table. Even Whipple's earlier enthusiasm for his breakfast dimmed as he set down his fork, the worry lines deepening around his eyes.

The steady patter against the windows filled the quiet, broken only by the occasional scrape of HG's spoon against her bowl. My own tea grew cold, forgotten as I watched my mentor lost in thought.

Whipple dabbed his mouth with a napkin, clearing his throat. 'Something's troubling you, HG.'

Her spoon continued its slow circles through the cooling porridge. The silence stretched until she pushed the bowl away with a gentle scrape against the tablecloth. A deep sigh escaped her as she met Whipple's concerned gaze.

'Today, Arthur, I must meet a man I detest with all my being. Both Rex and you have met the fellow. Remember the murder at Bircham Manor? Well, it's him. Rex and I shall meet the nasty piece of work at Claridge's in London at 2.30 pm today. Do you wish to join us?'

The inspector rubbed his temple as he considered her words. His usual cheerful demeanour dimmed at the memory of our previous encounter with Pinstripe.

'A kind invitation, but no, I'll leave that fellow to you. However, I will accompany you on the train and use the time in London to call in at the Yard to see how my lot are getting on with the tasks I set them yesterday.'

The tension in HG's shoulders eased slightly at his response. My own stomach tightened at the prospect of facing that particular individual again. The last meeting had left an impression none of us cared to repeat.

An hour later, our little group left Norwich behind, having secured a first-class carriage to ourselves on the London-bound train. The journey passed in uncharacteristic silence. HG gazed out the window at the passing Norfolk countryside, her thoughts clearly elsewhere. Whipple busied himself with case notes, though his usual enthusiastic annotations were absent. My own mind drifted between memories of last night's walk through Tombland and apprehension about our upcoming meeting.

Liverpool Street station greeted us with its familiar chaos - a symphony of hissing steam, clattering wheels, and shouting porters. The platforms teemed with passengers rushing in all directions, their footsteps echoing off the iron-and-glass ceiling high above. Steam billowed across the platforms, momentarily obscuring the scene before dissipating into the sooty air.

Porters weaved between the crowds with their sack trucks, emptying and refilling luggage compartments in a well-practiced dance. The cargo ranged from simple suitcases to elaborate hat boxes, tennis racquets, and even what appeared to be a parrot cage wrapped in cloth.

At the platform gate, a uniformed ticket inspector exam-

ined our tickets with methodical precision, his pencil moustache twitching as he scrutinised each one. Once through,
we made our way to the taxi rank, where a line of black
cabs awaited fares.

Whipple stepped forward to the first vehicle, leaning
into to the driver's open window.

'Scotland Yard, then Claridge's quick as you can, my
man.'

———

The opulent interior of Claridge's never failed to impress,
yet today its grandeur felt oppressive. HG and I found
ourselves tucked away in a discreet booth at the far end of
the coffee bar, the polished mahogany panelling creating a
barrier between us and the other patrons.

Steam rose from our Earl Grey tea in delicate wisps. HG
hadn't spoken since we'd been seated, her attention fixed on
the comings and goings of London's elite through the
hotel's entrance. Murmured conversations drifted around
us, punctuated by the occasional burst of refined laughter
from nearby tables.

A movement near the entrance caught my eye. The
figure's military bearing was unmistakable - ramrod straight
posture that spoke of years of parade ground discipline. His
Pinstripe suit fitted like a second skin, clearly the work of
Savile Row's finest. A polar-white shirt provided stark
contrast to the dark fabric, while his shoes reflected the light
from the crystal chandeliers above. Under one arm he
carried a bowler hat, his other hand gripping a tightly rolled
black umbrella.

He moved through the space as if on military
manoeuvres, ignoring other patrons as he strode towards

us. Upon reaching our table, he fixed his gaze solely on HG.

'Nice to see you again, Eleanor,' he said, sliding into the seat without invitation. His complete dismissal of my presence spoke volumes about the man's character.

HG's silence filled the space between us, her eyes boring into Pinstripe with the intensity of a carnivore stalking its prey. The tea before her remained untouched, wisps of steam curling into the air like question marks.

My mentor's voice cut through the refined atmosphere with precision. 'You forget to acknowledge my Ward. A most ungentlemanly thing to do, wouldn't you agree?'

Pinstripe's head swivelled towards me, his thin lips stretching into what might have passed for warmth had it been genuine. The expression reminded me of a snake preparing to strike.

'Rex, is it not?'

The calculated way he drew out my name left no doubt - he knew precisely who sat before him. Rather than challenge the obvious pretence, my response came measured and neutral. 'Indeed it is.'

The exchange hung in the air between us, weighted with unspoken tension. Pinstripe's fingers played with a cufflink at his wrist as if a metaphor for his behaviour toward me.

The ritual of tea preparation became a performance under Pinstripe's manicured hands. Each movement deliberate, precise, calculated to slow down time like a conductor leading an orchestra into an adagio. The silver teapot hovered above his cup, the amber liquid descending in an endless stream while HG remained motionless. Her gaze fixed upon him with an intensity I hadn't observed before.

The spoon clinked against the pot as he stirred, the

sound echoing through our corner of Claridge's. Three clockwise turns, pause, four counterclockwise, pause. Steam spiralled upward from his cup, dissipating into the air thick with unspoken accusations.

My fingers tightened around my own teacup as the silence stretched between us. The distant murmur of other patrons faded against the deliberate scraping of silver against porcelain.

'It was a delightful surprise to receive your call late last evening, Eleanor. And so direct. Of course, that is how you like to be, isn't it? direct?'

His words sliced through the air, each syllable polished to a shine by years at Eton or Harrow. As he spoke, his upper lip curled back just enough to reveal a flash of gold - a crown that glinted menacingly, reminiscent of a beast's lethal display of power.

The tension around our secluded table had shifted. HG's spine straightened, her shoulders squaring - telltale signs she'd grown weary of this verbal fencing match. Her teacup settled onto its saucer with a decisive clink.

'The Three Circles club. I assume you are a member?'

Pinstripe's lazy smile spread across his face like oil on water. 'You and I both know how dangerous it is to assume anything about anyone. In any event, why do you ask?'

He paused, lifting one manicured finger as though struck by sudden insight. 'Oh, yes. The young woman in Norwich. A fashion model with a big future ahead of her. So sad.'

My mentor's knuckles whitened around her teacup. The muscle in her jaw twitched - a rare display of barely contained fury that few would notice. Her voice remained steady, controlled, but carried an edge sharp enough to cut.

'You're remarkably well informed, as I knew you would be.'

Pinstripe's smile widened, showing more of that gold crown. 'As are you, or at least you think you are. I suppose that silly Leggit woman said too much?'

The corners of HG's mouth curved upward. 'As you knew, she would. Oh, not about you directly, but mention of Carstairs. I know you and he were...and perhaps still are, joined at the hip where the darker sciences are concerned.'

Pinstripe's facial expression morphed into something darker, more threatening. The transformation reminded me of a dog preparing to attack - subtle yet unmistakable. His eyes narrowed to dark slits beneath heavy lids.

'Do be careful, Eleanor. Lady Leggit's little mission at the Theatre Royal was delivered in good faith.'

The smile vanished from his face, replaced by an expression of cold calculation. 'Gift horses sometimes have a habit of biting back. To misquote Oscar Wilde: to ignore a warning once may be regarded as careless. To do so twice may be seen as a dangerous oversight.'

Before HG could respond, movement caught my eye. Two men materialised at our table, dressed in identical Pinstripe suits that matched our unwelcome companion's attire so precisely they could have been triplets. Their hands were clasped neatly in front of them, faces fixed with manufactured smiles that spoke of menace.

Pinstripe didn't acknowledge their presence, keeping his gaze fixed on HG. 'Speaking of which, my two colleagues and I should like you to come with us.'

HG's eyes flicked up to study the young men before returning to Pinstripe. 'And if we choose not to?'

That familiar curl of his upper lip returned, revealing

the gold crown once more. 'When I said, "should like", I was being polite. What I should have said is, "You will both be coming with us". Your preference is for plain speaking. And now you have it.'

Chapter Fifteen

ALL CAN BE DENIED

The black Daimler purred through the streets of London, its polished bodywork reflecting the afternoon sun. Our silent companions sat ramrod straight in the front seats, their matching Pinstripe suits creating an unsettling mirror image. My shoulder pressed against HG's as we navigated a sharp corner onto Oxford Street.

Intriguingly, Pinstripe remained at Claridge's, sipping his Earl Grey tea without acknowledging our leaving.

Neither young man had spoken since ushering us from Claridge's. Their movements possessed an uncanny synchronisation - like mechanical soldiers wound from the same key. Through the windscreen, pedestrians darted between motor cars and horse-drawn delivery wagons, while newspaper boys waved their afternoon editions at passing traffic.

We turned south onto Bond Street; the shops growing more exclusive with each passing block. HG's hand found mine in the shadows between us, giving it a brief squeeze before withdrawing. Her face remained impassive, studying the passing scenery as though we were merely on a pleasant afternoon drive.

The car slowed as we entered Mayfair, gliding past elegant townhouses with gleaming brass knockers and pristine white steps. Coming to a halt before a particularly grand residence, our escorts moved with that same mechanical precision - doors opening in perfect unison.

One held the door for HG while the other extended his arm, pointing towards number 68. The heavy black door stood slightly ajar, as though expecting our arrival. By the time we reached the top step and glanced back, both car and escort had vanished into the afternoon traffic, leaving only the echo of a well-oiled machine in their wake.

The heavy door yielded beneath my palm, its hinges releasing a low moan that echoed through the entrance. HG swept past, her steps muffled by the thick Persian carpet that stretched across the marble floor. Following close behind, my nostrils filled with the mingled scents of beeswax and leather.

Gilt-framed mirrors lined the walls, multiplying our reflections into infinity. Between them hung oil paintings of stern-faced aristocrats, their eyes following our progress across the lobby. A mahogany table dominated the centre of the space, its surface bearing nothing but our distorted reflections in its polished depths.

The tick of a long-case clock marked time somewhere deeper in the house, its steady rhythm emphasising the absolute silence. No footsteps creaked overhead, no distant murmur of servants going about their duties. The absence of staff struck an odd note - even the smallest of these Mayfair establishments typically maintained at least a skeleton household.

HG paused before a Gainsborough, her head tilted in

appreciation. The young woman in the portrait wore a blue silk gown that seemed to shimmer in the afternoon light filtering through the fanlight above the door. Crystal decanters on a nearby sideboard caught the same light, casting prismatic patterns across the damask wallpaper.

A pair of leather Chesterfields faced each other across an elaborate Turkish rug, their deep buttoning creating shadows in the rich brown leather. The space felt prepared for visitors, yet abandoned - as though the occupants had stepped out moments before our arrival, leaving everything arranged just so.

Our footsteps seemed inappropriately loud as we moved further into the lobby. The click of HG's heels against marble provided counterpoint to the persistent ticking of that unseen clock. Neither of us spoke, letting the weighted silence of the house settle around us like dust.

My fingers closed around the heavy brass doorknob; its patina worn smooth by generations of hands. The mechanism yielded to reveal a Morning Room that perfectly captured Georgian sensibilities. Pale green silk damask wallpaper caught the afternoon light streaming through tall sash windows. A Chippendale desk stood beneath one window, its mahogany surface gleaming. Delicate porcelain figurines posed on marble-topped side tables, while a pair of gilt-framed landscapes flanked the Adam fireplace.

The room breathed quiet wealth - from the subtle pattern of the Aubusson carpet to the carefully arranged fresh flowers in a crystal vase. A silver tea service waited on a low table between two wing chairs, though no steam rose from the pot's spout.

'Well, we might as well make ourselves comfortable,' HG said, settling into one of the chairs. 'I'm assuming we were brought to the correct address, which means our host will join us by and by.'

Twenty-five minutes later, footsteps echoed through the lobby - two distinct sets moving with measured pace across marble floors. Each click against stone stretched time like pulled toffee, drawing out the moments between steps until they felt endless. The sound grew closer yet maintained that deliberate slowness that set my teeth on edge.

Beside me, HG smoothed invisible creases from her skirts and straightened her already impeccable posture. Her fingers brushed briefly at her collar before settling on her lap.

The footsteps halted outside the door. Metal scraped against metal as the handle began to turn with agonising slowness. Hinges whispered as the heavy door swung inward, revealing a familiar figure silhouetted against the lobby's brightness.

'Arthur? What the devil is going on?' HG's voice carried equal measures of surprise and suspicion.

Whipple remained silent, stepping aside to allow another figure to enter. Tall and distinguished, the elderly gentleman moved with the easy confidence of someone accustomed to command. His perfectly tailored morning suit spoke of Savile Row, while his bearing suggested years of public service.

'Goodness me,' HG breathed, rising smoothly to her feet.

My confusion must have shown clearly on my face, for HG turned to me with a slight smile playing at the corners of her mouth.

'Rex, dear boy, may I introduce you to His Majesty's Home Secretary, Sir Edward Shortt.'

The Home Secretary's gaze fell on me, his smile warm

and genuine despite the gravity of our situation. Distinguished silver hair caught the afternoon light as he inclined his head in acknowledgement.

Crossing the room with measured steps, he embraced HG with the easy familiarity of old friends. The kiss he planted on her cheek spoke of years of shared history, while his perfectly pressed morning coat rustled softly against her dress.

'I see you've got yourself in a pickle again, HG? You could have waited a little longer to allow me to get my feet under my ministerial desk. The Prime Minister only appointed me a few days ago.' His voice carried the cultured tones of Oxford, tempered by genuine affection.

HG's shoulders relaxed fractionally at his familiar manner. 'And how is Mr Bonar Law?'

A rich chuckle escaped Shortt's lips. 'Jolly happy, considering the thumping majority, we've just won.'

Watching the exchange between HG and the Home Secretary, the warmth and familiarity of their reunion struck me as remarkable. Was there anyone of consequence that my mentor did not know?

The jovial atmosphere dissipated like morning mist when Sir Edward's expression shifted. His features hardened, mouth drawing into a thin line.

'Now, let me explain the reason Detective Inspector Whipple and I are here.'

Whipple stood near the doorway; his usual composed demeanour fractured by visible concern. Deep furrows marked his brow as he fixed HG with an intense stare that spoke volumes about the gravity of our situation.

HG's gaze darted between the two men; confusion evident in the slight tilt of her head. 'You sent those two young men to fetch us from Claridge's, presumably via that awful fellow of whom I shall not speak.'

The Home Secretary's fingers wrapped gently around HG's elbow as he guided her back to the wing chair. His tall frame loomed over her once she was seated, casting a long shadow across the polished oak floor.

'HG, it's rare for circumstances to come together as they have this day. I suppose one might describe it as serendipity. Well, whatever the circumstances, it's likely they saved the life of your ward and good self.'

Whipple shifted his weight from one foot to the other. 'Sir Edward, with your permission?'

The Home Secretary nodded, sinking into the chair opposite HG while adjusting his silver fob watch and chain.

'You see, HG, it was pure chance that Sir Edward happened to be present during my meeting with the commissioner this morning. As I briefed him about developments in Norwich, particularly when the Three Circles connection emerged-'

'Indeed,' Sir Edward interjected, 'The timing proved most fortuitous. I received an intelligence briefing earlier today containing some rather disturbing information about that organisation.'

Whipple's face had grown increasingly grave. 'The commissioner was about to dismiss the Three Circles as mere society gossip when Sir Edward stepped in.'

My fingers clenched the arm of my chair as the implications began to sink in. The synchronised movements of our pinstriped escorts took on a more sinister aspect considering this revelation.

HG's brow furrowed as she processed this information. 'But I still don't understand?'

The Home Secretary leaned forward, his hands clasped between his knees. 'Quite understandable, Eleanor. Let me put it like this, I keep a very close eye on...I believe you call him "Pinstripe"? Anyway, as part of that work, my predecessor, and now me, control one of the two young men that brought you here. He risks his life each day as he feeds back to the government what Pinstripe and his acolytes get up to. The meeting here today was contained in that briefing note to me. We did not know who the victim or victims were to be, but my intelligence sources told me they would be eliminated in this house today. So, you can see, when the inspector spoke about Pinstripe, I immediately put things together and ordered that certain actions took place to keep you safe.'

My breath caught in my throat. The elegant Morning Room suddenly felt confining, its Georgian refinements a thin veneer over darker purposes. HG's fingers whitened where they gripped the arm of her chair.

'And the assassin?' HG's voice remained steady despite the shock evident in her pale features.

The Home Secretary's gaze slid to Whipple.

'Not known to us, but as you can see, he failed. And before you ask, no, he didn't escape. I can't allow you to inspect the scene, but the unknown gentleman lies on the stone floor of the kitchen. We thought it better to get you into safe keeping before we remove the body and begin our investigations proper.'

HG leaned back in her chair; her face shorn of further reaction. After a few seconds of silence, the Home Secretary made a further devastating announcement.

'All we have to do now is get you out of here before Pinstripe, as you call him, sends in reinforcements. It won't be long before he'll expect to hear from his hired hand. In the absence of receiving news, the fellow will not hang about.'

Sir Edward's words hung in the air like gun smoke, their implications settling over us with leaden weight.

'The situation requires immediate action,' Sir Edward said, pulling a gold cigarette case from his waistcoat. 'Once Pinstripe discovers his man has failed, he'll move heaven and earth to finish what he started.'

HG's fingers drummed a restless pattern on the arm of her chair. 'Surely we can't simply vanish without raising suspicions back in Norwich?'

'Actually,' Whipple interjected, 'that might work in our favour. The investigation gives us perfect cover for your temporary disappearance.'

Sir Edward lit his cigarette with practiced elegance, the match flame briefly illuminating his grave expression. 'The inspector is correct. We need to manufacture a reason for your absence - something that won't raise eyebrows among the fashion set. If they don't know anything, they can't inadvertently betray you to your pursuer.'

'What about Detective Sergeant Muddleford?' Whipple asked. 'He could continue the visible investigation while we work behind the scenes and send Pinstripe on a wild goose chase trying to find you.'

HG's eyebrows rose. 'Muddleford? The name sounds familiar.'

'He's sharp as a tack,' Whipple assured her. 'Remember, he helped us on Hilltop's case.'

'Perfect,' Sir Edward nodded. 'He can be your public face while you two...' he paused, studying his cigarette thoughtfully, 'take an unexpected trip to investigate a lead in Scotland, perhaps?'

'Edinburgh would be suitable,' HG mused. 'Though naturally, we won't be going anywhere near Scotland.'

'Precisely.' Sir Edward tapped ash into a crystal ashtray. 'The further Pinstripe's attention is from your actual location, the better.'

The Home Secretary's matter-of-fact tone as he discussed our potential murder sent chills down my spine. The elegant room felt increasingly like a cage, albeit a gilded one, as we planned our own disappearance.

It was then that the Home Secretary made a comment that shook me to my foundations.

'I will do all I can to keep you updated on Pinstripe, beyond that I can't be seen to be involved...and I must advise you that if something dreadful happens to you or your people, I shall deny all knowledge of having met you here today.'

Sir Edward rose from his chair, adjusting his morning coat with practiced elegance. 'Good luck, Eleanor. Keep your wits sharp and your guard up.' He turned, nodding first to me, then to Whipple. His silver-topped cane caught the afternoon light as he executed a flourish worthy of the stage. The sharp tap-tap-tap of polished wood against marble echoed through the Morning Room and across the tiled hall. The heavy front door opened and closed with a solid clunk.

HG moved to the window, her fingers parting the heavy silk curtains just enough to observe the street below. The Home Secretary's gleaming Daimler merged seamlessly into the flow of traffic, vanishing between delivery vans, horse-drawn carts and motorcars as though it had never existed.

None of us spoke. The ticking of that unseen clock marked the passing seconds while we absorbed the gravity of our situation. My mind raced through the implications of the Home Secretary's words. We truly were on our own.

Beside me, Whipple's usually composed features betrayed an uncharacteristic uncertainty. His fingers drummed an irregular pattern against his thigh as he stared unseeing at the Gainsborough portrait.

HG remained at the window, her reflection ghostly in the glass. The afternoon light caught the silver threads in her hair, creating a halo effect that seemed strangely appropriate given our brush with mortality. Her shoulders carried the same squared determination I'd witnessed countless times before, but her fingers remained pressed against the curtain fabric as though seeking anchor in its solid reality.

Each of us stood frozen in our private contemplation, searching for the path forward through this unexpected maze of deception and danger.

Breaking the oppressive silence, HG turned from the window with a determined set to her jaw. 'I have an idea.'

HG's change in demeanour lifted Whipple and me no end.

'We shall use our invented excursion to Edinburgh to flush any fifth columnist still active among our Norwich suspects. It falls to you, Arthur, to let slip our imagined location…and your narks' network to report on Pinstripe's whereabouts. If the dreadful fellow makes for Scotland, it will be proof positive an informant is active. It should not be too difficult a job to work out who, if Detective Seargeant Muddleford can amass the local force in Norwich to keep tabs on our suspects.'

For the first time in a long time, I sensed a true opportunity to give our investigations the impetus it had lacked in recent days.

Whipple nodded, while looking deep in thought.

'The Three Circles connection to Lucy Daws' death appears undeniable now. If we're to get to the bottom of this, we have no option but to take Pinstripe head on. In asking myself why the fellow has become involved at all, I can only deduce that Lucy Daws had information, or something else that could do one or more people in high society immense harm. The suited one is either one of those persons or has been hired to protect others…no matter the cost.'

HG smirked, which Whipple observed.

'Please don't take this situation so lightly.' Whipple's face had grown even more serious, if such a thing were possible. 'The Home Secretary himself said-'

'You forget, Arthur,' HG bristled, drawing herself up to her full height, 'that Pinstripe and I go back some years, to the darkest days of the Great War, in fact.' Her fingers traced the ornate carved pattern on the chair she'd recently vacated. 'I know how he works; how he thinks. And I have one or two tricks up my sleeve.'

The set of her shoulders spoke volumes about her determination. My mentor had faced down countless dangerous situations before, but something in her bearing suggested this confrontation held personal significance beyond our current investigation.

A shrill ring of a telephone sliced through HG's words like a knife through butter. Its harsh metallic tone bounced off marble floors and wood-panelled walls, filling the cavernous space with echoing urgency. My heart leapt to my throat as the second ring reverberated through the house.

Whipple's face drained of colour. 'That'll be Pinstripe, wanting to know how things went.' He paced three steps towards the door, then back again. 'If we don't answer, he'll know something's wrong - probably send more men round to investigate.' His fingers worried at his collar. 'But if we do pick up...then what?'

HG's voice cut through his mounting panic. 'It would be perfectly natural for a police officer to answer the telephone at a crime scene, would it not?'

The telephone's third ring seemed to mock our indecision, its echo fading into loaded silence as we stared at each other across the elegant Morning Room.

Standing beside the Chippendale desk, watching these two seasoned investigators grapple with such a seemingly simple decision, brought home the gravity of our situation. The wrong choice now could have fatal consequences.

A fourth ring pierced the air.

The fifth ring barely started before Whipple strode from the room, his footsteps echoing across the marble tiles. Through the open doorway, HG and I crept forward, watching his tall frame reach for the telephone.

'Yes?' Whipple barked into the receiver, his tone uncharacteristically hostile. 'Who speaks?'

Pressed against the doorframe, my heart hammered against my ribs as we strained to hear the response. Whipple's face remained impassive, giving nothing away to the unknown caller.

'And the nature of your call?'

HG's fingers gripped my forearm, her nails digging through my jacket sleeve. The afternoon sun streaming through tall windows cast long shadows across the hallway's chequered floor, while dust motes danced in golden shafts of light.

'Can you come to the premises? Relatives, you say?' Whipple's performance proved masterful, each word measured and professional. 'No, that will not be possible.

This house is now a crime scene. However, I will take your details so that—'

He turned towards us, receiver still in hand. 'It was a woman. Very clever. She put the telephone down as soon as I mentioned taking her details. We don't have long to get out. I'll get a couple of squad cars and men over here with instruction not to remove the body. If my guess is correct, Pinstripe will have his people all over this...and he'll be expecting three bodies to be brought out. You two, plus his paid assassin since he hasn't heard from him. He'll assume the fellow died while carrying out his orders. We shall oblige by having three ambulances arrive and three stretchers taken out. That, at least, will give us time to spirit you two away before Pinstripe realises, he's been had.'

Chapter Sixteen

AN INVISIBLE PRESENCE

Relief flooded through me as Graham opened Thorpe Manor's heavy oak doors. The familiar scent of beeswax and leather welcomed us home after our harrowing escape from London. Lord Irvine's discrete private train carriage had proven the perfect sanctuary. No one would think to look for an ancient locomotive pulling two nondescript carriages slipping from a Southwick siding.

HG sank into her favourite armchair by the fireplace while Graham poured us both a much-needed brandy. The events of the past twenty-four hours felt like a fever dream. The dead assassin in that Mayfair kitchen. Sir Edward's grave warnings. Whipple's brilliant plan to stage our deaths using two unclaimed bodies from the morgue.

'Graham, ensure all the doors are secured,' HG said, her fingers cupping the crystal tumbler. 'And telephone Lady Margaret - she'll want to know we made it.'

Lady Margaret Irvine had been our salvation. One telephone call from HG and she'd arranged everything, even down to the simple clothes we now wore.

Through the library windows, darkness crept across Thorpe Manor's manicured lawns. Somewhere out there, Pinstripe's men searched London for our bodies, giving us precious time to escape and regroup. But for how long?

The brandy's warmth spread through my chest as I studied HG's composed features in the firelight. Despite everything, she appeared deep in thought rather than shaken by our brush with death.

Our intimate room cocooned us in its familiar embrace. Darkness pressed against the diamond-paned windows, held at bay by the blazing fire in the Tudor hearth. Flames danced and crackled, casting shifting shadows across centuries of leather-bound volumes that lined the oak shelves from floor to ceiling.

My armchair, positioned just right of the fireplace, had moulded itself to me over countless evenings spent in this sanctuary. HG occupied her preferred seat opposite, her profile outlined in the flickering orange light that played across her features.

Graham's quiet efficiency had produced a tea service that spoke of years of attention to HG's particular tastes. Her special Fortnum and Mason blend - a masterful combination of China, Ceylon and Assam leaves - released its complex aroma into the air.

The silver tray beside us held an array of perfectly formed pastries, their glazed surfaces catching and reflecting the firelight like precious gems. Graham had arranged them with architectural precision - a skill that never failed to impress.

'One almost forgets there's a world beyond these walls,' HG murmured, lifting her cup. The porcelain clinked against its saucer.

I realised while confined here for safety, there were far

worse places to hide than this book-lined haven. The weight of our London escape seemed to lift in the presence of such civilised comforts.

The question had burned in my mind since our London encounter. Now, safe in the library's embrace, the moment felt right to ask.

'HG, your history with Pinstripe?'

She lowered her teacup, her gaze fixed on the dancing flames. The firelight cast deep shadows across her face as she settled deeper into her armchair.

'Berlin, 1910,' she said at last. 'Such a vibrant city then - art, music, theatre. The cafes buzzed with intellectual discourse late into the night. Kandinsky had just finished his first abstract works. Schoenberg was revolutionising music. The air crackled with possibility.'

She paused, running her finger along the rim of her cup.

'But beneath that glittering surface, darker currents flowed. The government had asked me to... observe certain matters. Industrial developments, military preparations. Britain and Germany were locked in a naval arms race that seemed to have no end. Every week brought news of another dreadnought laid down, another fortress reinforced.'

The fire popped and crackled, sending sparks up the chimney.

'That's where I encountered him; as usual in his perfectly tailored Pinstripe suit. He moved through diplomatic circles like a shark through shallow waters. He recognised what I was doing, of course. We played our little game of cat and mouse through embassy parties and opera houses.'

She reached for the decanter of brandy Graham had thoughtfully provided.

'Such a foolish time, really. Nations building weapons they could never use - except, of course, they did use them. But in 1910, no one could imagine the horror to come. We were all too busy dancing on the edge of the abyss.'

The brandy's warmth spread through my chest as HG's words hung in the air. Her story of pre-war Berlin had sparked another question that had nagged at me since our encounter with Pinstripe.

'His accent puzzled me. Almost perfect English, but something wasn't quite right.'

HG's eyes sparkled over the rim of her glass. 'You noticed that?'

'If he were British, you'd know his family connections.'

'Quite right.' She settled back, a satisfied smile playing across her features. 'From what my sources tell me, he spent his formative years in South America. Among the polo-playing set.'

The pieces started falling into place. 'That explains the slight oddness in his vowels. Though most people wouldn't catch it.'

'Indeed. And have you noticed how little anyone really knows about him? Even those who claim to be close associates?'

'Just shadows and whispers.'

'Precisely.' HG swirled the amber liquid in her glass. 'That's how he's survived so long in his particular line of work. Impeccable connections, yet no one truly knows him. Selling those rather unorthodox skills of his to whoever can afford them.'

The fire crackled, sending a shower of sparks up the chimney as Graham entered with fresh tea.

After the butler retired, I asked HG if she thought he'd worked for our government.

'You can be sure of it,' HG purred as she looked deep into the crackling fire. 'You did notice that the Home Secretary said only that he would try to keep us safe, but that we were on our own if discovered of injured? Well, what does that tell you, dear Rex?'

HG's forthrightness took me by surprise. I hadn't considered that angle at all. Clearly, I still had much to learn about the body politic.

Her words hung in the air like pipe smoke, making me reconsider everything we'd witnessed in London. The Home Secretary's carefully chosen words now took on new meaning. Perhaps Pinstripe's connections ran deeper than any of us had imagined.

Graham's soft footsteps broke through my thoughts. 'Detective Sergeant Muddleford has arrived, Your Grace.'

My eyes flicked to the ornate clock above the Tudor fireplace. Twenty minutes past midnight - an unusual hour for visitors, even in these circumstances.

Muddleford's tall frame filled the doorway, his sharp features cast in stark relief by the library's warm lighting. Despite the late hour, his blonde hair remained perfectly combed, not a strand out of place.

'Thank you for making the journey at such an ungodly hour, Detective Sergeant.' HG's smile held genuine warmth.

Graham whisked away Muddleford's overcoat and hat with practiced efficiency. The detective settled into the remaining armchair, his long legs stretching towards the fire's warmth.

HG lifted the delicate teapot. 'Milk? Sugar?'

'Just milk, thank you.'

The detective's eyebrows rose slightly as he sipped the

aromatic brew. No doubt more accustomed to strong tea than HG's carefully curated blend from Fortnum's.

'How much do you know of our current situation?' HG asked, settling back into her chair.

Muddleford set his cup down with careful precision. 'Detective Inspector Whipple briefed me thoroughly before your departure. And I've developed several ideas about our next moves.'

The morning sun streamed through the tall windows of the Morning Room, casting long shadows across the breakfast table. HG stood by the window, teacup in hand, surveying the grounds of Thorpe Manor. Frost sparkled on the grass like scattered diamonds.

'What a glorious morning,' she breathed, her breath fogging the glass. 'The way the light catches the frost - quite magical.'

The breakfast spread before us was splendid: kippers, eggs prepared three ways, toast racks filled with perfectly browned bread, and rashers of bacon keeping warm under silver covers. The cook had outdone herself.

Detective Sergeant Muddleford methodically spread marmalade on his toast, his movements as precise and deliberate as everything else about him. The morning light caught his blonde hair, making it appear almost white.

'Have you given any thought to what the Detective Sergeant suggested last night, Rex?' HG turned from the window, settling into her chair. 'About becoming a Special Constable?'

My fork paused halfway to my mouth. The idea had kept me awake for hours. The prospect of official police powers, even in a limited capacity, was both thrilling and terrifying. But something in the way HG asked made me wonder if she'd already made up her mind about the matter.

'The position would grant you certain... advantages,' Muddleford added, carefully selecting another piece of toast. 'Access to information and resources that might prove useful in our current situation.'

Steam rose from the fresh pot of English breakfast tea Graham had just placed on the table. The familiar aroma helped ground my thoughts as both HG and Muddleford awaited my response.

Setting my teacup down, my fingers traced the rim while considering how to frame my response. The role would give me ways to protect HG while maintaining our investigation into Lucy's murder. More importantly, it meant staying close to Poppy without raising suspicion.

'The position makes sense,' my voice came out steadier than expected. 'Working undercover lets me keep you informed of developments, HG, while taking the necessary guidance. Plus...' The words caught slightly. 'Being a Special Constable provides legitimate reasons to frequent the crime scene.'

Muddleford's sharp features softened momentarily. 'Ah yes, Miss Poppy. Quite resourceful, that one.'

HG's eyes sparkled with amusement. 'Indeed. Though we'll need to make certain adjustments to your appearance, Rex. Can't have you recognised by anyone who might report back to Pinstripe's people, for he'll know if you're alive, then I am.'

She stood and walked to a painting of one of her male forebears in military uniform. 'What do you think, Detective Sergeant? Perhaps some impressive sideburns?'

'And a moustache,' Muddleford added, his usual serious expression cracking slightly. 'Nothing too elaborate - we want him to look like a proper bobby, not a music hall performer.'

The thought of sporting facial hair made me reach unconsciously for my clean-shaven chin. HG noticed and laughed.

'Don't fret, Rex. We'll make sure you look perfectly respectable. Graham knows a theatrical costumier in Norwich who can provide exactly what we need.'

Standing before the full-length mirror in Meredith Loveheart's cluttered shop, my reflection startled me. The stranger staring back bore little resemblance to the Rex Watson of yesterday. Gone was the clean-shaven chauffeur - in his place stood a proper bobby, complete with domed helmet and pressed uniform.

The sideburns changed everything. They framed my face perfectly, ageing me just enough to command respect without looking elderly. The moustache, neither too bushy nor too thin, completed the transformation. Rather handsome, if truth be told.

'Turn slowly,' Meredith commanded from somewhere behind a rack of theatrical costumes. 'Let me see how the light catches the adhesive.'

My movements in the mirror seemed both familiar and foreign. The blue and white striped armband on my left sleeve caught my attention - my new designation as Special Constable displayed proudly for all to see. The identification number and rank stood out clearly against the cloth.

'Remarkable work,' Muddleford's voice drifted from the shadows of the Tudor era galleried shop.

The uniform fit perfectly, each brass button gleaming in the morning light that filtered through the shop's leaded windows. The weight of it felt right somehow, as if I'd been meant to wear it all along.

'The adhesive will hold for days,' Meredith said, adjusting his wire-rimmed spectacles. 'But you'll need to return for maintenance. Can't have a policeman's face falling off in the middle of an arrest, can we? Always come around the back into the courtyard. That way, no one will know what's going on.'

I nodded, acknowledging the par-larva we'd had arriving today without being recognised.

Stepping from Meredith's dimly lit back room into the sunlit courtyard felt surreal. The ancient flint walls loomed above, their shadows dancing across worn cobblestones as we made our way through a narrow passage. My new boots clicked against the stone, each step echoing off the medieval buildings.

Emerging onto Elm Hill brought a rush of sensations. The bustling thoroughfare stretched before us, its Tudor buildings leaning precariously over the steep descent. The familiar street felt different now - or rather, people's reactions to me had changed.

'Good morning, Constable,' called a butcher, doffing his straw hat as we passed.

Another greeting came from a window cleaner balanced on his ladder. Then a newspaper vendor. Each acknowledgement caught me off guard, though my newly acquired police training kicked in. Back straight, chin up, measured nods in return.

The steep gradient of Elm Hill required careful footwork on the ancient cobbles. Muddleford walked beside me, his long stride matching mine as we navigated past busy shops and morning shoppers.

'Good morning, officer,' chirped a young mother, ushering her children to one side.

The weight of the uniform, the respectful nods, the subtle shifts in how people moved around us - it all felt like stepping into another person's life. Yet underneath the disguise beat the same heart, thought the same thoughts.

Glancing sideways, my attention caught on Muddleford's face. His usual stern expression cracked, revealing the ghost of a smile.

'Right, we'd better catch up with Miss Poppy to see what's been going on…and apply the next layer to Detective Inspector Whipple's subterfuge to flush out any remaining contacts this Pinstripe fellow may have in our proximity.'

The walk to the Railway Hotel took mere minutes, each step feeling more natural in my new persona. Already the weight of the uniform settled comfortably on my shoulders, and the respectful nods from passers-by no longer caught me off guard. My transformation into a Special Constable felt nearly complete.

Rounding the corner onto Prince of Wales Road, the Railway Hotel's imposing facade loomed ahead. Victorian grandeur in red brick and Portland stone stretched skyward, its windows gleaming in the afternoon sun. My hand reached for the brass door pull, ready to stride into the lobby with a purpose.

'Not so quick.' Muddleford's hand settled on my shoulder. 'Remember, you're a police officer now. Barrel into the hotel lobby like that and you'll have everyone think the place is on fire.'

Heat crept up my neck at the rookie mistake. Of course - a proper bobby wouldn't charge in like some eager puppy. Muddleford took point, his languid pace setting the proper tone as we approached the entrance.

'Helmet off, Watson,' he murmured over his shoulder.

Tucking the domed helmet under my arm, following Muddleford's measured steps across the marble floor towards reception. Behind the polished oak counter, a gentleman in an impeccable suit straightened his already ramrod posture. The desk lamp caught his brilliantined hair, creating an almost mirror-like sheen.

'Good afternoon, gentlemen. How may I help?'

As Muddleford explained our reason for calling, movement on the grand staircase caught my attention. Poppy descended with her usual bounce; her blue boiler suit replaced by an elegant day dress. My heart skipped - the perfect chance to test Meredith's handiwork.

She glided past, giving me nothing more than a fleeting glance before heading towards the hotel's lounge. Success! The disguise worked perfectly.

'Ah, Miss Poppy,' The gentleman behind the reception desk called out, his voice carrying just enough to command attention without disturbing the hushed atmosphere of the lobby.

She stopped mid-stride, turning to face us with curiosity written across her features.

'These gentlemen wish to have a word?'

A warm smile spread across her face as she looked first at Muddleford, then at me. Her gaze lingered this time, studying my features more intently. My pulse quickened as she stepped closer, her eyes narrowing slightly. Panic gripped me - surely she wouldn't give the game away?

With mounting desperation, my head moved in the

tiniest shake from side to side. Relief flooded through me as understanding flickered in her eyes.

'Of course, let's go somewhere more private, shall we?' Poppy's voice carried its usual playful lilt as she turned back to Muddleford with a girlish smile.

Following Poppy through the hotel's marble-floored lobby felt like watching a master class in poise. Her heels clicked a delicate rhythm against the polished stone, each step precise and graceful. The transformation from mechanic to socialite was remarkable - she'd traded motor oil for French perfume without missing a beat.

The elevator stood like a gilded cage. Muddleford's tall frame nearly brushed the ornate ceiling as we stepped inside. The operator, a young lad in a crisp uniform, pulled the latticed inner door closed with practiced efficiency.

'Top floor, please,' Poppy said, her voice carrying that hint of authority that seemed to work magic on everyone she encountered.

The lift ascended smoothly, its mechanical workings purring like a well-tuned engine. My new police boots felt suddenly conspicuous on the patterned floor tiles, but Poppy's assured presence kept my nerves steady.

Emerging onto the top floor, we followed her lead down a carpeted corridor that stretched the length of the building. Portraits of stern-faced Victorian gentlemen watched our progress from gilded frames. At the far end, a heavy oak door opened onto what appeared to be maintenance access to the roof.

The Norwich air hit us like a welcome embrace as we stepped onto the parapet. Below, the city spread out in all directions - a tapestry of red-tiled roofs, church spires, and ancient stonework. The cathedral's magnificent spire dominated the skyline, while the castle's square bulk loomed to our right.

Poppy moved to the stone balustrade, her skirts rippling in the breeze. 'I come out here when I want to get away from the girls. It's been over a week now and they're all getting restless.'

The city stretched before us, a medieval masterpiece painted in afternoon light. My voice felt rough as I explained the events in London - the setup at the Mayfair townhouse, the dead assassin, Sir Edward's warning, and Whipple's clever plan to fake our deaths.

'So Inspector Whipple's spreading word that you and HG are heading to Glasgow?' Poppy leaned against the stone balustrade, her blonde hair catching the breeze.

'The plan's quite elegant, really,' Muddleford said. 'We need you to casually mention to the other models that HG's gone north to investigate similar murders in Scotland. Let them draw their own conclusions.'

'That might work.' Poppy turned away from the view, her expression thoughtful. 'But we've got another problem. As I said, the girls are getting antsy. Every day they stay here is a day they're not earning. Clara's already talking about heading back to London, and the Cunliffs won't be far behind.'

The implications hit me like a punch to the gut. Without the models, we'd lose our best chance at uncovering the truth about Lucy's murder. The investigation would crumble.

'How long before they start leaving?' Muddleford's typically stern face showed genuine concern.

'Two days, maybe three.' Poppy shrugged. 'They're professional models - time is money. Unless someone's covering their lost wages...'

My mind raced ahead. HG needed to know about this immediately. We'd need funds to keep the models in Norwich, perhaps even arrange some local work to maintain their cover. The investigation couldn't afford to lose them now, not when we were so close to understanding the connection between Lucy's death and Pinstripe.

'Will you telephone HG straight away,' Muddleford said, as if reading my thoughts.

Before I had a chance to answer, a blood-curdling scream filled the street below us. It was as if the world had slipped into slow-motion. A woman lay motionless in the middle of the road; a black car sped off and vanished around a corner. After a few seconds, people began to gather around the crumpled figure.

'We need to get down there,' shouted Muddleford, leaving us in the dust of his shoes.

No time for the elevator now. We rushed down flight after flight of carpeted stairs. At last, we arrived in reception and sped across the marbled floor.

A group of horrified onlookers surrounded the frozen figure: a woman.

Strangers parted as they caught sight of my uniform. 'Please stand back', I commanded, surprised at the authority in my own voice.

Poppy and Muddleford moved forward to crouch beside the fallen figure.

Muddleford looked over his shoulder at me. His look told me the woman was dead. Then Poppy stood and whispered into my ear.

'It's Emily Brown; the fashion show director.'

Chapter Seventeen

CIRCLES WITHIN CIRCLES

The mortuary's harsh lights cast stark shadows across Emily Brown's pale face. Her stern features had softened in death, making her appear younger, more vulnerable than her demeanour just days ago.

Dr Phillips, Norwich's chief pathologist, pulled on his rubber gloves with practiced efficiency. The snap of latex against skin echoed off the cold tile walls. His assistant arranged gleaming stainless-steel instruments in precise rows on a metal tray, each catching the light.

Poppy stood motionless beside me; her usual confidence dimmed by the clinical horror of our surroundings. Muddleford kept checking his notebook, though what answers he expected to find remained unclear.

'Poor soul,' Dr Phillips murmured, examining the brutal damage to Emily's skull. 'Death came in a moment, at least.'

The mortician worked with gentle reverence, cleaning away street dirt and arranging Emily's limbs with the same care she had once used to organise her models on stage. Her grey bob lay matted with blood against the steel table.

'The vehicle struck her at considerable speed,' Muddleford opined. 'We saw it happen; no attempt to brake or swerve.'

'Deliberate then.' Phillip's voice carried the weight of certainty.

The antiseptic smell burned my nostrils as Dr Phillips positioned the overhead lamp. Emily Brown lay exposed beneath its merciless glare; her dignity stripped away. In death, she had become evidence - another piece in our expanding puzzle.

'Shall we begin?' Dr. Phillips lifted his scalpel, its edge catching the light.

We left the pathologist to his grim work, the mortuary doors swinging shut behind us with a metallic clang. The morning felt too bright after the clinical gloom inside.

'One hour,' Phillips had promised, his wire-rimmed spectacles glinting. 'My office, second floor.'

The walk to St Stephens Street cleared some of the mortuary's chill from my bones. Our unlikely trio drew sideways glances from passing shoppers - Poppy's innovative fashion, my borrowed police uniform, and Muddleford's sharp-featured authority.

A small cafe huddled between a tobacconist and a milliner's shop. Its bell above the door announced our arrival with a cheerful jingle that felt out-of-place given our morning's task. An aroma of fresh baked cakes wrapped itself around us.

The cafe fell silent. A pair of labourers at the counter, caps pulled low over their eyes, abandoned half-drunk cups of tea. They shouldered past us without meeting our gaze, the door's bell marking their hasty exit.

'Guilty consciences, I dare say,' Muddleford said with a thin smile.

The remaining patrons studied their cups with sudden fascination. A waitress approached our table, her pencil hovering above her notepad.

The cafe's interior spoke of decades of neglect. Pine panelling wrapped the lower walls like a nicotine-stained belt, its once-pristine surface dulled by countless clothes and dampened coats. Dark patches mapped generations of working men leaning against the timber while waiting for their morning tea. Cobwebs draped the corners where wall met ceiling, and a layer of grease coated the windowpanes, softening the morning light.

Our waitress delivered three cups of strong tea and over-browned toast, her sensible shoes squeaking against the worn linoleum floor. The few remaining customers in the small venue huddled over their cups, speaking in whispers.

'Miss Poppy?' Muddleford looked up from his notebook.

'Perhaps I'm seeing shadows where none exist.' Poppy set down her spoon. 'But consider - a black car makes no attempt to stop outside the Railway Hotel where the girls are staying.'

'Perhaps it is meant to frighten our remaining witnesses into silence,' I suggested.

Poppy's fingers traced the rim of her cup. 'Doesn't that seem a bit heavy-handed, even for that Pinstripe bloke you talk about?'

Muddleford's features hardened. 'The timing is suspicious.'

The ancient radiator beneath the window rattled and wheezed, struggling against the morning chill. A clock on the wall ticked toward our appointment with Dr Phillips, its brass face tarnished by years of cooking fumes.

Steam curled from our cups as Muddleford thumbed through his notebook, the pages dog-eared and stained with tea rings. The cafe's radiator continued its asthmatic wheeze while he gathered his thoughts.

'Ms Brown caught a glancing blow from the car. In some circumstances, this might point to a tragic accident. No doubt the car's speed played a critical factor in her death, whether intended or not. The truth of the matter is that until we apprehend the driver, and look at that car forensically, it's impossible to say. What makes me uneasy is that as a detective, I don't accept coincidences...and here we have one with bells on.'

The words hung in the stale air. My fingers traced the rough grain of the wooden table, mind replaying the sickening thud of Emily's body against metal. The black car had moved like a predator, purposeful and deadly in its approach, and the absence of tyre marks gave credence to the movement being maligned.

Poppy's hand found mine beneath the table, her grip steady and warm. The waitress bustled past with fresh tea, her rubber soles squeaking against the linoleum. Outside, a newspaper boy's cry echoed down St Stephen's Street, hawking the morning's headlines. None of it seemed real - the mortuary visit, Emily's broken body, this grimy cafe with its wretched fare and flighty patrons.

Poppy's teacup clinked against its saucer, the sound sharp as a gunshot in the hushed atmosphere. My new constable's uniform itched at the collar, the borrowed boots pinching my toes. The disguise felt like a cheap costume now, inadequate protection against whatever force had targeted Emily Brown.

Muddleford pushed his untouched tea away with a grimace, then wiped his fingers with a cotton handkerchief.

'I've had it.' He rose from his chair, straightening his long coat. 'The combined aroma of stale cigarettes and cooking grease is doing my lungs no good at all. I'd rather wait outside Dr Phillips' office rather than put up with another moment in this place.'

The ancient floorboards creaked beneath his sensible shoes as he gathered his belongings. A fresh wave of cooking smells wafted from the kitchen, making his nose wrinkle with distaste.

Poppy set down her teacup, her expression brightening with sudden inspiration. 'Perhaps I should head back to the Railway Hotel instead of joining you at the hospital. The girls must be in quite a state after Emily's death. Someone needs to keep them from bolting.'

Muddleford considered her proposition and nodded. 'Good idea to settle their nerves. Tell them I'll stop by later to address any concerns they have.'

I laid down two shillings and ninepence on the bare table, then followed the others out. The late morning air felt clean after the stuffy interior. Poppy squeezed my hand before heading toward the Railway Hotel, her confident stride drawing admiring glances from passing shopkeepers leaning against open doors awaiting their next customers.

Muddleford inhaled, the colour returning to his cheeks. 'Much better. Let's get to the hospital. We need to hear what Dr Phillips has to say.'

A late morning sun warmed my face as we walked along Ipswich Road toward the hospital. The red Victorian bricks blazed like a fortress against the autumn sky. Two identical wings spread from the central entrance, their windows reflecting a golden light.

Ornate stonework decorated the building's facade, telling tales of Victorian craftsmanship and pride. The nurses' quarters stood sentinel on the left, while the chapel's solid presence dominated the right.

My gaze drifted across the busy road where a row of distinguished yellow-brick houses lined up like soldiers on parade. Their manicured gardens and polished brass knockers spoke of the successful surgeons who, I assumed, called them home.

Muddleford's boots thumped against the flagstones as we approached the hospital's grand portico. Massive columns soared overhead, dwarfing us as we passed beneath their weathered capitals. Inside, the entrance hall stretched wide and welcoming. A young nurse looked up from her desk, offering a warm smile as we crossed the polished floor.

Our footsteps echoed off the gleaming walls as we climbed the broad staircase to the second floor. The banister felt smooth beneath my hand, worn by countless worried relatives and hopeful patients. The landing opened onto a long corridor that stretched away like a railway track, its end lost in shadow despite the tall windows lining one wall.

Dr Phillips appeared ahead, key in hand, his clinical white coat stark against the dark wooden door of his office. His wire-rimmed spectacles caught the light as he turned toward our approaching footsteps.

The pathologist stepped aside, his thin figure casting a shadow across the polished floor as he gestured us in. The neatness of his office struck me; everything appeared to have its place, from the stacked files on the mahogany desk to the framed certificates lining the walls. A faint smell of antiseptic hung in the air, mingling with a hint of something floral—perhaps a vase of flowers resting out of sight.

'Perfect timing,' he said, a slight smile breaking through his otherwise serious demeanour. 'I was just about to prepare my findings regarding Ms Brown's unfortunate demise.'

We filed into the office, and I chose a chair that faced him upholstered in dark leather, worn but comfortable enough. Muddleford sat beside me, his long frame comfortably fitting into the modest chair.

Phillips settled into his own chair behind the desk, backlit by the window's glow. The light framed him like an artist's portrait, emphasising the silver strands in his hair and deepening the lines etched into his face from years of disciplined work. He looked every bit the part of a man who had seen too much death but remained committed to uncovering truths.

'Now then,' he began, hands steepled before him. 'Emily Brown's injuries were severe.' He paused for effect, allowing us a moment to absorb what was coming. 'The impact was catastrophic—a blow to her head consistent with being struck by a vehicle at speed.'

Muddleford leaned forward, his eyes narrowing with focus. 'Do you think the driver meant to kill?'

Phillips adjusted his glasses. 'The nature of her wounds was not survivable.' His voice carried that icy edge of professionalism—a reminder that beneath every statistic lay a life extinguished too soon.

'Is there any way to ascertain whether the collision was planned?' Muddleford asked.

Dr Phillips paused, studying him, as if weighing the implications of the question against his professional obligations. His gaze flicked between Muddleford and me, the weight of his silence filling the room.

After a few seconds, he shrugged his shoulders and sighed. 'It's impossible to tell,' he replied, his voice tinged with resignation. 'That question lies more in your domain than mine, detective. It may have been a simple case of panic,' Phillips continued. 'Or perhaps a deliberate act to evade responsibility. The truth is often obscured in these tragic circumstances.'

Muddleford scribbled in his notebook, brow furrowed, deep in thought. A flicker of disappointment crossed his face. The thread connecting Emily's death to a calculated plot just out of reach—a tantalising lead we couldn't grasp.

The pathologist continued to regard us both, an inscrutable expression settling over him as if he were pondering something beyond our comprehension.

Muddleford broke the silence that had settled like dust over us. 'We'll need to gather more information about the vehicle involved—who owned it and where it went after impact.'

I nodded at the detective's suggestion while I leaned back in my chair, mapping out our next steps as an urgency grew within me—a need to push through this veil of uncertainty and uncover the truth behind Emily Brown's untimely death.

Muddleford rose from his chair. 'Thank you for your time, Doctor. Your insights will, I'm certain, assist our investigations. May I request a copy of the final autopsy report be sent across to Norwich police station?'

Dr Phillips adjusted his glasses, the thin wire frames catching the light as he considered the request. 'Of course, Detective Sergeant. I'll ensure it reaches you as soon as possible.'

With that settled, Dr Phillips extended his hand first to Muddleford, then to me.

As I held the door open for Muddleford, he paused at the threshold, glancing back at Phillips with a hint of curiosity in his eyes. 'By the way, Doctor,' he began, 'was there anything found on Ms Brown's clothing or person?'

Phillips gazed at the detective for a moment before responding. 'Yes. She had a purse in her coat pocket containing the usual assortment of coins.' He hesitated, then continued with an air of surprise creeping into his voice. 'I did find a tattoo. Not something I expected, although someone has had a good go at removing it.'

The words hung heavy in the air as we froze mid-motion. My mind raced back to our earlier conversations about Lucy Daws and that damned society whose emblem haunted us like a spectre.

Muddleford's brow furrowed as he took a pace towards the pathologist. 'It wasn't three interwoven rings on her shoulder blade, by any chance?'

Dr Phillips blinked, the surprise clear in his expression. Muddleford's words hung in the air, and I could sense the tension tightening around us like a noose. The pathologist's office felt smaller somehow, the walls closing in as he absorbed her statement.

'You believe,' he began, 'that Emily Brown was targeted?'

Muddleford stepped closer, his eyes sharp. 'I am afraid I do, and it gives me fresh reason to believe that the poor woman's demise was no accident. The world is a cruel enough place when a tragic accident occurs, Dr Phillips. However, when malice aforethought is in play, cruelty morphs into bestiality.'

The weight of his words settled over us. Dr Phillips straightened his posture, his previous composure replaced by a look of genuine concern. 'But why? What would anyone gain from harming her? She was the director of a fashion show—hardly someone of consequence.'

Muddleford's gaze flicked toward me before returning to Phillips, a spark igniting in his eyes. 'In this case, Doctor, it is because she was directing that fashion show that makes her pivotal. Her connections and influence could threaten many —a potential scandal involving the Three Circles Society and, therefore, the powerful figures who feature among the higher echelons of our society yet inhabit a dark secret world of avarice obtained by whatever means they deem necessary.'

Phillips ran a hand through his hair, worry clear on his features as he processed her implications. 'But who would go so far?'

'Those who fear exposure,' Muddleford replied. His voice took on an edge as if he were wielding it like a blade against unseen foes. 'Those who hold their power too tight to let it slip through their fingers.'

I shifted my weight as I watched the conversation unfold. My mind raced. Would there be a third victim?

'We must move at pace,' Muddleford added, determination flooding his voice once more. 'If there are more players involved than we suspect, we cannot afford to give them any time to cover their tracks.'

Phillips nodded; his earlier doubts seemed to dissolve beneath the detective's intensity.

Muddleford stepped back, adjusting the collar of his coat, before fixing his gaze on the pathologist once more. 'Again, thank you for your insight, Doctor.'

The hospital's car park lay quiet, the only sounds the distant murmur of traffic and the rustle of leaves in the autumn breeze. The air felt heavy, weighed down by the gravity of what we had just uncovered. No one broke the silence; it wrapped around us like a shroud.

Muddleford's expression remained inscrutable, his eyes fixed ahead, lips pressed into a thin line

The aged police car stood waiting in its spot; its dimming paintworks dull under the pale sunlight. I climbed into the driver's seat as Muddleford folded his tall frame into the passenger seat. The sparse interior offered little in the way of comfort that reflected our grim discussion moments earlier.

As I turned the key in the ignition, the engine spluttered into life, its noisy rumble giving little comfort that we might reach our next destination. I glanced at Muddleford and asked about our next move.

Instead of a destination, he posed a question. 'What are your thoughts on Emily's tattoo?'

Muddleford leaned back in his seat, a finger and thumb rubbing against his chin.

I thought about his question for several seconds before replying. 'There are two possibilities,' I replied. 'First, she could have been expelled from that wicked group—the Three Circles Society—perhaps as punishment for some transgression.'

I paused, allowing my theory to hang in the air like smoke from an extinguished candle before continuing. 'It stands to reason they would have spoiled her tattoo as a form of humiliation or warning.'

I exchanged glances with Muddleford's as I spoke. The weight of implication loomed large between us.

'Or,' I added with deliberate emphasis, 'it may be that she herself arranged for its removal after distancing herself from them—perhaps something members do not permit, and therefore making her a target for retribution and enforced silence.'

'You may be right. After all,' Muddleford intoned, 'The dead cannot speak.'

'No they cannot,' I agreed. 'But what they leave behind can. What about you telephoning Detective Inspector Whipple and ask him to check out Miss Brown's London home…and for him to get in touch with the French authorities to search her Paris apartment?'

'Consider it done,' Muddleford replied. 'Now, let's get back to the Railway Hotel. With luck, Miss Poppy will have done enough to stop them making a run for it.'

Chapter Eighteen

SOOTHING WORDS

The women filed into a private room to the rear of the Royal Hotel, their heels clicking against the polished floor like a nervous heartbeat. Tension pulled at their faces as they glanced around the well-appointed space. Against the far wall, a long table offered tea, coffee, and delicate pastries - an attempt to soften whatever news awaited them.

Clara Brightman settled into an emerald wingback chair, her fingers twisting the hem of her skirt. Amber Longstone perched on the edge of the sofa; her usual sharp demeanour dulled by clear exhaustion. The Cunliffs huddled together on a loveseat, whispering between themselves.

Muddleford stood near the fireplace, his tall frame casting a long shadow across the Persian rug. His expression remained neutral as he watched each model choose their place. The afternoon sun filtered through heavy curtains, casting the room in a subdued glow.

Poppy slipped in last, closing the door without a sound.

217

Her eyes met mine before she took up position near the refreshment table.

The Cunliffs picked at a plate of shortbread between them, leaving crumbs on their laps.

Muddleford waited, allowing the women time to settle. His patience eased some of the initial tension from the room, though worry still creased the women's brows. Clara sipped her tea with trembling hands while Amber's foot tapped an endless rhythm against the floor.

The last model found her seat and the shuffling of feet ceased. Muddleford cleared his throat. The sound drew every eye in the room to his commanding presence.

My heart slowed its frantic beating as Poppy's gaze swept past me without a flicker of recognition. She moved with casual grace to pour herself tea, not once glancing in my direction. The other models appeared oblivious to my true identity, focused instead on Muddleford.

The detective adjusted his collar and addressed the room in measured tones. 'I understand these past days have been hard. The loss of Miss Brown is tragic, but I assure you we have measures in place for your protection-'

'Protection?' Amber Longstone sprang to her feet. 'What protection? Two women are dead - Lucy shot in cold blood and Emily crushed beneath a motorcar. And where's the duchess? Where's that driver of hers - Rex Watson? Both vanished without a trace!'

My fingers tightened around my notepad, fighting the urge to react to my name. Sweat prickled beneath the false whiskers as Amber's accusatory gaze swept the room.

'What if they are next to snuff it? Or worse, and they're the ones behind everything!' Her voice cracked with hysteria.

Clara reached for Amber's arm. 'Please sit down. This is doing no good.'

'I will not sit down!' Amber yanked free of Clara's grasp. 'How are we supposed to feel safe when people keep snuffing it around us?'

The Cunliffs clutched each other's hands, their faces pale as milk. Even Poppy's maintained composure cracked as she set down her cup with trembling fingers.

Muddleford raised his hands in a calming gesture. 'Miss Longstone, please. Your concerns are valid, but-'

'The Dowager left for Edinburgh this morning,' I announced as part of our plan to flush out any informants.

Muddleford's sharp glance reinforced the dupe in persuading the woman I'd made the comment in error.

'Edinburgh?' Amber's eyes narrowed.'

Poppy stepped forward, her voice cutting through the rising tension. 'Rather than chase rumours, perhaps we might focus on facts? Detective Muddleford is here to answer our questions about the investigation.'

Relief flooded through me at her quick thinking. The models' attention shifted away from my slip as Clara raised her hand.

'What happens to Emily's clothes and stuff in her lodgings? Some of the dresses will be the ones used in the show.'

'Don't worry, we'll take care of all the arrangements, but thank you for your question.'

One of the Cunliffs - Margaret - spoke next. 'Were there any witnesses to the accident?'

'Several people saw a black motorcar, but none were able to identify the driver or provide the registration number.' Muddleford's tone remained steady and professional.

Amber, who had retaken her seat, leaned forward. 'What about Lucy's murder? Have you found the weapon yet…that is certain to help you, isn't it? You know, matching it to the bullet?'

'You've been watching too many moving pictures about American gangsters, you have,' Poppy said. Her ploy in lifting the mood for a few seconds worked as the women slipped back into their old habit of taking a rise out of each other. Once things settled, Muddleford answered Amber's question.

'A bullet recovered from the scene was fired from a custom-made pistol. We're tracking down potential sources of such a unique weapon.'

The mood in the room shifted like a spring breeze clearing winter fog. My pencil scratched across the police notebook, documenting their reactions while keeping my face angled down. The familiar scent of gum-arabic wafted up from my fake whiskers, making my nose twitch.

Clara moved to the refreshment table, selecting a fresh cup of tea and several Petits Fours. 'Anyone else need a top-up?'

Several models drifted over, their earlier tension dissolving into muted chatter. The Cunliffs abandoned their loveseat to join the gathering, Margaret reaching past Clara for a chocolate eclair.

My grip tightened on the pencil as Amber swept past, close enough for the rustle of her silk dress to brush my sleeve. The greasepaint around my jawline felt thick and obvious. Sweat prickled beneath the false sideburns.

Muddleford maintained his position by the fireplace, though his stern demeanour softened as he accepted a cup of tea from Clara. The women clustered in small groups, voices rising and falling in a more natural cadence.

Poppy circulated among them with practiced ease, her

undercover role perfect as she discussed the latest fashions from Paris. My pencil traced meaningless loops across the page, providing an excuse to keep my head down when any of the models glanced my way.

Each time someone passed too close, my heart skipped a beat. One whiff of the theatrical supplies might give the game away. The notebook became my shield, my reason to maintain distance without appearing suspicious.

Muddleford cleared his throat, drawing attention back from the scattered conversations. 'Ladies, thank you for sharing your concerns. Your cooperation has been invaluable to our-'

'Begging your pardon, detective.' Margaret Cunliff rose from her chair, shoulders squared. 'But speaking for everyone, we've had quite enough. None of us has worked in days. We're losing bookings and missing shows in London. We can't afford to stay here much longer.'

Heads nodded around the room. Clara dabbed her lips with a napkin while Amber crossed her arms, both agreeing with Margaret's assessment.

'You make an excellent point.' Muddleford raised his hands in a placating gesture. 'My sincere apologies for not addressing this sooner. The Dowager Duchess of Drakeford anticipated the issue and has already instructed her accountant to provide compensation for your lost earnings during the investigation.'

My pencil stilled against the notebook. Looking up, my gaze met Poppy's across the room for the first time. Her confusion mirrored my own. While HG had mentioned arranging for funds to be made available, neither of us knew of any actual transfer taking place. I viewed Poppy's concern as mirroring my own concerning the danger of his assertion backfiring.

Muddleford's mention of financial compensation worked like a charm. The earlier hostility melted away as the models huddled in small groups, whispering about potential amounts. Their animated chatter filled the room with speculation about allowances and compensation rates.

Clara's eyes sparkled as she discussed the Paris fashion houses with Margaret Cunliff. Even Amber's rigid posture softened while she chatted with several other models about missed bookings and future opportunities. The promise of money had transformed the atmosphere.

My pencil moved across the notebook, documenting the shift in mood. Several feet away, Poppy maintained her cover, joining discussions about upcoming shows and potential earnings.

After several minutes of pleasant conversation, Muddleford cleared his throat. 'Ladies, if there are no further questions, we'll bring the gathering to a close.' A sea of smiling faces looking at Muddleford gave witness to the success of his risky strategy.

The models filtered out; their spirits lifted. Soon only Muddleford, Poppy and I remained.

Poppy turned to Muddleford. 'About this money-'

'Thought you'd ask about that.' Muddleford cut her off, then faced me. 'After checking out Emily Brown's digs, we'll head back to Thorpe Manor to update the Dowager and sort the financial issue out.'

His gaze returned to Poppy. 'Perhaps you'd remain at the hotel? There's something rather...delicate I need your help with.' A flush crept up his neck. 'Might you perhaps find a way to check if any of the girls have that damned tattoo on their shoulder?'

Poppy's eyes danced with mischief. 'Why, Detective, are you asking me to get the girls to strip?'

Muddleford's face turned scarlet. 'No! That's not what I- I didn't mean-'

'Relax.' Poppy grinned. 'Know what you mean. Leave it to me.'

A Victorian mansion loomed before us, its red brick facade mellow and well maintained. White-painted box-sash window frames gleamed against the weathered surface, while pruned box hedges lined the path to the impressive front entrance. A brass plaque declared "Kett's House - Lodgings to the Professional Class" in flowing script.

Muddleford reached for the substantial brass door pull, its surface polished by countless hands. The resulting chime echoed somewhere in the depths of the building.

A maid in a black dress and starched white pinafore opened the door. Her eyes widened at my police uniform, and she dropped into a nervous curtsy.

'We need to speak with the proprietor,' Muddleford stated.

Without a word, the maid disappeared into the shadowy interior. Moments later, her place was taken by a stout woman dressed in severe Victorian black, complete with a high collar and cameo brooch. A substantial ring of keys hung from her leather belt; clicking as she moved.

'Mrs Harriet Pembroke.' Her voice carried the firm authority of someone used to maintaining order. 'How may I assist?'

Muddleford removed his hat. 'Madam, I regret to inform you that one of your guests, Miss Emily Brown, has been killed in a motor accident.'

Mrs Pembroke's expression remained unchanged,

though something flickered behind her eyes. The rigid posture and controlled reaction spoke of an upbringing where emotions were kept in check rather than any lack of feeling.

'I'd like to view her room, if possible?' Added Muddleford.

She gave a nod, turned on her heel, and proceeded up the stairs with military precision. Her back remained ramrod straight as we followed her to the second floor.

Stopping outside a door identical to the others lining the corridor, Mrs Pembroke lifted her ring of keys. She selected one and inserted it into the lock. The door swung open to reveal Miss Brown's quarters.

When my gaze shifted from the room back to the hall-way, Mrs Pembroke had vanished as silently as a ghost.

The room stretched wider than I expected, with high ceilings and tall windows draped in heavy burgundy curtains. Traditional furnishings filled the space - a mahogany writing desk, matching wardrobe, and a brass-framed bed with crisp white linens. Not a single item appeared out of place. The carpet beneath our feet showed deep brush marks, still visible from the morning's cleaning.

On an occasional table near the window, my attention caught a thick manila folder. The words "Show Directory and Running Order" were written across its cover in precise handwriting.

Muddleford moved through the space with careful delib-eration, his sharp eyes scanning every surface. Each step measured, as though he were mapping the room in his mind. The methodical way he worked reminded me of a chess player thinking several moves ahead.

From his jacket pocket, he produced a pristine white handkerchief. Using it to shield his fingers, he began opening drawers in the writing desk. The contents revealed nothing but stationery and correspondence materials, all stored in perfect order. Moving to the wardrobe, he used the same careful technique to examine its contents comprising fashionable dresses and coats, each hanging with military precision and each pocket checked.

His investigation led him to a narrow bedside cabinet. The top drawer opened with a soft whisper against its runners. Inside, concealed beneath some papers, lay a small book bound in black leather. The single word "Diary" gleamed in gold lettering across its surface, the book resting at an odd angle compared to the otherwise meticulous organisation of the room.

Muddleford's stern expression softened into a half-smile as his fingers reached for the leather-bound volume. The handkerchief cradled the diary with the delicate touch one might use to handle a rare butterfly specimen, preserving any potential fingerprints that lingered on its surface.

My eyes fixed on the small book, willing him to crack open its pages and reveal whatever secrets Emily Brown had deemed important enough to record. The spine showed signs of frequent use; its edges worn smooth from handling.

Catching my eager look, Muddleford's smile widened. 'Interrogating its contents can wait until we return to Thorpe Manor.'

He tucked the covered diary into his jacket pocket before resuming his methodical examination of the room. 'Watson, give the bed a thorough search while I satisfy myself there's nothing else of interest here,' Muddleford said, showing a rare flash of sardonic humour.

Approaching the bed, my hands moved with precision. The blankets peeled back one layer at a time - first the quilted coverlet, then the woollen blanket, and the crisp white sheet. The mattress revealed nothing but neat stitching and unmarked ticking fabric. Each pillow received equal scrutiny but yielded no hidden treasures.

With swift, practiced movements, I returned the bed to its original pristine state.

'Excellent hospital corners, Watson.' Muddleford nodded his approval.

The praise brought memories flooding back - matron's eyebrows lifting and lowering as she inspected row upon row of identical beds at the children's home, her white-gloved hand running along edges that had to be perfect. Those endless morning inspections had drilled the technique into my muscle memory.

'Nothing more to find here.' Muddleford pocketed his handkerchief. 'We'll head to Thorpe Manor, but first a quick stop in Wymondham.' Without waiting for acknowledgement, he strode from the room. 'Make sure that door's closed.'

Following his lead down the stairs, my footsteps echoed against the polished wood. Mrs Pembroke stood in the hallway, her arms folded as if about to bar our exit.

'Thank you for your cooperation,' Muddleford said, extending his hand. Our host chose not to return the courtesy and instead offered a brief nod.

'I shall ensure the room remains locked until you provide further instructions?'

Muddleford touched the rim of his cap as a mark of respect. 'That will do perfectly, Mrs Pembroke.'

With arrangements settled, the owner opened the front door and stood to one side. Muddleford stepped outside without a backward glance as his determined stride carried him straight to the police vehicle.

The aged car groaned in protest as the starter motor

engaged, the metallic whine piercing the morning quiet. After three attempts, each more laboured than the last, the engine spluttered to life, accompanied by a cloud of blue smoke from the exhaust that drifted across the road, a passer-by wafting the haze away from her face with a look of disgust. I caught a whiff of burning oil - another repair bill in the making.

'Keep watch for anyone following us out of the city,' Muddleford directed, his eyes fixed on the road ahead. I shifted in the driver's seat, the worn leather creaking beneath me as I turned to observe the sparse morning traffic through the rear-view mirror. A pair of cyclists wobbled past, and somewhere a church bell tolled the quarter hour.

The Norfolk countryside rolled past the windows, a patchwork of fields dotted with farm buildings and church spires piercing the horizon. Half an hour later, I brought the car to a stop outside an impressive Georgian building, its weathered brick facade speaking of centuries of history.

'Rather grand for a police station.'

'It is, isn't it?' Muddleford began. 'It used to be called "The Bridewell" and was a house of correction and prison. Local magistrates used it until 1878. The prison Governor lived in part of the building for centuries, hence how posh it looks. Now, the police station bobby and his family live here, as will we for a few days to keep away from prying eyes? I doubt it'll be a quiet stay since in addition to being a police station, the building also houses holding cells and the magistrate's court.

The heavy wooden door already stood open as we approached, revealing a tall young man in a police uniform, minus his hat. In his arms he cradled a baby, while somewhere in the depths of the building, another child wailed while a woman's voice murmured soothing words.

'Sergeant Featherstone, pleased to meet you,' announced Muddleford.

'And you, sir, and you, Mr Rex. Both of you, do come in.'

My eyebrows lifted at his knowledge of our arrival and names, though a smile tugged at my lips over the formal manner of address. Following the officer through a small corridor, we turned right into the police reception - a sparse space dominated by the tall counter, the likes of which are in every station across the country.

'Been expecting you, gentlemen,' Sergeant Featherstone said, bouncing the baby in his arms. 'Had word from a senior detective at Scotland Yard about keeping Mr Rex's true identity confidential.'

Muddleford's expression remained neutral. 'Might the detective be one Chief Inspector Whipple, by any chance?'

'The same.' A warm smile spread across the sergeant's face. 'A gentleman of repute, as you know.'

'As you say,' Muddleford replied without overdue reverence.

'Oh, and there's one other matter,' Sergeant Featherstone added. 'The Dowager Duchess of Drakeford telephoned - someone I understand you both know. She's requested one of you ring her as soon as possible.'

Our eyes met in silent communication. What matter might be of such import that it required an immediate telephone call?

As the sergeant and I waited in anticipation, Muddleford waited for his call to be answered. Seconds later I recognised the droll voice of HG's butler without being able to hear his precise words, then silence once more. After a brief pause, Muddleford spoke, turning from us as if attempting to keep a state secret.

'I see. Yes…yes, goodbye.'

Muddleford replaced the earpiece onto its cradle and turned.

'Detective Inspector Whipple was right. Two of Pinstripe's henchmen were seen boarding a train for Edinburgh less than an hour ago. You know what this means.'

Chapter Nineteen

DANGER WITHIN

The parlour at Thorpe Manor wrapped us in warmth, its oak-panelled walls gleaming in the late afternoon sun. A fire crackled in the stone hearth, casting dancing shadows across the Persian carpet. Graham had arranged an afternoon tea on the low table between the wing chairs.

HG settled into her favourite armchair, her silver hair catching in the firelight as she poured tea. Muddleford selected the settee, his long frame making the furniture appear almost doll-like in comparison.

'So they've taken the bait,' HG said, passing me a cup. 'Edinburgh will keep them occupied for at least a few days. Arthur's plan worked perfectly.'

I ventured to suggest that HG's timeline might be optimistic, given the henchmen were bound to spend their time aboard the train searching every carriage for her presence.

'A fair point,' HG began, 'yet they cannot be sure you and I took that particular train, or, indeed, any locomotive. After all, the Rolls is safely tucked away in the stable block and so away from prying eyes. For all Pinstripe's men know, we may have travelled by road - unlikely, I admit, but not out of the question.

Muddleford accepted his tea with a nod. 'Though I must admit, staging our deaths was rather theatrical. I sometimes think the best deceptions are the most obvious ones. In any event, Arthur has secured the cooperation of the Edinburgh Constabulary. They have agreed to put a tail on the two rogues when they alight at Waverly station.'

HG selected a scone, breaking it neatly in half. 'What news of Emily Brown's diary?'

The leather-bound volume sat in Muddleford's lap.

'Most entries are mundane - fashion show preparations, model schedules. But there's this.' His finger traced down a page. 'The day before her death, she wrote about meeting someone. If only she'd named the location.'

'I agree. Then again, she didn't know what fate awaited her.'

'She mentions someone she calls "P" - could be Pinstripe, it may refer to Pendlebury. But here's the odd thing, from then on the entry's written in some form of code.'

'Code,' HG responded, her tone markedly stark.

'And it's not the only time Emily uses it,' Muddleford said as he flicked through the well-thumbed pages. 'Here… and here. Also, at the end of this passage. The detective's fingers pointed to each position the strange characters appeared.

A burning timber slipped in the grate, scattering glowing embers on the stone hearth, briefly drawing our attention away from the captivating journal.

Graham moved silently through the parlour to tend the fire, sweeping away the scattered embers without fuss or noise.

'May I?' HG held out her hand for the diary.

Muddleford passed it across, and HG adjusted her reading glasses, peering at the pages with intense focus. My position in the armchair afforded a clear view as her fingers traced each line, moving back and forth between entries. The crease between her brows deepened with each page turn.

Minutes ticked by on the mantel clock while HG studied the cryptic text. Her tea grew cold, forgotten beside her on the small table. The scent of wood smoke mingled with leather as she worked, occasionally muttering under her breath or shaking her head at the puzzling passages.

Finally, she closed the diary with deliberate care, her fingers drumming a thoughtful pattern on its worn cover.

'We need someone with a particular type of brain to untangle this puzzle,' she said, 'and I have just such a person in mind.'

HG reached for the elegantly decorated teapot. Steam curled from the spout as she poured herself a fresh cup. Her movements were unhurried, deliberate, as though the pressing matter of Emily's coded diary held no urgency.

To accentuate the break in proceedings, a knife clinked against silver as she spread a generous layer of damson preserve, followed by a dollop of Devonshire clotted cream.

At last, HG settled back into her chair, taking a delicate bite of the scone. Her silver hair caught the late afternoon light streaming through the bay windows as she savoured each morsel with satisfaction. The diary lay forgotten on the side table, its secrets still locked within its pages.

The silence stretched on until my patience finally wore thin.

'You mentioned someone who might help with the code?'

HG lifted a finger in acknowledgement, dabbing at her lips with a napkin before responding. The last crumbs of scone disappeared as she gathered her thoughts.

HG's sudden giggle caught me off guard, breaking the weighty silence that had settled over the parlour.

'My sincere apologies for the dramatic pause,' she said, setting down her teacup. 'I was lost in memories of Berlin, 1910. You'll recall I mentioned that particular journey the other day?'

The fire popped and crackled as Muddleford shifted forward in his seat. 'Indeed, in connection with Pinstripe, if memory serves.'

'Quite right. During that period, among the diplomatic tensions, I encountered the most remarkable young woman.' HG's eyes sparkled with the recollection. 'Brilliant mind, absolutely brilliant.'

'How did your paths cross?' Muddleford asked, reaching for another sandwich.

A knowing smile played across HG's features. 'Oh, that's hardly relevant now. What matters is her extraordinary gift for languages and, more importantly, her exceptional talent for breaking codes.' She paused, adding sugar to her fresh cup of tea. 'Those skills proved rather invaluable in the years that followed.'

Muddleford's eyebrows rose. 'And you know where to find this code-breaking genius?'

'As a matter of fact, I do.' HG's smile widened as she stirred her tea.

A subtle movement caught my eye as HG reached toward the ornate wood panelling beside the fireplace. Her fingers found a concealed button.

A minute passed, marked only by the soft crackle of burning logs. The heavy oak door swung open, revealing

Graham's tall figure silhouetted against the hallway's dimness.

'Can you ask Miss Frodsham to join us if she's free?'

Graham gave a silent nod before he withdrew, the door closing behind him with barely a whisper.

Muddleford's puzzled expression mirrored my own as we exchanged glances. HG offered no explanation; instead, she focused her attention on finishing a scone with methodical precision. The silence stretched, broken only by the Muddleford's harrumphs.

Minutes later, the door opened again. A young woman stepped into the parlour, her appearance a stark contrast to the formal setting. Baggy trousers hung loosely on her frame, paired with an oversized woollen pullover that had seen better days. Mud-splattered galoshes squeaked against the polished floor with each step. A pencil perched precariously behind her right ear, nearly lost among wild curls with a mind of their own.

'Ah, there you are, Chunky. Do come and join us.' HG's warm greeting carried a hint of amusement.

'What ho, chaps and chapesses!'

The young woman flopped onto the sofa next to Muddleford, who instinctively moved as far to his right as possible. Her galoshes squeaked as she placed one leg across the other as she made herself comfortable, then getting up again as she spotted the scones..

My eyes darted between this peculiar newcomer and HG, searching for some explanation. Never in my time at Thorpe Manor had such an eccentric figure graced these formal rooms. Her wild hair looked to defy gravity itself, and that oversized jumper looked as though it had been borrowed from Goliath's wardrobe.

Muddleford appeared equally bewildered. His frame

stiffened as she settled deeper into the cushions beside him, crumbs from her scone falling onto her baggy trousers. The detective sergeant's usual composure cracked as he edged away from her, his expression a mixture of confusion and alarm.

HG sat in her armchair, enjoying our discomfort. Her eyes twinkled with mischievous mirth as she watched us grapple with the sudden appearance of this dishevelled creature. The contrast between Chunky's casual demeanour and the refined setting of the parlour couldn't have been starker.

Muddleford shot a pleading glance at HG. We both needed answers about this mysterious young woman.

HG's eyes met Chunky's, and they shared an identical mischievous grin that made me distinctly uneasy. Something in their matched expressions suggested they were enjoying our confusion far too much.

'Chunky, Rex and Detective Sergeant Muddleford are perplexed by your nickname... and indeed your presence. Shall we enlighten the gentlemen?'

Chunky turned toward Muddleford, beaming a smile that could have lit up Norwich Cathedral. She shuffled along the sofa, prompting the detective to press himself against the arm rest as though it might offer some escape.

'Pineapple Chunks,' she announced with cheerful confidence, as if those two words explained everything.

Muddleford's frown deepened. 'The fruit?'

A delighted giggle burst from Chunky. 'No, you old booby. The boiled sweet.'

Her hand disappeared into one of the numerous pockets adorning her baggy trousers, emerging with a crumpled paper bag. She untwisted the bag and thrust it toward Muddleford. The detective peered inside with the cautious expression of someone expecting a jack-in-the-box to spring forth, then declined with an awkward shake of his head.

HG's laugh rang through the parlour. 'Rather like Detective Inspector Whipple, Chunky is never without a supply of her favourite boiled sweet - hence, the nickname.'

Watching Chunky demolish another scone while Muddleford shifted uncomfortably beside her, my mind grappled with her unexpected presence at Thorpe Manor. The question must have shown on my face.

HG lifted a finger to acknowledge my unspoken query. 'In a word; serendipity.'

'I've been looking for a trained archivist for ages, and mentioned as much to a dear friend. Anyway, In a twist of fate, my friend recommended a young lady who had completed a similar project for her. When I invited the said person to visit, who should turn up but Chunky! I had been unaware of her real name, you see, since everyone called her by her nickname.

'Oh, you're far too kind,' Chunky interjected, brushing crumbs from her lap. 'I'd just finished a short assignment at Windsor Castle, sorting out the letter trail between George III and the then Prince of Wales, who as you know later became Regent, then, after his father died, George IV. Anyway, they really did not get on, the Prince of Wales always asking his father, the King, for money. George III often castigated his son as a wastrel, but usually relented and paid off his debts, anyway.'

'So, the "Dear Friend" you've just mentioned was, in fact…'

'A mere detail,' replied HG with a wicked smile. 'What a fascinating time archivists must have,' HG mused, 'peeling the layers of the life of the long dead. Good luck to whoever takes on the job of unwrapping my life at some future point.'

Chunky's face brightened. 'You're right, it is a fascinating work, and far safer than other jobs I've had-' She cut herself off abruptly, shooting HG a worried glance.

'There's no need to worry,' HG assured her. 'Rex and Detective Muddleford know the focus of your work during the Great War.'

HG's revelation about Chunky's wartime role eased the tension in her shoulders. The transformation was remarkable - like watching a coiled spring release.

'Talking about your previous role, I have something here that will be right up your street, so to speak.' HG reached for Emily Brown's diary and handed it to Chunky.

The young woman accepted the leather-bound volume, her fingers tracing the worn spine before opening it. Her brow furrowed as she scanned the first few pages, then looked up at HG with puzzlement etched across her features.

'No, not the ordinary entries. If you flick through, there are repeated occasions on which the writer uses a code of some sort. We want you to break that code and reveal what Emily considered it important to hide from prying eyes.'

Chunky began turning pages methodically, her eyes darting across each entry until she encountered the first section of coded text. The change in her demeanour was instantaneous and profound. Her previously animated expression settled into intense focus, her entire being absorbed by the cryptic messages before her.

She rose from the sofa, the movement so fluid it appeared unconscious. Muddleford relaxed as she drifted away, but Chunky paid no notice. Her feet carried her around the room while her attention remained fixed on the diary's pages.

The rest of us may as well have ceased to exist. She meandered past the fireplace, narrowly missing an antique side table, muttering under her breath as she went. Her fingers traced patterns in the air as she walked.

The inevitable collision with the door registered as nothing more than a minor inconvenience. Without looking up, or breaking stride, Chunky pushed through the doorway and disappeared into the hall beyond, the diary still commanding her complete attention.

The parlour settled into stillness after Chunky's abrupt departure. My eyes remained fixed on the doorway through which she'd vanished, half expecting her to reappear as suddenly as she'd left.

A soft giggle broke the silence. HG's shoulders shook with mirth as she dabbed at her eyes with a handkerchief.

The scene we'd witnessed defied conventional explanation. Never in my years with HG had anyone quite like Chunky crossed my path - a whirlwind of baggy clothes and a brilliant mind, sweeping through the formal setting like an autumn storm.

'I must confess,' Muddleford shifted in his seat, straightening his tie as though to restore order to his world, 'in all my years with the police force, I've never encountered anyone quite like... her.'

'Oh, Chunky transcends mere eccentricity.' HG's voice carried a note of pride. 'Her mind operates on levels few can comprehend. The beauty of it lies in her complete lack of pretence - she is who she is, without the tormented soul that so often accompanies genius.'

'How might her insights aid our investigation?' Muddleford leaned forward, his professional curiosity piqued.

'Three ways, I should think.' HG ticked them off on her fingers. 'First, if Emily encoded details about The Three Circles Society, we'll finally understand her connection to them. Second, there may be information about Lucy's murder - Emily was present that day, after all. And third,' she paused, 'Emily might have documented Pinstripe's involvement in her diary, perhaps without realising its significance.'

Muddleford nodded. 'If she managed to encode sensitive information before her death...'

'Precisely. 'Emily's final messages may prove invaluable.'

HG set down her teacup with finality. 'Perhaps we might take a turn about the gardens. The fresh air will help clear our minds.'

Minutes later, wrapped in warm coats against the autumn chill, we descended the wide stone steps from Thorpe Manor's entrance. The late afternoon sun cast long shadows across the grounds, while fallen leaves crunched beneath our feet.

The Tudor knot garden spread before us, its intricate patterns of box hedging still pristine despite the season. Our footsteps followed the gravel paths between the geometric designs as HG led us through the maze-like layout.

'Perhaps this is an opportune moment to run through our lines of enquiry and possible suspects, since the list appears to be growing.'

Muddleford pulled out his notebook, flipping through the pages as we walked. 'Starting with Lucy Daws's murder, we have several threads to follow. The Three Circles Society connection through her tattoo remains unexplained. Then there's Emily Brown's death - seemingly a hit-and-run. However, the timing suggests otherwise, especially given her partially removed tattoo.'

He paused at an intersection of paths. 'As for suspects, the list grows longer. We have Amber Longstone, who openly despised Lucy. Mr Daws, Lucy's estranged father with a violent temper. Milly Davenport, who fled suspiciously and appears connected to Pinstripe. Mr Pendlebury's behaviour around the storage room raises questions. The mysterious Phileas Cowpepper lurking beneath the runway. And now, potentially, members of The Three Circles Society itself.'

'There's also the matter of Emily Brown's coded diary entries,' Muddleford concluded, tucking his notebook away. 'And we mustn't forget Lucy's last words`, "Mason Drange" - perhaps the absent boyfriend?'

A raucous honking overhead drew our attention skyward. A vast V-formation of Pink-footed Geese carved through the autumn air, their distinctive calls echoing across the gardens. Muddleford's head tilted back, following their path as they began their long journey to Iceland.

His distraction proved costly. The detective's foot caught the low box hedging, sending him stumbling forward. His arms windmilled as he fought to regain his balance, his notebook flying from his grasp to land among the precisely trimmed shrubs.

HG's hand shot out to steady him. 'Not to worry, Detective Sergeant. You're not the first man to make that mistake.' Her eyes sparkled with amusement. 'In fact, Henry VIII apparently did the same thing and tore his silk hose - and you know how Henry liked to show off his ample calves.'

Muddleford straightened his jacket, a flush creeping up his neck as he retrieved his notebook.

'Apparently, everyone present held their breath to see

how the King reacted.' HG continued, clearly enjoying the parallel. 'When he began laughing, so did they!'

The detective took a moment to compose himself, brushing imaginary dirt from his sleeves. His usual stern expression softening as he acknowledged HG's tale with the barest hint of a smile.

Through the crisp autumn air, a commotion from the direction of the house caught our attention. Young Peter, one of the footmen, hurtled down the stone steps and across the lawn toward us, his livery flapping in the wind.

'Good gracious, Peter. What on earth occasions you to exhibit such a turn of speed?' HG called out as the lad approached.

Peter bent double, hands on his knees, drawing in great gulps of air. His face had turned a shade of crimson that matched the Tudor brickwork behind him. 'Mr Webb says their an urgent telephone call.'

HG's face softened with amusement at the boy's breathless state. 'Then we shall preambulate back to the house at pace. Now, Peter, I think you've earned a reward for your efforts. Why don't you nip into the kitchen. Tell cook I've sent you for a piece of cake and a nice cup of tea.'

The boy's face lit up like a Christmas tree. He bobbed his head in thanks before darting off toward the kitchen entrance with remarkable speed for someone whose chest was already heaving.

Back in the grand hallway, Webb, known as Graham to the family, stood ramrod straight beside the telephone table, holding out the earpiece with the dignity only a lifetime of service could instil. HG took the receiver while Muddleford and I waited, curiosity mounting, as we caught only her side of the conversation.

'I see... indeed... well-well.'

She returned the earpiece to its cradle and turned to face us, her expression unreadable. 'A second example of serendipity in one day, in itself, the definition of serendipity.'

Muddleford and I exchanged puzzled glances.

'Never mind,' HG waved away our confusion. 'A young gentleman walked into Norwich police station not half-an-hour ago claiming to be Lucy Daws' suiter.'

Chapter Twenty

GENIUS OR FOOL?

Through the Georgian windows of the small dining room, the last rays of autumn sunlight cast a broad shadow across the parquet floor. With my friends, I sat down at the small round table as the butler set up the buffet. The gentle clink of silver against porcelain provided a soothing backdrop to our gathering.

HG had foregone her usual evening attire, remaining in her day clothes to match Muddleford and me. Chunky slouched in her chair, her oversized jumper and baggy trousers a stark contrast to the refined surroundings. She continued scribbling in the margins of Emily's diary, pausing occasionally to mutter under her breath.

Chandelier light illuminated our group, reflecting off the walls, watched over by portraits of our ancestors. A fire crackled in the Adams fireplace, keeping the evening chill at bay.

Behind the screen, the butler's methodical movements punctuated the quiet as he arranged the serving dishes. The soft whirr of the dumb waiter signalled cook's preparations below stairs were complete.

HG straightened in her chair, setting aside her sherry glass. 'Now then, about this young man claiming to be Lucy Daws' beau. The timing seems rather convenient, wouldn't you say? According to the telephone message, he gave his name as Lucien Dupont.

'French, then,' Muddleford said.

'Indeed,' added HG.

The notion of Lucy's mysterious French suitor stirred memories of her last moments. Her dying word - not "Mason Drange", but perhaps her beau, or someone else; her killer? I toyed with my napkin while my mind wandered through the possibilities.

Graham glided from behind the screen bearing a silver tureen of mushroom soup. The rich, earthy aroma filled the dining room as he ladled portions into our bowls. Steam curled upward in delicate wisps, catching the last rays of daylight through the windows.

The butler offered crusty bread from a silver basket. Only Chunky declined, her nose buried in Emily's diary as she scrawled notes in the margins. Her soup sat untouched, cooling beside her elbow.

For several minutes, the only sound was the occasional rustle of Chunky turning pages. The starter's velvety texture and perfect seasoning spoke to cook's expertise.

'Most peculiar timing, wouldn't you say?' HG broke the silence. 'This Monsieur Dupont materialising just now. Perhaps they had plans to meet in Paris.' My spoon paused halfway to my mouth. 'When Lucy failed to appear, he might have come looking for her.'

Muddleford nodded, dabbing his mouth with a napkin. 'A reasonable theory. Though rather convenient that he surfaces at this precise moment.' He set down his spoon with a gentle clink. 'How do we know he wasn't in the country all the time - even in Norwich on the night of Lucy's murder?'

HG shook her head, setting down her spoon. 'There's no evidence placing him at the Assembly Hall that evening. Not one witness mentioned seeing a Frenchman lurking about.'

The grandfather clock in the corner ticked as we absorbed this point. Graham cleared our soup bowls, his movements precise and practiced.

Muddleford's sharp features took on a keen expression. 'What if he was the one that drove Milly Davenport away from the scene at great speed?'

The suggestion hit like a thunderbolt. Even Chunky looked up from her decoding work, her grey eyes wide with interest.

HG's face lit up. 'Muddleford, you're brilliant.' She leaned forward. 'If true, it opens the case of the first death right up. Though why would an accessory to murder effectively hand himself in to the police?'

The flames in the fireplace cast dancing shadows across the wallpaper as I raced through the implications.

I suggested that the fellow might be playing a clever game - or a dangerous one, depending on one's point of view. By coming forward now as Lucy's concerned suitor, he's trying to show he had nothing to do with her murder.

'A calculated risk,' Muddleford mused, 'but one that could pay off if we've no way to connect him to Milly's getaway.'

HG's eyes sparkled with that familiar gleam she displayed whenever pieces of a puzzle began falling into place. 'Our Monsieur Dupont is either remarkably foolish or astonishingly clever with this manoeuvre.' She paused, swirling the remaining sherry in her glass. 'Though in my experience, those two traits often occupy opposite sides of the same coin.'

The rich aroma of roasted potatoes wafted through the air as Graham emerged from behind the screen bearing a silver serving dish. He placed it in the centre of our circular table, followed by platters of grilled asparagus spears and golden corn on the cob. Steam rose from each dish, carrying promises of a memorable meal.

A gentle breeze through the half-open window carried the distinct scent of the Norfolk coast. HG's nostrils flared as she inhaled. 'Ah, I suspect we're having fresh Cromer crab.' Her hands clasped together in obvious delight.

Graham confirmed her prediction moments later, presenting each of us with a steaming plate of the local delicacy. The crab meat glistened invitingly, garnished with fresh herbs and accompanied by a wedge of lemon.

Conversation ceased as we passed the side dishes around the table. Even Chunky set aside Emily's diary, though she kept it within arm's reach as she helped herself to a generous portion of potatoes. The first taste of sweet crab meat dissolved any remaining tension in the room. Muddleford's usually stern features softened as he savoured each carefully selected morsel.

The delicate flavour of the Cromer crab melted on my tongue as HG dabbed her lips with her napkin and turned her piercing gaze toward Muddleford.

'Tell me, Detective, what are your thoughts on Emily Brown's killer - the driver of that black car?'

Muddleford paused, his fork hovering between plate and mouth, loaded with a perfect combination of crab and asparagus. He finished his mouthful with deliberate care before responding.

'Something's been nagging at me about the case.' He set down his cutlery. 'We keep referring to the driver as "he" - but what if we're working from a false assumption? The driver could just as easily have been a woman.'

Chunky's head snapped up from Emily's diary. 'Of course, women can drive and commit murder.' She pushed her wire-rimmed spectacles up her nose. 'Unlike men, we're rather good at doing two things simultaneously.'

HG's shoulders shook with mirth as she regarded Muddleford's bewildered expression. 'My dear Detective, I believe you've been properly schooled in your assumptions.'

'Er... yes... yes, of course.' Muddleford's sharp features showed confusion, clearly not grasping the stereotype he'd employed.

HG's expression grew serious. 'But you raise an excellent point. We've been rather narrow-minded about this.' She reached for her wine glass. 'Why shouldn't Pinstripe employ women for his diabolical schemes? It would be exactly like him to exploit our prejudices about such matters.'

Graham materialised at my elbow with fresh vegetables, but my attention remained fixed on this new thread of investigation. The possibility that our killer driver was a woman cast the case in a different light.

Sleep proved elusive at Wymondham police station. Young Timothy Featherstone's lungs rivalled those of an opera singer, his night-time performance echoing through the station's substantial walls. Between the infant's vocal exercises and my mind racing over yesterday's developments at Thorpe Manor, the rest came in fragments.

The morning brought welcome relief. After breakfast, which consisted of a combination of toasted egg soldiers and playing, "I spy with my little eye" with the Featherstone's eldest, Muddleford and I set out for Norwich. My new moustache itched, but the disguise felt more natural with each passing day.

'Dupont agreed to meet us?' The question had nagged at me since Daws.

'Rather eagerly, according to the desk sergeant,' Muddleford said as I navigated around a farmer's cart. 'Called back within ten minutes of the station's message.'

The Tin Hut emerged from the morning mist, its corrugated iron construction standing out like a sore thumb from the architectural splendour that surrounded the abomination. Inside, the familiar smell of damp wood hung in the air.

Lucien Dupont cut an elegant figure against the station's shabby backdrop. He stood as we entered, revealing his impressive height. Dark hair swept back from strong features, and his tailored suit spoke of Parisian craftsmanship.

'Messieurs.' His accent rolled through the greeting. 'We shall speak about Lucy, yes?'

Muddleford stepped forward. 'Detective Sergeant Muddleford.' They shook hands. 'This is Special Constable Watson.'

My grip met Dupont's firm handshake. Up close, his eyes carried a weight that belied his polished exterior. Something in his manner suggested more than mere concern for Lucy's death.

Muddleford led us down a narrow corridor to what

passed for an interview room. A small window offered the only respite from the oppressive atmosphere, though the breeze carried more coal smoke than fresh air. The sparse furnishings comprised a worn beech table, four matching chairs, and two oak filing cabinets that had seen better days.

Lucien's elegant appearance stood out in the simple room. His intertwined fingers pulsed with tension.

Muddleford cleared his throat. 'Mr Dupont, regarding the tragic circumstances of Miss Daws's passing-'

Lucien's face transformed. The colour drained from his features as his eyes widened in horror. 'Passing? Non, non...' His hands flew to his face, fingers splayed across his eyes. His head shook back and forth in denial.

Muddleford shot me a worried glance. We'd assumed he knew.

The detective leapt from his chair, producing a pristine handkerchief from his breast pocket. The detective's long fingers pressed the cotton square into Lucien's trembling hands.

'My deepest apologies, Mr Dupont. I made the mistake of believing you were informed.'

Lucien's shoulders shook. The handkerchief dabbed at his eyes while his other hand gripped the table edge. 'My beautiful Lucy. How could they do this to you?'

The raw anguish in his voice pierced the dreary room's atmosphere. My new disguise felt ridiculous in the face of such genuine grief. Muddleford placed a steadying hand on Lucien's shoulder, the gesture bridging the gap between detective and bereaved.

'Perhaps we should postpone this interview.' Muddleford's voice carried a gentleness at odds with his usual stern demeanour. 'Allow you time to process this terrible news.'

'Non.' Lucien straightened, squaring his shoulders

despite the tears still marking his cheeks. 'I must know everything. Please.'

The determination in his eyes matched the set of his jaw. Here sat a man who'd loved Lucy Daws, not the suave Parisian musician we'd expected to encounter. My hand moved unconsciously to the notebook in my pocket, but Muddleford caught my eye and gave an imperceptible shake of his head. The questions could wait.

'Some water first, I think.' Muddleford nodded towards the door, and my feet carried me into the corridor before conscious thought caught up.

By the time I returned with the glass of water, Muddleford and Dupont were engaged in hushed conversation, the detective's gentle tone carrying through the half-open door. Taking care not to disturb their exchange, my footsteps fell softly on the worn pine floorboards as I placed the tumbler before Lucien.

From my position across the table, the Frenchman's anguish struck me anew. His proud frame had crumpled like a discarded newspaper, shoulders hunched against the weight of grief. Dark eyes fixed on Muddleford as the detective recounted the terrible events at the Assembly Hall.

The sharp lines of Lucien's face tightened with each detail. His fingers traced absent patterns on the misted glass of water, leaving ghostly marks that faded into nothing.

'We knew Miss Daws had a lover,' Muddleford explained, leaning forward. 'Her frequent trips to Paris also known about. But her last words led us to believe we were looking for an Englishman.'

Lucien's head lifted a little. 'Why would you think this?'

'She spoke the words "Mason Drange" before...' Muddleford's voice tailed off.

The Frenchman shook his head.

Muddleford reached over the tabletop to touch Lucian's hand. 'I understand this is difficult for you to take in, but the very least you deserve is the truth as we know it.'

The room fell silent. Each tick of the austere wall clock punctuated the heavy atmosphere, marking time as Lucien wrestled with his thoughts. My new moustache itched, but the gravity of the moment kept my hands still in my lap.

The office door creaked open, revealing young Constable Peters. His face carried the serious expression of someone determined not to disturb a poignant moment. The tin tray in his hands held three steaming mugs and a pressed glass sugar bowl.

Muddleford's subtle head shake stopped Peters in his tracks. The young officer stood frozen, one foot still hovering above the threshold, before retreating with remarkable grace. The door closed with barely a whisper, as though the interruption had never occurred.

Across the table, Lucien's lips moved in silent conversation with himself, his words too muted to reach our ears. His hands folded and manipulated his handkerchief into squares, smoothing it flat before beginning again.

Time stretched like treacle until finally, Lucien's head lifted. His eyes, still bright with unshed tears, met Muddleford's steady gaze.

'What happens now?' His accent thickened with emotion. 'I tell you now that my beautiful girl never messed with other men. I know this for sure.'

Muddleford leaned back in his chair, the wood creaking beneath his weight. A deep sigh escaped him as he studied the Frenchman's face.

'When you feel ready, Mr Dupont, I must ask you everything you know about Lucy. When and how you met. Her friends, her acquaintances. Her interests and hopes for the future.'

Lucien dabbed his eyes one final time with Muddleford's handkerchief. His shoulders straightened; jaw set firm.

'Non, we must continue. There is no time to rest. We must find who did this terrible thing to my Lucy.'

My eyes met Muddleford's, sharing a moment of concern over the Frenchman's state of mind.

'Are you certain, Mr Dupont?' Muddleford's tone carried gentle hesitation. 'This can wait until-'

'I will not have it any other way.' Lucien's voice gained strength with each word.

Muddleford paused, studying the man before him. 'Very well.'

The detective's chair scraped against the floorboards as he pushed back from the table. Opening the drawer, he retrieved a pristine manila folder and several sheets of foolscap paper. The folder landed on the table with a soft thump, its crisp edges a stark contrast to the worn wood beneath.

The detective arranged the papers inside with methodical precision, then produced a fountain pen from his inner jacket pocket. The nib scratched against the paper as he recorded the date, time, and 'Lucien Dupont' in his neat hand at the top of the first page.

Looking up from his writing, Muddleford addressed our witness. 'I need to keep a written record, Mr Dupont. Any information you provide may open new lines of investigation for the police to follow.'

Lucien nodded; his eyes fixed on the blank page before him. Muddleford gestured for Lucian to begin.

'It was in Paris, last spring.' He smiled despite his grief, remembering that perfect moment. 'I played guitar at Le

Chat Noir in Montmartre. Not the famous one from the posters - a tiny place that borrowed the name. The sort where cats wander in through the windows and make themselves at home on patron's laps.'

Lucian's fingers traced the water glass's rim.

'That evening, a ginger tabby decided my guitar case was the perfect spot for a nap. Lucy stood in the doorway, laughing at my attempts to remove him without stopping mid-song. The more I tried to shoo him away, the more determined he became to stay.'

'She wore a blue dress that matched the twilight sky. When she sat down, the cat immediately abandoned my case to curl up in her lap instead. The traitor.'

Muddleford's pen scratched across the paper, his eyes occasionally meeting Lucian's to show empathy.

'We talked until Dawn. The owner kept bringing coffee. Lucy's French was perfect - she'd studied people all the time. My belle was...how do you say, magnificent. We walked along the Seine as the sun rose, sharing a warm baguette from the first bakery to open.'

'That sounds idyllic,' said Muddleford as he offered a gentle smile to the Frenchman.

'She had come to Paris to escape her father's plans for her future. She wanted to dance, to model, to live life on her own terms. Her spirit...' His voice caught. 'Her spirit was like watching a bird take flight.'

Lucian hesitated for a moment as though he recalled the memory of her laughter echoed in his mind.

'Do you know what she said when I asked to see her again? She reminded me about the sleeping cat in the cafe window and said, "Well, I can't disappoint our matchmaker, can I?"'

The pain of loss struck fresh as Lucian reached for the water glass, grateful for its coolness against his palm.

Muddleford showed an admirable skill at shorthand as he kept up with the Frenchman's recollections in real time.

'Do you want to take a rest, Lucian? I know how difficult this is for you.'

Mr Dupont offered the detective a half-smile. 'Non...I mean, no. This helps me to remember my love, and if it helps in finding the barbarian who hurt her, then it is all worth it.

'Then let's continue, shall we?' My colleague's pen touched the paper, ready to record every word spoken.

'After that first night, we were inseparable. I showed Lucy every corner of Paris - not the tourist spots, but the real Paris. The hidden cafes in Le Marais, the secret gardens behind ancient walls. We'd spend hours in tiny bookshops where the owners knew my name, and Lucy would curl up in worn armchairs, lost in French poetry.'

Lucian's fingers moved rhythmically on the table, mimicking a guitar melody.

'I tried teaching her guitar. Mon Dieu, she was terrible!'

A laugh escaped despite his grief.

'But her giggle when she hit wrong notes - it was like sunshine breaking through clouds. And those eyes... bleu-gris, like the Seine in winter. They changed with her moods - stormy when she spoke of her father, bright as stars when she talked about her dreams.'

Lucian paused, reaching for the water glass.

'She confided in me about her father one night at Montmartre. How he wanted her to stay in England and living at home with him. "I won't live in a cage," she told me. Her determination burned so bright. America was her dream. She'd read about the Ziegfeld Follies, about Broadway. "Just imagine," she'd say, "my name in lights on Times Square!" When she spoke like that, her face lit up. I'd never seen anyone with such...such fire.'

'Lucy was starting to make connections, too. The fashion shows were opening doors. There was an agent in New York who'd shown interest.'

His voice caught.

'She was so close to everything she wanted.'

Muddleford's pen scratched across the paper, recording every word.

'The last time I saw her...'

The words stuck in his throat.

'She was so excited about something. Said she had news that would change everything.'

'Ma belle Lucy.' Lucien's head dropped forward, the handkerchief rising to shield his eyes.

I leaned towards Muddleford and whispered, 'He asked where they took his beautiful Lucy from him.'

Chapter Twenty-One

AN AWAKENING

Lucien's gratitude to Muddleford came in soft, measured French, his musician's hands trembling as they gestured at the space.

Before we reached the main hall, Pendlebury materialised from a side door, straightening his jacket out of habit. The timing seemed uncanny.

'I'm certain that bloke has a sixth sense when someone crosses his threshold,' Muddleford muttered under his breath.

We navigated the post-fashion show mess across the polished floor, Pendlebury's gaze a persistent shadow on our progress. The runway stretched before us like a ghost ship's plank, its white surface dulled by days of neglect.

My boots echoed against the wooden stage as we climbed the steps. Lucien paused at the top, his shoulders rigid. Through the wings, past coils of rope and forgotten costume racks, the door to that fatal room stood part open. The sight stopped him cold.

As Pendlebury watched from above, Muddleford

supported the Frenchman. The small room waited, unchanged since that terrible evening. Dust danced in the cool breeze from the vast hall, the lingering perfume a ghostly memory of the fashion show's splendour.

The small room held more ghosts than just Lucy's memory, leaving us in weighted silence as Lucien stood at the threshold.

'So this is where it happened.' His voice barely carried above a whisper.

He remained motionless in the doorway, eyes fixed on some distant point within. The pain etched across his features told me he was seeing Lucy there - perhaps their last goodbye, their final shared moment before fate tore them apart.

'I smell her perfume.' Lucien drew in a deep breath, his eyes drifting closed. 'There are other notes here, too.'

Muddleford stepped forward. 'Your musical background must provide some comfort in these moments.'

Lucien's eyes snapped open, fixing on the detective. 'You misunderstand, Detective. My father was a perfumer in Paris. He taught me about notes - the different fragrances that create each unique scent. Every perfume tells its own story.'

'At least Clara Brightman was with her in those last moments,' Muddleford offered quietly. 'Providing what comfort she could.'

Lucien's nostrils flared as he sampled the air again. 'Lucy told me all about her friend, and what perfume she wore. There are two other notes in this room. Another woman has been here. I cannot name the perfume, but it has Oud, and Ambergris in it...it is an expensive perfume. I can tell you this.'

My nostrils detected nothing but musty air and stale

dust as I drew in a careful breath. Beside me, Muddleford performed the same exercise, his shoulders lifting in a silent shrug that spoke volumes.

'The models' dressing room sits just down the hall,' Muddleford said, gesturing toward the door. 'What you're picking up likely drifted from there.'

Lucien shook his head. 'Someone who wears Ambergris has means beyond a model's salary. It comes from sperm whales - one of the rarest perfume ingredients in the world. Only the most exclusive houses use it. Someone's lover has expensive taste.'

'Perhaps we should check the dressing room?' Muddleford suggested. 'See if you detect the same scent there?'

A cacophony of powder, rouge, and perfume filled the air as the heavy door creaked open. Lucien stepped into the centre of the space, his eyes falling shut in concentration.

'Non, it is not here.' His voice carried absolute certainty.

'Well, perhaps it's simply lingering from the show night,' Muddleford offered with forced lightness. However, the concern in his eyes told a different story. This extra detail added yet another layer of complexity to our already bewildering investigation.

Lucien cast one final, lingering glance at the small room where Lucy's life had ended. His shoulders slumped beneath the weight of grief as Muddleford guided us from the stage area. Our footsteps echoed through the empty hall, each step carrying us further from that chamber of memories and loss.

The foyer's grandeur seemed hollow now, its ornate columns and marble floors stripped of their usual splendour. Right on cue, Pendlebury materialised by the entrance, his perpetual presence as reliable as a church bell.

The autumn air hit us with a bracing chill as we stepped

outside. Muddleford turned to Lucien, his expression softening.

'Let us walk you to your lodgings.'

Lucien shook his head, his dark hair catching the weak sunlight. 'Non, Merci. My thoughts need ordering. A walk through your city will help clear my mind.' His attempt at a smile flickered briefly. 'Perhaps my feet will find traces of my Huguenot ancestors in these streets, non? They came here in the sixteenth century, after all.'

The smile faded as quickly as it had appeared. Without another word, he turned and vanished into the warren of Norwich's medieval streets, his tall figure growing smaller until the ancient buildings swallowed him completely.

Muddleford watched the space where Lucien had disappeared for several heartbeats before turning to me.

'We should head back to Thorpe Manor. See how Chunky's getting on with Emily's diary?'

The journey back to Thorpe Manor tested both patience and posteriors. The old police car shook and rattled along Norfolk's bumpy back roads.

Taking the scenic route seemed a polite way of describing our meandering path. The detective's insistence on doubling back and switching directions would have confused even the most determined tail, though the car's distinctive death rattle probably gave away our position to anyone within earshot.

Halfway through our circuitous journey, a flash of movement caught Muddleford's eye. A roe deer emerged from the thick hedgerow about fifty yards ahead, its delicate form frozen in the middle of the narrow lane.

Life or death hinged on our four-legged friend due to the erratic behaviour of the Morris's brakes. The deer cast us one disdainful glance before melting back into the hedgerow with elegant indifference.

After an hour of navigating lanes barely wide enough for a bicycle, let alone our wheezing chariot, the welcome sight of Thorpe Manor's gates appeared through the windscreen. Graham stood at the open front door, sporting a brown apron over his usual attire, as he attacked the brass doorknob with metal polish and vigour.

The car wheezed to a halt with a final shudder of protest. Extracting ourselves from the cramped confines proved an exercise in controlled contortion. My joints cracked in protest as I unfolded myself from the driver's seat.

'Her Grace awaits you both in the Morning Room, gentlemen,' Graham announced, moving to remove his apron.

'No need to interrupt you,' Muddleford said in a soft tone. 'We can find our own way.'

Graham acknowledged this with a nod as we passed into the grand hallway's embrace.

The Morning Room's warm glow enveloped us as we stepped through the doorway. My steps faltered at the unexpected sight before me - Inspector Whipple stood framed in the French doors, deep in conversation with Chunky.

HG rose from her wingback chair, her face lighting up with genuine warmth. 'Welcome back, gentlemen.'

Whipple and Chunky turned in unison, their matching smiles carrying hints of shared secrets. The inspector looked well-rested after his few days in London.

'And so, we're together at last,' HG declared, clasping her hands together. 'Time for tea and cake in celebration!'

The thought of Graham abandoning his passionate assault on the Manor's brassware prompted me to speak up. 'Graham is rather occupied at the moment. Perhaps I should pop down to the kitchen and arrange things with cook?'

'Don't be silly,' Chunky interjected, already moving towards the door. 'I need to nip back to my room for a minute, anyway. I'll sort everything with the kitchen on my way - back in a jiffy.'

She slipped past me, the familiar sight of baggy trousers and an oversized jumper disguising her frame.

'Only Poppy missing now,' HG mused, settling back into her chair. 'Though that's about to be corrected, I think.'

The distant growl of a motorcycle engine caught my attention. The sound grew steadily louder until a familiar BSA pulled up outside the French doors, its chrome work gleaming in the afternoon sun.

My heart skipped as the rider removed helmet and goggles, revealing Poppy's radiant smile. Without conscious thought, my feet carried me to the doors, fingers fumbling with the brass handle in my haste.

HG's laughter rang out behind me. 'Do you think he's keen, Arthur?' she said with unmistakable mirth.

Whipple glanced between HG and me, his usual stern expression softening. 'I rather think "keenness" might be an understatement.'

Poppy stepped through the doorway, her hand finding mine with natural ease. The leather of her riding gloves was still warm from the journey.

'Afternoon,' she called out cheerfully, then nodded towards the inspector. 'Whipple.'

Poppy unzipped her leather jacket, draping it over a

nearby armchair. Her helmet and goggles found a temporary home on the polished floorboards beside her feet.

Her arm brushed against mine as we stood by the French doors, sending a subtle current of warmth through my body. The early afternoon sun cast long shadows across the Morning Room, while conversation flowed easily between us all.

Amid the pleasantries, Chunky reappeared with a trolly ladened with edible delights.

Poppy's face lit up with curiosity. 'So, you're the famous Chunky I've been hearing so much about. Pleased to meet you, I'm—'

'And you're Poppy.' Chunky's eyes sparkled with mischief. 'I, too, have had my listening ears on.'

Laughter rippled through the room. Even Whipple's stern features cracked into a smile.

Moving to help Chunky with the tea things, my hands reached for the familiar ritual of setting up the side table. Delicate cups clinked as they found saucers, while cook's famous Victoria sponge took pride of place on a silver cake stand.

The group settled into comfortable chairs as Chunky, and I distributed cups of steaming Earl Grey. Poppy perched on the arm of my chair, close enough that her knee pressed against me.

Strange how tragedy could forge such unlikely bonds. Conversation flowed as smoothly as the tea. Chunky's quirky personality appeared to captivate the entire room, with her humour eliciting soft laughter from Muddleford, who typically maintained such rigid composure. Poppy's presence beside me felt natural, comfortable, as though she'd always been part of our peculiar circle.

Half an hour slipped past in pleasant discourse until

Whipple cleared his throat, his expression shifting. 'Pleasant as this is, we should turn our minds to business.'

The change in atmosphere was immediate. Teacups found their way back to saucers, and plates set aside as everyone adjusted their positions. Poppy slid from the arm of my chair into a proper seat, though her hand remained close enough that our fingers still brushed occasionally.

Whipple extracted a worn notebook from his jacket pocket, its pages ruffled and dog-eared from constant use. Muddleford followed suit, producing an identical notebook that looked considerably newer.

Chunky dug deep into one of her voluminous trouser pockets, fishing around until she emerged triumphant with Emily Brown's diary. The leather-bound volume looked almost dainty in her large hands, its pages marked with various bits of paper poking out at odd angles.

HG settled back in her chair; hands folded in her lap. Her grey eyes swept across our assembled group, taking in each face in turn. 'Now, where shall we begin?'

Muddleford settled deeper into his armchair. 'Young Monsieur Dupont proved most illuminating. His reaction to Lucy's death couldn't have been more genuine.'

The detective's assessment piqued HG's curiosity. 'How can you be so certain?'

'Several factors. First, there's the matter of his collapse upon hearing the news. Not the theatrical swooning one might expect from someone playing a part, but a proper physical shutdown. The colour drained from his face so rapidly as the fellow swayed in his chair.'

'Grief can be performed,' HG pointed out.

'True enough.' Muddleford nodded. 'But it's the smaller details that convinced me. During our conversation, he kept touching a small silver locket - Lucy's gift to him. More telling was his extensive knowledge of French perfumery. He spoke at length about Lucy's favourite scent, Essence Royale. He even identified the precise notes she preferred - jasmine and tuberose over the more common rose base.'

'And this proves his innocence?' HG responded.

'Combined with his genuine shock at the news, yes. A man planning murder rarely memorises his victim's perfume preferences down to the individual scent notes. His grief was raw, unscripted.'

HG's gaze shifted to Whipple, who gave an almost imperceptible nod of agreement. The inspector's usual scepticism seemed satisfied by Muddleford's assessment.

'Besides,' Muddleford added, 'he provided train tickets and hotel receipts proving he was in Paris the night of Lucy's murder. The French police have already confirmed his alibi.'

Poppy leaned forward, her elbows resting on her knees. 'From what you've described, Lucien's alibi seems water-tight. The French police wouldn't confirm his whereabouts without thorough checking.'

'Perhaps so,' HG replied, looking thoughtful. 'Let's set that thread aside for now. While you've been investigating Monsieur Dupont, my time hasn't been idle.'

'Graham and I have been combing through the Manor's archives. Several interesting documents surfaced regarding the Three Circles Society. It seems my great-uncle Augustus kept detailed records of their activities during the 1860s.'

The mention of Augustus caught my attention. The portrait of that stern-faced gentleman hung in the library, his penetrating gaze following visitors across the room.

'His journals describe meetings held right here at Thorpe Manor.' HG gestured towards the window. 'The Society apparently favoured the old summer house for their gatherings. Augustus noted particular interest in their distinctive ring ceremony.'

Chunky perked up. 'Ring ceremony?'

'Yes. New members received a silver ring bearing the three interlocking circles. Augustus doodled different versions in his journal. HG picked a chocolate biscuit. 'What's interesting is his observation that women were excluded from full membership until 1890.'

'That timing correlates with Queen Victoria's influence,' Whipple noted. 'She took quite an interest in secret societies during that period.'

'Precisely.' HG nodded. 'Augustus documented everything. Dates, names, locations. He even preserved correspondence between founding members. The thing is, from what I read, the group's aims were altruistic…at least then. If that's the case, one wonders what happened. '

My gaze drifted to the window, where the old summer house stood visible through the shrubbery. If only the weathered structure could tell its secrets.

Chunky shifted forward in her chair, the oversized jumper bunching around her shoulders. 'Your findings about the rings dovetail perfectly with what Emily's diary revealed.'

She flipped open the leather-bound volume, various paper markers fluttering. The document's pages were filled with a mix of random letters, numbers, and drawings.

'Emily used a variation of the Vigenère cipher. Most people would have missed the key entirely, but she left subtle clues in her sketches. Little circular patterns hidden in the margins, always in groups of three.'

Her fingers traced one such drawing. 'The cipher key was "THREE CIRCLES" - rather on the nose, but effective.

Once I had that, the rest fell into place. I do like a good polyalphabetic substitution cipher.'

'A what?' coughed Whipple.

'Oh, sorry,' Chunky began. 'I do so get carried away with this sort of thing. To explain, the cipher uses multiple substitution alphabets to encrypt the text, see?'

'Er...not really, but then that doesn't matter as long as you do,' Whipple replied, scratching his chin in bemusement.

Chunky smiled at Whipple. 'The decoded entries paint quite a picture. Emily had been tasked with tracking certain society members who'd gone rogue. She mentions several people receiving silver rings; always followed by the phrase "bound to silence".'

The room had grown silent, everyone engrossed as Chunky continued. 'But here's where it gets interesting - Emily wrote about someone called "P" who was corrupting the society's original purpose. According to her notes, this "P" person had started selling membership rings to wealthy individuals who hadn't gone through the proper initiation...but it gave them access to significant power and influence.

My shoulder brushed against Poppy's as she leaned closer to examine the diary pages Chunky held out. The familiar aroma of motor oil and lavender momentarily distracted my thoughts.

'Emily was clearly onto something,' Chunky continued. 'The question is, what did she discover about those rings that got her killed?'

The weight of Chunky's revelation settled over the Morning Room like a heavy fog. Even the cheerful afternoon sunlight streaming through the French doors seemed subdued.

Whipple took up the discussion; his notebook rustling as he flipped through its well-worn pages.

'My time in London proved rather enlightening,' he began, adjusting his position in the leather armchair. 'Scotland Yard's archives revealed some interesting connections. Our friend Pinstripe has quite the colourful history - though pinning him down proved as difficult as knitting smoke.'

My fingers found Poppy's hand resting on the chair arm between us. Her warmth anchored me as Whipple continued.

'The Yard's intelligence suggests he operates through a network of carefully placed associates, both here and abroad. Never directly involved, always three steps removed from any situation. They've tracked his movements across Europe, South America, even as far as Singapore - though we can never quite catch up.'

HG's expression remained neutral, though her fingers tightened as her hands remained in her lap.

'As for our other persons of interest,' Whipple continued, 'several promising leads emerged. The Cunliffs' alibis check out - they were photographed at the precise time of Lucy's death, posing with the Lord Mayor's wife. However, Amber Longstone's background raises some red flags. Her claimed modelling experience in Paris? Completely fabricated.'

Sunlight shone on HG's steaming tea while Graham silently reappeared with more drinks. The familiar ritual seemed at odds with the gravity of Whipple's words.

Whipple's voice carried across the Morning Room, his words measured and precise. Poppy's hand remained warm in mine, her thumb tracing patterns on my palm.

A single pair of shoes was the most concerning discovery, Whipple explained.

'Shoes?' HG exclaimed.

Whipple shot his host a serious look. 'I checked the photographs taken by forensics on the night. There were several shoe prints on the dusty floor of that tiny room. While in London, I asked the local team in Norwich to check every shoe that the fashion models brought with them. We found a match to four out of five prints. One set remains unaccounted for…our task now it to find those shoes, and their owner.'

Chapter Twenty-Two

A STRANGER RETURNS

HG's suggestion that we each retire for a couple of hours allowed the afternoon's revelations to swirl through my mind as I lay on the familiar bed. Next door, HG would do what she always did; arrange the facts in that remarkable mind of hers, piecing together the puzzle while the rest of us struggled to see the complete picture.

The clues—Chunky's diary, Whipple's discoveries, and a shoe print—were significant, but their link was a mystery. The Three Circles Society's corruption by this 'P' figure, Emily Brown's final discovery about the rings, Lucy's murder - they had to be connected, but how?

My thoughts drifted to Poppy, her hand in mine during Whipple's revelations. A bright spot in this dark business.

Sleep tugged at the edges of consciousness, and father stood beside me, just as he had that day at those gates. His worn tweed jacket smelled of pipe tobacco and leather, his kind eyes filled with tears he tried to hide.

'It's for the best, son,' his voice echoed somewhere in my unconsciousness. 'Your mother gone, and I need to keep you safe. This place will give you what I cannot - a proper life, education, purpose.'

'You could have stayed,' my dream-self whispered.

'No, lad. Some things can't be mended. But look at you now - solving murders, protecting the innocent. Your mother would be proud.'

The scent of his tobacco faded as sleep properly took hold, his words floating like smoke rings in the still air: 'You found your path, Rex. That's all a father could want.'

The dream shifted, and father's expression changed - that familiar mix of pride and pain I'd seen the day he left me.

'But why did you really go?' My childhood self, reached for answers that had eluded me for decades.

Father's hands moved restlessly, performing one of his old coin tricks - making a silver coin disappear and reappear between his fingers. 'All shows must end, my boy. The curtain falls, the audience leaves, and the theatre grows dark.'

'You could have taught me your magic.'

'The greatest trick is to keep those we love safe.' His voice caught. 'Sometimes, the only way to protect someone is to let them go. Like your mother always said - better a clean break than a festering wound.'

The silver coin vanished one final time. 'There are men in this world who deal with darker magic than mine. They take everything - hopes, dreams, futures. I couldn't let them take you too.'

'Were you in trouble, father?'

His eyes grew distant. 'Trouble? No, son. Just the last act of a tired old performer who couldn't keep up with the changing times. The world moves on, and so must you.' But his trembling hands betrayed the lie.

'You were protecting me from something.'

'From growing up too fast. From seeing the ugliness behind the curtain.' He squeezed my shoulder. 'I gave you to people who could offer security, education - a chance at a better life than a travelling player could provide.'

The scent of greasepaint and sawdust drifted through the dream, bringing with it memories of touring with father's magic show. His hands, rough from years of sleight-of-hand practice, moved through the familiar motions of the cup-and-ball trick.

'Remember this one?' His eyes crinkled at the corners. 'You used to beg me to teach you.'

The red velvet balls danced between the brass cups, their movement hypnotic. Each tap of metal against wood echoed with the weight of unspoken truths.

'There were other tricks you never showed me.'

His shoulders tensed. The cups stilled. 'Some secrets are better left buried, son.'

The dream shifted, and we stood in the wings of a theatre. The same theatre where mother had collapsed during father's performance. The musty curtains pressed against my face, their texture both familiar and suffocating.

'You left because of her death, didn't you?'

Father's fingers traced the edge of his top hat, the same one he'd worn that final night. 'Death has many faces, Rex.'

The theatre lights dimmed, casting strange shadows across his features. In that moment, he looked older than his years, burdened by knowledge he couldn't share.

'The Three Circles Society - did they-'

His hand gripped my arm with sudden force. 'Some questions lead down dangerous paths.' His voice dropped to a whisper. 'Remember what I taught you about misdirection? Sometimes the truth hides in plain sight, like a coin beneath a cup. Trust your instincts, son. You've always known how to spot the trick behind the magic.'

The dream began dissolving around the edges, father's form growing translucent. 'Tell me the truth,' I pleaded.

'I already have, in the only way I can.' His smile was sad. 'Some truths are better left in shadows, young 'un. Like any good magic trick - the mystery is kinder than the revelation.'

'Are you still alive, father?' The question escaped before I could stop it.

Father's smile held all the warmth of those long-ago summer evenings when we'd practice card tricks in the garden. 'I'll always be alive for you, son.'

'I don't understand.'

'You will.' He touched my shoulder. 'When you have children of your own?'

A familiar figure materialised beside him - Poppy, radiant in a summer dress, yet a grease smudge on one cheek. She and father exchanged glances filled with such natural affection, such easy understanding, as though they'd known each other forever.

'What's troubling you, Rex?' Poppy's voice carried that gentle, teasing note I'd grown to cherish.

Tears welled up, hot and unexpected. The terror of abandonment, of being left behind again, rose like a tide. Memories flooded back - watching father walk away, the cold iron gates of Horizons closing behind him, years of wondering why I wasn't enough to make him stay.

Poppy's fingers stroked through my hair, cool and soothing. The simple gesture unleashed more tears.

'You'll never be alone again, son.' Father's voice held absolute certainty.

Another voice cut through the dream-haze, familiar and insistent. HG, calling my name with increasing urgency...

'Rex... Rex...'

The gentle pressure of fingers through my hair drew me from the dream's depths. HG's smiling face swam into focus, perched on the edge of my bed.

'That nightmare, dear boy?' Her silk handkerchief dabbed at my forehead, cool against fevered skin. The familiar scent of rose water wafted from the fabric.

'It's always the same dream.' My voice cracked. 'Father leaving me at those gates. But this time...'

HG's eyes crinkled with warmth. 'This time?'

'Poppy was there. She and father seemed to know each other, though they've never met. It felt... right somehow.'

A knowing smile spread across HG's face, deepening the fine lines around her eyes. 'What a lovely thing that is.'

The confusion must have shown on my face. Dreams of father usually left me hollow, aching with a yearning for him. Yet this time, despite the tears, something felt different. Warmer.

HG's hand brushed my cheek with maternal tenderness. 'When Poppy feels the time is right, then you'll understand.'

HG's gentle expression shifted to something lighter, mischievous even. 'Now then, what would you like cook to prepare for dinner? Anything you fancy.'

The question pulled me from the lingering traces of sleep. After a moment's consideration, my lips curved into a smile. 'Let's have cook make Whipple's favourites: eel soup, sausage and mash with peas, and bread pudding.'

A rich laugh burst from HG as she ruffled my hair with her open palm, the gesture so motherly it made my chest tight. 'Trying to get into Arthur's good books, are we?'

'Not sure that's even possible.'

'Oh, my dear boy.' HG's voice softened. 'You should know by now that Arthur holds you in the highest regard. He'd never tell you so directly, of course - not his way at all.'

The revelation settled warm in my chest, like a good brandy on a cold evening.

Rising from her perch on my bed, HG smoothed her skirts. 'I'll see you in the Drawing Room for pre-dinner drinks after the first gong.'

She crossed to the jib door connecting our rooms, the hidden opening blending seamlessly with the wall's wooden panelling when closed. The door clicked shut behind her, leaving me alone with thoughts considerably lighter than before my impromptu nap.

The library's warmth enveloped us in its familiar embrace. Relaxed in his armchair, Whipple enjoyed his favourite childhood foods. His waistcoat buttons strained slightly as he settled deeper into the cushions, brandy balloon cupped in both hands.

The fire crackled, sending dancing shadows across the oak-panelled walls. Graham had followed HG's instructions. Only three lamps cast their gentle glow, creating intimate pools of amber light that made the spacious room feel snug and welcoming.

'About the fashion show, HG,' Poppy's voice carried across the comfortable silence. 'Are we still planning to go ahead with it? As a tribute to Lucy, and now, Emily?'

Firelight glinted on HG's crystal glass as she swirled her whisky. 'Initially, the show was meant to smoke out our killer.' She paused, studying the dancing liquid. 'But now... now everything's more complex.'

Whipple, softened by brandy. 'The Three Circles' involvement made a big difference.

'Perhaps we could arrange something smaller?' Muddleford suggested from his position by the fireplace. 'A private memorial service instead?'

'The models are getting restless,' Poppy noted. 'Most want to return to London, even though HG sorted the money issue out. Clara's the only one truly invested in honouring Lucy's memory.'

HG's gaze remained fixed on her glass, though her mind was clearly elsewhere. 'We need something that serves both purposes - paying proper respect while exposing the killer.'

The fire popped, sending a shower of sparks up the chimney. The sound seemed to punctuate the gravity of our situation.

'What if we made sure everyone that we're interested in knows about whatever we decide to do?' The words came slowly as Poppy's idea took shape.

HG's eyebrows lifted; her whisky forgotten in mid-swirl. 'Go on.'

'A soiree. Here at Thorpe Manor. They'd have to respond somehow, wouldn't they?'

Muddleford straightened from his position by the fire. 'That's rather clever. The last thing anyone might expect.'

'We could position it as an update on the investigation,' Poppy added, her eyes bright. 'Get ahead of the rumours already circulating.'

'But we'd need to know who we're dealing with first,' Whipple cautioned, setting his brandy aside. 'Otherwise, we're just shooting in the dark.'

HG's expression shifted from contemplative to determined. 'Poppy is right. A soiree is perfect - but not just as an update.' She set her glass down with a clunk as it contacted the mahogany side table. 'We'll use it to expose them. The perpetrators will come expecting platitudes and vague assurances. Instead, they shall walk into our trap.'

'The element of surprise,' Muddleford nodded. 'They won't have time to prepare or react.'

'Precisely,' HG's eyes gleamed. 'And with the press there to witness everything, there'll be nowhere for them to hide.'

The warm glow of brandy settled in my stomach as I watched the interplay between my companions. Chunky shifted forward, her sharp features catching the firelight.

'Hold on a moment,' she raised her hand, cutting through the enthusiasm. 'We're getting ahead of ourselves, aren't we? We've got two deaths, multiple suspects, and a shadowy organisation that may or may not be involved. What exactly would we expose at this soiree?'

My gaze drifted to Muddleford, who nodded. 'She's right. We can't risk a gathering only to present theories and speculation.'

The fire crackled in the silence that followed. HG's eyes sparkled with that familiar look - the one that meant she was several steps ahead of us all.

'On the contrary,' she gathered up her glass and swirled its contents. 'Announcing the soiree now is precisely what we need. Think of it as setting the stage.'

'But without concrete evidence-' Chunky began.

'The evidence will come,' HG insisted, her voice dropping to that compelling tone she used when sharing her most brilliant insights. 'By announcing our intentions early, we force their hand. They'll think we're closing in, even if we're not there yet. The pressure of an impending public revelation will make them desperate.'

'And desperate people make mistakes,' Muddleford took a deep breath; understanding dawning across his features.

The logic was beautiful in its simplicity. Even Chunky's sceptical expression softened as she considered the strategy.

Poppy stood to stretch her legs by taking a turn about the library, before turning back to HG. 'When were you thinking of holding this intimate gathering?'

Muddleford spoke before HG could answer. 'We'll need at least three more days to be certain about our suspect. There are still loose ends to tie up.'

Chunky's oversized jumper rustled as she shifted position. 'The task ahead is enormous. We need to verify alibis, connect all these disparate threads, and develop a watertight plan. Perhaps we should wait until we're absolutely certain?'

HG's silver hair gleamed as she shook her head. 'Saturday evening. That gives us three days to solve both cases.'

My eyebrows rose without intention. The timeline seemed ambitious, even by HG's standards.

'Rex, Muddleford,' HG continued, 'you'd best stay here at the Manor rather than returning to Wymondham. We can't afford to waste time travelling back and forth.'

Whipple set down his brandy glass with a soft clink. 'It's almost certain we're being watched. Someone will have noticed both of you are here.'

The fire popped, making me jump. Through the window, darkness pressed against the glass. For a moment, the sensation of being observed sent a chill down my spine despite the room's warmth. Poppy caught my eye and offered a reassuring smile that did more to settle my nerves than any amount of brandy could manage.

The familiar comfort of my bedroom at Thorpe Manor offered little solace tonight. Even the cherished photographs of my parents seemed to watch me with concerned expressions as I paced the carpet. My mind refused to settle, spinning through the day's revelations like a motor running too fast.

The hand-painted Chinese wallpaper, with its delicate birds and flowers, was usually calming. Tonight, the stylised patterns only reminded me of Emily Brown's coded diary entries. Each elegant brush stroke morphed into another potential clue we might have missed.

Perhaps a hot bath would help. The Manor's ancient plumbing groaned as I turned towards the connecting bathroom. That's when the sound caught my attention - a muffled voice from HG's room next door.

The familiar cadence of her voice when deep in thought was something I knew well. Many nights I'd heard her working through cases aloud, each problem dissected with surgical precision. But this was different. The tone carried an edge of urgency I'd rarely heard before.

My hand hesitated on the brass bathroom door handle. The voice continued, too muted to make out words but clear enough to raise the hairs on the back of my neck. Something about it felt wrong. After the events in London and Emily Brown's death, I'd come to expect the worst.

The floorboard beneath my foot creaked as I stepped away from the bathroom. Standing still in the darkness, I held my breath and listened.

The voice from HG's room fell silent. Fear gripped me as I pictured Pinstripe's men already inside, waiting. Was this a kidnap, or worse?

Muddleford's room lay just thirty feet down the corridor. Whipple's quarters were further, near the east wing. The jib door between my room and HG's offered the quickest access, but those damned squeaky hinges would give me away.

My gaze fell on the bathroom's porcelain soap dish. The bar of Palmolive soap might work. Moving with careful steps, bare feet silent on the floorboards, my fingers closed around the smooth soap.

The jib door's brass hinges gave off a dull gleam in the darkness. Working quickly but quietly, I ran the soap along each hinge point, praying the waxy lubricant would do its job. A bead of sweat rolled down my temple as muffled voices continued from HG's room.

Gripping the door handle, I eased it forward inch by inch. The soap worked - no betraying squeak came from the hinges. Through the widening gap, faint light spilled from beneath HG's door, creating strange shadows in the short passage between our rooms.

Her voice grew clearer now, speaking in measured tones to someone else present. My fingers tightened on the heavy door as I continued to ease it open, stopping every few inches to apply more soap to the hinges.

Finally I pressed myself against the wall in the cramped space. The gap around HG's door threw thin ribbons of light across my feet. She was speaking to another person, the words still indistinct but the cadence clear.

Without warning, the handle of her door turned with a metallic click.

My heart nearly stopped as the door opened, revealing the same pinstriped figure from Claridge's. The dim lamplight made him appear more menacing than our previous encounter.

The bar of soap felt childish in my hand now. Heat

crept up my neck as he gestured towards HG's sitting room with an almost theatrical flourish.

'Do join us, Rex. The soap was a good idea, but not quite good enough.'

Looking down at the fragrant bar still clutched in my right hand, embarrassment washed over me. The situation felt childish, like a schoolboy prank gone wrong.

HG stood still, her face an unreadable mask. Our eyes met briefly as I sought some indication of the situation's gravity.

Turning back to our uninvited guest, I kept my voice steady. 'Do you have a real name, or should I keep calling you Pinstripe?'

His smile widened, revealing perfectly aligned teeth. 'My name is of no concern, a mere detail. Though I must thank you for the non-de-plume. Rather caught on, hasn't it? Far nicer than some things I've been called over the years.'

Without dignifying his attempt at levity with a response, I stepped through the doorway and moved to stand beside HG. The familiar scent of her French perfume provided an odd comfort in this surreal moment.

'Do sit down.' His tone made it clear this wasn't a request.

HG settled onto her chaise-lounge while I chose a silk-covered carver chair, keeping both of them in my line of sight. Pinstripe perched himself on the edge of the bed between us.

'Now,' he said, 'to begin.'

Pinstripe stood, his pristine suit barely showed a wrinkle despite the late hour and his unannounced arrival.

'What fun it's been,' he drawled, 'watching you all

scurry about these past few days.' His gaze fixed on HG. 'Even drafting in a code breaker. Quite resourceful.'

My fingers gripped the arms of the carver chair, the wood's smooth finish offering little comfort. The urge to leap up and tackle this smug intruder grew stronger with each passing second.

'I met her in Berlin, just as you did - imagine my surprise. Small world, wouldn't you say, Eleanor?'

HG's expression remained impassive, though her shoulders tensed at mention of Berlin.

'And Edinburgh.' His thin lips curved into a knowing smile. 'That was quite a ruse, wasn't it?'

The muscles in my legs coiled, ready to spring. But what good would that do? He'd likely anticipated such a move and no doubt he had a pistol about his person.

HG's voice cut through the tension like ice. 'A necessary precaution, given your attempt to have us killed in London.'

Pinstripe's shoulders shook with suppressed laughter. 'That's the funny thing. You see, that wasn't me. In fact, you're mistaken about my actions on every count.' He leaned forward, his voice dropping to just above a whisper. 'The truth is, Eleanor, I've been busy keeping you and yours alive all this time.

The silk-covered chair felt cold beneath my fingers as Pinstripe's words hung in the air. His pristine suit caught the lamplight as he moved across the room, each step measured and precise.

'Money talks, Eleanor. You know this better than most.' He paused by the window, his reflection ghosting across the dark glass. 'The highest bidder gets my services. That's how it's always been.'

HG harrumphed 'Berlin taught me that lesson well enough.'

'Indeed, but that's in the past.' Pinstripe turned from the window. 'A certain person made quite the generous offer to keep you away from this investigation. To ensure the truth remained buried.'

The muscles in my neck tightened.

'But something changed.' His voice dropped lower. 'The Three Circles - or rather, a faction within it - has become something else. Something even I cannot stomach.'

HG's eyebrow arched. 'You expect us to believe you developed a conscience?'

'Believe what you will.' Pinstripe straightened his cuffs. 'The British government paints me as some sort of monster, yet hires my services from time to time. You yourself think me capable of any evil. But even devils have their limits.'

The night air grew thick with tension as he moved closer to HG's seat. My hand gripped the chair arm tighter, ready to spring.

'That's why I've been protecting you both. Keeping watch while you piece together this puzzle.' His lips curved into a thin smile. 'Though I must say, your methods leave much to be desired.'

Now shall I tell you who really wants your guts for garters?'

Chapter Twenty-Three

CONSPIRACY OF SILENCE

The room seemed to shift and blur around me as Pinstripe's words sank in. My grip loosened on the carver chair's arms, mind racing to reconcile this new reality with everything we'd believed true.

His revelation hung in the air between us, heavy as lead. HG remained perfectly still, but her fingers had stopped their usual rhythmic tapping on the chaise longue's curved arm.

My certainties crumbled like sand. If Pinstripe spoke the truth, who had tried to kill us in London? Who had arranged for the assassin in that Mayfair mansion?

A soft tap at the bedroom door broke through my spiralling thoughts.

Pinstripe's thin lips curved into an amused smile. 'Do you make a habit of having night-time visitors to your bedroom, Eleanor?'

HG's spine stiffened at his use of her first name. Her voice carried that familiar edge of steel when she spoke. 'Rex, would you be so kind as to see who that is?'

Rising from the carver chair, my legs felt oddly unsteady. The whole scene carried a dreamlike quality - the sort of nightmare where nothing quite makes sense, but everything feels terribly important. The tap came again, more insistent this time.

Moving towards the door, my hand hesitated on the handle. Behind me, Pinstripe's soft chuckle raised the hair on my neck. Everything we'd thought we knew about Lucy's murder, about Emily Brown's death, about the Three Circles Society - all of it wrong.

Opening the door, Whipple's worried face greeted me, his forehead creased with concern. His hand rested near his jacket pocket, where he kept his service revolver.

'Rex? What are you-' His eyes widened as he peered past my shoulder? 'Heard voices passing by. Wanted to ensure HG is...'

'Do come in, Arthur.' HG's voice floated across the room, calm but carrying that particular tone she used when situations grew delicate.

As the door opened wider, Whipple caught sight of Pinstripe. His entire demeanour changed in an instant. His shoulders tensed, jaw clenched, and he moved with the speed of a man twenty years younger.

'Arthur!' HG's sharp command froze him mid-stride. 'Stand down.'

Closing the door quietly behind Whipple, I returned to the carver chair. The atmosphere in the room had shifted from tense to explosive. Whipple remained rigid, his eyes never leaving Pinstripe's face.

'Our gentleman visitor brings rather surprising news.' HG's voice held a note of weariness. 'It seems we've been operating under some... misconceptions.'

Whipple's expression mirrored my own internal struggle

- disbelief warring with years of trained observation and deduction. His gaze darted between HG and Pinstripe, seeking any sign of coercion or threat.

The golden light from the table lamp cast strange shadows across our faces as HG began explaining Pinstripe's revelation. My mind wandered to all our careful plans, our theories about Lucy's murder, Emily's death - how much of what we thought we knew needed to be re-examined?

Whipple settled into the chair nearest the door, his posture still alert, ready. Though his expression remained neutral, the slight tremor in his left hand betrayed his agitation. Like myself, he must have questioned every assumption we'd made since that fatal gunshot at the Assembly Hall.

Through the dim lamplight, Pinstripe's angular features cast strange shadows across the room. 'Ah, it's nice to see the old team back together again.'

Whipple's face darkened like storm clouds gathering over the Norfolk coast. His hand still hovered near his revolver, knuckles white with tension.

'Now, now, Detective, don't be so grumpy - it's a compliment.' Pinstripe's mouth curled into that familiar, unsettling smile.

The muscles in Whipple's jaw twitched as he turned to HG, seeking guidance. My heart hammered against my ribs, caught between years of distrust and this bewildering new reality.

HG shifted on her chaise-lounge, her grey eyes evaluating Pinstripe with careful consideration. 'Our friend always did have an odd sense of humour. However, let us give him the benefit of the doubt. We have much ground to cover and if the gentleman can assist, then so much the better.'

Pinstripe's laugh held no warmth. 'And think about it, why else would I place myself in the same room as Scotland Yard's finest, Detective, if it were not to help your enquiries?'

The room felt smaller somehow, the air heavy with unspoken histories. Whipple's expression remained thunderous, but something in HG's calm demeanour seemed to steady him.

Pinstripe's signet ring sparkled as he gestured, sending brief flashes across the Chinese wallpaper. Each flash reminded me of the gunshot in the Assembly Hall, of Lucy's last words - 'Mason Drange' - and Emily Brown's coded diary. How many of our carefully constructed theories would crumble under this new light?

The radiator's metallic groan punctuated the silence, its warmth slowly seeping into the room's tense atmosphere.

HG's hands, which had been locked together like a steel trap, loosened their death grip. Her shoulders dropped a fraction, though her eyes never left Pinstripe's face. The subtle change in her posture allowed my own muscles to relax a little.

Whipple's transformation was equally telling. His right leg swung over his left, settling into a more casual pose, though his hand remained within easy reach of his service weapon. The detective's sharp features softened marginally as he observed HG's apparent acceptance of the situation.

The soft whisper of fabric accompanied Pinstripe's movements as he reached inside his immaculate jacket. The silver cigarette case caught the lamplight as it emerged, its polished surface reflecting distorted images of our gathering. His eyebrows raised slightly in HG's direction - a silent request that spoke volumes about their complicated history.

HG's nod was barely perceptible, but Pinstripe caught it

immediately. The case opened with a satisfying click, revealing a row of Cuban cigarillos nestled in purple silk. His selection practiced and deliberate - each movement calculated for maximum effect.

The match flared in the dim room, briefly illuminating Pinstripe's angular features. Sweet, pungent smoke curled upward, creating ghostly shapes. He settled back into his chair with the air of a man completely at ease, though his eyes held a predatory gleam that set my teeth on edge.

'Now,' Pinstripe drawled, smoke wreathing his words, 'let me tell you what I know. Then, perhaps you will believe why I'm here.'

The smoke from Pinstripe's cigarillo drifted across the room, carrying memories of countless similar encounters in drawing rooms and studies across England.

'Let me be clear,' Pinstripe's voice cut through the haze. 'The Three Circles have never counted me among its members.' He paused, studying the glowing end of his cigarillo. 'When I found out I had also become of interest to the group, it forced my hand, you see. Made me look closer at an organisation I'd previously dismissed as harmless do-gooders.'

'And how did you come by such information?' HG asked in a clipped tone.

'My information source is of no consequence. However, the news did make me take your safety more seriously. That's why I concocted the charade of having those two gentlemen escort Rex and you to that mansion. You see, I suspected we were all being watched. Do forgive me for any overacting I may have displayed.'

He looked across to Whipple, 'I guessed the good detective here would have you disappear for a while. I didn't anticipate the Edinburgh ruse, which I thought exceptional.'

Whipple flushed a little at the compliment.

HG glanced at the detective to show her appreciation, then turned back to our guest. 'And the body in the kitchen…the would-be assassin?'

Pinstripe's levity faded. 'Yes, I thought you might ask about that. Let us just say officialdom can be a useful ally at times.'

Whipple's facial features looked strained at the admission. 'Wait a minute,' he began. 'Are you saying you planted that body?'

Pinstripe gave a curious smile, given the topic. 'All in a day's work, Detective Inspector.'

My throat tightened at his words. He spoke so casually about death.

After a moment of reflection, HG went back on the offensive.

'You occupy a most peculiar place among humankind; however, I shall not dwell on the subject. For now, prey tell us what you discovered about those who may have killed and now, according to your testimony, wish to harm us.'

'The Three Circles present themselves as philanthropists, charitable souls doing good works.' Pinstripe's long fingers tapped ash into a crystal ashtray. 'But something has changed. Or…' He leaned forward, shadows deepening the hollows of his face. 'Perhaps the charitable facade merely conceals darker purposes.'

The air felt heavy with implications. HG had also mentioned that the group's founding principles were those of a charitable organisation of the great and the good. What caused the change, and who lay behind its latterly evil intent?

Somewhere in the distance, church bells tolled midnight, their sonorous notes barely penetrating the thick

Manor walls. Each chime seemed to mark another certainty, falling away, leaving only questions in their wake.

Attention in HG's bedroom shifted as Whipple broke his stoic silence. His question about the Three Circles' corruption hung in the air like Pinstripe's cigar smoke.

Pinstripe rose with fluid grace. The wool-silk blend of his suit glinted as he moved to the window. He held open a curtain with his left hand, darkness pressed against the glass. The grounds of Thorpe Manor lay silent beyond, shrouded in Norfolk's particular brand of midnight black.

The cigarillo's ember glowed brighter as Pinstripe drew on it, his silhouette stark against the window. Rather than answer Whipple, he turned back to us with that familiar, unsettling smile. My skin prickled at the calculated pause before he addressed HG.

The name he spoke - Comte Charles-Henri de Rohan - meant nothing to me, but HG's reaction proved fascinating. She remembered the snooty snuff-user from a Berlin party in 1910, and a playful expression crossed her face.

Something in the way Pinstripe watched HG's response reminded me of a cat watching a mouse hole - patient, focused, certain of eventual success. The familiar scent of his Cuban cigarillo mingled with the leather and wood polish that pervaded the Manor's rooms.

HG's finger rose in that characteristic gesture she used when pieces of a puzzle began falling into place. The connection she made about the Comte's casual reference to "circles" sent a chill down my spine. The innocent comment about his social connections in England took on a different meaning, considering recent events.

My mind raced back to Emily Brown's coded diary entries, to Lucy's murder, to the Three Circles tattoo. How many casual conversations had we dismissed that might have held similar hidden meanings?

The room fell silent as HG leaned forward; her eyes fixed on Pinstripe. 'Tell me, do you believe the Comte has corrupted the Three Circles' group for his own malevolent purposes?'

My fingers gripped the arm of the chair as Pinstripe's expression shifted from calculated amusement to something darker. The smoke from his cigarillo curled around him like a serpent.

'Indeed. As far as I can tell, the takeover began in 1908.' Pinstripe's voice carried a note of grudging admiration. 'Through his English connections, the Comte managed to position himself perfectly. Rather clever, really.'

'As you say,' HG responded.

De Rohan, a small, harmless-looking man with a monocle, pretended to be a perfect gentleman, but Pinstripe was suspicious. He won over existing members by sharing their charitable goals, while also recruiting new members who were just as cunning.

My stomach churned as Pinstripe detailed how the Comte operated his parallel organisation. Unaware they were covering up extortion and worse, the original Three Circles members carried on with their charitable activities. The Comte's carefully selected recruits carried out his darker bidding while he maintained his cheerful, aristocratic facade.

The horror of it struck me - how many deaths, how many ruined lives lay at the feet of this jovial French aristocrat? The room felt colder somehow as Pinstripe described the Comte's network of influence spreading across Europe like a poisonous web.

HG's hands clasped tightly in her lap as Pinstripe

revealed how the Comte worked for the highest bidder, his services extending to murder when the price was right. The familiar scent of leather and wood polish that usually brought comfort to this room now felt suffocating.

The gentle tap at the door barely registered above the hum of conversation, yet Pinstripe's head turned like a predator sensing movement. His thin lips curved into that familiar mocking smile.

'Another gentleman caller at this hour, Eleanor? Your reputation will be ruined.'

My hand hesitated on the doorknob, glancing back to see HG's perfectly composed expression. She didn't dignify Pinstripe's comment with a response, merely nodding for me to open the door.

Graham stood in the darkened hallway, silver tray balanced in one hand, palm up at chin height. Steam rose from a gleaming silver teapot, and - most remarkably, four cups and saucers sat arranged with perfect harmony. My mouth opened, then closed as words failed me. Stepping aside, warmth spread through my chest at the quiet competence of HG's butler.

Graham glided into the room as if serving tea to a mysterious gathering near midnight was the most natural thing in the world. His polished shoes made no sound on the carpet as he moved towards HG's bed.

'I thought light refreshments might be in order, Your Grace.'

The silver tray settled on the bed's foot with barely a clink. Graham's face remained impassive as he completed his task. A slight nod to HG, another as he passed my position by the door, and he was gone.

'Never underestimate the secret intelligence one's butler holds.' HG's voice held warm amusement. 'Dark art or guesswork. I've never been brave enough to ask the man.'

The scent of Earl Grey tea mingled with Pinstripe's cigar smoke, creating an oddly comforting atmosphere despite the tension still crackling through the room. My mind whirled with questions about Graham's uncanny timing and perfectly counted teacups, but HG's small smile suggested such mysteries were best left unexplored.

Pinstripe took charge of the tea service. His movements held a grace that seemed at odds with his dangerous reputation.

'How do you take yours, Detective?' The question floated across to Whipple, whose expression remained guarded.

'Milk, no sugar.'

Steam curled from the spout as Pinstripe poured with theatrical precision. My own preference for milk and two sugars came next, followed by HG's customary splash of milk.

The familiar ritual felt surreal in the context of our midnight gathering. Pinstripe's attention to detail - the perfect measure of milk, the careful placement of each cup - carried an almost hypnotic quality.

Once settled back in his chair, teacup balanced briefly in hand, Pinstripe took a measured sip before placing his cup and saucer on the floor. His focus shifted to Whipple, eyes gleaming with interest.

'Now then, Detective. Share your thoughts on our suspects. Who concerns you most?'

Whipple's jaw tightened before he spoke. The list of suspects rolled out like items in an evidence log - each name accompanied by careful reasoning.

'And we plan to hold a soiree on Saturday,' HG added once Whipple finished.

Surprise flickered across Pinstripe's angular features, soon replaced by obvious amusement. 'Rather bold, Eleanor. Nothing concrete to announce yet...' His lips curved into that familiar calculating smile. 'Though provoking the killer is rather the point, isn't it?'

HG's answering smile held equal measures of acknowledgement and challenge. The silent exchange spoke volumes about their shared history - two master strategists recognising each other's intelligence in an endless game of chess.

The tea in my cup had grown cold, forgotten in the tension of the moment. Outside, an owl's cry pierced the Norfolk night, a reminder of the real world beyond our strange gathering.

The familiar scent of Cuban tobacco drifted through HG's bedroom as Pinstripe absorbed every detail from Whipple. My fingers traced the cold rim of the teacup while the detective's precise descriptions filled the air. Each suspect, each piece of evidence, laid bare under Pinstripe's keen scrutiny.

'And the shoe print?' Pinstripe's question cut through Whipple's explanation about Emily Brown's diary.

'Size seven, distinctive heel wear pattern on the right side.' Whipple's response came without hesitation, his earlier hostility tempered by professional focus.

The detective's confidence grew with each query, his answers becoming more detailed, more assured.

My shoulders tensed as Pinstripe rose again, the movement fluid despite his tall frame. The wool of his suit whispered against the leather chair. His reflection appeared ghost-like in the windowpane, overlaying the darkness beyond Thorpe Manor's grounds.

The stub of his cigarillo glowed one final time before meeting its end in the crystal ashtray held in his left hand. Sweet smoke curled upward, adding another layer to the room's already complex atmosphere of tea, leather, and tension.

Without turning from his vigil at the window, Pinstripe's voice carried across the room. 'Then we must spend the next two days going over the evidence and preparing for your little gathering, Eleanor. Let us see if our French aristocrat also makes an appearance.'

The reference to France lit a spark as HG rose from the chaise longue and paced about the room. I asked if HG was well. HG wafted a hand and muttered under her breath. At last, she proclaimed, 'It all makes sense now. Lucy Daws last words were not, "Mason…Drange". I'll wager she was not referring to a man, but a place. She spoke fluent French, didn't she?'

Whipple nodded. 'That's what Lucian said.'

HG clasped her hands with excitement. 'For "Mason… Drange", read "Maison des étrangers"'

'A house…strange?' Pinstripe said with a confused look.

HG smiled for the first time. 'Try that the other way around. I think she tried to say strange house.'

Whipple shook his head. 'How does that help us?'

HG's smile broadened. 'It doesn't if you say it like that. Let's take a linguistic leap, shall we? I say Lucy was trying to say "Stranger's House". Now let's think about why she said that. If we believe, as we do, that poor Lucy had been sucked into the orbit of the Three Circles group evil side, she probably assumed they shot her. What if she attempted to expose them with her last words?'

Whipple scratched his head. 'But I still don't get the link?'

'We have a reference to a place. The murder took place in Norwich. I assume there are very many strange houses... But there is only one Strangers Hall.'

HG's delight in her own deductions stood out for all to see. If true, my mentor had made a momentous stride in connecting the dots.

'I think the Three Circles group, or at least the part involved in Comte Charles-Henri Rohan's evil plans, meets at Stranger's Hall.'

HG resumed her seat, flopping onto the chaise longue exhausted with her intellectual gymnastics.

'But the place is owned by Norwich Council. I'd have thought they might have noticed a gang of thugs using the premises?' Whipple asserted.

'Why should they suspect say, a sub-committee meeting of the charitable Three Circle group? Because that's how I suspect they get away with hiding in plain sight?'

HG nodded as she recovered her normal demeanour.

'I'll get a team of Bobbies down there tomorrow morning,' Whipple began. 'If there's anything to find, they'll uncover it.'

Pinstripe appeared to agree. 'That's a good plan. The only thing I would say is, might it be better to adopt a low-key approach? The last thing we want is the council panicking and it getting into the press before we're ready to reveal our cards.'

Whipple thought for a moment. 'Your right. I'll have Poppy and Muddleford to visit as a couple - as tourists interested in the history of the place. That way they can scrabble about to their heart's content without raising suspicion.'

HG sat up and smiled. 'What a wonderful idea, Arthur. Trust you to come up with an exciting plan.'

Whipple blushed but accepted HG's compliment. What a clever mentor I had.

'There's something else we should check,' said HG. 'Do you know the one place we haven't looked into at the Assembly Hall?'

The question appeared to be rhetorical.

'Under the stage. I don't mean the show runway, I mean the "real" stage. I doubt the space will reveal anything other than dust and old props. Nevertheless, let's make sure.'

In the excitement, Pinstripe's dour face had escaped us. Slowly, we transferred our attention to the fellow, now sitting bolt upright in his chair.

'What's the matter?' HG began. 'We've made huge progress this evening. Just then, a single bell tolled from the church. One o'clock.

Pinstripe looked up from his polished shoes, hands in his jacket pocket.

'It occurs to me that you'll have but one chance to catch our man...or woman at Thorpe Manor. That's assuming we get to them, before they get to you.'

'And what of you?' asked HG pointedly.

Pinstripe rose to his feet and began making his way to the bedroom door. He paused as he reached HG's position and gave her an enigmatic smile. 'You will not see me again...at least not in relation to your current adventure. I have accomplished my task, and it is time for me to frequent another life.'

'Another life?' quizzed HG.

Pinstripe's smile broadened. 'I exist in many forms, Your Grace. You see only what I allow you to see.'

He gave a polite bow without making any further

comment, before opening the bedroom door and passing into the corridor. With hardly an audible click of the door receiver the fellow was gone.

I enquired what my mentor thought of Pinstripe's strange exit.

'He will be true to his word, and we shall see no more of him for the present. That gentleman may be many things, but consider his words a true testament, for that is how he has remained of this earth for so long.'

Whipple shrugged his shoulders. 'I suppose he'll be looking for some favour or other in the future for watching over you too?'

HG shook her head. 'For all his many faults and discreditable actions, the fellow's actions are purely transactional. He asks no favours because he is paid to do what he does. Good luck, favours, and happy coincidences do not form any part of his thought process. He is paid to do this or that, and he delivers. No more, no less. He knows that compassion and sentimentality have but one outcome for him: *his death*.

Chapter Twenty-Four

A COMING TOGETHER

Sunlight streamed through the breakfast room's tall windows, causing all present to relax into a pleasant mood. Kippers, kedgeree, and poached eggs nestled among silver serving dishes. The aroma of fresh coffee mingled with wood smoke from the fireplace.

My thoughts drifted to the previous evening's uninvited visitor.

Poppy sat across from me, her mechanic's hands now holding a coffee cup. The transformation from her usual boiler suit to a fashionable dress still caught me off guard. Beside her, Chunky hunched over a plate of toast, her over-sized jumper collecting crumbs.

'So he just...vanished?' Muddleford's alert features creased with concern as he addressed HG.

HG dabbed her lips with a napkin. 'Rather his way, I'm afraid. Graham tells me the bed wasn't touched.'

'What a strange...and dangerous man that fellow is,' Whipple intoned. 'Do you truly believe he's on our side, HG?'

I'd been turning over the same conundrum and pondered what my mentor felt.

'On the balance of probability, I'd say what that "gentleman" intoned last evening is the truth. I know him too well to think he is motivated by doing the right thing. I suspect he's being paid by this country to get closer to the Three Circle's group with a view to destroying their malevolence. If I had to place a bet, I'd say our investigations have crossed his own, and he's been ordered to keep us out of it.'

Poppy set down her coffee cup with a sharp clink. 'Does this mean we're to abandon our investigation?' Her grey eyes flashed with disappointment.

HG's lips curved into that familiar, knowing smile. 'My dear girl, quite the opposite. We shall redouble our efforts. Pinstripe's involvement only confirms we're closing in on something significant.'

'But surely if the government-' Poppy began.

'The government's interests and justice are not the same thing,' HG said, reaching for the coffeepot. 'Lucy and Emily deserve answers regardless of who prefers them to remain buried. It cannot be right or think the destruction of the group must be at the expense of the deaths of two individuals. We seek the same end, except our order of priority is catching a murderer.'

Whipple nodded. 'The killer wrongly thought they could hide behind the charity's records of good works. They also, underestimate HG's determination.'

My gaze met Poppy's across the table. The spark of enthusiasm had returned to her features, replacing the momentary doubt.

'Then we proceed as planned?' Muddleford asked, helping himself to another kipper.

'Indeed.' HG's voice carried that steel-edged tone that

brooked no argument. 'The soiree remains scheduled for Saturday. By then, we shall have our killer.'

Whipple finished the last of his kipper and mopped the remnants of his plate dry with a piece of bread. HG's friendship with Arthur prevented her from criticising his eating habits, even though she disapproved.

'Right then,' began Whipple, blissfully unaware of his social gaff. 'We've two days until the event, so we must get on with things. Muddleford, you and Poppy will visit Stranger's Hall this morning. I understand that the owner just gifted Norwich Corporation the place. From what I've learned, it's in a state of disrepair, so it should be easy for you to wangle your way in. Perhaps you might suggest you are surveyor and assistant if you come across anyone, if you catch my drift . The rest of us need to-'

A clatter interrupted as Chunky dropped her fork. 'Got it! This section of the code translates as, "House of merchants past". It must mean Stranger's Hall.'

'Excellent work, Chunky.' HG beamed. That reinforces my deduction as to what poor Lucy tried to say with her dying breath. Now, Arthur, please continue with our assignments.'

My attention drifted to Poppy, who caught my eye and smiled. For a moment, the gravity of our investigation faded away.

'Are you with us?'

Whipple's comment drew me back to reality as I noticed several smiling faces looking back at me. Thankfully, having exposed my preoccupation, the inspector returned to the subject at hand.

'Muddleford, Miss Poppy, any questions about your assignment? Remember, you must gain access to every part of that building. Your purpose is to establish what the malevolent side of the Three Circles group gets up to during their meetings - understood?'

'Gotcha,' said Poppy. Muddleford nodded.

'Chunky, will you be able to complete the transcript of the code by this evening?

'Rather, old boy,' chirped an enthusiastic Chunky.

'HG and Rex? I'd like you to revisit the Assembly Hall and take a last look around. Have we missed *anything* that might point the way to the evil behind Lucy's, and by extension, Emily's, murder?'

'And you, dear Arthur,' asked HG.

'I have one or two loose ends to tie up with Scotland Yard. I suggest we all meet back here this evening when we can share the outcomes of our intelligence missions, agreed?'

A collective nod gave Whipple the response he sought.

It should be incorrect to say the Assembly Hall had started to feel like a second home, however, its familiar interior had a strange effect on me; as if the structure called out, *"Look again, there's more to find."*

The Assembly Hall's musty air carried memories of that fatal night. My footsteps echoed across the empty auditorium as HG and I surveyed the scene once more. Discarded programmes littered the floor, frozen in time since Lucy's murder - testament to how swiftly joy had turned to horror.

'One must wonder what we missed,' HG mused, her fingers trailing along a velvet seat back. 'The smallest detail could change everything.'

The fashion runway stretched before us like an accusing finger, its low curtains rustling in the draft. My boots crunched on scattered sequins that had fallen from the models' gowns.

A scampering sound broke our contemplation. Pendlebury burst through the double doors, clutching a vanilla folder to his chest as if it contained the Crown Jewels. His face glowed with barely contained excitement.

'The information you asked for?' He thrust the folder towards HG, who looked momentarily puzzled.

Recognition dawned. 'Ah yes! Mr Pendlebury, your efforts are truly magnificent. This shall not be forgotten.'

Pendlebury's chest swelled with pride. He executed an elaborate bow that would have suited a royal court, then practically danced his way out of the auditorium, his footsteps growing fainter as he disappeared through the double doors.

'I'll look at this later. For now let us get on with the matter in hand,' said HG as she passed the folder to me.

The Assembly Hall's vastness swallowed us as we split up to search. My torch beam caught dust motes dancing in the air while HG methodically worked her way along the left side of the hall. Papers rustled beneath my feet - forgotten programmes, torn tickets, the detritus of that tragic evening.

Stooping to retrieve a crumpled sheet near the third row, my fingers smoothed out what appeared to be a hastily sketched diagram. The pencil marks had smudged beyond recognition. Into my pocket it went - every scrap might matter.

'Hold this back a moment,' I called to HG, gesturing at the heavy curtain blocking access beneath the runway.

She obliged, creating a slice of light that illuminated the cramped space. The musty smell of old wood and fabric intensified as I crawled forward on hands and knees. My torch revealed nothing but newly formed cobwebs and a selection of sweet wrappers scrunched into a neat pile. No evidence existed that the small man HG had scolded during her first visit had left anything behind, nor had anyone else to find.

'Anything of note?' HG's voice drifted down.

'Just dust and disappointment.' My knees protested as I backed out, brushing off my trousers.

The space felt oppressive, as if the walls themselves concealed secrets. Every shadow seemed to hide potential answers, yet our careful search yielded nothing but more questions.

Within a minute, we both stood on the building's stage, from which the temporary runway jutted out at ninety degrees. I ponded about the worthy individuals who have given an oration to interested parties from the spot I now occupied. Also, the number of musicians and other artists who had plied their trade upon the worn pine boards. As for fresh evidence; none became apparent. HG and I exchanged frustrated glances.

'This is hopeless,' intoned HG with a weary sigh. 'One more inspection of the dressing room and that's it. I'm done and shall report as much to Arthur this evening.'

As I opened the dressing room door to allow HG's progress, a heady mixture of perfume and stage makeup assaulted my nostrils. The room was the untidy mess we had observed during our previous visits. This time, we took care to inspect every item. Our efforts came to nought. Reluctantly, I concurred with HG that our time might be better spent following other leads. As we sat in chairs last occupied by the fashion models.

'Look, all I have to show for our efforts is a broken shoe

strap. HG lifted her skirts a couple of inches to reveal the offending strap, lying out of position.

HG leaned forward in her chair to secure the truculent strap. As she did so, I noticed she became fixated on a spot somewhere in front of her position.

'I wonder what that is?' she pondered.

It took me a few seconds to latch on to what my mentor observed, and only then because I, too, lowered my body position to match HG's. Now I understood…an item sticking out from behind a steel cupboard by the rear door.

We covered the few steps together. HG bent to inspect the item.

'Do you know what? I think it's a…'

She pulled out the almost totally hidden objects. I use the plural since HG now held a pair of shoes in her hands.

'I wonder if…Can they be the missing shoes? You know, the pair Arthur spoke of?'

I had to admit to some excitement. What other reason was there to hide such items?

'They can't of fallen and lodged where we found them. Someone has stuffed these shoes behind the cupboard to hide their existence.

I ventured that the position of the cupboard by the door added weight to HG's hypothesis.

'Could it be that our murderer hid them in haste, to cover their tracks…literally?' said HG, observing every inch of the canvas foot ware.

HG realised to her horror that she had handled important evidence with her bare hands.

'Oh, dear,' she began. 'Arthur will be most displeased with me. Pass me one of those towels, will you, dear boy? The least I can do is to wrap the items up to prevent further contamination.

The vanilla folder's contents lay across my lap until HG snatched it; her earlier dismay at contaminating evidence, forgotten in her sudden enthusiasm. Papers rustled as she devoured the contents.

My mentor's eyes lit up while scanning the yellowed documents. 'Fascinating! This building began its life as a theatre, not an Assembly Hall at all.'

The architectural drawings caught her attention. Then she raised her gaze to the heavens.

'Behind all that modern boarding and paint lies a magnificent proscenium arch,' she declared, glancing up at the ceiling, then back to the plans. 'The Victorians never did anything by halves. This place was originally built as a theatre!'

Following her gaze, my eyes traced the current plain walls and modern fixtures. Somewhere beneath those austere surfaces lay hidden grandeur, waiting to be rediscovered. Like the building itself, this case seemed to have layers upon layers of secrets.

'Look here,' HG pointed to detailed sketches of the under-stage area. 'All the theatrical gubbins to make a show work. I wonder how much still exists beneath our feet?'

Her earlier frustration had vanished, replaced by that familiar gleam of discovery in her eyes.

'What do you say we take a look at what lies beneath?' She was already gathering the papers, her movements quick and purposeful. 'There may be more to this building than meets the eye.'

The search for access beneath the stage proved frustrating. My hands traced along wooden panels, seeking any hint of a hidden entrance. The building's conversion from theatre to Assembly Hall had masked its original features well.

Finally, tucked behind a loose section of skirting board, my fingers caught the edge of something. A small door, barely visible in the dim light, lay cunningly concealed at floor level. The craftsmanship was remarkable - without knowing where to look, one would walk past it a hundred times.

I eased the door open, bracing for the expected shower of cobwebs and scuttling spiders. None came. The space beyond yawned black with a hint of damp.

'Most peculiar,' HG murmured beside me. 'This entrance has seen recent use. The lack of dust and debris speaks volumes.'

Reaching for my lighter, I flicked the wheel. The flame cast dancing shadows across ancient wooden struts and mysterious shapes lurking in the darkness.

'Put that out immediately!' HG's sharp whisper made me jump. 'One spark in here could set the entire building ablaze.'

I snapped the lighter closed. Now only weak light filtered through the small doorway. As my eyes adjusted, indistinct forms emerged from the shadows - old scenery flats perhaps, or forgotten props.

My foot connected with something that rolled away with a metallic clank. Crouching down, my hands found a familiar shape - an old paraffin lamp. I gave it an experimental shake, rewarded by the sound of liquid sloshing inside. The wick had been trimmed, ready for use.

'Look at this.' I passed the lamp to HG.

'More evidence of a recent visitor, I'm sure of it,' intoned HG.

The paraffin lamp's warm glow filled my hands as the match caught the wick. Strange how a small flame could provide such comfort against the pressing darkness beneath the stage. Holding it before me like the Link Boys of old London, my feet found uncertain purchase on the dusty boards.

HG followed close behind as mysterious shapes emerged from the gloom. The lamp cast wild shadows across discarded scenery and mysterious mechanical contraptions. My head passed under the low-hanging beams by less than an inch while navigating the cramped space. The musty air carried hints of greasepaint and sawdust, lingering remnants of the building's theatrical past.

A sharp intake of breath from HG made me pause. Her coat had caught on a protruding nail, the rich fabric making a soft tearing sound as she carefully freed herself. The soft, edgeless beam of light from the lamp revealed her frustrated expression.

My boots scuffed against something solid, nearly sending me sprawling. Steadying myself, the lamp illuminated what appeared to be an old winch, its metal dulled with age but still solid. More mechanical forms loomed in the darkness beyond our small circle of light. Ropes and pulleys hung like forgotten spider webs, while painted backdrops leaned against the walls in various states of decay.

The space felt alive somehow, as if the ghosts of past performances still lingered in these shadowy depths. Each step brought new discoveries - a broken chair here, a mysterious lever there. The lamp's glow caught glimpses of gilt and faded paint, hinting at former grandeur now lost to time and neglect.

At its centre, the underground maze cleared, allowing us to stand more comfortably.

The dank air made breathing difficult, yet HG seemed unaffected by our subterranean environment. My arms ached from holding the lamp at the perfect height - not too low to read the plans, not high enough to singe my mentor's prized hat feather.

Her fingers traced lines on the faded blueprint while my gaze wandered across the cramped space. Something felt wrong here. The wooden beams overhead should have matched the stage dimensions exactly, yet shadows stretched further than seemed possible.

'Hold steady,' HG murmured, her eyes darting between paper and reality. The lamp's glow highlighted her furrowed brow as she compared measurements. 'This doesn't add up at all.'

My boots shifted on the uneven floor, sending a small cascade of debris skittering into darkness. The sound echoed, suggesting hidden depths beyond our small circle of light.

'The stage above appears smaller than this space below.' HG's voice carried that familiar tone of discovery. Her gloved finger tapped the plan. 'See here? The original drawings show additional width we can't account for from above.'

She turned, examining our surroundings with a new purpose. The lamp's beam caught glimpses of old machinery and forgotten props, but nothing to explain the dimensional discrepancy. Until HG's hand shot out, pointing left into the gloom.

'That way,' she commanded, already moving. Following close behind, the lamp's glow hardly penetrated the pressing darkness ahead. The musty theatre smell grew stronger with each step.

The darkness ahead seemed impenetrable until HG's outstretched hand guided my lamp towards a mass looming before us. A wooden structure dominated the confined space. Its weathered planks bore the patina of age.

My boots scraped against the rough floor, ready to step closer, when HG's sharp command froze me mid-stride.

'Don't move another inch!'

The urgency in her voice halted my progress. Following her pointed finger, my gaze dropped to the floor. There, preserved in the thick layer of grime, stood a pair of footprints facing away from the wooden behemoth. The lamp's glow caught their crisp edges, untouched by time or disturbance.

'Arthur must see these exactly as they are,' HG whispered, her excitement barely contained. 'He'll have them photographed before anything else.'

The footprints held my attention, their presence both eerie and compelling. Each impression showed a distinctive pattern, strikingly clear in the undisturbed dust. My mind flashed to the canvas shoes we'd discovered hidden behind the cupboard upstairs.

'Could these match...' My words trailed off as HG nodded vigorously.

'Precisely what I'm thinking,' she replied, crouching carefully beside the prints without disturbing them. 'The size appears consistent, though we'll need proper measurements to be certain.'

The flickering lamplight cast dancing shadows on the wood and footprints. The air felt heavy with possibility, each breath carrying the weight of discovery. Here, in this forgotten space beneath the Assembly Hall's respectable facade, lay another piece of our murderous puzzle.

The rough wood beneath my palm felt damp, its surface worn smooth by time and countless hands. Seeing the structure brought back painful memories of Lucy's death and the chaos that night.

The lamp's glow caught HG's profile as she studied the

architectural plans with fierce concentration. Her gloved finger traced lines across the yellowed paper while her other hand gestured at the wooden framework before us. The musty air pressed close, heavy with decades of theatrical secrets.

Sweat prickled at my collar despite the underground chill. The space felt different now, knowing what lay above. Those footprints in the dust took on new significance - silent witnesses to murder. My mind raced through calculations, trying to navigate this hidden space with the room where Lucy met her end.

The answer hit like a physical blow. Blood rushed in my ears as pieces clicked into place. Above our heads, separated by layers of wood and time, lay that fatal room. The same space where we'd found Lucy, where that mysterious perfume lingered.

Words formed on my lips, but HG spoke first, her voice cutting through my revelation. Her interruption confirmed my suspicions. HG moved closer to the wooden structure, her keen eyes examining every aspect of its construction. Her posture radiated the familiar energy of imminent discovery. She spoke with steely determination.

'That's it. I know how it was done.'

Chapter Twenty-Five

REVELATIONS

HG's desperate urge to telephone Whipple almost led to catastrophe as we hastened from our musty refuge beneath the platform. While guiding our path, clutching the paraffin lantern, I stumbled and sent the flickering light tumbling forwards. My heart seized as the crystal vessel splintered upon impact and rolled to rest beside a timber support. The bare flame now touched the debris-coated beam, permitting the raw fire to caress the detritus.

The narrow flame shot upwards as my fingers scrabbled against the rough floorboards. Before my hand could reach the burning debris, a force knocked me sideways. My shoulder struck the wooden planking, sending splinters of pain through my arm.

The basement's musty air swirled with dust and smoke while my mind struggled to grasp what was happening. Through watering eyes, HG's silhouette emerged from the gloom. Her hands moved with grace, smothering the creeping flames with what appeared to be old costume material. She dragged the heavy fabric down the wooden upright as methodically as her butler polishing the Manor's finest silverware.

My chest heaved as I watched her set the lamp upright. The immediate danger had passed, but my heart continued its frantic rhythm against my ribs.

'Less haste, more speed, dear Rex.' HG's voice carried its usual calm authority as she brushed dust from her skirts. 'Now, let us proceed calmly to a public telephone...' She paused; head tilted. 'By the way, have you brought any pennies?'

Never was I so pleased to experience the cold drizzle of an English autumn as in the minutes following our departure from the Assembly Hall. All around us, the city's populace went about their business, unaware of the deadly drama HG and I had just experienced.

'Ah, over there,' said HG as she simultaneously brushed some soot from the cuff of her coat and pointed to the Post Office building.

Upon entering the busy establishment, HG spotted a coin-in-the-slot telephone and made a beeline for it before anyone could cut across her path.

'Ah,' sighed HG. 'Have you any idea how the machine works?'

It should be impertinent of me to comment on my mentor's incapacity to avail herself of such modern technology. Persons of HG's standing could have no reasonable expectation of having to utilise such equipment. Therefore, I made no comment as I lifted the receiver from its hanger and place one penny into the slot on the top of the mahogany case.

'What would I do without you, dear Rex? You are my knight in shining armour if ever such a thing ever existed.'

HG relieved me of the handset and dialled the number for Thorpe Manor. At length, I heard a droll voice of Graham, HG's loyal butler crackling over the line.

After a further brief delay, the authoritative voice of Whipple filled the receiver.

'Arthur, I have splendid news to report. You might like to know that—'

HG withdrew the receiver from her ear. A confused look had displaced her elated features.

What had caused such a change?

'I see,' said HG, her response urgent. Then we must act upon it…yes, we can do that…my news?, oh, that can wait awhile.'

The handset appeared to float midway between HG and its hook as HG stood frozen to the spot.

I could wait no longer for an explanation and asked HG what on earth had caused her change in demeanour?

'Lucy Daws' father's been detained by the police.'

––––––––

The Tin Hut that constituted Norwich's main police station had not improved its welcome since I'd last set foot in the eccentric construction. As we entered the small reception area, the desk sergeant held his hand up in recognition of HG as he spoke into a telephone. It soon emerged that the fellow was speaking to Whipple. On completing his call, the Sargeant said as much and bade us wait, pending the arrival of his superior.

A small office served as our rest area and two mugs of tea soon arrived via a young constable. On seeing the grandeur of HG, the lad blushed, before apologising for the earthenware mug.

'Worry not, Constable. I daresay you'd be astonished to learn of the various containers from which I've sampled such delightful refreshment as you've graciously provided.'

The constable offered an embarrassed smile before scuttling from the sparse room.

And now we waited...and waited. In the meantime, we listened to various conversations emanating from the small reception through a crack in the door. One involved a request that His Majesty's Constabulary keep a lookout for "Albert," the beloved tabby cat of one Miss Perbright of Gas Hill. A second, less cordial exchange, pertained to an inebriated gentleman destined for the cells until he sobered up. "It was the milk that was off," protested the fellow in a far from melodious drawl. "Milk my foot. One more word from you and I'll tell your Agness what you've been up," threatened the desk sergeant, which appeared to hit the spot since not a peep followed.

HG tutted, 'And not yet eleven-of-the-clock.'

Our entertainment continued until, at last, Whipple rushed through the door like a man possessed.

Whipple collapsed into the chair opposite us, his hat becoming an impromptu fan as he worked to catch his breath. His coat fell open, revealing a crumpled waistcoat beneath. The usually composed inspector looked thoroughly dishevelled.

'Getting too ancient for all this running about,' he panted, mopping his brow with a handkerchief. 'My constitution simply isn't what it used to be.'

'Nonsense,' HG replied, her eyes twinkling. 'You're merely in need of more exercise, Arthur. Perhaps some morning constitutionals would serve you well.'

Whipple shot her a look that suggested he'd rather drink

vinegar than take up morning walks. After taking several deep breaths, he collected himself.

'Now then,' HG leaned forward. 'Do enlighten us about this business with Mr Daws.'

Whipple's expression turned grave. 'Received an anonymous tip about a firearm in his possession - a war trophy, supposedly. When officers called round, he freely admitted to having it and handed it over without any fuss.'

My stomach tightened as Whipple continued.

'The weapon had been fired recently, and here's the clincher - the bullets match our evidence from the Assembly Hall perfectly. The old boy's in custody now.'

The tea had grown cold, forgotten as the weight of this revelation settled over the small office.

HG's fingers traced the rim of her mug as she considered Whipple's words. The small office felt even more confined now.

My thoughts drifted to Lucy's father, alone in his cell. The man who'd shown such hostility during our visit to his home now sat silently behind bars, his war trophy weapon becoming his undoing. The image of him freely handing over the gun puzzled me as much as it clearly troubled HG.

'A father taking his own daughter's life, then surrendering himself to the noose?' HG's voice carried that particular tone she used when pieces refused to fit together. 'It strikes me as peculiar, Arthur. Most peculiar indeed.'

Whipple shifted in his chair, the ancient wood creaking beneath him. 'Guilt can drive a man to strange extremes. Perhaps he simply couldn't live with what he'd done.'

'And yet he maintains this stubborn silence?' HG's eyebrow arched. 'A man seeking absolution through punishment typically wishes to unburden his soul. Does the man have legal representation?'

HG's question brought a grimace to Whipple's face. Through the gap in the door, the desk sergeant's voice drifted in, still dealing with the morning's parade of minor infractions and lost cats. The contrast between those trivial matters and the weight of Mr Daws' situation struck me forcefully.

'Pro-bono work for a confessed murderer?' Whipple shook his head. 'I wouldn't count on it. Not in a case like this.'

HG's frown deepened. Her eyes taking on that distant look that meant her mind was racing down paths the rest of us had yet to spot.

'Then I shall fund his defence myself,' announced HG.

The declaration hung in the cramped office air. Whipple's eyebrows shot up, while my own surprise must have shown plainly on my face.

'No person should face a capital charge without proper representation,' HG continued. 'I'll engage Sir Walter Egbert-Fostrot. He's never lost a murder defence case yet... mind, he will only take on the case if he, himself, believes Mr Daws to be innocent.'

The name sparked recognition. Sir Walter's reputation preceded him - one of England's most formidable QCs, known for taking on seemingly impossible cases.

'That's... extraordinarily generous of you, HG,' Whipple managed.

HG waved away his words. 'Nonsense. I'd do precisely the same for you, Arthur, should such circumstances ever arise.'

Whipple nodded his thanks, then his features creased in thought as the full meaning of her words sank in.

'Now then,' HG straightened in her chair. 'Might we

revisit Mr Daws' residence before returning to Thorpe Manor? The team will be waiting for our debrief, but I'd like one more look at his home first.'

Whipple consulted his pocket watch. The ticking seemed unnaturally loud in the small space as he considered her request.

My thoughts turned to Thorpe Manor, where Muddleford, Poppy and the others would be gathering. The pieces of this puzzle remained frustratingly scattered, but something in HG's tone suggested she was beginning to see a pattern emerging from the chaos.

———————

The Daws residence felt cold. A fire in the living room grate had long since burned out, leaving only a layer of grey ash and the odd potato peeling to witness its demise.

My footsteps creaked on each wooden stair tread as we climbed to the upper floor. The landing offered little room for three adults to manoeuvre, forcing me to press against the wall while HG and Whipple discussed which bedroom to enter first.

Mr Daws' room struck me as a shrine. Lace doilies adorned every surface, and a faint trace of lavender lingered in the air. The curtains hung perfectly pressed, their floral pattern faded but clean. A pair of silver-framed photographs caught the weak afternoon light. One showed a kind-faced woman with Lucy's eyes, the other capturing Lucy herself in what must have been her early teens.

Whipple moved to the tallboy; his fingers pulled at the handle of the third drawer. The wood scraped against its runners with a hollow sound. HG stood beside him, peering into the drawer's depths before methodically opening and closing the others in turn.

'Have you noticed how ruffled the contents are in the drawers?'

Whipple's brow furrowed. 'We didn't go through them. Why should we have? Daws brought my officers into the room and went straight to this drawer to retrieve the gun.'

'So, no one except Mr Daws has been in these drawers?'

'That's correct.'

HG's lips curved into a knowing smile. 'Then you may wish to look at that.'

———

Graham served tea as we gathered in Thorpe Manor's Morning Room. The late afternoon sun slanted through tall windows, casting a lazy shadow across everything it touched.

Chunky perched on the edge of her chair; fingers thumbing a stack of papers covered in her cryptic notes. Poppy sat closest to the fireplace, welcoming the fire's warmth on a chilly afternoon. Muddleford stood on the opposite side, resting against the mantelpiece, notebook at the ready.

The room hummed with anticipation as Whipple thumped his pen on the notebook. 'Let's begin with the Assembly Hall, shall we? Over to you, HG.'

HG set down her teacup and thought for a few seconds. 'Rex and I made a thorough search of the main hall. I'm afraid nothing new presented itself.'

News that there was, apparently, no news, let loose a communal groan.

'However,' HG continued, 'We did discover the building

had originally been a theatre. And thanks to plans furnished by that unusual fellow, Mr Pendlebury, we discovered the one location no one had investigated. I refer to the cramped space under the original stage. I shall spare Rex's blushes concerning our interrogation of that place for now...'

I felt my cheeks flush and our companions gazed at me with expectant grins and raised eyebrows.

'So to the point,' HG continued. 'Rex and I discovered an ancient contraption that I believe explains why the killer thinks they will get away with their heinous crime. My only concern is that there must have been an accomplice. A person, as yet, unknown, although I do not believe that person will take much to unmask.'

HG's briefing left the room buzzing as she continued with her analysis. And how we might unveil the perpetrator, or indeed perpetrators?

Next, Whipple invited Muddleford and Poppy to speak on their visit to Strangers Hall.

Muddleford straightened his tie and cleared his throat. 'Strangers Hall proved most illuminating. The building stands as a testament to Norwich's medieval prosperity, though now its grandeur has faded considerably.'

Poppy leaned forward; her eyes bright with excitement. 'The merchant's house spans three floors, with the most fascinating timber-frame construction. Though parts of it have fallen into disrepair, you can still see how magnificent it must have been. An old shop front faces the Charing Cross, but the exciting discovery came round the back.'

My attention fixed on her animated gestures as she described their findings. The warmth from the fireplace seemed to intensify as she spoke.

'There's this small door,' Muddleford interjected, 'Barely noticeable unless you know where to look. It faces the River Wensum, where merchants would have loaded and dispatched their wares centuries ago.'

'The under croft beneath was the real prize,' Poppy continued. 'We found fresh candle wax drippings, cigarette ends, and this.' She produced a small medallion bearing three interlocked circles.

'Not only that,' Muddleford added, 'but we discovered recent footprints in the dust. Someone's been using that space regularly.'

HG's fingers traced the medallion's edge as Poppy passed it to her. 'The Three Circles have indeed made themselves at home there. Did you find any documentation?'

'Better than that,' Poppy smiled. 'We found a scribbled note about a meeting on a scrunched up piece of paper in a paper bag filled with other rubbish…they're gathering there tonight.'

The room fell silent as we absorbed this revelation. Even the crackling fire seemed to pause in anticipation of HG's response.

The medallion caught the late afternoon sun as it passed between hands. HG's fingers traced the three interlocked circles while her mind worked through possibilities.

'We could expose them all tonight,' she said, setting the medallion on the side table. 'Think of it - catching them red-handed in their corruption of an otherwise honourable organisation.'

Whipple shook his head. 'Too risky. We don't know how many will attend or if they're armed.'

'But we have the element of surprise,' Poppy countered. 'If we coordinate with local police-'

'And risk someone warning them?' Muddleford interrupted. 'They may have an informer among their ranks for all we know; alas, it wouldn't be the first time a copper needed a bit of extra cash.'

The fire crackled, filling a moment of tense silence. My gaze drifted between their faces, each deep in thought.

'What about the floor above?' HG's eyes lit up. 'The merchant's house has multiple levels. If someone positioned themselves immediately above the meeting during their meeting...'

Poppy nodded. 'The floorboards were quite thin in places. We could hear footsteps clearly when the caretaker walked overhead.'

'Perfect for gathering intelligence without risking confrontation,' Whipple agreed. 'Then we can choose what to reveal at Saturday's gathering.'

'But who should listen in?' Muddleford asked.

'An individual they'd never suspect,' HG responded. Her eyes fell upon Chunky, who'd stayed muted during our exchange.

Our whizz code breaker looked up from her papers, adjusting her oversized jumper. 'Oh yes, I'd love to. Nobody ever notices the odd one lurking about.'

The plan took shape: Chunky would position herself above the meeting room while Whipple, Muddleford, and I waited nearby in case of trouble.

'And talking of you, Chunky,' said Whipple, 'have you managed to finish the decoding?'

Next came the odd scene of Chunky slipping a pineapple chunk boiled sweet into her mouth, while Whipple fished an Everton mint from his pocket and spun it between his teeth.

'Yes, I have,' responded Chunky in a slurpy sort of way. 'Most of the entries are about private stuff; too much to recount now, and not pertinent to the case. However, those entries pertinent to the Three Circle group are telling. Emily talks about what a fool she'd been to get involved. It seems, quite reasonably, that she thought they wanted her expertise for a charitable event of some sort. Not until Emily met "The Count" and one other did she understand they'd scrutinised her past and would blackmail her unless she complied.'

'Does Emily say what the fellows bade her do?' Asked HG

Chunky gave an uneasy sigh. 'Yes…to kill Lucy.'

A startled moan filled the room.

'But she wouldn't do it?' prompted Whipple.

'Correct. She flat refused, knowing she'd put herself in danger.'

'No wonder the poor woman was in bits when we first arrived at the dress rehearsal last Saturday,' began HG. 'When I comforted her, she gave no clue about the burden she carried. Later, when Lucy died, Emily must have known the Count couldn't leave her alive to tell the police what she knew. How awful.'

Whipple moved from the hearth and sat on a nearby carver chair. 'The big problem is, we have no evidence, other than a few diary entries, that Comte Charles-Henry de Rohan has done anything illegal…he's a clever one, alright.'

The news was too much to take in. We'd heard so much new information over the previous hour that HG suggested we take a break for half-an-hour to recuperate and gather or thoughts. My mentor's announcement hit the spot as our gathering scattered to the winds. Some left for a breath of fresh air; others retired to their bedroom.

Soon, we all gathered back in our cosy retreat to continue our work. A sense of fresh enthusiasm filled the space as Whipple briefed us on the work he'd completed while everyone else completed their assigned tasks.

The room settled as Whipple settled into his chair. His demeanour suggested what followed might prove less dramatic than our previous revelations.

'After the excitement of the afternoon, my report feels rather minor in comparison,' Whipple began thumbing through his notebook. 'Those two fellows we sent on a wild goose chase to Edinburgh turned out to be common criminals - pickpockets and confidence tricksters. No connection to the Three Circles that we can establish.'

His finger jabbed the notebook entry. 'Still worth knowing.'

'There are two other matters,' Whipple continued. 'First, some interesting details about Miss Davenport have surfaced. Scotland Yard should provide confirmation shortly, but it may - and I stress may - have some bearing on our case.'

Muddleford leaned forward. 'Care to elaborate?'

'Better to wait until we have concrete facts,' Whipple replied. 'The second matter concerns Miss Longstone. She claimed to have modelled extensively in France, yet our inquiries suggest otherwise. Not a single agency or fashion house recalls her.'

'Why lie about something so trivial?' Poppy asked, voicing my own thoughts.

'Perhaps jealousy,' Whipple suggested. 'Many of her colleagues have genuine Parisian experience. Though why fabricate such an easily disproven story?'

The question hung in the air as Graham entered with a fresh pot of tea. He then moved next to HG and whispered something. HG nodded and accompanied the butler out of the room, leaving the gathering to conjecture what the sudden interruption might mean.

After what seemed like an age, HG returned. By her side stood a gentleman.

Dear friends,' began HG. 'Allow me to introduce investigative journalist, Mr Peter Walsall.'

Chapter Twenty-Six

AN INVITED AUDIENCE

Peter Walsall stepped into the room, appearing nonplussed by the welcome party. He turned, as if seeking reassurance from HG. A warm smile and gesture to sit eased the fellow's discomfiture.

The slight man in neutral clothes settled into the chair beside HG. My initial assessment of his dress and manner allowed the fellow to fade into the background. However, his piercing gaze held an intensity that belied his unremarkable appearance.

Steam rose from the tea HG poured as Peter Walsall gathered his thoughts. The room fell silent; even Chunky's usual fidgeting stilled.

'Perhaps you might inform my friends what you divulged to me at the door, Peter?'

He accepted the cup with a nod, his hands steady despite the weight of what he was about to share. 'Since 1918, I've been tracking the Three Circles group. A trusted source revealed criminals had infiltrated an otherwise respectable organisation of long standing.'

The journalist's voice carried no particular accent, yet commanded attention. His revelation about Lucy's Paris meeting with the Comte sent a chill through me. The way he described befriending her, gaining her trust - it painted a picture of a young woman caught in something far darker than she'd realised.

'Lucy thought she was joining a charitable organisation.' His face darkened. 'When they started asking about the storage location of new Paris fashion collections for 1922, she knew something was off and had told the Comte she wanted out. That decision signed her death warrant. He couldn't risk Lucy telling the authorities about his plan. Too much money, and his reputation among his "clients" rested on complete secrecy.'

My gaze drifted to HG, noting how her fingers clenched around her cup. We already identified the means and opportunity leading to Lucy's murder. Now we had the motive. But what about Emily's sad demise? Peter answered that question, too.

Peter's words hung in the Morning Room's stale air. My left side rested against the arm of the chair, watching him pull a notebook from his jacket pocket.

'Emily sought me out after discovering Lucy's predicament.' He flipped through dog-eared pages. 'The Comte used identical methods on both women - flattery, followed by threats once they were in too deep.'

The journalist's thin frame tensed as Whipple shot up from his chair. The inspector's face flushed red beneath his moustache.

'You sat on this information while two women died?' Whipple's fist struck the table, rattling teacups. 'Give me one reason I shouldn't arrest you this minute for obstruction?'

HG's hand touched Whipple's sleeve. 'Arthur, please.'

The gentle reproach in her voice deflated his anger. Whipple dropped back into his seat, though his glare remained fixed on Peter.

'The story became an obsession.' Peter's shoulders slumped. 'After years tracking the Three Circles, I convinced myself gathering more evidence mattered more than...' His voice trailed off.

'Than two lives?' Whipple's words cut like steel.

'I picked up a rumour about Saturday's gathering. I knew I couldn't stay silent.' Peter met HG's steady gaze. 'Emily trusted me with Lucy's secret. My failure to act cost them both...'

The weight of his confession crushed the sullen fellow. Through the window, clouds gathered over the Manor grounds, matching the darkness of our thoughts.

A chill settled over us after Peter's confession.

HG's presence anchored the room as she had done countless times before. Her grey eyes swept across our gathering - Whipple's rigid posture, Chunky's restless hands, Peter's bowed head.

A distant clock chimed ten, its sound muffled through oak-panelled walls. Graham appeared at the doorway with fresh tea, his measured steps and careful movements a stark contrast to the tension crackling between Whipple and Peter.

'The soiree requires careful orchestration.' HG's voice cut through the silence. 'Peter, your knowledge of the Three Circles could prove invaluable.'

Whipple shifted in his chair, his earlier anger giving way to professional focus. 'We'll need more than circumstantial evidence to trap the guilty.'

'The trap's already set.' HG placed her cup down with

precision. 'Our murderer believes they've covered their tracks. Saturday's distraction will flush them into the open.'

Peter leaned forward, his investigative instincts piqued. 'How can you be certain the killer will attend?'

The familiar twitch at the corner of HG's mouth signalled her satisfaction at the question. My years beside her had taught me to recognise that expression - she held all the cards and knew it.

'Our murderer possesses that most dangerous of qualities - pride.' HG's fingers drummed a gentle rhythm on her armrest. 'Not appearing would be tantamount to admission of guilt.'

The morning light caught the silver threads in her hair as she turned toward the window. 'These types share a peculiar trait with fire-setters. They must return to admire their handiwork.'

The comparison struck home. My mind flashed to the Assembly Hall's hidden passages, the carefully planned escape routes. Each detail spoke of meticulous planning followed by theatrical flair.

Whipple pulled out his notebook, pen poised. 'The guest list?'

HG extracted a folded paper from her sleeve. 'Every name serves a purpose. The seating arrangement will ensure our person of interest remains within sight of your officers, and us.'

Peter studied the list, his reporter's eye scanning for details. 'You've thought of everything.'

'Almost.' HG's gaze swept across our gathering. 'Success depends on absolute secrecy. The slightest hint could spook our quarry.'

HG's plan seemed watertight, yet something nagged at

the edges of my thoughts. The killer had proven clever, adaptable. Would they truly walk into such an obvious trap?

Over the two days since our briefing at Thorpe Manor and the adoption of Peter Walsall into our eclectic band, life had been hectic. Chunky had carried out her observations at Strangers Hall with aplomb. Our plan had worked a treat. Her report, together with the outside team, in which I took part, remained out of sight and not called upon to intervene.

Now we had a list of Three Circle members who'd gone rogue and confirmed their leader. Our earlier intelligence about his identity proved accurate.

With the active investigation over, HG had insisted we go over her plan for the soiree several times. Meanwhile, the others continued to check the evidence and known facts. Now, each knew the part they would play, what was to be said, and our individual positions within the gathering.

I witnessed the tension between HG and Whipple as they rehearsed their orations, and the points at which one was to give way to the other.

And now the moment had arrived.

The Manor bustled with people as they located their assigned seats in the spacious saloon of the magnificent House. Necks craned to see who else attended the gathering.

Midway down the vast space, two chairs rested two feet apart. Invited guests sat in an arc on either side of the two chairs.

From my position at the side of the saloon, the assembled crowd formed a sea of expectant faces. The air held that peculiar stillness that comes before a thunderstorm.

The ormolu clock sat high on an overmantel, ticked towards eight. Right on cue, HG emerged from the left door at one end of the grand room while Whipple stepped out from an identical entrance on the right. They met centre stage, their footsteps echoing on the oak floor in the hushed space. Together, they moved with purpose towards their chairs.

Not a cough, not a rustle of fabric disturbed the silence that fell over the saloon. The invited gathering sat transfixed as HG and Whipple took their seats.

The clock of the village church struck eight. HG rose to her feet, her presence commanding every eye in the room. Her gaze swept across those present, lingering here and there as she took a measure of each face before her. Some leaned forward in anticipation, others shifted uneasily beneath her scrutiny.

'My Lords, Ladies, and gentlemen,' HG's voice carried clear and strong. 'Two deaths have cast a shadow over the fine city of Norwich. The fashion show that should have celebrated that city's artistic spirit, instead became a scene of tragedy when Lucy Daws lost her life. Emily Brown's subsequent death compounds our grief. Powerful forces are at play, hidden beneath the surface of society, as tonight shall reveal. You are here because each of you holds a piece of a tragic puzzle, whether you know it or not.'

The audience hung on her every word. Her presence captivated even the experienced journalist, Peter Walsall.

HG continued her address. Her voice carried to every corner of the portrait-hung room, each word measured and precise.

'On that fateful evening, we gathered at the Assembly

Hall to celebrate the creative spirit of Norwich's fashion community. The models had completed their preparations, the music stood ready to play, and champagne waited on ice. None suspected the darkness that lurked beneath the surface of such a bright occasion.'

My gaze drifted to Clara Brightman, whose hands twisted in her lap. The pearls at her throat caught the light as she swallowed hard. The terrible ordeal of that night remained on her tortured features, and, no doubt, the experience of holding her best friend as Lucy lay dying in her arms.

'Lucy Daws arrived early that evening, her golden hair swept up in the latest style. She moved through those halls with grace, greeting friends and adjusting her costume. The show began as planned - models strutted down the runway, showcasing the finest designs our nation had to offer.'

HG's hand brushed the edge of her chair. 'Then came the sound that shattered our revelry. A single gunshot rang.' She pointed to the right, conjuring up the sight of that awful room. 'Lucy lay dead, struck down in her prime, her last words a mystery that would lead us down unexpected paths.'

Her audience leaned forward as one. Peter Walsall's pen had ceased its scratching across his notepad.

'The killer moved with purpose that night, knowing the layout of the venue, understanding how to slip away unseen. But they made one crucial mistake.'

My fingers curled around the arm of my chair. The memory of that night surged fresh in my mind - the chaos, the screams, the sight of Lucy's body sprawled across the floor. Whipple's face remained impassive, but his knuckles whitened where they gripped his knees. On cue, the detective stood while HG resumed her seat.

Whipple's measured steps on the oak floorboards echoed through the saloon. His tall frame cast a long shadow across the faces that flanked him. His sharp features remained fixed, unblinking, as he scanned the crowd.

My pulse quickened. Each tick of the clock marked another heartbeat of anticipation.

The detective's gaze settled on someone. His voice cut through the stillness with cold precision. 'A woman fled the Assembly Hall moments after the fatal shot. 'Outside, she climbed into a waiting taxi and vanished into the night. 'Isn't that so, Miss Davenport?'

Whispers rippled through the gathering. Heads turned toward Milly's seat. Her gloved hands gripped the chair arms, knuckles white against the dark wood.

'Please stand, Miss Davenport.'

She rose on trembling legs, her usual confidence stripped away. Her wide eyes, so often deployed to her advantage, darted between Whipple and the exit doors, like a trapped animal seeking escape.

Accusing eyes fell upon the famous Norfolk debutante, known for her cutting remarks. Her carefully constructed facade had shattered under Whipple's steely gaze.

Milly's distress became a palpable presence. Her shoulders trembled beneath her fashionable silk dress, and the feather in her hat quivered with each shaking breath.

Whipple's tone held none of its usual gruffness. 'Miss Davenport, perhaps you might share with everyone what drove your actions that night?'

'But Inspector...' Her voice came out thin, reedy. 'We discussed this the other day?'

'For the benefit of those present, if you would be so kind?'

The silence stretched. Milly's hand fluttered to her

throat, fingers playing with the string of pearls there. Her gaze darted around the room like a trapped bird.

'The fashion show was a disaster,' she began. 'That dreadful argument between the Fairbridge twins and then Emily Brown's breakdown... it was all too much. My reputation would suffer by association.'

The explanation rang hollow in the historical space. Even those who knew nothing displayed scepticism.

'So you fled?' Whipple pressed.

'Yes... no... There was a telephone call I needed to make. An urgent matter concerning my father's business interests.'

Her words tumbled faster now, each explanation more tangled than the last. She went pale, describing unbelievable coincidences: a parked taxicab, a missed appointment, and an urgent need to be in London that night.

The pearls at her throat clinked together as her trembling increased. Her knees buckled. Her contemporaries remained riveted by her growing distress.

'And the man who helped you escape?' Whipple's question cut through her rambling explanation.

Milly's mouth opened and closed without a sound. Her eyes rolled back, and she swayed on her feet.

The scene unfolded like a play. A constable gave Milly water; she held the glass before her face, as if it might hide her from Whipple.

My gaze swept across the assembled faces - some held pity, others scorn for the fallen socialite. Others observed the queen bee crumble before their eyes.

The click of Whipple's shoes echoed throughout the saloon as he turned to face the Fairbridge twins. Dressed alike in blue, they appeared poised and sophisticated, but a subtle nervousness was present.

'Would one of you ladies care to enlighten us about this alleged argument?' Whipple's voice carried across the hushed room.

Adelaide Fairbridge rose to her feet, her blonde curls bouncing with the movement. 'There was no argument, Detective Inspector. My sister and I never quarrel. We wished only for the evening to be successful for Her Grace's charity when we heard the shot.'

The words hung in the air as heads turned back to Milly. She kept her eyes fixed on the tumbler, her fingers tracing patterns in the condensation that had formed on its surface. The proud tilt of her chin, which had commanded so many social gatherings, now drooped in defeat.

'Thank you, Miss Fairbridge,' Whipple said. 'So, Miss Davenport, it appears there was no argument to flee from, was there?'

Milly's head moved in a slow shake, her gaze never leaving the glass in her hands. The woman sat mute, reduced to cradling her water glass like a lifebuoy.

The temperature in the spacious room felt cool as HG took over from her co-interrogator. She began her oration by drawing the attention of everyone to Mr Pendlebury, the Assembly Hall's General Manager.

'I doubt the venue would survive at all without the diligent work of that gentleman,' HG began. 'I think it fair to say our Mr Pendlebury is the mainstay of that august building, and it should be a lesser place without his loyalty and guiding hand.'

Pendlebury stood without invitation, his rotund frame casting a squat shadow across those seated near him. Beads of sweat dotted his forehead despite the room's chill. His oiled hair gleamed under a crystal chandelier as he preened at HG's initial words of praise.

The fellow's chest puffed with pride, his waxed moustache twitching as he basked in the attention. But his expression froze mid-smile as HG's tone changed. His hands began their familiar wringing motion - that nervous habit which had struck me as odd from our first meeting.

Blood drained from his face as HG spoke of his constant presence in the building. His high-pitched voice cracked when he tried to interject, but HG continued without pause. The gathered crowd turned as one to stare at the venue manager, their collective gaze boring into him as HG's words stripped away his carefully maintained facade.

His legs trembled beneath his weight as HG posed her devastating question about Lucy. 'Perhaps you became infatuated with Lucy Daws, but she rejected you. In a fit of jealous rage, you killed her. After all, it should not have been the first time such a scenario has played out? And then there is poor Emily Brown. Perhaps she observed your crime, so she too had to be disposed of?'

The mention of Emily Brown's name caused him to grab the chair before him for support. His knuckles whitened against the dark wood as he struggled to maintain his composure.

The silence in the saloon felt shocking in its intensity. Even the usual creaks and groans of the Tudor building seemed muted, as though the structure itself held its breath. Through the stillness came the soft click of Muddleford's shoes as he moved to block Pendlebury's path to the exit.

'Prey, do not leave us just yet. I'm sure whatever urgent business calls you can wait awhile. Besides, we have much yet to say on the subject of Lucy and Emily's tragic demise. Mr Pendlebury...sit down.'

HG's last sentence had not been uttered by way of an invitation. Pendlebury knew as much and slithered back into his chair. The guests sitting next to him, left and right, shuffled their chairs to put a little distance between them and a double-murderer.

'Others could have harmed the girls,' HG said, looking away from Pendlebury. 'Perhaps chief among them, Lucy Daws father.'

The room erupted into a cacophony of noise. The thought of a father killing his own daughter hit home like a steam engine crashing through the safety buffers at a train station. An outcome too dreadful to contemplate, yet that is exactly what HG had done.

My attention focused on Muddleford as he positioned himself behind Lucy's father.

Mr Daws remained seated, but his complexion turned ashen. The proud set of his shoulders that had marked our first meeting at his home crumpled under HG's steady gaze. His hands lay flat on his thighs, trembling against the dark fabric of his only suit.

HG's voice carried through the saloon with brutal precision as she detailed the bitter falling out between father and daughter. The audience hung on each word; necks craned forward to catch every detail of the family drama unfolding before them.

When HG mentioned the gun, Mr Daws' head snapped up. The movement caught the light, highlighting beads of sweat on his forehead. His throat worked as he swallowed, Adam's Apple bobbing beneath his starched collar.

The evidence mounted with each passing moment. HG's words about the matching bullets struck him like physical blows. His shoulders hunched further with each revelation, his body folding in on itself as though trying to disappear.

Through it all, Muddleford maintained his position, a

silent sentinel ready to intervene should Mr Daws attempt to flee. The detective's presence seemed to press down on the accused man, whose breathing grew more laboured with each passing moment.

The rustle of fabric and creak of chairs provided a restless backdrop to HG's devastating presentation. Their collective gaze bore into Mr Daws' back, their judgement as palpable as the evening heat.

'So, it is true,' continued HG. 'You murdered your own daughter, then took the life of Emily Brown.'

Chapter Twenty-Seven

IT CAN'T BE?

Hostility towards Lucy's father grew to the point Whipple felt it necessary to bring calm back into the room. 'That's enough!' he shouted. Realising his order had failed to penetrate the pandemonium, Whipple signalled to a constable to blow his whistle. The high-pitched tone did the trick. The din lessened until Whipple's repeated order took effect.

Furtive looks continued to fly in Mr Daws' direction as Whipple sat, allowing HG to continue.

The mood in the saloon shifted as HG released Mr Daws from her scrutiny. My fingers traced the edge of my notebook while she pivoted to address the broader motives behind Lucy's death.

Amber Longstone's face blanched at HG's command to stand. The young woman clutched the arms of her chair; reluctant to let go until she had no choice.

The question about France hit home. Amber Longstone's mouth opened, closed, opened again - no sound emerged.

My gaze darted between HG and Amber, noting how

the model's shoulders hunched forward, her previous poise crumbling under HG's steady stare.

'Your story you told us about visiting France was rather detailed, Miss Longstone.' HG's voice carried to every corner of the room. 'Yet when Inspector Whipple checked with the fashion houses, not one establishment remembered you.'

Amber's lower lip trembled. The sharp tap of her heel against the wooden floor echoed through the silent room.

'Perhaps you fabricated that tale to hide your jealousy of Lucy?' HG paused. 'Was it such feelings that drove you to kill? Lucy's rising star, her handsome French admirer - did it all become too much to bear?'

The model's composure cracked. A tear cut through her rouge, leaving a pale track down her cheek.

'The time for tears has passed, Miss Longthorn. You made no secret of your hatred for Lucy. I wonder why you harboured such feelings towards a woman who'd done you no harm?'

Amber trembled as the tears tumbled; her voice silent as the dread accusation hit home. Among the other guests, confusion reigned. What were they to think? Alleged murderers stacked up like the elements of a Russian Doll.

The tension in my shoulders eased as HG turned to Whipple. Her nod spoke volumes - time for phase two of the event.

Whipple rose, straightening his ill-fitting jacket. The movement drew every eye in the room. Amber remained fixed in place, her shoulders quaking.

'Miss Longstone.' Whipple's voice carried none of its usual warmth. 'Do you drive a motor car?'

The question hung in the air. Amber's hands clenched,

her face a mask of misery. Fresh tears tracked down her cheeks.

'Miss Longstone.' Whipple's tone hardened. 'Can you drive a motor car?'

Her head bobbed once, a bare movement that offered confirmation.

'Then you had opportunity and motive.' Whipple paced three steps closer. 'As for the means, we shall return to that shortly.'

Amber collapsed back into her chair, her blonde hair falling forward to shield her face.

The saloon held its breath, waiting for further revelations. My gaze swept the assembly - some betrayed shock, others calculation. Clara Brightman's expression remained unreadable, while Mr Daws stared at his hands.

Through it all, HG maintained her poise. The day's light had faded into the darkest of nights. Norfolk's big sky showcased the heavens in all their majesty as a full moon shone a ghoulish hue through the tall bay windows.

'For now, I wish to turn to someone that has remained elusive, yet a thread that runs through this entire investigation.'

The room garnered itself for yet more explosive revelations. Who would be next to fall under the brutal scrutiny of Detective Whipple of Scotland Yard?

'I speak not of a native of this fair land, but one of Galic origin.'

Confused faces filled the room.

'Let me introduce you all to Comte Charles-Henri de Rohan.'

Heads turned, attempting to locate the French aristocrat.

Whipple pointed out a heavyset man in a white flannel suit, which I thought odd attire for a chilly British evening.

'Perhaps you might stand so that we might all admire your presence?'

The man smiled, embodying the essence of haute couture. 'I shall remain seated, if I may, Inspector,' began the fellow in perfect English. 'The dampness of your British climate has seeped into my old bones and precludes compliance with your request.'

The Comte's refusal to stand sent a ripple of murmurs through the crowd. My fingers tightened on the notebook as HG rose from her chair, her bearing regal, commanding. Whipple stepped back, surrendering the floor to her.

A strange smile played across HG's face. Not the warm expression she shared with friends, but something sharp, dangerous.

'Comte de Rohan. Our paths crossed once before, did they not? Munich, 1910.' HG's voice resonated around the sumptuous space. 'You held court at that little cafe near the Residenz, regaling everyone with tales of your ancestors losing their heads to Madame Guillotine.'

The Comte's lips twitched beneath his groomed moustache. 'Such a pleasure to be remembered.'

'Behind that jovial mask lies something far darker, doesn't it?' HG's words cut through his forced bonhomie. 'A man who manipulates others to commit crimes while keeping his own hands clean.'

The Comte's face hardened, though his smile remained fixed.

'You infiltrated the Three Circles group.' HG's accusation rang out. 'A respected British institution dedicated to charitable works. Yet under your influence, it became a front for extortion, blackmail - and murder. All this while the "old membership" remained ignorant of the evil antics.'

My gaze darted between them. HG stood tall and resolute, the Comte attempting to maintain his facade of aristocratic indifference.

The fellow inspected his pudgy fingers, betraying the tension beneath his cultivated air of boredom. His monocle caught the light as he tilted his head, studying HG with cold calculation.

HG continued her assault on the Comte. The gathered crowd hung on every word as she detailed the police surveillance of his movements.

The Comte's smile never wavered, though something cold lurked behind those eyes. HG spoke of his manipulation of the Three Circles Society. The monocle glinted in the harsh electric light as he tilted his head, studying HG with the detached interest of a scientist examining a specimen.

'You flatter me with such attention,' he purred, his English perfect despite a thick Gallic accent.

The atmosphere shifted when HG mentioned Strangers Hall. The Comte's smile faltered. Even from where I stood, the change in his demeanour became clear - gone was the apparent boredom, replaced by something darker.

'Ah, I've hit a nerve, have I?' HG's eyebrows rose as she delivered the blow.

The Comte's scowl transformed his face. The mask of genteel aristocracy slipped, revealing something cruel beneath. His monocle dropped from his eye, swinging on its black ribbon.

The audience stirred, sensing the shift in power. Clara Brightman pressed back in her seat while Amber Longstone's tears dried on her cheeks as she stared at the unfolding scene.

'I shall not listen to such manufactured tittle-tattle,' protested the Comte.

'Charles-Henri, you shall do as I say, unless you wish to spend the night in a cold, damp British prison cell?'

Defeated, the Comte averted his gaze from HG. He appeared not to bask in the attention heaped upon him; a marked change from before.

'Excellent,' chirped HG, 'After all, we aristocrats must stick together in looking after each other's health, yes?'

A ripple of low laughter spread throughout the room. The Comte's thunderous face told me this was not a situation he expected to find himself in at our gathering. This was a fellow used to the total control of others. Now he sat ridiculed by the droll sense of humour he clearly hated in the British.

Just as she had done once before this evening, HG moved the conversation on without once looking at her current victim.

'And now we must bring all our evidence together. So far, the Inspector and I have shown you the threads that wove their despicable web about us as we strained to uncover the truth of not one, but two murders.'

Whipple moved forward so that he stood beside HG. He ruffled his moustache as he gazed around for the person he wished to address.

'Ah, there you are, Clara. I know this evening will not have been easy for you, as Lucy's close and trusted friend. You have witnessed Her Grace, and I highlight the comings and goings of several people. Some you know; others you may not be familiar with. What I'd like you to do, if you feel strong enough, is to explain just what Lucy Daws' death means to you.'

Heads turned in a familiar frenzy to locate the person Whipple addressed. After several seconds, Clara stood; a sad expression masked the beauty of youth.

Everyone waited with bated breath for Clara to speak. Instead, she looked forlorn.

'Take your time, Clara. I know this is difficult for you,' said Whipple in a soft tone.

At last, Clara spoke. Her voice wavered as she spoke of her friendship with Lucy. Their first meeting, life in Norwich, dreams and fears—they'd talked about it all. My chest tightened as she described their bond, two young women navigating the cutthroat world of the fashion industry.

Clara revealed Lucy's terror of her controlling father. Mr Daws slumped in his chair, tears tracking down his weathered face. His hands trembled as Clara spoke of Lucy's desperate escape to London.

Amid her tears, Clara depicted happier memories, tea and cakes, clothes swaps, and whispered secrets about their romantic interests. The room hung on every word as she described their last exchange, full of Lucy's excitement about some wonderful news she couldn't wait to share.

My gaze drifted to the Comte. He toyed with his monocle, eyes fixed on Clara as she spoke. The hair on my neck prickled at his predatory attention.

Clara's voice dropped to a whisper as she turned to face Mr Daws. Her next words cut through the silence like a knife: 'Why did you hurt my Lucy?'

The question sent a ricochet around the saloon. Mr Daws crumpled in his chair, face buried in his hands as his shoulders shook with silent sobs. Around us, handkerchiefs appeared as several of the models dabbed at their eyes.

'Why indeed,' began HG. 'Perhaps the more pertinent question is, Clara, why did *you* hurt Lucy. More to the point, what drove you to murder your best friend, and then arrange for Emily Brown to be run down and killed?'

The room erupted for a second time. Clara's voice vanished beneath a cacophony of noise as the shocked crowd attempted to take in HG's assertion. I noticed Muddleford's hands on the Comte's shoulder from his position behind the scoundrel, thwarting a second attempt at escape. In the far corner, a small, rotund gentleman attempted to persuade a constable to open the door; which met with a resolute response.

The room settled into an uneasy quiet. Clara's shoulders drooped, the confident posture of moments ago replaced by a defensive, uncertain posture.

HG's unwavering stare pinned Clara in place. 'You were saying?'

Clara's hands fluttered like trapped birds. 'This is stupid. Lucy and I were closer than sisters. Everyone knew that. Ask the other girls - we shared everything. Why would I harm her?'

The ormolu clock ticked upon the overmantel of an Adams fireplace, marking each painful second.

'It was him!' Clara thrust an accusing finger at Mr Daws. 'He's the one with the gun. How many times did he say he didn't have a daughter anymore? Lucy told me herself!'

HG's smile held no warmth. 'An interesting point you raise, Miss Brightman. Tell me - how did you know Mr Daws possessed a gun?'

The collective intake of breath from the crowd stirred

the air. My gaze caught the Comte's face - a sick smirk split his features.

Clara's mouth worked without sound. Her complexion paled to match the greyish walls behind her. 'Lucy told me.'

The lie hung in the air between them. Clara's hands twisted the fabric of her dress, knuckles white with tension.

'Lucy told you?' HG's voice dripped with false sympathy. 'When exactly did she share this information?'

Clara's composure cracked. Tears welled in her eyes as she struggled to expand on her answer. The silence stretched, broken only by the soft rustle of clothing as the audience waited.

'And did Lucy tell you where the gun was?'

'No, why should she?'

'Interesting,' responded HG. 'Then perhaps you can explain how we came to find this in the very drawer in which the gun lay?'

HG reached into her silver chain shoulder bag and withdrew a small, sparkling object. 'Is this your earing?'

'No,' responded Clara, without looking at the exquisite object.

'I thought you might say that, so the police took the precaution of searching your room at the Railway Hotel. Do you know what they found? Oh, let's not prolong this nonsense. They found its match. Now, I wonder how such a precious item came to find itself in Mr Daws' bedroom tallboy resting next to a gun. A gun that had recently discharged a bullet, and whose ammunition matched the bullet used to murder Lucy. What was it you called Lucy, ah, yes, your best friend?'

Clara's demeanour went from defiance to desperation.

'I remember now. Lucy borrowed them.'

HG laughed aloud. 'You mean "it", not "them". Now

why should a person borrow just one earing? it doesn't make sense, does it?'

Clara's fingers clutched at her necklace; her other hand pressed against her stomach. The pearls twisted between her fingers as she glanced around the room, seeking support that wasn't there.

'Lucy borrowed the earring because...because she wanted to match it to a necklace she planned to buy.'

The explanation rang hollow. Even Amber Longstone rolled her eyes at the transparent misrepresentation.

'She said she'd return it after the show.' Clara's voice rose an octave. 'But then everything happened so fast and—'

'Enough,' shouted HG in a rare moment of anger. 'Mr Daws told us of your visit two weeks ago to give him news of his daughter and persuading him to allow you to look at Lucy's bedroom. You told him, "Lucy had asked you to check her room was as she left it". Instead, you tuned left at the top of the stairs. You knew what you were looking for because, in fact, Lucy had told you were her father kept the gun You stole it.'

'That's not true!' Clara shouted in terror. 'So how did it find its way back then?

HG shot back her answer. 'We are ahead of you, dear girl. You played the loyal friend and visited Mr Daws again. This time to offer your condolences. Then, you pulled the same trick a second time. You said you'd like a memento of Lucy, if only you could visit her room one last time. Mr Daws, heartbroken and bereft, agreed. That was your passport to put the gun back...except that you dropped an earing into the drawer in your haste to accomplish your evil task.

Clara's face crumpled. 'No, that's not... I mean, Lucy must have...'

'Must have what?' HG stepped closer. 'Broken into her own father's house, stolen his gun, then returned it after her death? Rather difficult, wouldn't you say?'

A low hubbub swirled around the voluminous room.

'Perhaps,' she stammered, 'perhaps someone else took my earring and-'

'Again, enough.' HG's command struck like a thunderclap.

Clara tried one last gambit. 'Alright then, explain this. How could I have shot Lucy? Just because I was first in the room after the gun went off doesn't mean I did it. You saw me yourself. Lucy lay across my knees on the floor. I comforted her in her last seconds. She spoke to me, and I told you what she said. Why would a guilty person do that?'

HG clapped her hands, much to the amazement of the crowd. 'Ah, yes, the "How could I have done it?" ruse. In fact, you couldn't, at least not on your own.'

The hubbub grew louder at this latest revelation.

'You see, the police know you had an accomplice.'

HG turned to her audience. 'Do you know, my Lords, Ladies, and gentlemen, that the Assembly Room was once a theatre?'

Most shook their heads. The older among the crowd nodded.

'And so the stage you observed on that fateful night, in its original form, spanned the full width of the room. In fact, a most beautiful proscenium arch remains hidden under a thick layer of ornate plasterwork.

'I know this,' HG continued, 'because Mr Pendlebury furnished me with the original plans for the building...and you know what? The document also indicated an interesting space beneath the stage. I shall not bore you with the details of my exploration, but together with a colleague, I discovered a most remarkable machine.'

HG turned back to Clara. 'Can you think what that might be?'

The accused failed to engage in eye contact with my mentor.

'Well, I'll tell you. We found a lifting machine, a common piece of equipment beneath the stage floor in every large theatre. Its use? To deliver and remove an actor to and from the stage at a moment's notice. Have not we all felt wonderment at the puzzling arrival and vanishing of a performer? The Geni surrounded by mists of steam during Christmas presentations of Alibaba and the Forty Thieves at theatres across our country.

Clara shook her head. 'That's ridiculous.'

'Is it?' shot HG. 'You see, the most confusing question the Inspector, and I had to answer was how you got into that tiny room…and out again without anyone seeing you. Well, one might say you turned into a genie. You knew there was no apparent entry to that room without being seen. No door, no windows. So how could someone materialise and vanish without being observed doing so? Once you know the secret, the answer is simple. You enticed Lucy into that room on the pretext of gaining privacy to deliver a message from her father; something Lucy had longed for. Once alone, you mercilessly shot her, at which your accomplice triggered the mechanism to spirit you way. Isn't that so?'

Clara shook her head. 'This is a fantasy.'

'Is it? Replied HG.

'You have no proof,' began Clara. 'This is just assumption after assumption.'

HG smiled again. 'Oh, Clara, do you think Scotland

Yard's finest detective deals in conjecture? You see, we found several footprints in that dusty little room. Remnants of the scrape marks were confusing. However, police experts gleaned enough information to warrant comparing them to everyone's modelling shoes. And do you know what? One set couldn't be located…at first.'

Clara's defiant gaze dimmed.

'There's something to be said for the phrase, "More haste, less speed." You see, in your panic to change your shoes on re-entering the changing room, you knew you had to dispose of the shoes you wore to escape the understage area. The problem? Time. So you stuffed them behind a cupboard by the door…only as time went by as the police got involved, you could not retrieve them. However, by pure chance, I did.

'You see, Clara, your vanishing act, and sudden reappearance wasn't magic, just a simple wooden lift. And this is where your partner in crime came into his own. Isn't that so, Mr Cowpepper?'

Confusion raised its head again as HG's guests searched for a person they did not know. Finally, a nervous-looking man got to his feet. He wore a look as if waiting outside the headmaster's office for the punishment he knew awaited within.

'Allow me to introduce Mr Cowpepper,' continued HG. Sometime stage assistant whom I first met when he emerged from beneath the runway at the Assembly Hall. You see, when we first looked into the gentleman's past, we thought he'd developed an obsession with Lucy Daws; that she had rejected him and, in a jealous rage, he'd killed her. In truth, his proclivities focused on Clara Brightman. When Clara realised she could manipulate the fellow, she roped him in to her evil plot with the promise of love to follow…if they were successful. Some might say Mr Cowpepper had every incentive to make sure he played his part to perfection. Like a fool, he fell for the ruse and even agreed to kill Emily Brown to make sure their tracks remained covered, so that they might elope together.'

HG's gaze fell on the hapless fellow. 'Yes, Mr Cowpepper, we found the car, but congratulations on hiding it so well. If only you'd set the vehicle on fire, the police would never have been able to lift your fingerprints. After several of the other models told the Inspector of you following Clara like a lapdog, the tragic connection fell into place.'

Before Cowpepper could react, two police constables grabbed an arm each and placed handcuffs on the startled man.

'You stupid old fool!' screamed Clara. 'I told you to—'

Clara's composure shattered. Her face contorted with rage as she spun to face Mr Daws.

'You killed her! Your own daughter - and now you're trying to blame me! Everyone knows how you treated her, how she fled to London to escape your control.'

The raw hatred in her voice made my skin crawl. Her finger jabbed the air as she wheeled to face Amber Longstone.

'Or what about you? You hated Lucy because she got all the best assignments. The jealousy ate at you every day!'

Amber recoiled, but Clara had already turned her venom toward Emily's empty chair.

'And that pathetic Emily Brown - always fawning over Lucy, giving her special treatment. She deserved what she got!'

The room fell silent at this slip. Clara's eyes widened as she realised her mistake.

'No...that's not what I...'

Her desperate gaze darted around the room like a trapped animal. The pearls at her throat snapped, scattering across the floor as she clawed at her collar.

'The Comte! He's the one behind it all - him and his Three Circles! They made me do it!'

The Comte's smirk never wavered. Clara's chest heaved as panic overtook her.

'None of you understand! Lucy had everything - the looks, the talent, the mysterious French boyfriend. She was going to America without me! After everything I did for her!'

Spittle flew from her lips as she screamed. Her perfectly coiffed hair came loose, falling around her face in wild tangles.

'She betrayed me! She was going to leave me behind in this miserable place. I couldn't let her...'

Clara's voice cracked. The fight drained from her body as the truth of her actions crashed down.

'So you did order poor Emily's murder?' interrupted HG. 'Your words condemn you.'

The startling revelation caused the saloon to erupt. In the confusion, a portly gentleman made for an exit door.

'Arrest that man,' shouted Whipple at the top of his voice. In a flash, the officers apprehended the fellow; his struggles useless. In seconds, he felt a pair of handcuffs tightening around his wrists.

As the room settled, HG turned to Clara. 'What on earth led you down this awful path?'

Clara looked at the floor and shrugged her shoulders. 'What chance have my type got?' she began. 'I work all the hours God sends, work hard, and do as I'm told. And what have I got to show for it? A shabby, damp, room to rest my head. Living from one payday to the next. Never enough to buy the clothes I model for rich people. It stinks…all of it.'

The room fell quiet. Coughs stifled; sniffing noses, silenced.

'But Lucy? Of all people, Lucy?'

Silent tears flowed. Clara's cheeks reddened. 'Lucy was the only genuine friend I ever had…I would have done anything to—'

'And yet you killed that friend. Why?'

I knew what HG was up to. She needed Clara to implicate the one person we had failed to find evidence that would pass the test of a judge and jury.

Clara moved her gaze from HG, hesitant at first; then with anger. She pointed to the man held by two constables.

'Say his name, Clara,' said HG in a gentle tone.

'Comte Charles-Henri de Rohan. He followed me around for weeks, paid me nice compliments; took me to fancy restaurants. I trusted him when he said he'd look after me. Then he started asking about Lucy. After a while, he turned nasty. He'd found out about my past, and some serious stuff I'd done, but not caught for. The Comte threatened to tell the police if I didn't do as he asked. He said if I did it, he'd take me to America and make me a movie star…he knew all the studio bosses and I believed him. When I stole the gun and showed him, he took it from me. Later, when he returned it, he said he'd put special bullets in it that would only bruise Lucy. Just enough to scare her into keeping her mouth closed about something.'

'But they turned out to be real bullets, didn't they?' Responded HG.

Clara ran out of words. She sobbed and lowered her head.

'And Emily?'

'It had gone too far. Emily told me she knew who'd ordered Lucy's killing and was closing in on who the person was. I couldn't take the chance and knew Mr Cowpepper would do anything I asked. Now I'm just glad it's all over. I know what will happen to me. At least I'll be out of this lot. God will forgive me, won't he…'

HG gathered her thoughts as she gazed at the guilty woman. 'I hope so, Clara. If you are truly repentant, I believe that He will…but that is in your hands. No earthly being can take that from you.'

Despite the evil Clara had perpetrated, several women, high and low born, shed a tear for the wretch who stood before them.

HG looked at Whipple. She knew what he had to do.

'Look at me.'

Clara obeyed without complaint.

'Clara Brightman. You are hereby arrested on suspicion of the alleged murder of Lucy Daws, and alleged accessory to the murder of Emily Brown. You will come with me.'

Epilogue

Two weeks had passed since the fateful evening during which HG and Whipple unmasked Clara Brightman. Her vile murder of Lucy Daws. Not content with one killing, Clara had inveigled Mr Cowpepper, her besotted admirer, to kill Emily Brown.

This evening's gatherings at Thorpe Manor was, in no sense, a celebratory affair. However, HG, ever aware of others, decided she should call our little group together by way of thanks for the excellent work we had all put in.

Graham's polished shoes whispered across the Persian carpet as he offered champagne from a silver tray. The library's oak panels glowed in the lamplight, casting warm shadows across familiar faces. Poppy caught my eye and winked from her perch on a leather wingback chair, her modern outfit a stark contrast to the room's centuries of tradition.

The crystal glasses sparkled as HG raised hers, tapping it with delicate precision. The clear note rang through the comfortable silence. Her grey eyes swept across our gathering - Whipple lounging against the mantelpiece, Muddle-ford's tall frame bent into an armchair, Chunky perched cross-legged on a footstool, and Peter Walsall standing near the window, notebook tucked away for once.

'My dear friends,' HG's voice carried its usual quiet authority. 'We've weathered quite the storm these past weeks. From fashion show tragedy to international intrigue, each of you proved invaluable.'

She detailed our journey - the Assembly Hall murder, Emily Brown's death, the Three Circles Society's web of deceit. The champagne bubbles tickled my nose as she praised Chunky's code-breaking genius and Poppy's under-cover work.

'Without Muddleford's steady hand and Arthur's London connections, we might never have unmasked Clara Brightman's betrayal.' HG paused, nodding to Peter Walsall. 'And Mr Walsall's years of investigation gave us the final pieces of this dark puzzle.'

The fire crackled in the grate, its warmth matching the glow of accomplishment in the room. Graham appeared at my elbow with fresh champagne, his practiced movements part of the Manor's eternal rhythm.

My champagne glass caught the dancing flames, creating prisms of light across its crystal surface.

Chunky fidgeted on her footstool, her oversized jumper bunching at the elbows. 'How did you manage to get everyone to play their parts so well, HG?'

HG's lips curved into that familiar smile that spoke of both triumph and compassion. 'It proved more complex than expected. Mr Daws showed remarkable courage, knowing the accusations would cut deep.'

The mention of Lucy's father brought a hush to the room. The poor man had endured public scrutiny, all to help us trap his daughter's killer. My fingers tightened around the stem of my glass.

'Others fell into their roles with natural talent,' HG continued. 'Though Mr Pendlebury's theatrical flourishes nearly threw me off balance.'

Peter Walsall gave a short laugh. 'The look on the Comte's face made it worthwhile. His mask slipped rather spectacularly.'

Poppy slid from the arm of her chair into the comfortable embrace of the plush leather seat. 'What about Clara? How did someone like her end up tangled in all this?'

HG's expression darkened as she gazed into the fire. 'A desperate young woman from humble beginnings, dreaming of wealth and fame. The Comte recognised her vulnerability, exploited it. But murder is murder, regardless of circumstance.'

We all knew what fate awaited Clara Brightman as she sat in her cold cell awaiting trial. There could be but one outcome, which sent a chill down my spine.

After a deep-felt silence, Peter Walsall asked HG a question; I think to move the conversation on.

'I've heard much said about that fellow the Inspector and you call, "Pinstripe". Can you tell us anything of his real name?'

This had been a question I'd wanted to ask HG for some time. However, the moment never seemed to present itself. Or perhaps if I'm being honest with myself, knowing HG's hatred of the besuited fellow, I hadn't been brave enough to raise the question. If Whipple knew the stranger's name, which I assumed he did from the resources at his fingertips, he wasn't saying anything.

'Ah, that one,' began HG. 'It is true that I know the braggart's name, which is an entirely different proposition from speaking it. In fact, I promised myself many years ago to never utter his name. To do so would lend credibility to a creature of the night, not worthy of formal identification.'

'But he saved your life last week?' Poppy's statement had an urgency about it.

'It is true,' began HG while glancing at Whipple. 'But only because he received payment by…well, let us leave that question aside, to do so. Be under no misapprehension, Poppy, had the "other side" paid more to kill Rex and I, then that is what should have happened.'

Whipple gave a silent nod as he swigged the last of his champagne, only for his flute to be immediately refilled by Graham, much to the fellow's pleasure.

For the remainder of the evening, a relaxed atmosphere held sway, in which we played Charades and Twenty-questions. Eventually everyone sat in silence, or talking quietly to another as the fire settled into a deep reddish glow.

HG, Whipple, and I sat to one side, musing about past cases and what the world might have in store for us next.

It was then that HG asked Whipple and I to draw closer.

'I've been thinking,' she began as Whipple, and I exchanged curious glances. 'What say you both that we go on a little adventure?'

'Isn't that what we do all the time?' expressed Whipple in a sardonic tone.

HG smiled and patted Whipple's arm. 'Oh, Arthur, you are a wag. No, I mean a proper…what do people call it… ah, yes. A "holiday"'.

I had to stop myself from giggling. HG had a vast knowledge of the world, politics, and the workings of her own class. Yet, for her compassion, of which I had been a significant recipient, she knew little of the *real* lives of working people.

'I have in mind,' continued HG without breaking breath, 'a short trip to America and back, you know, by ocean liner. We shall sail on the Aquitania; also known as "The Ship Beautiful", and one of Cunard's finest vessels.

Whipple and I shared a dumbstruck look. The largest boat I'd ever been on was the Liverpool ferry that sailed the ten-minute journey to New Brighton, where my father was appearing on stage at the New Brighton Palace theatre.

Whipple spoke first. 'You mean across the Atlantic…in Winter?'

'Tish,' said HG. 'It is late autumn, not winter. Anyway, these large vessels are so safe these days, you'll hardly feel a thing.'

Whipple gave HG a serious look. 'Isn't that what they said about the—'

'Do not say that name. You are being irrational. You never know, we might find a case or two to investigate on board.'

Whipple blinked in a slow, rhythmic fashion. 'You mean a bit like a busman's holiday?'

HG offered Whipple a confused look. 'Arthur, you do say the strangest of things sometimes. What does he mean, Rex?'

It only took a few seconds for HG to recognise her social naivety, at which point the three of us broke into a raucous laughter, made all the more hilarious at the sight of the stoical Graham attempting to refill our shaking champaign flutes.

Also by Keith Finney

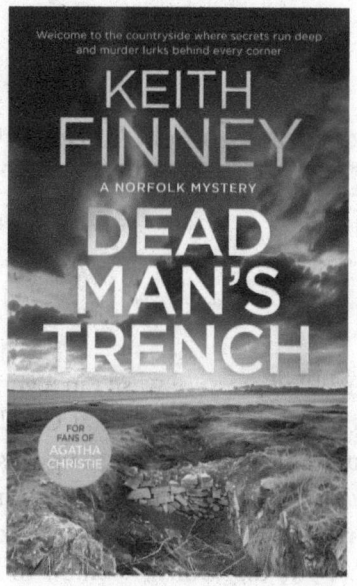

vinci-books.com/deadmanstrench

A quiet village. A deadly secret. Two unlikely allies racing against a killer.

When a suspicious death is brushed aside as an accident, landowner Ant Stanton and headteacher Lyn Blackthorn dig deeper—unearthing buried grudges and a murderer who's not done yet.

Turn the page for a free preview…

Dead Man's Trench: Chapter One

IN A HOLE

Alan Fairchild's blood pressure wasn't in a good place.

Getting the head of archaeology at Cambridge University to meet Stanton Parva's history group was a coup.

Why on earth turn up if they won't listen? Alan fumed in his thoughts. Did no one care that he'd sweated blood to secure a private tour of the dig, which he knew to be of national importance?

"May I emphasise again," said Professor Pullman, as heads swivelled and old friends chatted, "on no account interfere with the excavations you will see this morning."

It was an unequal battle. The gentle waters of Stanton Broad, glistening in the morning sun, had much more appeal than a dusty academic. Add in a golden carpet of Norfolk reed swaying rhythmically in the breeze, and the result was inevitable.

"Our hypothesis is that this vast Roman villa complex was wantonly destroyed. All the signs point to Boudica, queen of the Iceni tribe. In around AD 60 she led a revolt against the Roman legions. Also…"

The professor's words failed to impress one section of the group as they soaked up the latest village gossip. First amongst equals was Phyllis Abbott, a sprite eighty-two-year-old whose loss of hearing caused her to shout then accuse others of not speaking the queen's English.

Alan tried a flanking manoeuvre to work his way around the rebels so he could get close to Phyllis, who was in deep discussion with her best friend, Betty.

Phyllis was lamenting the post office's move from the village shop, which she'd run until she was age seventy-one, to the petrol station on the outskirts of Stanton Parva.

"Modernising the post office is what they call it. How can making things worse be better for the customer? And what Her Majesty must think about it, well, I just don't know. What do you think, Betty?"

Betty nodded as she attempted a reply. "Well, yes... I suppose..."

Phyllis was having none of it. "There's no supposing about it. How do I get to Flatley's petrol station with my leg? Then there's the price of a first-class stamp. Shocking, that's what I say."

By now, Alan had sidled up to the pair and knew from Betty's scowl that she'd given up any hope of challenging her friend's views on the subject.

"Shush," said Alan, a wobble in his voice letting slip that his nerves were getting the better of him.

Phyllis shot Alan a cold stare. "Who are you shushing, young man? Just like your mother, you are." The old woman dismissed Alan with an imperious wave of her hand before turning back to Betty. "And you know what?"

"No. What, dear?" offered Betty, pleased to be asked her opinion.

"When I went to pay for my Jiffy bag, that stupid boy

asked which pump I was using. Well, I thought he was talking about the thing Dr Bridlington prescribed me. I told him to mind his own business. Then…"

The rest of the group were torn between Boudica chasing out the Romans and Phyllis' medicinal pump.

Alan had had enough. "Er, excuse me, Phyllis, but I'm sixty-five, and my mother's been dead for fifteen years."

Half turning, she switched conversation from Betty to Alan without missing a beat. "I remember you when you were in shorts. They called you Snot-Sleeve, didn't they? And your mother still owes me for a pint of milk," said Phyllis, before once more engaging Betty in the thorny issue of Jiffy bags.

Alan withdrew, trying hard to act as if his run-in with Phyllis hadn't happened.

Keen to regain a measure of control, he turned to the professor. "May I ask if the expanse of open water had anything to do with the villa's location ?"

It was a question to which he already knew the answer, but anything was better than another rebuke from Phyllis.

"Ah," replied the professor, pleased once more to be the centre of attention. "In fact, the Broads weren't dug until the twelfth century when the growing population needed peat for cooking and heating."

Alan's relief was palpable as the academic gave a positive response to his question.

Professor Pullman waxed lyrical about the abandoned peat diggings being filled over time by rising water levels to form the Broads, until the manic laughter of a Minions mobile ringtone interrupted his flow.

Alan strained to see where the sound was coming from and meandered through the group until he came across

Angela Simms, who was rummaging through her enormous shoulder bag to silence the din.

"Can you manage?" asked Alan, sensing Angela's embarrassment.

"Never you mind this lot. They can tut all they like."

Alan shook his head in admonishment at two male members of the group. "You can moan all you like, but just think, what if someone was trying to get an urgent message to you? Until you take the call, you don't know why they're ringing, do you?"

The two men half turned from Alan, shrugging their shoulders like two naughty schoolboys.

Alan turned back towards Angela just in time to see her retrieve the mobile and scurry from the group, her face etched with concern.

As Professor Pullman seized his opportunity to round off his introduction to the site, he turned from the group, lifted his right arm, and urged the assembly to follow as he set a blistering pace towards a small mound in the middle distance.

It took a couple of minutes for Alan to realise Angela hadn't rejoined the group. Fearful she had received bad news, he scanned the field to see where she might be.

He noticed a hundred yards or so to his left the young woman standing ramrod straight, frozen to the spot.

Alan quietly backed away from the group and ambled towards the woman, not wanting to draw attention to himself—or to Angela.

As he neared, he noticed Angela held both arms to her sides. Her phone hung limply in one hand.

Oh Lord, he thought.

"Is everything okay, Ang?" said Alan in a low, quiet tone, keen not to startle her.

She didn't respond.

Alan slipped the mobile from her hand and raised it to his ear. Angela offered no resistance. He turned and walked a few paces back towards the distant group.

"Ang, are you still there? How's the signal? Can you hear me?"

Alan spoke into the handset, trying his best not to alarm the caller. "Hi, she's fine but tied up for a minute or two. I'll get her to give you a ring back. Is that okay?"

Alan didn't wait for a response. Instead, he ended the call, switched the mobile to silent, and slipped it into his shirt pocket.

He retraced his steps towards Angela and both now stood at the edge of a deep excavation.

Alan saw what she saw.

The body of a man.

Dead Man's Trench: Chapter Two

THE WALLED GARDEN

The eyes were open, face drained of colour. A trickle of congealed blood puddled in the dusty ground to the side of his head.

"I knew that bugger would come to a sticky end one day."

Alan, startled at the sudden sound of voices, turned to see Phyllis at the head of a small group of club members who had wandered over, curious at Alan's earlier departure.

The old woman showed no sign of shock. It wasn't the first time Phyllis had observed violent death. War service had seen to that.

Alan instinctively moved closer to Angela, who hadn't moved a muscle.

He looked across to Phyllis, admiring her composure but puzzled by her comment. "What do you mean?"

"Well, they don't… or should I say, didn't, call Fred Collins 'Narky' for nothing. He was a bad-tempered bully, that one."

"Mrs Abbott," Alan responded, not sure of how to

finish the sentence. Simultaneously, he turned Angela away from the horror. She offered no resistance.

"It's true," Phyllis continued, her voice quiet now yet still lacking any trace of sympathy for the dead man. "He always picked on the young'uns from the 'big house'. He knew they couldn't answer back."

Alan returned to the edge of the excavation. He shook his head. "What a waste."

Phyllis fumed. "Waste? What do you mean? He thought he was God's gift to women. Always trying to paw them. I've seen him do it. Given him a piece of my mind more than once, I have."

Phyllis kicked some loose earth into the trench, watching it settle like unwanted confetti on the dead man's exposed cheek and shoulder.

Alan recoiled, at last summoning the courage to challenge the old woman. "For the love of God, Phyllis. Show some humanity, will you? No one deserves to die like *that*."

The old woman tilted her head upward and sniffed the air, dismissing his show of sympathy for the dead man.

She pointed a spindly finger towards the corpse. "Seen this in the war. Men who lord it over other lads. Try it on with their girlfriends. When a jealous man gets his blood up, he can do anything. And from what I know, plenty had it in for that fat sod."

Before Alan could respond, he noticed the remainder of the group approaching and headed them off before they reached the excavation.

"There's been a terrible accident," said Alan. "We need to call the police. I'll try and get through on my mobile, but as backup, I need someone to run over to the big house and raise the alarm."

All eyes descended on Sid. He was the youngest by decades.

"I'll do it," replied Sid, making off at a sprint towards Stanton Hall.

Enjoying the solitude of the Hall's walled garden, Anthony Stanton filled his lungs with a riot of heady scents. As the dew lifted into Norfolk's big sky, the effect seemed all the stronger.

This place is about as far from work as I can get, he thought.

Anthony kicked a spray of gravel from the pathway, which cut its way through blazing beds of late-summer flowers.

He flopped onto a rickety, cast-iron bench and tilted his head backwards. A warming sun had the desired effect.

For the first time in a long time, he pushed painful memories to the back of his mind.

The quiet didn't last long. Reacting in an instant to the sharp crack of a rusty gate latch lifting, he hunched over as if to make himself as small as possible, his attention focused on a dark outline filling the gate opening.

Anthony squinted at the silhouetted figure of a woman.

"Excuse me, this area is private." The voice was assertive. He expected compliance.

Ignoring his words, the woman continued to close the distance between them. "So it's true. You're back, Anthony… and in one piece too. Lucky for you they couldn't shoot straight."

He recognised the voice. Using the long form of his first name was a giveaway. She always did that to provoke him.

He chose not to react. "Military training has its uses."

"Hello, you," said Lyn.

"Hello, you," he replied.

The ease of their exchanges had all the familiarity of a long-married couple, relaxed in each other's company.

"Still breaking the rules, Lyn. Just like at school... and the Hall still isn't open to the public today."

Lyn smiled, unmoved by his halfhearted rebuke. "Just as well I'm not Joe Public, then, isn't it? And as for school, we couldn't all be the class swot, could we?"

Lyn's barbed comment rolled back the years to a time when they were at Stanton Primary together.

He gave a throaty laugh. Time had passed, but the constant ribbing he got from his classmates had stayed with him. He'd always seemed to come top in exams, but it wasn't the only reason he stuck out. Ant spoke differently and lived in "the big house".

His smile widened as he recalled how she was the one who controlled the others. A talent, he suspected, Lyn still possessed, judging by the confidence in her voice and the way she held herself.

"Wasn't my fault my parents bought into that swinging sixties hippie thing, and sent me to the local primary school for oiks instead of public school."

Lyn gave him a sideways look and shook her head in that dismissive way only she could get away with. "Playing the victim doesn't suit you, Ant, and anyway, you wouldn't have suited pinstriped trousers or a straw boater. At least your parents spoke to each other in words with more than one syllable and lived in the same place."

"Things any better now?" Ant responded.

Lyn let out an almost inaudible sigh. "Let's put it this way, at least Mum has stopped throwing things at Dad. Mind you, living at opposite ends of the village helps."

Ant didn't pursue the point and broke eye contact, knowing the damage went deeper than Lyn would ever admit.

"Anyway, I popped over to drop off a chocolate cake to your parents. It's their favourite, you know. I bring one over every Saturday."

Ant smiled as Lyn flopped next to him on the bench.

"I didn't think you'd come back after Greg's death."

Ant rolled his head as if to make sure his exposed skin captured every ray the sun had to offer. His arms hung across the back rail of the bench. Lyn didn't try to avoid contact as she settled back.

"I didn't intend to stay away for so long. At eighteen you think your parents will live forever. I'm still not sure if I'm back for good, even though…" Ant faltered. He shuffled his feet in the gravel.

Lyn stared into the distance, looking at nothing in particular. "A flying visit, then? Your brother's been dead a long time, and the estate seems to run itself from what I can see."

Ant gave a short, sharp laugh. "That's just the problem, Lyn. You know better than me how frail Mum and Dad are. They've both suffered bad luck with their health for years, and I don't suppose it helped that they had Greg and me comparatively late in life because of all the travelling they did. But still, to tell you the truth, it was a shock."

He stopped, sensing Lyn's reaction.

Another telling-off coming.

"For heaven's sake, Ant. They're both in their seventies, and the man had a heart attack a few months ago. What did you expect?"

Ant shrugged his shoulders and changed tack. It was easier than thinking about his parents not being around forever. "The thing is, Lyn, the estate's in a right mess, and I'm not cut out to fix it."

Lyn sensed his unease.

"That was Greg's job. And what happens? He flips his car into Stanton Broad, and goodnight Vienna."

"Sounds like you're feeling sorry for yourself again, Anthony."

There she goes again.

"Not at all," replied Ant. "I'm just stating a fact. It was Greg's inheritance, not mine. Turns out the estate income has been slipping for years, and the Hall is in a hell of a state. You've seen the water damage. Dad's tried, but it's too much. To make things worse, the people paid to look after the place just haven't done their jobs."

Lyn's expression softened.

Ant settled back into the bench, his head once more falling backwards as the sun bathed his face.

"Isn't it strange, Lyn? You know, when you're a kid, you look up to your parents and assume they know it all. Then whether it's poor health or just getting older, you realise they're not invincible after all. You must see it all the time." Ant opened an eye and squinted into a bright Norfolk sky. "Dad mentioned you started as head teacher at our old school in September. Spooky or what!" He let out a throaty laugh.

"Come to think of it, it's kind of strange, dealing with stuff in classrooms I sat in as a child," replied Lyn. "But you're right. I see kids affected by things at home. There's a familiar look in their eyes when voices are raised—a rabbit caught in the headlights type of look. Despite working like stink, sometimes we can't fix things. But we try. That's all anyone can do."

Ant sensed her sudden nervousness and could have

kicked himself for making her remember her own child-hood traumas. "Sorry, Lyn. Didn't mean to do that; I know you had it tough at home."

After a few moments of uneasy silence, Lyn gave Ant a sideways glance as she playfully pinched the skin of his arm between two fingers.

Ant winced in mock pain but made no move to distance himself from the attack.

"That's something else you did in class, remember?" said Ant. "I never understood why."

Lyn smiled. "Let's just say it was my way of toughening you up," she replied.

Ant had to admit Lyn had got him out of several sticky situations with Jezza, the class bully.

"Of course, there's another explanation."

Lyn gave Ant a puzzled look. She was at risk of overacting. "And that would be?"

"Affection, Lyn. I asked my father once why you kept hitting me when you spent most of your time fending off Hillier and his thugs. Dad was clear about it, and seeing as I didn't have a better explanation, I believed him!"

Lyn waved at Ant dismissively. "In your dreams, Anthony Stanton. My older brother used to pinch me, so I took it out on you. One snotty boy was just the same as any other to me. Anyhow, you sat next to me and were daft enough not to fight back."

Both laughed, the interlude having served as a conve-nient pressure valve for less happy memories.

"Right. Time for a piece of chocolate cake and a cup of tea with your parents." As she spoke, Lyn sprang from the rickety bench and launched herself towards the gate.

"Haven't I endured enough pain for one day without being exposed to your baking?" moaned Ant as he sprinted to make up the distance between them. "Remember that nut caramel toffee you made with salted peanuts in year four? Yuck!"

Without stopping, Lyn bent down, scooped a handful of gravel and tossed it over her head. "And before you say anything, if I'd have wanted to hit you, I would have. You're not the only one who's a crack shot."

The levity didn't last long. As Lyn reached out to lift the latch of the gate, it moved towards her at speed, causing Lyn to cry out in pain as the heavy construction smacked into her.

"Oh, er... sorry, miss. Only..."

Ant's instinct was to shout at the lad. The look of panic on the youth's face stopped him from doing so.

The boy didn't wait for either a welcome or reprimand. "It's your land agent, sir. He's, er... sort of... dead."

Ant felt a swell of frustration at the youth's nervous ramblings. "What do you mean, 'sort of'? Either someone is dead, or they are not dead."

Ant glimpsed Lyn's look of disapproval and knew he'd gone too far.

Sid looked no less frustrated as he tried to make himself understood. "Up at the dig site. He's in a ditch. They told me to fetch the police."

Ant pointed towards the elegant columns fronting the imposing entrance to the Hall. "The phone's in the hallway. And you'd better ask for an ambulance."

Grab your copy...
vinci-books.com/deadmanstrench

About the Author

Keith's fascinating novels skillfully combine the heart of a retired assistant principal with the imagination of a gifted author, taking readers on a captivating journey through Norfolk's scenic landscapes and rich history.

Acknowledgments

The author is thankful for the following, whose contribution added to the historical authenticity of the book:

Norfolk Police Historical Society, in particular, David Chilvers, for his invaluable information of Norwich's "Tin Hut" police headquarters

Norwich Theatre Royal Archives, and the immense assistance Maria Andrew provided on the history of the theatre – and for tutoring me on use of a maniacal machine within Norwich's Archive Centre within the Millennium Library!